PRAISE FO[...]

"*Seven Forges* is a per[...] brutal fighting, beguiling magic and assassinations. [It] *has* the WOW factor."
The Book Plank

"A hell of a read."
The Baryon Review

"James A Moore entertained the hell out of me with *Seven Forges* and also made me think. If he writes more books in this world, I'll definitely read them."
Shelf Inflicted

"I highly recommend this and all of his books."
The Crows Caw on Smile No More

"*Deeper* is pulp fiction at its most exciting, but it's Moore's talented writing style that raises the novel above just another forgettable monster-romp."
Dark Scribe Magazine

JAMES A MOORE

Seven Forges

**ANGRY
ROBOT**

ANGRY ROBOT
An imprint of Watkins Media Ltd

Lace Market House,
54-56 High Pavement,
Nottingham,
NG1 1HW
UK

angryrobotbooks.com
twitter.com/angryrobotbooks
Too many gods

An Angry Robot paperback original 2013

Cover by Alejandro Colucci
Set in Meridien by Epub Services

Distributed in the United States by Penguin Random House, Inc., New York.

ISBN 978 0 85766 383 2
Ebook ISBN 978 0 85766 384 9

Printed in the United States of America

9 8 7 6

The book is dedicated to and to Charles R. Rutledge for all of his help, and to the memory of Fritz Leiber and Robert R. Howard for the inspiration.

ONE

An unfortunate fact about the Pra-Moresh: they tend to run in packs. The damned things are not only large, but they are also violent to a fault. The good news for most people is that they are rare. The bad news for Merros Dulver is that they still show up from time to time, and just at that moment, they'd decided to make their presence known.

Seventy-three days into the expedition across the Blasted Lands and they'd run across no sign of another living thing, unless one qualified the dust and the ice storms as being alive merely because they moved with such violence. Merros was many things, but stupid wasn't among them – his present situation excluded, as he would have argued the intelligence of his decision to lead the trip to the distant Seven Forges mountain range.

Seventy-three days of bitter cold and constant twilight and the same number of nights wasted as they moved slowly through the near-complete darkness toward the stone towers in the distance, their light the only source of illumination under a near-constant blanket of clouds that spewed ice on some occasions and a bitter tasting dust on others. The parts of him that weren't numbed by the cold were still aching with a deep and abiding chill that refused to go away. If it weren't for the thick furs he wore, he'd have been worried about frostbite and worse. If the money hadn't been such a sweet offer he'd have never considered this insanity.

And now Morello, the damned cook of all people, had alerted him to the howling screams of the Pra-Moresh. He wasn't upset with the cook for noticing; quite to the contrary, he was very grateful. He was also extremely annoyed that neither he nor any of the twenty soldiers with him had heard them first.

Merros stared out into the darkness of the afternoon and looked at the shapes where they moved, slowly circling around the camp, their low moans and high-pitched cackles grating on his nerves and sickening him with the odd noises that crept past even the sharp winds that tried to snatch all sounds away.

There has been a great deal of debate among the scholarly as to exactly what the Pra-Moresh are and where they came from. There have been no definitive answers, but most people accept that they're damned scary, damned big, and capable of eating roughly five times their not inconsiderable body weight in a single meal.

Merros had no desire to be dinner. To that end he called for his soldiers to get their asses in gear. The group had stopped for the night – day, whatever – only a little over an hour earlier and now they gathered their weapons and wits as quickly as they could, knowing by Merros' tone that this was not a drill or an exercise, but a serious issue that had to be dealt with immediately.

They were none of them pups anymore. Each of the soldiers he'd chosen to bring along had been chosen for several reasons, not the least of which was experience. The Empire demanded service from all of the men who lived within its reach, but this was different. The men he'd chosen were lifers, the sort who'd spent ten or more years in the ranks. Some of them had even seen real combat in various border skirmishes over the years, though not many, to be fair. It had been close to a century since the last major war involving the Empire had occurred. The Empire had won, so really there wasn't much to fight about.

Still, most of them had fought alongside him in a few bar skirmishes, and all of them had done combat in numerous exercises. He trusted them to know what end of the sword to use on the brutes that were looking at them from a distance, and more importantly, he trusted them to know how to use the crossbows. He didn't want to get close enough to the Pra-Moresh to get himself chewed on. He'd only ever seen illustrations of the damned things and one skull on display at the duke's palace. They were a great deal larger than he'd imagined.

"How damned long for the bows?" He was pleased that his voice didn't crack as he feared it might. Certainly his heart was pounding well enough to break his sternum.

Wollis loped in his direction, his game leg giving a twinge that did nothing to stop the man from coming along at a hard jog. His second carried a crossbow in each hand and a quiver of bolts was slapping against each hip. "Got 'em. Just had to dig them out of the extra blankets."

"Seriously, Wollis? Did you not think they might be a little more important than a damned blanket or two?"

The man looked at him and smirked. "You're the one that wanted extra blankets. It's been over two months and no encounters, so don't go getting all bitchy with me when something finally happens."

Anyone else and he would have been offended. Wollis knew him too well. Wollis was a northerner; he was used to the cold and to the heavy steppes that led to the Blasted Lands. He had also been on two previous expeditions into the great frozen waste, and as a result was invaluable as an asset. He had, however, never once encountered any living thing on his treks across the least hospitable part of the Empire.

Wollis looked at the shapes and let a low whistle spill from between his chapped lips. "I always figured the heads were, I dunno, properly sized to the bodies…"

The heads and faces of the beasts were large, but nearly tiny in comparison to the rest of them. The savage jaws of the things belonged to an animal the size of a bear, but the bodies? They didn't make bears that big.

Even as they assessed the creatures in the distance, the rest of the soldiers followed years of practice and loaded their crossbows, set their shields in the ready positions, and laid out spears and swords alike. None of them looked the least bit confident in their actions, which made perfect sense, really. The Pra-Moresh hadn't even attacked yet and their voices were making every last one of the trained veterans edgy. The creatures – whether they were smart enough to be called intelligent or not – had uncanny voices that called out in different tones and seemingly from different locations. One of the damned things sounded like a room full of people crying and laughing both. Several together sounded more like a small gathering of the damned.

From almost fifty yards away one of the things reared up onto its hind legs and let out a roar that warbled and shook through the air, calling in a dozen voices, challenging and demanding and weeping all at once. Even from that distance, Merros could feel the bones in his chest rattle with the sounds.

And then the damned things charged as one, their heavy claws carving trenches into the ice, allowing them purchase, whereas the soldiers had to balance themselves carefully or kneel in order to use their crossbows.

"At will! Take out their vile eyes!" Merros' voice was calm and loud despite a desire to hide away and do whatever he could to avoid being noticed. It was automatic after the years in a position of command. He was very grateful for the ability to sound like he wasn't ready to piss himself as he took careful aim and fired.

He watched the heavy wooden missile cut through the air, noticed how the feathers gave just the right spin to the shaft, allowing the bolt to stay true and go farther than he'd have hoped in the bitter winds. The metal tip of the bolt drove into the wrinkled fur of the creature's muzzle, driving deep and cutting through the muscles before stopping against the bone of the skull underneath. The Pra-Moresh shrieked-wailed-screamed and shook its head, but did not stop charging.

"Oh, shit." It was all he could think to say.

Wollis' missile took the creature in the eye and it reared back, the screaming noise replaced by a different sound, a single note of pain that was loud and clear and almost deafening.

There wasn't time to celebrate. The damned things were still charging. They moved hard and fast and lowered their heads, showing mostly the thick hide of their skulls and their impossibly broad backs. There would be no time to reload the bows. Instead it was down to using the spears.

The spears were designed to take down horsemen, and the soldiers knew how to use them. They braced the long poles in the hard-packed ground, digging in with the short spikes designed to help on the icy surface, and waited, holding to the places where they knew they might well die. Running would be a guarantee of death, something they'd all been taught in the army. More than one fool had tried and been executed for his troubles in the time that Merros had been with the army. He'd killed a few such men himself, a sad side effect of being an officer.

Damn it, they were big creatures. The ground shook as they came closer and every last one of his men was looking as nervous as he felt. "No one moves! No one runs, or I'll kill you myself, do you hear me?"

"Aye! Ho, sir!" The answer was automatic and belied the fear he saw on their faces. They would not run. They had never been trained for cowardice.

The first of the Pra-Moresh hit the line three soldiers away, and the spear that Kallir Lundt held drove in deep, puncturing flesh, cutting meat and stopping only when it reached the shoulder blade on the monster's other side. The beast shrieked – a sound that made Merros' teeth ache from this range, and his eyes vibrate in their sockets – and slapped one gigantic paw across Kallir's face and chest, carving his face away in one stroke. Kallir lived through it, which only made the situation worse.

And then there was only time to look at the nightmare in front of him, the enormous wall of charging teeth and claws that filled his entire world with a cacophony of screams that seemed designed solely to drive him mad. The spear in his hands shuddered with impact and then, damn every imaginable imp of ill fortune, broke in his grip. The splintering oak stung his fingers and shredded his gloves and the flesh on his palms as the beast drove forward, the wide, yellowed teeth snapping shut scant inches from his face. Wollis was there again, his spear pushing the beast back as it sank deep into the thing's side. It looked toward Wollis for a second, shriek-cry-roaring, and then lunged for Merros a second time.

He was a dead man. Nothing to be done but accept it. He had lived a good life, with women and friends and the occasional special moments that made everything feel right for however fleeting a time. He would miss the world; he would certainly miss not having raised a family, but it was alright. This was at least a worthy death, better than dying in a pool of his own vomit like that fool lieutenant he'd known when he was just starting his training.

The axe ripped past his head in a savage arc, cleaving the air hard enough to make a sharp whistling note he heard even over the demented noises of the Pra-Moresh. An instant later the animal that was about to end his existence was throwing itself back, trying to escape the blade that took out both of its eyes and drove deep into its brain. The haft of the weapon vibrated in the monster's ruined face and Merros looked at the thing as if he'd never seen an axe before. Mostly because this one was nothing quite like what he'd seen in his years of training. The metal was thin and black; the design spoke of a weapon meant to be thrown like a knife, despite the grip. Even as he took in the sudden save – *Alive! How the hell?* – and considered the odd-looking weapon, he saw another of the monsters fall, driven down by his men. The pain in his hands stopped him from attacking anything. Instead he looked at the heavy splinters which had pierced his flesh in a dozen places and tried to wrap his mind around being alive.

A second axe whistled past his head close enough for the blade to almost part his hair, and crashed into the face of another beast that had been turning toward Wollis with every intention of biting his second in half.

Merros frowned. One axe was strange. Two was simply crazy. He finally put the thoughts together and turned his head sharply, assessing where the axes had come from.

The rider hurled a short spear past him and Merros stared at the long cord that trailed from the thing back to the rider and the strange mount he rode. Everything was happening too damned fast, and he didn't like it. He stared at the rider for only a moment and then looked at the long streamer of rope that led past him and toward something behind him where the monsters were. Where he should have been looking all along if it weren't for the axes moving past his shoulder. Too much to see, to take in. He didn't like it at all, damn it.

The spear was buried deep in the neck of one of the monsters, which was roaring-shrieking-sobbing as it tried to get away from the barbed point that refused to come free.

Rider and mount backed up abruptly, and the beast let out a louder series of noises as the cord drew tight and then tighter still. The Pra-Moresh tried to get away, but the hooks in its neck were stubborn. As it started to slash at the tether leading back to the rider, the man pulled a preposterously long bow and drew back with a strength and speed that was unsettling. Merros didn't much like bows. He preferred crossbows because he felt the accuracy was better and the lack of range was easily compensated for by the ability to steady the weapon, even when mounted and riding. The man behind him apparently did not agree. The arrow he fired buried itself in the screaming thing's eye, and the creature fell hard and fast, very likely dead before the arrow had finished its journey.

While he watched the single rider slaughtering his enemy, four of Merros' soldiers died horribly at the hands of the Pra-Moresh. Tardu, Hanliss, Mox and the southerner, Alcard Hammil, were torn apart, the creatures hungrily shoving mouthfuls of their bleeding flesh into mouths that snapped and slavered. How long had it been since the creatures had eaten? Even with all of the supplies they'd brought with them, he and his men had to be careful. The beasts had brought nothing. For all he knew they'd been starving for weeks.

Merros drew his sword and held it tightly, looking from one fallen beast to the next. His men had killed three of the things. The single man behind him had killed three more. No. Four. The arrow whizzed past his ear and took out the last of the things as it came from up from behind the supply wagons. He prayed it hadn't gotten to the women. He hadn't even had a chance to think about them. Everything had happened too damned fast.

The rider again. Merros turned back toward the stranger just in time to watch him pull three more of his short spears from a strange-looking holster on the saddle of his mount. The spears were all barbed, much like the first one had been, and with unsettling accuracy he launched them hard and fast, each slamming into the thick fur and fat of the Pra-Moresh the man had killed.

"Wait! What are you doing?" The words left his mouth without any conscious thought. He damned near flinched at the hostile tone he found himself using. The rider had to be part demon. He'd killed four of the things and never even entered the combat save at a distance.

Also, frankly, he looked very, very large sitting atop the odd beast he was riding. It could have been the creature itself, which was substantially larger than any of the horses, even those bred for hauling the supply wagons.

The rider ignored him completely and turned his mount, which began moving slowly forward, the thick claws on its feet getting purchase on the slick, icy surface before it began pulling the four dead beasts behind it.

Wollis, faithful, sturdy and sometimes a little stupid, pulled his spear from the side of the dead nightmare he'd impaled and held it at the ready. "Captain Dulver asked you a question! You'd do well to answer it!"

He wanted to yell a loud no, wanted so much to stop Wollis from being so damnably efficient before it cost the man his life. Because while the facts weren't adding up for his second, Merros was having no trouble at all doing the math. The rider was a terror. No one should be that fast, that good at killing. No one.

The rider turned his head slowly to look first at Wollis and then at Merros. He wore a helmet, which in turn was partially covered by a thick fabric hood. The night was almost upon them and the little light that existed was fading, until they had only their torches and the distant Seven Forges to grant them meager illumination. That meant Merros couldn't truly see the face of the rider, but he saw the eyes clearly enough. They gave off their own light: a dead, gray color that shone out from under hood and helm alike, letting each man see clearly when he was being stared at.

Merros stood his ground. Wollis did too, but he looked a bit like running seemed a fair notion.

Before either of them could have done so, the rider's hand lashed out and a long line of leather unfolded like a frog's tongue. From seemingly nowhere the man had found and unfurled a whip, which cut the air. Had Wollis moved he would surely have regretted it. The whip caught the head of the spear and the rider tugged. Wollis squawked as the spear sailed away from him, his hands obviously stinging from the strength the rider used.

They stood that way for several heartbeats, Wollis staring at the rider, Merros doing the same, while the dark figure and his unnatural mount stood their ground and waited.

When no more words were forthcoming, the rider turned his odd mount around and they moved, pulling the four cooling corpses along as their prize.

"What the hell was that?" Wollis' voice was subdued.

Merros stared at the retreating figure, watched as it moved toward the distant Seven Forges. He took his time answering, seriously considering everything that had just happened.

"I have no idea. Gather the men. Gather the dead. Do it quickly. We're going to follow that rider until we get some answers." It was the sort of response he hadn't planned on giving. Not really. He'd have preferred to say something wiser, perhaps to have suggested that they forget all about the strange rider and his preposterous mount. Instead he'd said something that bordered on responsible.

Damned if his training wasn't going to get him killed.

Wollis looked at him for another long moment and responded. "Aye. Ho, Captain."

Damned if Wollis' training wasn't going to get them killed too.

Naturally they couldn't merely get on with what was planned. That would require participation from the people who'd hired them, in this case the three women who worked for Desh Krohan. Krohan was a legendary sorcerer. According to the stories he was not only old enough to remember the third Emperor, he was also powerful enough to kill his enemies from hundreds of miles away. The annoying thing about those sorts of claims was that they were damned hard to disprove. Maybe the wizard had killed an enemy in another part of the world and maybe he was just saying he had. What was known for certain was that a few people who'd angered him had died under unusual circumstances. Also, just because the books of lore claimed that a wizard named Desh Krohan lived four hundred years back didn't guarantee it was the same man. Merros was hardly the only soldier to have borne his name, and yet no one mistook him for his great grandfather or his second cousin. Hard to prove.

What Merros knew for certain was that the alleged sorcerer paid in gold, and that whatever the hell was hiding under the cloak had offered him a very large sum of money and paid him enough in advance to supply the wagons. What he suspected was that the man was probably adept at certain magicks and had built a reputation for himself that was at least half false claims. In any event the money was good and it was best not to refuse a man who could just possibly destroy your entire bloodline with little more than a few drops of blood and the very large cauldron he'd seen delivered to the sorcerer's domicile.

Even if that meant dealing with the three women who were now heading in his direction, while the surviving soldiers and workers gathered their dead and their belongings.

They were distractingly attractive women. Even dressed for the cold as they were, the soldiers turned and looked as the three approached Merros. He set his jaw and did his best not to look into their eyes. Despite extremely shapely forms – shapely enough that the furs seemed only to emphasize rather than detract from them – it was when he looked at their faces that he tended to forget how to think and to reason without wanting to—

Enough of that.

The brunette, Pella, spoke to him, her voice clear despite the wind. "Desh asks that you gather the bodies of the Pra-Moresh and take them with you as you follow the rider."

"What? How does he know about the beasts? About the rider for that matter." He didn't mean to be curt, but he'd seen and heard nothing from the sorcerer in over a month, and had only encountered the women who served the wizard when they left their wagon to tend to nature's call or to eat.

The blonde this time, her hair almost as white as the snow, her eyes so light a blue as to make him want to stare. Her lips full of promises and temptations best not thought about. Her name was – he looked away from that mouth with an effort – Goriah. "Desh has seen the battle with the Pra-Moresh. He has also seen your meeting with the rider."

"Really? Would you care to tell me what happens then?" Even he heard the skeptical tone in his voice. He believed in the abilities of wizards. It was sorcery that had destroyed the land he stood on, magic that had raised the City of Wonders from the ashes of old Canhoon. Still, the claims of seeing the future always left him doubtful. How could it be proved after the fact? He had heard far too many claim they could see the future.

The red-haired one responded, waving one delicate hand dismissively. "What has been seen will come to pass. Your inability to believe in the Sooth does not change it."

"So he knows nothing then?" Merros shook his head and damned near bit his own tongue. What had he been saying to himself ever since he took the commission? Angering mages is a wonderful way to end a life or twelve.

The redhead, Tataya, stared at him with hazel eyes that glittered in the cold. "You will lose your hand, find your fist and gain an ally. You will also meet your enemy face-to-face."

Without another word the woman spun away, heading slowly back toward her wagon. He stared for a moment, cursing her shape for being distracting, cursing his tongue for asking questions and his mind for immediately trying to interpret the riddle of her words.

"Wait. What does that mean?" His voice was harsh, bordered on demanding as he looked to the other women.

Both of them lowered their eyes, lowered their faces, and then stepped back toward the wagon, not quite as dismissively as the redhead, but their postures told him he would get no more answers.

He gave thought to spitting, but it was cold enough that the damned stuff would likely freeze to his skin. Instead he pulled his scarf back over his lower face and moved to join the men as they readied the horses.

Fifteen minutes after the rider had left the campsite, Merros and his people did the same, following behind the stranger as best they could in the near-darkness of the late afternoon. They'd have surely lost him but the bodies of the Pra-Moresh left long trails to follow and even the constant winds of the Blasted Lands weren't enough to scour away the heavy marks left in the occasional drifts of snow and ash.

The ride was long, and better men than Merros were in charge of following the trail and taking care of poor Lundt, who was sobbing softly as he fought to keep his life for himself and not for the great darkness. He left them to it. Instead he reflected on exactly how he'd come to this point and what it meant.

Retirement from the army meant a stipend. Not enough to live comfortably, but enough to eke out a living. As Merros had hired on when he was barely of age, he'd retired while young enough to do other things with his life. The sad fact was, however, that there was little he was good at aside from being a soldier. Little that interested him for that matter. So when the three women came to him and made their offer on behalf of the wizard, he said yes. There was a real possibility that he might not have said yes quite as quickly had they not been very attractive women, but the odds were still that he would have. The money was good and he was on the edge of going out to the pubs and looking for fights to join into, or worse, signing on with the City Guard to keep himself from getting too bored. The City Guard: as far as he was concerned they were the worst sorts of rabble. Most of them couldn't make it as soldiers and so they had signed up as local enforcement and bullied their way around, believing that made up for their lack of actual skill. He'd lived in a dozen towns and as far as he was concerned it was the same in all of them.

He didn't know why the wizard wanted to examine the Seven Forges. He didn't much care, either. He understood the reasoning well enough. There were, according to the legends, numerous treasures just waiting to be recaptured: great war machines, cold and sorcerous weapons lost during the great Annihilation that founded the Empire of Fellein, hundreds of years ago – possibly more than a thousand, though, of course, no one could say with certainty any longer. Too many years, too many wars and catastrophes had happened to guarantee the accuracy of anything written in the history books.

All he needed to know was that gold was involved. If that sounded mercenary, then so be it. The fact was simple: he was taking on a very dangerous assignment and he had every intention of finishing it as quickly and efficiently as he could.

The rider they were following, however, did not go with any of the ideas he'd had for how this would play out. There were expeditions that had not come back in the past. Some did; Wollis was a perfect example of successful expeditions. He'd spoken with his second at length regarding what to expect and so far they'd encountered exactly what was supposed to be out here. Nothing.

Now Pra-Moresh came out of the damned shadows and strange riders came along to kill the monsters and take the bodies. He looked behind the last wagon and saw that the remaining carcasses were still chained to the end of the wagon, as they should be. Wollis had another rider with him, both trailing behind the wagons, and his second nodded before moving forward. He hadn't meant to summon the man, but didn't much mind the company.

Wollis pulled up next to him, the horse under him looking as calm as could be, despite the way all of the animals had acted earlier when the Pra-Moresh came for them. That was good. The animals being skittish would have made everything worse.

"Do you think we'll catch him?" Wollis' voice was brusque. It was always brusque.

"Maybe not for a few more hours." He squinted and looked toward the distant smear on the horizon. "Whatever that thing is he's riding, it's faster than the horses."

"Damned well should be. Did you see the size of it?"

"It's pulling four Pra-Moresh. Our best horses are struggling with the weight of three."

"Well, they've also got a wagon." Wollis looked back at the team of four horses. "Alright. And his mount is pulling four…" The man looked from the team toward the distant shape. He let out a low grunt of disbelief.

"So you can see why I think he might outdistance us with ease."

"I don't suppose we could take half the soldiers and catch up with him?"

Merros shook his head. "Much as I would like that, I don't feel we can safely leave our supplies and our charges undefended." Wollis opened his mouth to protest and Merros countered before he could. "We have just survived an attack by seven particularly large beasts. I don't want to take a chance that there are more of them out there. Also, I don't want to offend that rider without having a great deal of back up."

"But–"

"He killed four of the beasts. Four. Think that through. We lost six men. Seven if you count poor Lundt. We killed three of the damned things."

Wollis nodded his head and sighed. They rode in silence for a while and finally Wollis spoke up again. "I've been out here twice and never seen so much as a shrub growing. In one day we've seen more than I have seen in over a year of my life spent out here."

"What do you suppose that means, Wollis?"

The man looked out at the distant mountains. The glow from the Seven Forges was lighting the sky in that direction a dark, angry red. Even from miles away the light from each mountain was distinct.

There were seven red stains on the underbelly of the clouds.

"Honestly? I think it means I was lucky."

"Why's that?"

Wollis reached into his saddlebag and pulled a stick of dried meat from its depths. He brushed it clean of lint and dust and then clamped it between his teeth before he answered. "Either it means I've never had the misfortune of running across the Pra-Moresh before, or I've never had the misfortune of running across the sort of man who hunts them."

"Hunts them?" Merros looked hard at him.

Wollis chewed on his dried meat for a moment while his eyes scanned the horizon. Best to be careful, a lesson they'd almost forgotten earlier. "Hunts them."

"Why the hell would anyone hunt those things?"

"Merros, why would anyone come out to this gods-forgotten land and kill those things and then take the bodies with them? They wouldn't, unless they were actively hunting them down to kill and keep."

Merros stared hard at the distant shape. The shape they were following, because he'd ordered it.

"Well, that's… that's…"

"Insane? Maybe." Wollis finally had the meat softened enough to actually tear a chunk free. The rest he put back in his saddlebag. "Now tell me, Captain, what does that say about the sort of fools who then follow the man who goes hunting after that sort of creature?"

Merros had no answer to that. Wollis drifted back to the end of the caravan, and Merros let him. He had to think. He had a lot to think about.

They kept riding, not quite immune to the cold, the ash and the wind, but close enough that they seldom noticed unless the winds gusted. Merros didn't like to think about how long it had been since he'd had a proper bath. Back in the capital city of Tyrne he had bathed nearly every day, and when he was younger, before the army moved him to a different place, he had bathed every day in the river at the edge of the family farm. A smile crept across his face as he thought about a few of the encounters he'd had with Delih, the girl who'd lived just down the road from his family back then. He didn't let himself dwell on those memories for too long, however, as the only women he'd seen in far too long were decidedly unavailable for his needs.

Not married. Never married. He told himself he was fine with that, but sometimes there was that little ghost of a voice that wondered how different his world would have been with a family of his own: a wife, children, possibly even a son among them.

Enough. The dot in the distance was growing a bit larger. Either the rider had stopped to rest, or he was waiting for them. Either way, he wanted this done.

No. There was one option he hadn't considered. The rider was coming back. He gestured over his shoulder and a moment later Wollis pulled up beside him again, not the least bit inconvenienced by the change of plans.

"Is it me? Or is he coming back our way?"

Wollis stared long and hard and finally spat a wad of dark phlegm into the snow. Wollis was from a people that spat to show their dissatisfaction. In this case, however, he was merely clearing his mouth of the ash that constantly blew through the air of the Blasted Lands.

"It's not you. He's definitely coming back."

"Right then. Alert the others and be ready." He looked at Wollis long and hard. "I'm going to meet him."

"Do you want company?"

"No." He looked back at the Pra-Moresh being dragged behind the last wagon. "But I want those bodies. Have Lomma catch up with me."

"He'll be delighted, I'm sure." The sarcasm was obvious, even through the winds. Lomma was not a fighter. He was a whiner. He'd been damned near crying at every opportunity since they'd started this fool's expedition. That was the problem with hiring civilians for a trip, but in this case the man also owned the wagon and the horses. He had come along to protect his property.

"He's not that bad, is he?"

"He is, and you know he is. I swear he whines more than my wife did when she gave birth to our ass-first son."

Merros chuckled and shook his head. "Does Nolan know you call him that?"

Wollis rolled his eyes. "Gods no. If he did he'd have slit my throat in my sleep."

That was probably true. At fourteen the lad was constantly in a bad mood. "Get on with it and wish me well."

"Oh, I wish you very well. Make a friend, not a foe. I should rather not die today." Wollis turned his horse and rode back at a fast trot, while the captain shook his head, checked his sword and weapons, and then charged forward, quickly moving past the caravan. He spared one look behind him to see that Lomma was indeed following, though not quite as quickly.

He had long enough to consider what he wanted to say to the stranger. Having seen the man kill four of the fiercest creatures he'd ever seen in motion, he wanted very much for their meeting to be friendly.

The wagon lurched to a halt next to his horse, and Lomma looked toward him, a worried sneer on the lame man's round face. Lomma had been a soldier once, but hadn't fared well in a border skirmish to the south. The end result was a right foot that was missing all of the toes, and a knee that refused to hold him in an upright position unless he was bracing himself with a cane. To that end, the man seldom left his wagon if he could avoid it.

"That the one I saw earlier killing all those things?"

"Oh, yes."

"I just wanted to make sure." He very calmly reached over and held up his crossbow: a massive thing, with a bolt large enough to take down a bear. It was also only good for one shot, because to reload it required the use of a pulley system.

"You plan on using that, don't even raise it unless he attacks me first."

"Don't plan on using it at all, but if he kills you, I'll give it a try." Lomma didn't even bother looking at him. Instead he focused on the rider coming closer. Merros took the time to look the rider over again as well, and was not made more comfortable on the second assessment.

The man was large. Not gigantic, but decidedly large. Though like everyone else he was bundled up against the cold, his forearms were exposed to the elements, and even from a distance Merros could see the muscles moving smoothly under the skin as the rider casually moved the reins and rested one hand near the hilt of a well-worn sword pommel. His face was still covered by both a veil to protect from the ash and by the heavy helmet he wore under the hood of his cloak.

The thing he rode, first taken for a horse, was anything but. Closer up he could see the thick fur of the thing, the heavy, padded feet and claws designed for gripping the rough, icy surface, and the metal latticework over the face that both helped protect from the elements and, unfortunately, hid away the features of the thing. Merros thought he'd imagined the claws on the feet of the beast earlier, but now knew better. What the hell was he getting himself into?

Merros might well have continued staring at the man, but motion at the edge of his vision caught his attention and made him look to his left, where the three women of the mage were walking closer, their cloaks whipping in the strong winds.

"Why are you here?" His words were demanding. They were not here except to report to their damnable wizard. He didn't like that they were suddenly comfortable walking where they pleased after so long keeping to themselves.

Their faces were too well-covered, but he recognized the blue eyes of the blonde woman. "In case you cannot speak his tongue. In case you need someone to speak on your behalf, Captain."

"You know about this man? About the thing he rides?" The notion was preposterous. How could they know of him when they'd never been out here before?

She shook her head. "Desh Krohan has suspicions about the rider. He believes we might be able to translate if the need arises." Her words were a lie. He felt it in the beating of his heart. Still, he had no choice in this. What if the rider wanted to speak and they had no common tongue? What then?

"We can aid you or leave you with your rider, but decide now, Merros Dulver." There was no anger or recrimination in the woman's voice. She was merely stating a fact. "Your rider is almost here."

He looked away from her and was startled by how much closer the man was. The great beast under him stopped moving and the rider swayed softly as he compensated for the change. Beyond that he was motionless for a long moment.

Lomma made a noise in his throat that could have been a cough or a worried note.

The rider slid from the saddle and landed with ease, the armor and leather on his body jostled and the cloak covering him opened enough to reveal that he was carrying still more weapons.

One of the other women spoke; Merros didn't have the inclination to look away from his opponent to determine which one. "Captain? What is your decision?"

"Speak to him."

Before any of them could attempt it, the rider came closer; his stride was efficient, but not overly cocky. He stopped well within reach of the blade he wore on his hip, a fact that Merros did not miss.

The rider's voice was low and harsh, the words a nonsensical blend of sibilance and barking noises that obviously formed language, but one completely unknown to the captain. The tone was dark enough that Lomma's hand moved toward the crossbow and Merros stopped him with a gesture.

"He demands to know why you follow him." The woman's voice was not completely confident.

"Is that a guess or are you sure?" He made himself look at the woman. It was the redhead speaking this time. He could see the dark red curls of her hair flowing from the edge of her hood.

"A near certainty."

"That's not comforting." He was aware of the rider, knew the man was staring hard at the back of his head, could damned near feel the man's eyes looking for the best place to bury the blade of his sword.

"It is what it is, Captain." He forced himself to look away from her eyes and whatever secrets they might be holding.

"Then tell him we wish to offer our thanks for his assistance, to gift him with the kills he left behind."

The brunette spoke, calling out in a strong, steady voice that was easily heard over the sound of the winds. The rider tilted his head, listening to her words, and Merros wished again that he could see the face buried under shadows, to know what the man was thinking. The eyes that looked him over still shined with that odd gray light, but gave away nothing, no hint of what the rider might be thinking.

Another exchange, the words that snapped from the rider's mouth were harsh, guttural, and had an undercurrent of odd sounds that made him think of the Pra-Moresh, as if more than one voice was being heard. He felt the fine hairs along his neck rise at the very thought.

All three women spoke at the same time, their voices spiraling around each other in an odd harmony that once again brought the savage beasts to mind.

This time, when the rider answered, it was with laughter, loud and rough. He lifted both of his hands over his head and waved them almost daintily, and though he had no correlation to the gesture, Merros understood it was a sign of humor, simply because that notion fit.

The redhead turned toward Merros and sidled closer. He lowered his head until he was closer to her level, despite still being on his horse.

"He has invited us to join him in a meal." She paused for a moment. "I offered him the beasts and he accepted."

"What did you say that made him laugh?"

"Initially he was offended. He took insult to the notion that we thought he could not kill his own dinner."

They eat those things? The thought was slightly sickening.

"What made him change his mind?"

"I told him he caught you and your men on the chamber pot. For that reason you felt you did not deserve the kills."

"So, you insulted me to the rider?"

She nodded slowly but shrugged at the same time. "No. I insulted you on your behalf."

"I'm not sure how I feel about that." Merros frowned as he stared at the rider. The man was a brute, and it was best not to be fighting him. Still, it was hard to accept.

"You should feel very good about it. Had I not allowed humor to take the place of what he saw as a challenge, he had every intention of challenging you to a blood match."

His eyes took in the arsenal of weapons surrounding the rider. "Fair enough. Please thank him for the hospitality and accept on our behalf."

Her eyes smiled and she nodded again. "Consider it done."

A few moments later the caravan began moving, led by the rider. No one moved very quickly as the winds grew stronger. The women who served the wizard walked across the landscape, seemingly unfazed by the elements, while Merros and his men huddled in their cloaks and did their best not to be blown from their horses.

Magic. Maybe the women were protected by it. Whatever the case, they seemed far more at ease than he felt as they rode ever on toward the Seven Forges in the distance.

TWO

The entire caravan was forced to stop when the storm came, a howling, furious thing that made standing in the open a near guarantee of a savage battering. The men worked hard and quickly, covering the horses with the padded blankets that would have never been brought along had it not been for Wollis' insistence. Merros was glad he'd listened to his second. The wind brought harsh blades of stone and ice that slid across the ground and skipped through the air, cutting at flesh wherever they touched. Between the cuts and bruises he'd received on his hands while fighting the Pra-Moresh, and the three slashes that graced his neck and face when the storm first hit, it seemed like every part of him was aching and miserable. Then again, that much hadn't changed since the trek had started.

Still and all, he hardly had anything to complain about. The rider sat across from him in the center of the wagon – that also carried the three servants of Desh Krohan – the interior of which was decorated in thick furs and a scattering of pillows, save where they managed a small fire in a metal contraption that allowed them to cook and heat the wagon without catching the whole thing aflame. The women had cooked for them, an unexpected treat – several delicacies that shouldn't have been possible in the frozen wasteland – and now they sat facing each other in the insulated interior, safe from the worst of the winds and the cold.

Which, so far, had done nothing to reveal anything at all about the rider. He had taken off the helmet protecting his head, had pulled down the hood of his cloak, but only revealed that his head and face were covered with a thick layer of insulating cloths that he did not remove. It was still impossible to see much aside from his eyes and the skin around them, which had a gray tint and was well weathered. Even when he ate, the rider merely slid whatever morsel he was eating under the cloth that covered his lower face and chewed slowly.

Merros resisted the urge to pull the damned cloths away. Curiosity wasn't worth getting himself killed over.

As they finished the meal, Pella settled herself down on the cushions to the left of the rider and touched his gauntleted arm with her long, delicate fingers. She spoke softly, but the foul language distorted her voice and made her normally pleasant tones uncomfortable.

The rider listened and responded in kind, and though Pella looked at Merros, it was Tataya, the redhead, who spoke to the captain. "His name is Drask. His title is Silver Hand." She frowned. "I have no idea what the title means." She shrugged and poured a strong, hot elixir into several small cups. He had watched her settle tealeaves into the pot, but seen a few other liquids and plants tossed in as well. Though he was suspicious by nature – it was almost a requirement among officers in the army – Merros took the offered drink and sipped at it carefully. The heat of the brew was pleasant, and whatever had been added to the tea had the muscles in his body relaxing in a decidedly comfortable way.

Drask drank without hesitation as well. Despite his earlier attitude at being followed, he seemed a trusting enough soul. It was the blonde who spoke next – and if he couldn't remember her name soon, it was going to drive him into a rage. It was on the tip of his tongue, damn it – her voice carrying an odd, nearly lazy quality. "This is tiresome. Better if you could speak to each other, I think, without our interference."

Merros frowned. "I've yet to learn how to speak new languages without years of practice."

Tataya touched his forehead and Pella brushed her fingers over the exposed skin of Drask's eyes at the same time. Then the two women reached out and touched their free hands to each other, palm to palm, fingertips to fingertips.

And the blonde whispered something into the air. For a moment the pressure in the cabin seemed to triple and Merros blinked, gasped, struggled to breathe. And then everything was fine again.

"What did you do to me?" He was thinking the words, even as Drask spoke them.

The blonde waved her hand and moved to sit in a thick pile of furs. "A trifle. You can speak freely now, and understand each other."

"You've used sorcery on me?" Merros' skin suddenly felt clammy and chilled again, the pleasant heat from the fire and the drink alike fading to nothing.

"A minor thing. Only so that you can speak to each other without having to speak through us. This way the words you hear are as they were meant to be heard." Tataya spoke, her tones soft, placating, her eyes as nearly hypnotic as ever. And he had to concede her point. There had certainly been occasions where translators had made errors. For that reason alone he forced himself to calm down. There was a man here. For all he knew him, Drask, lived alone, but he doubted it. The weapons, the armor, they all bespoke a soldier, and very few soldiers ever lived off by themselves. He was here to map out the Seven Forges mountains. There was always the possibility that meeting a people who lived near the mountains would be worthy of extra rewards. Haste was a foolish waste of energy. So, too, anger at what was already done.

"Should the need arise again, Tataya, I'd ask that you and yours ask before gifting me with any form of sorcery." That sounded properly polite. He was annoyed, yes, but not foolish enough to taunt someone who could use enchantments. His childhood was filled with stories of people who crossed wizards, and all one had to do was look around to see what happened when the greatest of them warred between each other.

Tataya opened her mouth to speak, but Drask talked first. "You have fed me. You have sheltered me. We should rest. When the winds have calmed, I'll take you to meet with my elders." His words were for Pella. His eyes looked to Merros.

Merros was a captain in the army. He had long since developed a skill for knowing when he should answer and when he should hold his tongue. In this case, he let the woman answer.

"We were glad to offer you the shelter, Drask and we are far more grateful to meet your elders, your family." He couldn't have said it better himself.

The wagon rocked in the savage winds, and the wood creaked as the air outside roared its frustration at not getting inside. Despite their protection, Merros wondered if the horses would be well when the storm abated. Without the horses, they were as good as dead. They couldn't possibly carry the supplies, and the journey had already left them far away from any form of shelter save whatever Drask and his people might offer. And while they were, for the moment at least, speaking civilly, he had to remember that several expeditions had come this way previously. For all he knew the ones that had never showed again had fallen victim to whatever hospitalities were waiting at the Seven Forges.

"I am curious, Drask. If I may, why do you carry the title 'Silver Hand?'" He asked mostly just to keep the conversation going while he pondered the possibilities of what lay ahead.

Drask looked at him for a moment, his eyes unreadable, and then raised his right hand to eye level before he pulled away the armored glove that covered it. The skin of his forearm and wrist, as with his face, had a gray tinge that looked unhealthy, but from the edge of his wrist up, his entire hand changed. The texture, the color, was unmistakably metallic. Merros leaned in closer and stared hard at the appendage, fascinated. The hand was not real. It couldn't be. The flesh was silver; it shone with the warmth of the fire, but the skin where the hand connected to the rest of the arm was rough, scarred, and twisted with lines of silver that shot directly into the rider's natural flesh. Though they seemed organic in nature, there were deep scars running across the silver surface, runes and markings that had to be etched in place when the limb was forged, or before the metal had completely cooled.

"How on earth…?" His voice trailed away. Magic, of course. Not a sorcery he was familiar with, but what else could it be?

Drask very casually reached out and worked his glove back over the metallic surface. "A gift. A replacement for what was taken from me." Drask's tone wasn't quite brusque, but Merros nodded his head and forced himself to ask nothing else. Whatever had happened to the rider's hand, it was apparently a private thing. The captain chose to understand that. Why antagonize the man?

There was no more speech that night. The storm was far too severe for anyone to brave heading out into it, and so the five of them stayed the night together in the wagon. Merros settled himself near the door, and the three women slept together in a pile of furs he couldn't help but envy. The rider, Drask of the unnatural hand, placed himself in a corner – a proper spot for anyone who was left in uncomfortable surroundings – and soon drifted into silence if not sleep.

Merros was considering how likely it was that he'd never get to sleep when he drifted away into a deep rest.

The morning brought the sort of calm that seldom shows up save before or after a storm, and Merros crept carefully from the wagon to inspect the damage. Most everything was fine, save that the bodies of the Pra-Moresh had been stripped of half their fur in the blasting winds. If that was the worst thing that happened, he was glad to call the storm a successful encounter.

They were ready and on their way again in short order, with Drask riding at the front and Merros keeping the strange man company. They mostly rode in silence.

Three hours or more into the day's journey the sun managed to force itself through the nearly perpetual twilight brought by the clouds, and changed the way that damned near everything around them looked. The bright rays struck the land, and, in turn, the land retaliated with a thousand shimmering reflections. Even from a distance, he could see the ruins as they approached them.

There were stories, of course. But that was all most people would ever have when it came to the Blasted Lands. The tales of his youth told that the land had once been populated by great cities, and until the sun broke through the cloud cover, Merros would have thought the stories little more than myths. That changed when he saw the mounds to the west of them.

He stared, unable to look away, drawn to the shadows that hinted at other things buried in the fractured, broken glass towers that had been worn nearly smooth by centuries of harsh winds, but that still survived against the impossible odds. The glinting sunlight made him squint, which only made the half-shapes buried in the glass seem even more... organic.

"What are they?" He was barely aware that he'd spoken aloud.

Drask answered him with an oddly detached tone, as if the answer should have been obvious, but still he had trouble looking away. "The Mounds. Death."

"Death?" That seemed a bit dramatic.

"Nothing that goes too near the Mounds survives. Nothing. No one." Drask shrugged. "Things live there. Things that only come out in the darkness."

"How do you know that?"

"Your kind has tried to explore them before, looking for treasures. They have never come back."

"You've seen my kind before?"

Drask chuckled. "Only from a distance."

"Why is that?"

"They always want to explore the Mounds."

Merros opened his mouth to ask another question but the query faded from his lips, his mind, as the sound came from the Mounds. It was a low, deep noise, so low that he nearly felt it more in his teeth than heard it. A long, deep ululation, a mournful tone that made the horse under him dance nervously, and the steed he rode was a well-trained animal, not known for being skittish.

The beast under Drask did not get skittish, but it turned to face the Mounds and a loud hiss escaped from under its armored mask. The thick claws of the thing scratched at the ground and everything about its posture made Merros think it wanted little more than to attack whatever was making the impossible noise.

Drask cuffed the beast between its ears and screamed something that sounded like a different language altogether. The animal immediately calmed down.

"What the hell is that?" The noise was fading away at last, and the scrawling sensation that Merros had barely been aware of eased on his flesh.

"The Mounds." Drask shrugged. "Things live there."

"Have you ever seen the things that live there?"

"No."

"Aren't you curious?" A foolish question. He might be curious himself; on the other hand he had a strong sense of self-preservation that said exploring the Mounds would be a hideous notion.

"Of course. But it is forbidden."

"Who forbids it?" This was a chance, just possibly, to hear about the authorities of Drask's people. The lawmakers, the enforcers. Merros was looking forward to making his encounter with the strangers but a little knowledge would have made him feel a good deal more comfortable.

Drask looked at him, his face still hidden, but the eyes that stared at him expressed their surprise well enough, as did the tone of his voice. "The gods. Who else?"

They rode on a while longer in silence while Merros considered that answer. As they rode, the darkness crept back in and obscured the Mounds, but not before Merros could recognize some of the distant debris for what it was: there was at least one wagon over there, broken, yes, but the design was familiar enough. He'd been living in one just like it for the last two and a half months.

"So, none of my people ever made it to your home before, Drask?"

Drask looked back at him, his face once again lost. His eyes glowing dully. "Not that I have met."

Vagaries. He hated that. "Have you ever heard of any making it?"

Drask did not answer.

When they finally stopped for the day Merros' body ached from the long ride. He knew the horses were probably exhausted, and that the soldiers were as tired as he was and in fact they'd ridden for close to three hours longer than he would have preferred, but there are many ways to learn about the people you deal with and one thing he didn't feel he could do was offer any weakness to the rider. Drask was a worthy fighter and more, and he could not allow the man to think that he and his would tire sooner than Drask or his people. It went against his training.

While the soldiers set the wagons for the night, preparing for the possibility of another storm after Drask warned them, Merros rode a small distance away with the rider and they observed the mountains, closer now than ever.

"How long until we reach your home?"

Drask rolled his shoulders and stretched his arms. For a moment the area where his flesh arm met his metal hand was bared and Merros stared, mesmerized by the odd fusion of skin and silver. Scar tissue and weaving strands of metal and muscle were visible. What sort of man could withstand the pain that had surely been a part of the marriage? The very notion made him want to shiver.

"Two more days to the mountains. One more day to get through the pass and then we are there."

"What took you so far from your home in the first place? Surely you weren't merely looking for the Pra-Moresh."

"Hunting."

"For the beasts?"

Drask slid easily from the saddle on his mount, his hand touching the beast the entire time he descended, a reminder to the animal that he was there and not a threat. He was a big man, a brute, to be sure, but next to his animal he seemed small. The great creature yawned and bared wide, predatory teeth as it did.

"No. The Cacklers are just a bonus." Cacklers. A nickname they had for the Pra-Moresh. It seemed almost a term of affection for creatures that could kill a dozen men with ease.

"Then what were you hunting for?"

"You." Drask slipped his hand into the saddlebag on his mount's side and dug around and as he did so, the skin on Merros' body crawled again. Sometimes the doubling effect of the rider's voice still unsettled him. His hand moved toward his sword without conscious thought. He rested his fingers on the hilt.

Drask pulled out a metal horn that was neither elegant nor elaborate. "Who do you plan to call, Drask?"

"My people. They will meet us here. To come further without their permission would be foolish." Damned if his voice didn't seem even more unsettling, more alien than before.

"Why is that?"

"We do not see strangers often." With no more warning the rider turned toward the mountains and pulled the cloths from his face. Merros nearly cursed under his breath because the man's face remained hidden, turned away from him as the horn was lifted and then sounded. The note was clear and sharp, unexpectedly loud.

Less than a minute passed before a horn sounded in the distance, faint, but still clear enough to be heard over the winds. There was no mistaking the sound.

"Now what?"

"We wait. They will come."

"We have to wait three days for them?"

"No." Drask pointed toward the north, toward the mountains. "They will be here in hours. They will ride as fast as they can to meet you."

"Why were you waiting for us, Drask?" He shook his head. "Why were you looking for us?"

"What the gods command, we do. It is our way."

"Are your people very religious, Drask?"

"Aren't yours?"

"Some of us are, I suppose."

Drask patted his animal and slid the horn back into his saddlebag, his face once again obscured by the cloth and the helm alike. He did not look at Merros as he spoke again, but instead made himself busy checking the buckles and straps that held his saddle on his mount. "When the world was younger and our people were separated from yours, we expected to die. We were prepared for it. Do you understand?"

Merros blinked and slowly nodded. He hadn't expected to hear that Drask and his people remembered the Great Annihilation, though he supposed he should have.

"We readied ourselves for death, but death did not come. Instead the Seven Gods awoke and took us in. They offered us life if we served them, and so, we have served them well and faithfully and they have given us life for these many years."

"The Seven Gods?"

Drask gestured toward the distant mountains. "You call them the Seven Forges. We call them the Hearts of the Gods."

Merros shook his head and kept his tongue. He'd heard of savages worshiping fire before, but had never thought to meet any. Like so many things he'd heard about, he thought the tales were merely stories meant to entertain children. Or possibly to frighten them.

"Do your gods speak to you?"

"They speak when they want to speak, and to whom they want to speak." Drask looked out at the darkness, his eyes scanning the horizon for signs of approaching riders, perhaps, or just for any sign of change.

"Have they ever spoken to you?"

"Of course. I am here. I would not be here if they did not tell me to go out and find you."

"Just you?"

"No. Others rode out as well. It was my fortune to find you." His tone was exasperated, as if he were explaining to a child and rapidly growing bored, but still Merros had to ask more questions.

"And your gods, they wanted you to meet us?" He mulled that over as he asked.

Drask turned and looked him over from head to toe. "No."

"But you said—"

"Not 'us.' You. I was sent to meet you."

"Me? Personally?"

"Yes."

"Why?" The notion was absurd. He didn't believe in his own gods, let alone the gods of a stranger.

Drask scuffed at a rock with his foot and the stone skipped and skittered away into the darkness. In the distance a few of the horses whinnied, but there were no other sounds to hear in the oddly still air.

When Drask finally answered he did so with an odd finality that put an end to the conversation. "I do not question the gods. I obey the gods."

Merros was puzzling over those words when Drask spoke again. "They come." He pointed out into the distance where several shapes moved toward them, dark riders on dark beasts that looked much like Drask and his mount.

They rode hard, tearing up the distance, their bodies low over their mounts, their cloaks whipping frantically in the air.

"Why are they in such a hurry?"

Drask stared at the distant riders and a sigh escaped him, long and drawn out. "We are expected. You are expected. It is time."

Merros shook his head. "Time for what?"

Drask shook his head. "Only the gods can say."

Merros checked the weapons on his body, making sure he had easy access to all of them. "Honestly, Drask. I truly hate this cryptic nonsense. You either know why they're coming for me in particular or you do not know."

He turned his horse and moved back toward the camp at a canter. "Wollis! I need you!"

Wollis nodded and moved to meet him, still on foot. "Aye! Ho, sir!"

"There are riders coming. Apparently they're interested in meeting me. I have no idea why. Whatever the case, you're in charge until I return. If I don't return, it might be best to assume we're dealing with hostiles."

"Do you want us to come after you?"

Merros muttered faint laughter. "Of course I do. I've no death wish. But if the numbers look too outrageous, retreat."

All three of the mage's women came toward them. Sometimes he thought they were just waiting for him to act in any sort of official capacity before they came over to add in their own comments. Other times he bloody well knew it.

Pella spoke up, her voice urgent. "This is a time of great opportunity for you, Captain Dulver. Desh Krohan believes you are supposed to meet your destiny here."

"Really?" He rolled his eyes. "Your great sorcerer feels I need to meet my destiny here. Has he told you what that destiny might be?" He leaned down in the saddle until he was closer to her face. She was beautiful, but just then he wasn't much worried about her looks. He was worried about the forces coming for him, because if they were anything like the single rider he'd been talking with, he was fairly sure his destiny would involve getting cut into so many shreds of meat. "Has he told you why a rider out hunting the most dangerous animals I've ever seen might feel the need to bring a few friends along for me to meet this destiny?"

She shook her head.

"Then with all due respect to Desh Krohan as my employer, I'd ask that in the future he either keep his opinions to himself or give me a little more advanced warning when I'm about to get myself killed." Merros hissed the words. He was nervous. He was very nervous, but he also knew he had to keep his calm well enough to make sure that the women and the other people he was in charge of were kept as safe as possible.

He looked to Wollis again. "Stay here. Get the men armed and ready. If I live through 'meeting my destiny' you might need to get out of here in a hurry."

"Do you think they mean to kill you?"

"I have no idea, but let's just assume they're riding over here at high speed to do something a little worse than shake my hand, shall we?"

With that he turned his horse again and tapped with his heels, giving the command to move faster.

The horse listened and started toward the riders coming their way. Merros was a little unsettled to see how much closer they'd gotten while he had his conversation.

Throughout the entire exchange Drask had remained where he was, but as Merros started riding toward the approaching group, he quickly climbed back onto his mount and moved to pace alongside him. The damned beast he rode was still unsettling to watch; it was too big and too predatory for his happiness. And the men coming toward him were riding more of the same things.

Merros was not a religious man; just the same, he said a quick prayer to the gods he was familiar with and left the gods of the Seven Forges out of the equation. Better the deity you know, after all.

It seemed like the riders should have been hours away, but the distances were distorted out in the darkness of the Blasted Lands, and despite any hopes he might have had for more time to prepare himself they were soon within hailing range. Drask did not hail them. Instead he kept riding. Merros resisted the urge to reach for his sword. It was a nervous notion, surely, and he didn't like the idea of appearing any more nervous than he had to.

The riders stopped their mounts, the great beasts snorting and panting steamy breaths into the air. They looked tired and Merros was grateful for that. Maybe that meant they'd only want to kill him and his horse, and not play with their food first. Whatever doubts he'd had about the beasts before were removed as he looked them over. They were definitely predators.

They had teeth that were as long as daggers and the masks they wore to shelter them from the wind, while different from the one on Drask's mount, were still heavily armored.

So too were the men who'd been riding them. The riders dismounted with a small clatter of arms and armor alike. All of them wore helmets, great metallic contraptions that bore ornamental horns in some cases, or were sculpted to look like the skulls of great beasts in others. Years of service to the Emperor's army and he'd never seen a more intimidating lot of men in his life. They did not move with menace, but rather with the sort of grace that spoke of hard years learning to move in their armor and to wield their weapons while encumbered. Worse, even in the darkness of the Blasted Lands, he could see the scars and pit marks on the armor. It wasn't for show; it was for function.

One of the riders stepped in front of the others, tilting his head slightly as he looked Merros over from his boots to the hood he was using to stay warm. His eyes gave the same unsettling light as Drask's.

When he spoke his voice was calm, and he spoke the Emperor's tongue, but with a thick accent that was harsh but intelligible. "You are Merros Dulver." It wasn't a question.

"I am." He swallowed his heart, which was doing its level best to sneak out of his throat and make a run for it.

"We are here for you."

"What do you want of me?" His hand slid closer to the hilt of his sword and he saw the eyes of the speaker flicker briefly down to observe the motion. That wasn't a comforting notion at all.

"Tarag Paedori, Chosen of the Forge and King in Iron asks that we escort you to him. Beyond that I know nothing."

"'King in Iron?' He's the king of your people?" Stupid question. He knew it as soon as he said it and the look that the rider offered him made clear that they knew it too.

"He is the king of our people. Will you join us?"

"What about my people?"

The speaker looked around and nodded to the horizon, in the direction from which they'd come. "Another storm comes, a powerful one, by the looks of the clouds." Merros looked. The clouds seemed no different to him. "Your people are welcome. They will be our guests as well, but I would urge that we move quickly, before the storms reach us." He lowered his head as he spoke, possibly as a sign of courtesy, but it wasn't easy to say one way or the other. They were a different people and likely had different customs. He'd once seen a merchant from Freeholdt nearly get himself slaughtered for using a gesture that was a greeting in his homeland and a request for sex near the docks where he employed it. Happily he'd been a better fighter than the offended sailor, or he might not have lived long enough to make it to captain.

He'd come here to map out the Seven Forges and now he was meeting people who very likely already had maps and might be willing to share. In any event he had little doubt that saying no would not go well. One does not, as a rule, turn down the offers of kings without risking life or a few years in a dungeon. The men he was looking at didn't seem the sort to look at a stone cell as a good idea of how to settle a disagreement.

Merros lowered his head as the speaker had done. "I am honored that Tarag Paedori, the Chosen of the Forge and King in Iron would invite me to his hearth. I thank you for your offer of escort."

The men around him relaxed just the smallest amount. That in turn made him relax little. Good to know they were a little nervous, too.

The riders followed him back to the camp and Wollis and the soldiers gaped as the group approached. Within half an hour they were on their way, riding toward the mountains again.

What they encountered was nothing at all like what Merros had expected.

THREE

They rode hard, driving the horses and the steeds of their escorts with a nearly reckless abandon that worried Merros. If the horses took lame, they wouldn't be able to get home, assuming that was still a possibility. He had to consider that this was a journey with no return destination. Taking away from that worry was the sight that awaited them when they finally got their first real look at the first of the mountains, which Drask informed him was called the Forge of Durhallem.

There were illustrations, of course. There were maps and sketches, and the mage had made absolutely certain that Merros and his people had the very latest of them to examine as they approached the Seven Forges. That did not change the absolute shock of seeing the mountains up close for the first time.

Pictures seldom do justice to the reality. The Forges were immense, great, black towers that rose from the uneven ground and continued to rise until it seemed scarcely possible that they could have an ending. Merros had traveled a good deal of Fellein, had served the Empire for two full decades, and in all of his travels he had never seen mountains that looked so fresh. The stone was hard, glazed and black, and looked as clear and sharp as the insides of a gem he'd once seen shattered by a jeweler's hammer. That was the part that unsettled him the most: not the impressive size of the mountain range, but the feeling that the Forges were somehow more vital than the land around them. From far above, the sky was lit up with color, an angry red of a stormy sunset, though there was no sign of the sun itself. There were some who believed the Forges were volcanic. Merros could understand why.

He did not mention that fact to the men who escorted him. Instead he took a hint from them and simply rode with his thoughts, occasionally looking back to make sure the caravan was still there.

Where the mountains met the plain it was easy to see why they were called the Forges. The air held a smoky quality, and the air was much hotter than which they'd been forced to grow accustomed to over the months of travel. Certainly it wasn't uncomfortable, but instead a welcome reminder that there were places in the world where one didn't have to cover the entire body in layers of fur and cloth.

The Forge of Durhallem held an unexpected surprise: a massive cave entrance that opened at the base of the mountain and had obviously been used for a good number of years, maybe even centuries, as a method of getting into the mountain itself. Though Merros was tired, and knew the other riders were feeling the same level of exhaustion as he was, they continued on at the same insane pace, riding hard into the dark mouth of the cavern. He'd expected darkness, of course. He'd expected to be nearly completely blinded even after the weeks of riding in constant cloud cover that left the world in perpetual twilight, but instead a new source of light took the place of the sun. The walls of the cavern, the ceiling above, even the ground below glowed sporadically. He stared hard at one of the stripes of light that spilled down from above them – not letting himself consider what would happen if the rocks should suddenly fall or the cavern crack while they were riding beneath the largest mountain he had ever seen in his life. Though a great deal of the cave was lost in darkness, the warm orange glow let him see that the tunnel around him was either made of glass or crystal, or shot through with translucent rock. The light came from within the mountain itself, and shone out through the transparent portions of the nearly smooth tunnel.

Had he trusted his horse to do the work of guiding itself he'd have closed his eyes and kept them that way until they reached the other side. Instead, he focused on the back of Drask's animal and looked away from the glowing walls that defied all logic and hurt his sense of balance as they ripped past.

And then the glow of the walls faded, lost behind the brightest glare he'd seen since they'd reached the desolate plains of the Blasted Lands, a warm glow that brought to mind the hearth in winter, a bright, inviting light that seemed impossible after so long in the cold.

Up ahead, the other end of the cavern came into view and revealed that warm, wondrous light. And so much more.

The group rode just as hard through the exit of the tunnel, unwary, perhaps even uncaring if there should be anyone or anything in their path, and as soon as they had passed through the tunnel they veered hard to the right, down a strong slope for another half mile at least, where the walls of rock rose on both sides of them, natural outcroppings that had formed the path they followed. There was no reason to worry about obstacles, as the road was smooth and clear of any debris.

Merros ground his teeth. He was tired and his body ached from the long, hard ride. He was worried about the horses, the supplies, the people, and whether or not his hosts would ever stop moving at a hard run.

He needn't have worried. The curving path they followed suddenly opened up on a level field and just as it did, the riders brought their animals to a halt, the great beasts all panting, grunting for breath in air that was fresh and sweet, and felt as alien as the sight revealed by the plateau.

They had stopped on a ridge, easily large enough for a fortress, though there was, instead, a small collection of buildings left in the open. The buildings themselves were squat, built from the same black stone as the walls of the mountain, though without the odd glazed areas of nearly transparent rock. A fenced-in pen waited for the mounts, next to stables that Merros suspected would hold their horses. Unlike the other buildings, the stables looked newly built from wood that had only recently been cut and planed. He knew fresh wood when he saw it. He'd spent two years in the forests of Trecharch, and had watched on three separate occasions as the people there felled trees that rose hundreds of feet into the air.

The riders dropped from their beasts, moving with ease that seemed impossible for Merros himself as he half-crawled from the saddle. He almost expected to hear the soldiers laughing at his discomfort, but instead they were silent and began to efficiently strip their animals of saddles and supplies.

All of which meant nothing at all to Merros as he looked out across the valley below, seeing the land that had been hidden by the Seven Forges. Drask removed his great helmet and moved toward the edge of the land where it abruptly dropped down into the valley, and despite his exhaustion, Merros moved to join him.

The sky above was lighter in color than he'd expected, as if the clouds themselves were held at bay by the height of the mountains. The light was not as strong as he'd been familiar with, but after the long time in near darkness it was strong enough to make him squint. And below that brightness, the black stone walls of the mountains cradled what seemed like a dream.

The valley below was lush with vegetation, trees and fields that had obviously been cultivated and carefully tended for a long while. Several streams and rivers fell from the sides of the mountains, merging in lakes that, from this distance, seemed like mirrors reflecting the glare of the sky back in defiance. And spread here and there, too far distant to see clearly, he could see towns, possibly even cities.

"How can this be here?" He spoke to himself, his voice breathless, stunned.

Drask answered him, shrugging his heavy shoulders. "The Daxar Taalor are kind to us." Daxar Taalor. The words meant the Gods of the Forges as near as Merros could tell. Most words seemed to translate with more ease, but those were different. They sounded wrong in his mind.

Wollis stepped toward them, clearing his throat and pulling down his cowl and his hood. Baring his face to the gentler temperatures they were experiencing. There was sweat on Merros' neck. He hadn't felt sweat in what seemed like forever. "We're stopping for the night. There are rooms and food." His face split into a grin and he shook his curly dark hair. "They have beds, Captain. Enough for all of us."

Merros could understand his second's enthusiasm. The ground was hard, even with blankets and furs to soften the rough land.

Drask nodded. "This is an outpost. Any riders coming through who plan to leave the valley stop here first. Those that come back almost always rest here."

"That happen a lot? The people not returning?" He looked toward Drask as he spoke, curious about what the man looked like now that he was in his home area. He needn't have wasted his time as the man's features were still hidden behind layers of cloth.

Drask regarded him silently for a moment and then lowered his head in a way that spoke of formality.

"The Daxar Taalor are kind to us. The land beyond the Forges is not as forgiving."

Wollis slapped him on the shoulder. "I'm sending the men for rest. They've earned it."

Drask finally looked away from the view, away from the home he had not seen in the gods knew how long. Merros envied him that glance. It had been too long since he'd had a decent meal or slept with a woman. If he survived this trip he would be wealthy. That was the part he had to remember. Without glancing in his direction, Drask made a final comment before heading toward the distant buildings. "The structure to the left, the one closest to the pass, is where you and your men will stay the night. There will be baths and food. Then you should rest. We'll rise early."

Merros tried to listen. He ate food: fresh meat and fresh vegetables – a delight after the last few weeks – and then he took a long, luxurious bath in warm clean water and scrubbed his flesh until it was pink. He had not bathed in so long he feared the color of the gray grit would never leave his skin.

And after that, he tried to sleep, but rest was elusive. He had seen the strangers, yes, but he had not met their people, nor had he met Tarag Paedori, their so called King in Iron. How long had it been since anyone from the Empire had met a new people? One mistake, one stupid blunder, and he could cause not only his own death, but the death of every person in his command. One foolish misstep and he could very well cause the start of a war between his people and the people he was just meeting for the first time.

Frankly, if they were all as good as Drask, that was a terrifying notion.

Sleep did not come easily.

Desh Krohan settled himself at the marble table with ease. He had been here before, many times, and while the world was about to change, he felt no reason to suddenly be uncomfortable in the company of kings, or emperors for that matter.

Pathra Krous, the Emperor of Fellein, sat across from him in the small dining chamber. The man's hair fell in well-oiled ringlets, a fashion that Desh refused to follow himself. The Emperor didn't much seem to care what his hair looked like as long as the girl who was taking care of his appearance was the one handling the matter. To that end he currently had long oiled locks and a mustache that ran down to his chin. At least his face was long enough and narrow enough to carry it off. Several men trying for the same look had come across as little more than comical in Desh's eyes. Desh kept his graying hair short, because there was less effort in maintaining it every day. He had little enough spare time on the average.

There was no gathering for this meal, there were no followers on, or family members to get in the way. That was what Pathra wanted, and what he wanted, he usually got.

"Have you news of your little expedition?" The Emperor started almost every conversation with the same question. It wasn't a matter of manners, so much as the powerful desire the man held in his heart to be on the trip himself. Since he was a child, almost five decades earlier, the man had suffered from a nearly insatiable wanderlust. Sadly the duties of his crown had kept him from traveling the world. He was, unlike so many of his family, a man who took his station very seriously.

Desh nodded his head and smiled, reaching for a particularly juicy looking piece of pabba fruit. Most would have waited for permission to eat in the presence of the Emperor. Desh asked permission of no one. To his credit, Pathra couldn't have cared less about etiquette when it came to the sorcerer. The sweet essence of the stuff perfumed the air as he peeled it and he offered half to the head of the nation before he took a bite. The man took the fruit gratefully. He knew he needn't worry about any sort of dangers with the mage in his presence. "They have reached the Seven Forges."

The Emperor smiled. "Have they indeed? And have they found anything interesting?"

"Not that they've shared with me, not yet at least, but perhaps we'll know more tomorrow."

Pathra looked out the window down into the courtyard far below, his eyes once again taking on the wistful look that Desh knew so very well. "I envy them."

"Don't envy them yet, highness. If they should find Korwa there's no way to know what might be waiting for them."

The rumors and innuendo did not come from mortal sources, but from the spirits themselves. Desh knew better than most that spirits tended to lie and even the ones that were telling the truth often had no idea what they were describing. Everything he'd tried pointed to Korwa waiting in the Blasted Lands, and that was not a pleasant notion.

"I don't see how the wreckage of the First Empire could be of any concern, Desh." Pathra shook his head and scratched idly at his chin. "A thousand years ago there was a war. What could possibly be left now that would matter?"

The wizard chewed on a wedge of the sweet citrus and then licked his lips before he answered. "Where is your capital located?"

The man looked at him as if he'd just possibly grown a second nose. "Where it has always been. Right here."

"And where was Korwa located?"

"Is this really the time for a geography lesson, old man?" Pathra scowled and looked out the window. Most would have thought the Emperor had suddenly grown addled. The wizard looked to be the same age. Then again, the man had not aged in the five decades that the Emperor had known him.

Desh ignored the slight barb. Only he knew exactly how old he was, and he chose not to share that information. "There is always time for lessons, Pathra. Don't ever forget that." Pathra Krous was the Emperor, born and bred into a family that had ruled for centuries. Some had ruled wisely, some had not, but one thing had not changed much in that time. The Emperors accepted the word of their advisor and they accepted his calling them by their first names. Desh ate another piece of fruit and wiped the excess juice across his wrist. "Korwa was a very large city. It was the seat of power just as Tyrne is the seat of your Empire. No one has seen any sign of Korwa in the Blasted Lands. No one has looked. Still, the spirits are telling me that Korwa is near the Seven Forges. They won't tell me what's left of it, or where exactly it is, and as I have said before, the spirits often lie, but they seldom do so without a reason. If they say Korwa still exists, then I believe them."

This time it was the Emperor who chewed at his fruit before answering. "Even if it does, what is the possible threat of a city without people, Desh?"

"The Blasted Lands, Pathra. What have we seen come out of the Blasted Lands in the last thousand years?"

"Plague Winds, the Pra-Moresh and an astonishing amount of dust."

"The Plague Winds are long past, thank the gods. The Pra-Moresh are different. They've come from the Blasted Lands for centuries. Not often, but when they do they always bring destruction and death in their wake."

Pathra waved an impatient hand. "Make your point."

"How many expeditions have we… no, have *I* sent into the Blasted Lands? Dozens? Hundreds? Even I lose count." Desh shrugged. "In all that time we've never had anyone come back from the Seven Forges, or even make it all the way to the mountains before now. They've never run across anything before, or if they did whatever they ran across killed them. The Pra-Moresh come and go, they don't interfere with us too often. But they're out there and they have to feed on something more than dust and snow. I've studied their bodies at the behest of your family in the past and I can tell you, they need to eat a great deal of food to stay alive. That means they've been feeding on something out in the Blasted Lands."

"And?" Again the Emperor made his gesture, waving his fingers for Desh to get to his point.

"Whatever they've been feeding on might come from somewhere beyond the Seven Forges. Or it might come from the forges themselves. Or it might come from Korwa." And here Desh leaned toward the Emperor and stared hard at him. "Or they might have been sent from Korwa to test what might be found on the other side of the Blasted Lands."

Pathra Krous leaned back in his seat and scowled in thought. "Is that what your spirits tell you?"

"No. The spirits refuse to tell me much beyond the fact that Korwa still exists. But, Pathra, how can we know for sure that Korwa and the people of the First Empire haven't been waiting on the other side of the Seven Forges for centuries, sending occasional expeditions out to see if anything still remains of the upstarts who tried to take the Empire from them so long ago?"

Pathra Krous tossed aside the portion of his fruit that he had not yet consumed, his appetite destroyed.

Desh Krohan reached to the roast in the center of the small table and cut off a slab of rare meat that was perfectly seasoned. "You have ruled Fellein very well, Pathra. You have been wise and you have ended almost every conflict with minimal losses. Like your father before you, you are a good and decent man."

Desh's voice was kind. "But the fact remains that we have no idea what lies beyond the Blasted Lands, and the fact remains that, though the process is slow, the Blasted Lands have been receding. Perhaps the damage from the Great Annihilation is mending itself. For all we know, the very world is growing smaller. Whatever the case, within a hundred years it's possible that the Seven Forges will be only a few days away through lands that are almost recovered from the damage done."

Krous shook his head, uncomfortable with the talk of the table though they'd certainly had the conversation before. "What's out there, Desh?"

"I'm working on finding out. Whatever the case, you need to prepare yourself for the possibility that we could well be facing enemies who are not only unknown to us, but who control creatures like the Pra-Moresh and who knows what else."

He took a look at the Emperor's worried expression and sighed.

"I don't think you have to worry at just this moment, Pathra. I simply want to make sure you're contemplating the need to strengthen and train your armies. I can't imagine that things will change too quickly, but just the same, I'll let you know what the expedition has to say."

Far below where the likes of emperors and sorcerers had conversations, Tyrne swarmed with business and life. Shopkeepers dealt with patrons, the City Guard dealt with squabbles and thieves, and Andover Lashk prayed to the gods he didn't believe in for a miracle.

Andover was sixteen, legally an adult in the eyes of the land. His parents would have disagreed completely had they not already cast him out into the world to fend for himself. You steal enough from your parents, and even they can turn their backs on you. Andover was learning that lesson, but he was learning it very slowly.

"There has been a misunderstanding! I don't know what you think I did, but I assure you, it wasn't me!" Lies, all of it. He was caught good and proper, and he knew it, but circumstance was forcing him to lie if he wanted to keep his hands, and he desperately wanted to keep them. He had not stolen from a shop. That would have been a few lashes in the square – he still had the scars to remind him that three pabba fruit up a billowing sleeve was not worth the cost of recovering from a good whipping, thank you just the same. So, no, it wasn't trying to be a thief that had him in trouble this time around.

It was the other thing that normally got him in trouble. It was a girl. Actually, to be precise, it was her fiancé. Tega of the blonde hair and green eyes, with freckles aplenty dusted across her nose and cheeks, and a smile that tended to lead him to distraction, was not a problem at all, except for the distraction part. And how the City Guard who fancied her decided he didn't much like Andover looking at the girl.

Currently, that meant that half of the City Guardsmen who should have been stopping crime were instead standing around Andover while one of them held his arms over his head and two more held his legs. He had an excellent view of the towering giants as he was currently pinned to the ground, his hair half-submerged in a puddle he didn't want to consider too carefully. They were near the abattoir, after all. A beating he could have accepted. He'd had his share, to be sure. It wasn't their fists they were planning to use today.

The one with the nasty smile, complete with a broken tooth to match his often broken nose, was the one who claimed Tega as his own. He couldn't for the life of him – just possibly in a literal sense – remember the man's name. Still, that didn't mean the man wasn't willing to talk to him.

"Purb, over here…" He jerked a thumb in the direction of a man who seemed to have no neck. His head just sort of fused into his shoulders, which were preposterously wide – "He says you've been trailing after Tega like she was a bitch in heat." He had the thick accent of a west-ender, a guttural quality that did nothing but make him sound ignorant in Andover's eyes.

"Purb is mistaken. If we happen to travel the same way from time to time, I can't help that."

Purb, a stout fellow who wore a corporal's rank on his chest, stepped forward, squatted and slammed his exceedingly large fist into Andover's groin. "Don't you never call me a liar, boy!"

Andover would have curled into fetal position had his arms and legs been free. Instead he merely coughed and gasped and tried to think of anything other than the waves of pain and nausea fighting for his attention.

"I warned you twice before." The offended fiancé shook his head and picked up the hammer he'd brought with him. "I told you if I saw you so much as looking at Tega, I'd take from you." Andover shook his head, his eyes wide and round as he looked at the hammer's head. It was a well-worn piece, a smith's hammer, to be sure. He knew them well enough, having worked the last two months as an apprentice to Burk, the very smith who supplied the City Guard with their weapons. He had, in fact, probably held that very hammer on more than one occasion while contemplating the living he would make when he was done apprenticing. There were different hammers, of course, some for the finer work and some for pounding the hot metal into a shape that was vaguely like what it should eventually become. The heavier hammers did rough work. The smaller, lighter hammers shaped and perfected. The thing being shown to him was for rough work.

There was a part of his mind that knew this had to be a jest. Surely the men who kept the peace and protected the citizens wouldn't consider striking a man in his privates, breaking him for life with such ease. Just the same, Andover's breaths hitched in his chest and his throat constricted.

"Please. Please, no." he wanted to scream, but past experiences had told him that would merely annoy the guards.

"Wreck his hopes of fathering runts, Menock." Purb's voice grated and he grinned as he looked at the very area he had recently done his best to shatter with his fist. Andover tried in vain to pull his legs together and protect himself. He was desperate enough that the man holding his ankles had to fight to keep him still.

He looked at Menock, saw the dark look in the man's eyes, and began to doubt that there was anything of the jesting nature in the City Guard at all. Oh, how he wished he could think it was all just a joke, or another warning.

"I'd never do that to a man. Not unless he'd done more than look at my woman." Menock shook his head as he spoke. Andover almost sobbed with relief. Almost. He still didn't quite trust the way this was happening. He was wise that way. Women could make him foolish, but men merely made him cautious.

Menock hefted the hammer high above his head and looked at Andover's face, an ugly sneer making him seem nearly an animal. There was something in his eyes, something not quite right, but Andover didn't have time to consider that. He was too busy realizing that the man had just lied to him. The hammer was going to come down, and there was nothing he could do about it save fight to get free. He bucked, he strained, but the guards were simply too strong. Menock shifted as he held the weapon and then he brought the hammer down with a roar, swinging at the hips and causing the guard holding Andover's hands to scream in shock.

Andover's scream was not from shock. It was from the pain of having the bones in both of his hands shattered under the hammer blow. The guards holding him let go, screaming out themselves.

"Have you lost your damned brains, Menock? It was supposed to be for a scare!" Purb's voice broke as he talked, his eyes looking down at Andover then looking away from the wreckage of his hands.

Andover could see that the man was stunned. He could not clearly acknowledge that shock, however, as the pain of the first hammer blow overtook him.

He screamed again, his throat hot from the sound, and tried to raise his hands, but Menock was not done with him. The man's booted foot came down on his wrist and held his right arm down again as the hammer came down and pulped the pinned limb for a second time. After that the world went gray and then black. He heard the other guards fighting back against their friend, stopping him from bringing the hammer down a third time. After that he heard nothing for quite a long time.

For a while the only sensation he knew was pain, intermingled with the fever dreams brought on by the infection that set into his hands. Eventually, however, Andover woke to find himself not in the street but in a bed with sheets that were clean. His hands flared with pain to remind him of what he'd gone through. Foolishly, he raised his hands to look at them and immediately wished that he had not.

The left hand was ruined, that was all there was to it. The fingers were misshapen and swollen and the skin was mottled a dozen shades of blue and black, where it was actually intact. He could feel the pain move through each finger along with the pulse of his heartbeat.

His right hand was worse. It was gone. Missing. Replaced by a bundle of tightly wound wrappings that were surrounding a white-hot pain strong enough to steal his breath away.

Andover closed his eyes again and prayed for the pain to go away. Instead the darkness claimed him and muted the pain to almost tolerable levels. There were voices then, but they were distant, inconsequential things that made no sense to him. He thought he heard Tega's voice and that was enough to make him force his eyes open.

And lo, there she was, Tega, looking away from him, but he'd know that hair anywhere. What a delicious explosion of curls. "He never did anything to me, that one. He only ever spoke to me politely and then when our paths crossed." Her voice was weak, strained. The man she was talking to listened intently. He was dressed in the uniform of a City Guard, but not the worn, frayed things he was used to seeing. This man was capable of keeping himself clean, at least. Unlike the swine near Andover's home.

Andover felt himself blink at that. He'd never thought of any man as a swine before. His hands throbbed as he moved a bit on the bed, and that was enough to brush aside the curiosity of the names he chose to call anyone in the privacy of his own head. They were little more than animals that would ruin his hands the way they had.

An attempt to sit up in his bed ended with a deep moan and little else accomplished, but Tega and the City Guard both looked in his direction. Tega's eyes grew wide in her face as she saw that he was awake, and she approached him carefully, like he was a wounded beast that might bite at her.

"Andover? I didn't think you'd ever wake." She moved closer still and he let himself drown in her for a moment, deep and lost, beyond the pain of his ruined hands as he looked at her. How was it possible for anyone to be so spectacular?

He tried to speak, but nothing came out of his parched throat save a grunt. The City Guard moved past Tega, gently sliding her aside, and poured water into a simple cup. The sound of water running was enough to make him realize how desperately thirsty he was. A moment later the guard's hand held the cup to his lips and let him drink a maddeningly small dose of the sweetest thing he had ever tasted. The water was cool and soothing and then it was gone.

When he gasped again, his voice was present again. "Where am I?" He looked from the guard to Tega and the words came out on their own. "I didn't even know you knew my name."

The City Guard spoke gently. "I'll give you a few minutes. Then I need to talk to the lad, yes?"

Tega nodded her thanks and then watched as the man walked away. Then she looked back to Andover and shook her head. "I'm told that Menock did this to you. That he…" She looked to his hand and the bandages that surrounded whatever was left of his other hand.

"He did. While his friends in the City Guard held me in place." He looked at her without realizing he was looking, lost in the past, in the memory of what it felt like to have his hands destroyed.

"Oh. Oh, Andover, I'm so very sorry." She looked away from him, face painted with shame as she sought anything at all that could distract her from staring at his hands.

"You didn't do this." His eyes stung. Pain came back and chewed on his wrists, gnawed at the bones and muscles, even the ones he could clearly see weren't there any longer. "You didn't take from me. He did. Menock." He was shocked at the venom in his voice, a tone so unfamiliar as to sound like it came from another person's mouth entirely.

Tega shook her head again and rose from her seat. Before he could ask her what was wrong, she was gone, fleeing, no doubt, from being around the ruin that he'd become.

And he was a ruin. He knew that. He wasn't a fool. His apprenticeship to Burk was gone, to be sure. All he could do was pump the bellows, and then, only with one hand that felt and looked as if it would never be able to close into a workable grip again.

The City Guard came back a moment later, his face set like stone, his thick mustache well-groomed and as gray as the hair he wore short to his scalp. He was older, to be sure. And likely at least a sergeant. Of course, that bastard Purb had been a corporal...

"I am Libari Welliso. I am the commander of the City Guard where you were attacked."

Andover nodded his head, unwilling to risk saying anything that would cause the man to strike him. He was furious, yes, and in pain to be sure, but he was also absolutely terrified. Most of that was simply that Welliso had an aura around him that spoke of combat-readiness and strength.

Welliso looked him over from head to toe with an unreadable expression. "I understand that it was members of the guard who did this to you, is that correct?"

Questions had to be answered, especially if you were dealing with someone like Welliso, so he nodded. "Yes."

"Do you know their names?"

"Only two." He paused for a moment, nauseated, as the pain grew worse in his hands, his arms. "Menock and Purb."

Welliso nodded again. "I'd heard as much, but I wanted to be sure."

His eyes narrowed. "I didn't deserve this." Despite the agony, he raised his hands above him, showed them to the man. "I didn't steal anything, I never touched anyone. I didn't deserve this." Anger only went so far. The pain came back and he settled his arms as gently as he could on his chest again.

Pity. The man looked at him and his features softened, and he knew the look, even if he didn't know the man well enough to be sure. He knew pity from what he felt when he saw the beggars on the street, or the forgotten who were too old to tend to themselves and had no one to aid them.

He hated it.

Pity.

Sometimes it's all you have.

"I know, son. One of the others reported them. They've been locked away."

"What will happen to them?"

Welliso looked at him for a long moment. "At the very least, they'll stay locked away."

"What will happen to me?" He wasn't sure he wanted to know. Without hands, he was little more than a beggar waiting to happen.

"Well. That's the rough one, isn't it? But there might be someone who can help you."

He grunted. No one could fix hands. It wasn't possible. "Who?"

"Your friend, the girl, has connections you would not believe." He shook his head. Tega barely knew him. Owed him nothing. "She should have sent my runner to assist in trying to find a way to help you."

Andover closed his eyes and drifted again. There was nothing else to be done.

In the darkness of his troubled, fitful half-sleep, his mind wandered, sorted through the memories of his pain and the damage done to him. In his heart he had long known a wistful, fanciful love for Tega, a girl who had a lovely smile and seemed incapable of bad thoughts, regardless of his lowly station. That childish love comforted him, but it also hid a small seed of hatred, a troublesome spot of rage for the bastards who had ruined his hands. The gods taught that anger was a chance for happiness wasted and mostly Andover agreed with that belief.

But deep within him that small seed burned and seethed and festered, hidden by the pain in his ruined hands and the affection he had for a pretty stranger.

And far away in the valley between the Seven Forges, the fertile soil for that particular seed was tilled and prepared.

FOUR

They travelled through the valley for three days, moving at a steady pace, but one that held less of the urgency that had seen them tearing across the frozen wastes of the Blasted Lands on their way.

Much as he knew he should have a stronger sense of urgency – he was to meet with a king very soon and the most he'd ever managed before that was guarding the house of a rather impoverished duke – Merros couldn't help but enjoy the scenery. After months of traveling in the perpetual twilight he was enjoying the valley's lush terrain and warmth to a level he'd have thought almost impossible before the trip started. Not that there weren't a few sour notes, to be sure. Kallir Lundt, who was still hanging on to his life despite the grave wounds dealt him by the Pra-Moresh, was fading. There was nothing that Merros or any of his team could do about that, and it bothered him deeply.

Wollis rode next to him, and ahead of them rode the men taking them to meet the king of the valley. They were in the light now, and the air was clear of debris and shadows. That meant it was ridiculously easy to see exactly how large each of the strangers was.

Wollis shook his head. "Do you really think this is wise, Captain?"

"Which part? Going to see a king who we've never heard of in a land we didn't know existed? Or traveling with a band of warriors who seem perfectly willing to ignore us now that they have taken us where we needed to go in the first place?"

Wollis stared at him darkly.

"No, Wollis. I don't think any of this is wise, but it is necessary."

The road ahead of them was well-tended, but the side of the mountain hid a great deal of what lay ahead until they took one more turn. As they were moving around that curve, Merros continued his argument. "We have an opportunity, with luck mind you, to get an accurate and detailed map of the area we were paid to explore. We are also, whether or not we like it, the first emissaries of the Fellein Empire to meet the people who live here. Depending on who you ask it's been several hundred to over a thousand years since contact was made with anyone in this area, because no one was supposed to be able to live up this way. And yet, here we are."

Wollis would normally have argued with him by that point. He'd come to anticipate the man's responses after the years they'd been together. So when he got no response, he looked toward his second-in-command and frowned when he saw the look of growing surprise on the man's face.

Wollis said, "Here we are, indeed."

The sound of the horns drew Merros' attention to the road ahead, to where Wollis was already looking, and he found himself staring at the vast structure that now stood revealed.

Merros Dulver had spent a good amount of his adult life traveling to different parts of the Empire. He had been to Canhoon, Trecharch and a dozen other cities, and more towns than he could remember. As a rule, the towns were old, the streets long since worn down by time and by thousands of people treading on their cobblestones over the years. The fortress ahead of him spoke of a greater age than any place he had ever been to, but still stood unbowed by the centuries he could sense within the great bricks. The structure was built directly into the side of the mountain, carved, it seemed, from the black stone of the volcanic barrier. The walls were easily eighty or more feet in height, and even though they obscured a great deal, he could see the towering buildings behind those walls, all of them black and gray marble, adorned with almost no colors save whatever natural striations were offered by the stone. Unlike in the pass they had used to reach the valley, there was no glow from the great furnace of the volcano itself. The wall was almost smooth, save where the great doors stood sealed against any possible attack. Though they were still a distance away, the guards spotted them and either heralded their arrival or blew out warning notes. Either way, Merros felt his heart beat faster. They were here.

One of the men in front of him pulled a heavy iron horn from his saddle and blew out a harsh note that echoed and merged with the sounds coming from the great walled structure. A moment later the heavy doors opened, sliding smoothly into the sides of the walls rather than opening outward.

Drask turned in his saddle and looked back toward them. "It is time now." He pointed a gauntleted hand toward Merros. "Prepare yourself."

Like there was any possible doubt.

They rode forward again, the long caravan moving in fits and jerks. Merros did not have that luxury. The riders moved faster and a moment later he waved for Wollis to stay behind with their charges.

Apparently he was to meet the King in Iron without the benefit of any retinue. That was just as well. He was only a retired captain at any rate. At least that was what he kept telling himself, as the people who claimed the gods had sent them out into a frozen hell to find him led him to meet their ruler.

They rode hard, moving past the massive gates protecting the city – though for the life of him, Merros had no idea what they might need protection from in a valley that no one in the entire Empire knew existed – and along streets that were paved with more volcanic stones. There was little by way of decoration to be found anywhere, and the people they passed seldom bothered to look up or take any note of them, not that there was time for anyone to notice much beyond the escorts heading for the castle at the center of the walled city.

The path they took led directly to the main structure, a castle within another courtyard, a last bastion of defense against any possible attacks. Several blasts of horns heralded their approach and when the entourage finally stopped, Merros stared at the vast structure ahead of him and did his best to take the entire place in.

The outer wall of the city had been easily eighty feet in height, and the walls of the castle were almost as tall. Hewn again of the black and gray stone, the building was both grandiose and intimidating, with patterns carved directly into the walls that were too large to easily absorb. No less than a hundred men stood along the walls looking down on the courtyard. A small army stood at the one building. How many soldiers did they have here? Merros wasn't sure he wanted to know.

His guides, Drask among them, moved at a hard pace, and Merros was forced to jog in order to keep up with them. Their cloaks snapped like half-furled wings behind them and the men entered the building without stopping to announce themselves or to check with any of the armed guards around them.

If there was any rhyme or reason to the armor that every single person he'd met wore, it was lost on Merros. None of them seemed to wear symbols of rank, and while they all wore helmets and carried weapons, it seemed that nothing was standard issue for the guard.

Once past the guards, the men slowed down. A great hall spread out before them, and again Merros felt small in his surroundings. Had he ever been in any structure as vast? Not that he could think of. The hall was a long affair, with polished stone walls and floors and columns that rose easily fifteen feet to a dark ceiling. Whatever was lacking by way of decoration outside of the hall, the opposite was true of the inside. Heavy wooden tables were spaced throughout the room with chairs enough to accommodate every guard he'd seen along the wall. All of which was impressive enough, but easily ignored for the throne that waited at the far end of the hall.

The seat of power, no doubt, for the king. The throne was carved from black stone and inlaid with precious metals. The seat was lined with a thick fur that Merros couldn't identify and on either side of the throne was an array of weapons: swords, knives, axes, and spears, each well-used and well-cared for. Possibly the most unsettling aspect of the weapons was that they were very obviously meant for function and not merely appearance.

Four men in armor stood on either side of the throne. Like the men escorting him they wore armor that was unique to each of them. Some wore chainmail, others heavier plated armor. All of them wore red tunics, which seemed to be the only indication they were associated. The tunics were clean and new enough in appearance that they almost seemed an afterthought.

None of which was nearly as significant as the man who came striding into the room from the left. The first thought Merros had when he met Drask was that the man was a giant – an image partially cemented by the massive creature he rode into battle, but having stood next to him and stared the man in his shoulder, the impression stuck.

Tarag Paedori, Chosen of the Forge and King in Iron, was actually even bigger and he was not riding on a war-beast. Unlike his followers, the man was not dressed in armor. He wore dark leather breeches, a thick black vest, and a cloak that looked decidedly ceremonial in nature. The heavy black material was adorned with gold and silver in a pattern that was lost in the folds of the cloth and kept in place by a heavy gold cord. He wore an iron crown on his head, simple and unadorned with extras, save for a veil that covered most of his face. Only his eyes were easily seen, and the dark hair that fell out of the crown in loose coils. Thick, muscular arms were crossed over a barrel chest. Heavy scars could be seen on the bared arms, across the massive hands, and on the powerful shoulders, and all of the flesh that could be seen bore the odd gray tint that Merros had originally assumed was grit from the cold wastelands outside of the valley when he first met Drask.

All of them had the same gray skin. It looked unhealthy, nearly dead. All of them hid their faces behind veils or masks. All of them had eyes that were a flat gray when seen in light and seemed to issue their own luminescence when seen otherwise.

As one, the men escorting Merros dropped to one knee before their king, and in a fluid move that was unsettling in its efficiency, they drew their swords from the sheaths at their hips – or in a few cases across their backs – and held the weapons out. Their hands held the blades of the weapons with the points to their chests, and the pommels offered to the King in Iron, a sign of fealty and/or an offer to let him take their lives should he feel the need. Whatever the case, the men seemed unified in the offer they made.

Tarag Paedori nodded acknowledgement of the men, but his eyes sought Merros and pinned him with the force of his stare. If his carriage and his confidence were not enough to make his station known, the man's will, forceful and demanding of attention, would have clarified his position.

The King in Iron spoke softly but his words carried. Like Drask before him, his voice had an odd echo that made the traveler's skin crawl. "Merros Dulver of the Fellein Empire. We have waited a very long time to meet you."

FIVE

Andover Lashk suffered a fever for almost three weeks as the infection from his mangled hands ran through his body. He would very likely have died from the illness, but, as the captain of the city watch had said, the girl he adored, Tega, had interesting connections. He had never met Desh Krohan, but no one in the capital city of the Empire failed to recognize the name when it was whispered. Krohan was supposed to be a powerful sorcerer, and even if he weren't he was certainly a powerful man. He was advisor to the Emperor, and according to most rumors had been advisor to the last seven emperors at the very least.

Not that Andover cared much. During his weeks of deep fever he had slept for the most part. He remained unconscious save when Krohan came to his room to administer different medications and run his hands over Andover's body, muttering impossible words even as his fingers pushed and kneaded flesh that burned with fever.

And he dreamed a great deal. Oh, the dreams he had were far removed from his regular life.

He dreamed of fire and metal and great hammers that struck his body again and again, pounding against his rigid form and forcing him to take a new shape even as he cooled. Hammers large and small struck him, shaped him, until his skin gleamed and the delicate symbols carved carefully into his surface were a permanent part of him.

He dreamed that the very earth had a pulse, and that every beat of the planet's heartbeat moved through him and carried him along the tides of the ocean. In the dream that made perfect sense. When he woke from the dream he was puzzled by the entire affair, especially since he had never seen the ocean in his life. Tyrne was a hundred leagues from the closest ocean, accessible by the sprawling Freeholdt River, but as vast as that stretch of water was, it wasn't anything like the great oceans he saw in his dream.

He dreamed that he was at the heart of Korwa when the First Empire fell, and he felt the very air around him shatter as the explosions ripped the land into new shapes and drove the remains of the city down into the molten ground beneath him. The shockwaves leveled towns, burned away armies, consumed the air and the forests, and boiled away the truths once known by the world around him along with rivers and lakes.

And when he awoke once more, Tega was there with the man who had loomed over him again and again. Desh Krohan looked to be somewhere in his forties, perhaps, with silver-shot blond hair and a jaw line that needed a good shave. He seemed tall, but Andover was flat on a bed and looking up. Even

Tega seemed tall, and she was as short as she was pretty.

And all of the gods, his hands were screaming in agony. He grimaced and did his best not to yelp. Tega's eyes spoke volumes of pity and said nothing of love, and that too caused him a deep and abiding pain. He looked into those perfect eyes, and for the second time in moments had to resist the urge to let out a pained noise. Really, it was hard to say which was more exquisite, the torture of shattered hands or a broken heart. Poets and physicians each have their own answers.

The wizard put his hand on Tega's shoulder. "Give us a moment, would you, Tega?"

She nodded and rose, a flash of relief on her face, perhaps, or merely a sign that she had been sitting in one place for far too long.

When she'd left the room Krohan sat where she had been, a weary half-smile on his face. "She's been here every day, you know. She'd camp here at night if her parents would permit it."

Andover shook his head. "Why?"

"Why?" The man frowned. "I suppose because she feels responsible." There must have been something on Andover's face, perhaps merely that he wasn't really old enough to hide his feelings as well as he'd like. "No, she hasn't told anyone that she loves you. Neither has she said that she knows you very well at all." The man's face was annoyingly knowing. "She's a beautiful girl. She's had numerous suitors. None of them have gotten very far. She's far more interested in her studies."

"Studies?"

"Tega is my apprentice, Andover. That's why I'm here. She asked me to see if I could help with what was done to you."

"She wants to be a wizard?"

Krohan smiled. "Something like that, I suppose."

He stared at the man above him and sighed. Apprenticeship meant hard work. To be apprentice to a sorcerer? Hard work and possibly the cost of a soul? That was one of the rumors.

"What Tega studies takes a great deal of time and effort. She's already gotten behind on her studies as a result of what's happened to you." Krohan held up a hand before Andover could protest. "I'm not accusing you of anything or saying that she's in trouble; I merely want you to understand that she's been very dedicated to helping you recover."

And there it was, an instant flash of anger. Pain lashed through Andover's ruined hands and he held up the bandaged messes. "What's left of them to help get better?" His voice broke as he spoke.

The man looked at the carefully bandaged bundles for a moment. "You already know the answer to that. There's not much left to save and not much I can do to help you." He looked at Andover and studied his face eyes in silence for several moments. "But you are alive, Andover. And I am investigating possibilities."

"Possibilities?" He shook his head. "What does that mean?"

"It means I have messengers on the road who have… located a possible method for making your hands better. Under most circumstances I would not even bring the matter up, but Tega is a very good student and what happened to you has her worried. If I can learn more of what is needed, I might be able to mend your hands. If I can mend your hands there might be a cost to you." He once again held up a hand to stop any possible questions or comments. "Not a cost that I would charge you. What I've done and will do for you has already been paid. The cost would be to you, yes, but emotional cost, not any other sort that I know of."

"If you can do it, then do it." His eyes stung. "Whatever it is, I don't want to be a beggar in the streets."

The man stood up, moving with the sort of care normally reserved to the decrepit. "You say that, like being a beggar is the worst that could possibly happen. There's much worse, believe me." The mage looked toward the door. "I'll get Tega for you. If there's anything to be done, I'll do it, Andover Lashk. But don't talk to anyone other than Tega about this. Not yet. First we have to see what we can do."

The man left the room a moment later and Andover thought about the possibility of getting back his hands. He could feel them even now. He could move them under the swaddled cloth and protection, though he already knew that there was little left to move. If he closed his eyes he could feel his fingers waggling in the air. When he opened them he could see the air where they should have been according to what his mind told him. Right hand completely missing, left hand little more than a lump of meat, but he could feel the fingers. Could damn near feel the slight breeze playing on the hair on the backs of his hands.

Anger blossomed again in his chest, his heart; a deep heat that simmered and spit an occasional cinder. But in that seemingly endless well of hatred there was something else.

Hope.

What would he do to get his hands back? Damned near anything.

Desh Krohan had only just left the boy's room and nodded to Tega that she could visit him when the storm-crow came through the open window in the Healer's Hall and flew right at him. A good number of people might have been terrified by the sight of one of the great gray birds, but Desh knew them well and had raised this one from the time it had escaped the confines of its egg.

He raised one arm and winced a little as the bird's talons scraped through fabric and across the flesh of his forearm. "Gently, Goriah. Tell me what you know."

The bird cocked its head and looked at him intently with one startlingly blue eye. From a great distance away the communication took place. Goriah's voice whispered into his head and he listened, nodding.

"I would very much like to meet them. Yes."

The storm-crow leaned in closer still until he could smell the carrion taint of its breath and its eye nearly touched his own. So much information after so long with little more than reports of ice and dust. The knowledge came so fast that it hurt his skull. There is always a price to pay for knowledge.

"Really?" He opened his eyes and looked back toward the room he had left a few moments earlier. In it the girl he had accepted as an apprentice sat with the young man she had decided needed special help. "No, that's perfect, really. That's ideal. What would they like in exchange?"

He almost dropped the bird. It hopped impatiently and reminded him that it was there right before he would have lowered his arm. "Well, that's... problematic. But no, I think we can make it work. I don't think it's impossible at all." He looked away from the room and nodded his head. "I think I know exactly who to choose."

Desh Krohan moved away from the door he'd been staring at and then down the hallway where the window opened on the courtyard far below. He held his arm out and the storm-crow bobbed its head several times while looking at him. "Go on then. Tell them that we accept their terms."

The great bird launched itself from his limb and almost immediately headed for the north and the wastelands beyond the last towns of the Empire. From where he stood, the wizard could see nothing of the Seven Forges, not even the clouds they so constantly generated. But he knew they were there, and now he knew so very much more than he had before.

They rode across the Blasted Lands in the direction of home, this time taking the distances at a far greater speed. Merros Dulver looked around and frowned. A moment later he gestured and Wollis rode forward to keep pace with him. As always the northerner's expression was glum. It wasn't that he was in a bad mood, really, it was just the sort of face the man had.

"Are we speaking again, Captain?"

"I wasn't aware we were giving each other the silent treatment, Wollis."

"Neither was I, but aside from yelling that it was time to go home you've had remarkably little to say since you met up with hizzoner the King of Fancy Pants." The tone of his voice didn't change at all, but Wollis sniffed his disapproval.

Merros looked toward the entourage of soldiers who were escorting them on their trek home. "I'm going to suggest very strongly that you not keep that sort of chatter right now."

"Afraid your new friends might hear?"

"I've grown rather fond of you over the last few months, Wollis. I would rather not have to explain to Dretta or Nolan why I had to leave your body here in the frozen wastes."

"You saying you wouldn't have the decency to bury me properly?" Wollis was only half-joking.

"I don't think I'm strong enough to break the ice out here." The area they were moving over was more than half-submerged under ice. There were rocks, true enough, but they were few and far between.

Wollis nodded his head. "I'll keep my tongue. But before this is said and done, I want to know why we're now traveling with an additional fifty men."

Merros nodded in response. The winds were harsh, but he didn't trust that the soldiers escorting them wouldn't find a way to hear the conversation. The Sa'ba Taalor – the People of the Forges was the way his mind immediately translated the words, and though he didn't think that was completely accurate, it seemed fairly close – had a way of hearing things out in the wind-torn desolation that seemed nearly mystical in nature.

"Here's why we're traveling with fifty extra men. Their king asked me politely to offer several gifts to the Emperor on his behalf. Those ten boxes being hauled by those insanely large animals of theirs, those are part of the gifts being offered. The fifty large armored men with many, many weapons? They are his way of making sure that the gifts being offered get to the Emperor intact." Merros leaned in closer to his second. "Why am I doing this? Because apparently the Gods of the Forges predicted I would be arriving and seem to feel I've got a destiny with the Sa'ba Taalor."

"Is that what this has all been about?"

"No, not really." Merros looked toward the south, where they were headed. Up ahead of him five men in heavy armor rode their great beasts – they rode them like horses, but surely they were something else entirely – and seemed to look at nothing but the promise of what lay beyond the horizon. "It's about the maps they gave us, and the monies we were promised by Desh Krohan." He looked to Wollis again and saw a rider coming toward them from the caravan. "I'm not an ambassador, nor am I a soldier of the Empire. I'm a mercenary same as you and we've been promised a solid wage for a map of the Seven Forges and the surrounding lands. Anything else we bring back is a bonus." He nodded toward the approaching rider and Wollis took the hint.

A moment later the fur-bundled form of one of Krohan's women rode in closer. Red hair whispered from the hood. Tataya looked up at him with her intoxicating eyes. "I leave you now, Captain."

"Excuse me?"

"I leave you now," she repeated. "I am expected in Tyrne."

"Well, we're moving as fast as we can." What else could he say? She'd lost her mind. Pity, what with her mind being wrapped in such a lovely package.

"I suspect we will meet with you when you arrive, but for now Drask Silver Hand comes with me. We are to meet with Desh sooner than the caravan."

"How the hell are you going to manage that?" They were already moving at a pace he was uncomfortable with, propelled on by the urgency of the fifty soldiers who were "escorting" them home.

The redhead offered him an enigmatic smile that, as with almost every expression the woman wore, smoldered with promises best not considered too carefully. "Be safe on your journeys, Captain."

She veered away, and as he watched, the great mount of Drask Silver Hand broke from the caravan and came closer, charging forward with unsettling speed. The man's silvery eyes regarded him from within his horned helmet's shadows, and the horns nodded a brief greeting before he reached down and grabbed Tataya's proffered arm. The man lifted her from her saddle with frightening ease and she swung her weight onto the saddle in front of him, nearly swallowed by his bulk.

The woman leaned forward and her gloved hands grabbed at the mane of the creature she straddled. A moment later Drask leaned forward as well, and then the dark mount under him surged forward, nearly tripling its speed as it started to move at a full out run. The damned thing let out a roar that shook the air and a moment later the trio were dwindling into the distance, cutting between two of the soldiers escorting them. The soldiers waved casually as if watching an animal that size move with that sort of speed was perfectly normal, thanks just the same.

"Well that's depressing." Wollis' voice took Merros by surprise.

"What's that?"

"I rather liked Drask. He seemed so cheerful."

Merros thought about that for a moment and nodded. In comparison to most of his brethren that was true. "Let you in on something. I know for a fact that Drask is carrying something meant for Desh Krohan."

"I'd hardly call that comforting."

"I meant what I said before, Wollis. I'm a mercenary, same as you. We served in the Emperor's army. We did our job. Then we were hired by the Emperor's advisor for this job. Either way, we're getting paid. The difference here is that we're going to be paid much better than we were before."

His second looked around them, noticed the men on their odd mounts and nodded his head. "Man brings a plague back with him on a ship, he's still going to have the plague named after him."

"Alright, that only ever happened once, and none of us has developed any weeping sores since entering the Blasted Lands. Hell, we're actually on our way out of the Blasted Lands. That already makes us the exception to the rule here."

"We also met the Pra-Moresh and the fine gentlemen leading us home. Those are exceptions, too." Wollis looked around for a moment as if making sure that none of the strangers with them could hear him. "And what about Lundt?"

Merros looked away. "What about him? They said they'd try to save him."

Wollis stared at him. "So they did. We've left him in a strange land with strange people, dying or dead for all we know."

"Aye. And if we'd brought him back, we'd be hauling nothing but his corpse by now and you know it." He shook his head and felt his teeth clench. "Gods, Wollis, the poor bastard's face was half torn away. It's a wonder he's alive at all. If they can help mend him then I say we let them."

"And how will we know of it, Captain? How will we know if he's mended or if he dies?" Wollis' voice snapped at last, an angry lash of harsh words.

"What choice, Wollis?" He snapped back. Oh, there was guilt, yes, but what could he do? The King in Iron said they'd save the man's life. While Merros was hardly nobility, he knew well enough that one didn't exactly decline the offers of kings without risking a swift death or a life in the dungeons. "What would you have done differently?"

Far in the western distances, the Mounds rose from the frozen wastes, misshapen pillars of darkness that rumbled and shuddered and issued sounds somewhere between monstrous and merely terrifying. Closer in, three of their armored escorts looked toward the distant edifices and their hands slid to the closest weapons. Merros felt his own hand reaching for his sword, seeking the cold comfort of steel.

"I don't know what I would have done differently, Merros. I have no idea. But I know I'm not comfortable with how this has come down."

Merros thought about leaving one of his soldiers behind in a place where none of them had ever ventured before, where they might never have a chance to venture again, and resisted the urge to spit the foul taste of failure from his mouth. Failure, or the ruined ashes that fell from the blackened skies above; either way he hated the flavor.

"At the current speeds we're only fifteen days from home. Twenty days from Tyrne. We'll have our answers soon enough."

Wollis nodded his head and looked toward home. "And the pay. Don't forget that part. We're mercenaries now. It's all about the gold."

Wollis slowed his horse a bit before Merros could comment, leaving the captain alone with his thoughts.

They spoke almost constantly as they rode toward the distant Empire, Drask learning the words of a language he'd have never heard had his gods not blessed him with being the first of his kind to meet with the people of Fellein.

The woman before him was tiny, but she spoke with confidence and seemed comfortable enough with him and with his mount. From time to time she leaned down and spoke directly into Brackka's ear and the great beast rumbled with pleasure each time. Whatever she said, Brackka approved. That was enough for Drask. Tataya spoke of the customs of her people and Drask listened, knowing that it was important he understand the ways of Fellein.

They rode for three days before finally resting. While Brackka was a sturdy beast and a fine companion, even the greatest of the mounts needed time to recover from a great run and they had covered more than half the distance before they stopped. The air here was calmer, the winds less violent and the taint of ash from above milder than anywhere Drask had been when outside of the valley.

Tataya offered him fresh food and water from her satchel. He took both, moving the flask and then the hearty bread under the layers that covered his face. Even as he chewed on the bread, he opened a sealed package of meat and threw it to Brackka, who grumbled a note of thanks and then tore into the feast. What the Fellein called Pra-Moresh was a musky-tasting meat, to be sure, but it was nourishing and layered with enough fat to make the mount happy. Brackka chattered happily as he ate.

Drask ignored the noises and focused on the woman instead. They were decidedly different peoples. They might have come from the same places once, but the thousand years that divided them as surely as the Blasted Lands separated their people had made changes to one or both species. Her skin was soft and pale, her hair was bright red, and her eyes were a color that seemed impossible.

"You hide your face." Her words were not a question.

"The Daxar Taalor say your kind are not ready to see us yet."

She nodded her understanding and said no more of it. He admired that. One did not question the gods. "Tell me of the Daxar Taalor."

"They saved us. When the Cataclysm happened, they came to us and saved us from the great destruction."

"How?" Her eyes were unusual, to be sure, but he stared at them and found it hard to look away from her.

"According to the legends the ground was shattered. The air burned. The seas boiled away and left behind oceans of molten glass and rivers of ash. And in this great chaos, we would surely have died, but the Hearts of the Gods rose from the destruction and sheltered us from the great storms, from the burning skies and the winds that peeled flesh from bones."

"How did your people survive before the mountains rose?"

Drask lowered his head. "That I do not know. The Daxar Taalor have not spoken to me of this."

"The Daxar Taalor are your gods, yes?"

"Of course."

"Have you names for them?"

"Of course." He shrugged. "Durhallem, Ydramil, Wrommish, Paedle, Truska-Pren, Wheklam, and Ordna."

"Does one god rule all of the gods?"

What bizarre questions she asked. Still, he had been told to answer all questions posed and he saw no reason not to. "We know only what the Daxar Taalor tell us, and they have never spoken of a hierarchy among their kind."

She reached for his face and he started to pull away. "Drask, you were told you could not show me your face. I do not ask you to show it to me. I merely wish to touch it." He was hardly a fool. Fingers could see, too, but still, he approved of her unique approach and felt Ydramil would approve as well. For that reason he did not stop her hand from moving under the veil over his face. Her fingers were soft, warm, and perfumed with the faintest scent of exotic flowers. The soft tips felt the contours of his jaw, his nose, his lips, and she stared into his eyes as she touched his face and studied him in ways that none of her kind ever had before. She touched his lips and traced them softly.

"How?" She was not horrified. He had been puzzled when he first saw the strangers; they were… different.

"It is the will of the Daxar Taalor." He paused while she continued examining and when her fingers moved on, spoke again. "We must speak with their tongues."

"You are very handsome. You are surely very blessed."

He removed the gauntlet from his flesh hand and touched her face, her lips, fascinated by the warmth he felt. Her lips kissed the tips of his fingers and she smiled at him with a certain pleasant mischief. The fire was not the only source of warmth that night.

The following morning they rode on, neither speaking of the intimacy they had shared. Instead they spoke of the gift that Drask was bringing for one of the people. "Will it work, do you think?" she asked.

"The Daxar Taalor have willed it. It will work."

"Will it hurt, do you suppose?"

"Oh yes, a great deal. But the rewards speak for themselves."

"Your gods are very kind."

Drask laughed then, the comment catching him off guard.

"That is amusing to you?"

"Lady Tataya, the Daxar Taalor are not kind. They are just. There is a difference."

"What do you mean?"

"They are gods, Tataya." His arm slipped around her waist as Brackka started moving faster, running closer to the ground and fairly leaping instead of merely walking. "All gods offer blessings. All gods demand sacrifices. All gods demand a price, yes?"

On the fifth day they left the Blasted Lands, moving through a country that was green and living, the only one he had ever seen outside of the valley. They passed farms and once, in the distance, they passed a city that seemed pale and weak in comparison to the vast cities in the valley. As the air grew warmer, Tataya shed her cloak and after several hours of running time, the heat became great enough for Drask to follow suit. He even removed the helm he normally sported away from home and let the air run through his thick hair.

They stopped that night as well, and rested near a river in the woods. Brackka found his own food to eat in the darkness and the woods around them were silent as the creatures around them sought to adjust to the strangers beneath the canopy of the trees. Tataya offered food again and Drask took it. Brackka did not offer to share and Drask was not foolish enough to ask. The beast was hungry from days of nearly no food and nearly endless running.

Another day of travel and they reached a city that nearly dwarfed the cities of the valley. Drask stared with wide eyes, barely believing that so many could live in one spot.

"This is Tyrne, the capital of Fellein." Tataya's voice was a comfort. He had thought himself prepared for almost any sight, but this was altogether a grander scale than Drask had thought possible. Even from a distance he could see the rolling hills of manmade structures, small buildings furthest out, as if they had not yet had a chance to grow to their full height. Closer to the center of the city there were walls and towers and great structures that seemed almost as tall as the Forges themselves.

"Tyrne has been building on itself since before the Cataclysm." Tataya spoke softly and placed a hand on his forearm. "This is the very heart of the Empire and is much larger than most towns."

"Where do we go from here?"

"Desh Krohan knows we are coming. He has prepared the way."

He did not question the fact, but merely accepted it.

"Ride forward and I will tell you where to go."

Drask nodded and spurred Brackka onward. The mount grunted out a rude noise but obeyed. It was time to offer gifts and forge a new destiny, as ordered by the Daxar Taalor. Drask was many things, but foolish was not among them. When the gods directed, he obeyed. The gods demanded their due and he would pay them as he always had, regardless of what they might cost.

SIX

Little known fact: sometimes wizards do things just because it amuses them. At least they do if their name is Desh Krohan. There were many rumors about the sorcerer, quite a few of which were blatant lies he'd created himself, but one rumor that was true was that he'd been around for centuries. Sometimes that meant he had to find ways to drive away boredom.

When he first met Merros Dulver he hid himself in a thick cloak that he'd created years before. The fabric was as tough as steel and, as an added bonus, the material tended to move of its own volition, leading people to wonder exactly what he looked like under the mantle that covered his head and hid his face in dark shadows. He still liked to wear the robes whenever meeting someone for the first time, because he wanted them to be uncertain about him.

He called the robe to him when Tataya whispered in his mind that they were almost upon him. The great cloak obeyed and wrapped itself to him. He'd just drawn the hood over his head when the flame-haired beauty entered the castle.

Desh watched from his window as his assistant moved through the great hall and led her attendee toward his chambers. While most of the officials in the Empire had their own homes – Desh Krohan had several, actually – the wizard was also the formal Advisor to the Emperor and as such had offices within the castle that were his alone. That hadn't always been the case, but over the centuries the various rulers of Fellein had realized that having a sorcerer in residence had its benefits, especially when the man in question tended to handle a good number of bothersome issues for them.

Rather than wait for them to come to him, Desh moved out of his chambers and into the main hall, standing at his full height as Tataya brought the first of the Sa'ba Taalor into the Emperor's offices.

There was no fanfare. Not yet, not at this point. This particular meeting was not exactly clandestine, but neither was it meant to be announced to the general populace.

That was just as well. The man she brought with her was a true terror. A few centuries is long enough a time to let a man know how to read the strangers he meets. Perhaps he could not guess a man's name, or even that man's intent without careful study, but Desh could normally judge a man's mettle with ease. The stranger was enormous to begin with. Drask Silver Hand had, per Tataya's requests, removed his armor, save for the leather vest and thick leather breeches. He sported a heavy traveling cloak and though he did not brandish them, Desh could see that several weapons were sheathed on his body.

He carried a satchel over one shoulder that swayed
lightly with his steps, though by the way it moved,
Desh suspected it was anything but light. The muscles
on the man's body were hard and rippled like those
of a great cat as he walked toward the wizard, and his
skin, as had been reported to Desh, bore a gray tint
and was crosshatched with scars both thick and fine.
Though they had traveled a great distance, Tataya
must have taken the time to stop to let both of them
clean up properly because the man's thick black hair
had been recently washed. The hair fell nearly to his
shoulders. His eyes looked everywhere and he studied
everything he saw.

Most of the people who first approached the
castle were understandably intimidated. The size
of the structure, the symbols of office, and the
guards who stood throughout the building, all of
these things lent an immediate air of authority that
cowed most people. That was the purpose, really. In
addition to being the seat of the government, the
entire structure was designed to hold off armies if
it came to that. Nothing about it was meant to be
warming so much as it was designed to let all who
approached know that the Emperor of all they saw
was close by and capable of leading his people. Desh
knew all of that because he had helped design the
bloody structure.

Drask Silver Hand took it in with a casual glance.
Though the stranger's face was mostly hidden, his
eyes showed no sign of being impressed by what he
saw. The man's stance was relaxed, calmer than most
who came before Desh or the Emperor. The stranger

was about to meet both and didn't seem the least bit worried about the notion.

And that very fact worried Desh just a little. It went against the norm.

Desh stepped from his office and stood before Tataya and her charge. The man looked at him for a moment and his eyes narrowed a touch as he assessed the potential threat of the man in the shifting cloak. His fingers twitched within their gloves. Desh knew enough to understand that he was checking himself, resisting the urge to reach for a weapon. That was good. The man was properly uncertain of what lay under the dark, heavily shadowed cowl and the fabric that seemed to breathe and shift of its own will. He was not intimidated, no, but he was cautious.

"Desh Krohan, this is Drask Silver Hand of the Sa'ba Taalor, emissary of Tarag Paedori, Chosen of the Forge and King in Iron." Tataya's voice was confident and warm and Desh resisted the urge to hug her to him. She was precious, as were all of the women he chose to work with. Instead he stepped back with his left leg and bowed from the waist, holding his arms wide open.

The stranger looked at him for one moment and then returned the gesture.

"Drask Silver Hand, this is Desh Krohan, Advisor to the Empire of Fellein and Emperor Pathra Krous." She placed one delicate hand on the thickly muscled forearm of the stranger and spoke in a softer voice. "He is also my friend and the reason you are welcomed here."

When Drask spoke his voice was accented; although there was an odd tone to them that confused the wizard's ears, his words were easily understood. That was good. He wanted the man to make a good first impression on the Emperor. "It is the hopes of my king that your people and mine can meet in peace and honor." The words were obviously rehearsed. That too was as it should be.

"That is the hope of our Emperor as well." Desh nodded his head. "Do you come as formal representative? Or do you come to prepare the way for your people?"

Drask tilted his head the slightest bit and looked around the room again, his eyes tracking two guards who moved into the area and stared for a moment. They knew exactly who Desh was and were wise enough to not interfere. "I come to prepare the way, and I bring with me a show of faith meant for you, Desh Krohan, as promised by Goriah."

His left hand tapped the satchel he carried.

Desh smiled. "We have a few preparations to make, Drask Silver Hand. When we are done with these small tasks, I shall introduce you to the Emperor and hopefully we will begin a great friendship between our peoples."

"As the Daxar Taalor will it." The man bowed again and waited for Desh's instructions.

Really, there were only a few things that had to be done. Desh wanted to make sure that everything was in proper order. This was to be a monumental occasion and he wanted nothing to go wrong.

How very seldom we get what we most desire.

••••

Andover was in the small garden when they found him. The weather was bright and the air was warm, and if he had stayed in the room for a moment longer he was sure he would go mad. Also, no matter that the sorcerer had done wonders for keeping his muscles conditioned while Andover slept, his legs felt restless. All of him felt restless. The anger inside him had grown, had bloomed when he wasn't paying attention. While Tega still occupied his mind a great deal, so did his rage for what had been done to him. It had been long enough that his mind had, mercifully, hidden away most of his recollections of the pain of having his hands destroyed, but while the actual pain was a thing of the past – give or take the ghosts that still ran through his arms and told him his hands were still there and still shattered – the memory of the look on Menock's face as he brought the hammer down was still burned into his eyelids. He couldn't even close his eyes to escape the look on the bastard's face as he ruined Andover's world.

Tega came out into the garden, a flower brighter than the rest around them, and offered him a nervous smile. That was the only sort of smile she could offer him, really. He scared her or shamed her. Andover was never quite sure which.

Despite the feelings she always inspired in him, he could barely muster a return smile for the girl. Still he tried. She was not at fault, not for his hands and not for the fact that she did not feel the same way toward him. That much he knew in his mind, even if his heart did not always agree.

Tega's eyes shone with excitement. "Andover! Come quickly! Desh Krohan wants to see you!"

Her excitement cut through the clouds of his sullen mood and he looked toward her with renewed interest. "Does he then?" He nodded and moved toward her. It was unusual to see her enthusiastic about much of anything, at least in his presence. He'd seen her talking to others, seen her smile more times than he could easily count, just not around him. It was refreshing.

He allowed her to lead him, her delicate hands gripping his arm at the elbow. "Calmly, Tega. My legs aren't as strong as they used to be. Too much time spent in that bed."

"Never mind that! Come on, come on!" She half pulled him through the corridors, past the Healer's Hall and further still. Tega knew her way around the palace but Andover had never been beyond the chambers where he slept and the small garden down one corridor. His eyes widened at the sheer size of the place. It was one thing to know he was in the Emperor's Palace and another to actually comprehend what that knowledge meant.

Before he could truly adjust to the size of the palace, he was hauled by the girl he adored into another chamber, this one substantially larger than even the garden he'd been walking in. The ceiling had to be at least three times his height, and though there were no windows within the room, there was light aplenty from several torches and a blazing pit.

He recognized the wizard immediately. Most of him was hidden but his hands were now familiar to Andover, as were the rings he sometimes wore. And even under the mantle of his cloak the man carried a certain authority that made him recognizable. If anything, the odd cerements he wore made him even more intimidating than he usually was. It was true that Andover felt a certain level of familiarity with the mage, had even spoken his mind to the man, but he had never forgot exactly who he was dealing with. Three others stood with the sorcerer: a striking woman with red hair, a very large man with who hid his face behind a veil, and–

The Emperor himself!

Andover froze as surely as if he were staring a Pra-Moresh in the face. The Emperor! One thing to see the man at a distance – though Andover himself had not done so in over five years – another to see the man who ruled over all of them in the flesh.

Tega recovered faster. Either she had expected to see the man or she was merely more familiar with protocol. She lowered her gaze, stepped back on her left leg and bent at the waist. The pressure of her grip on his arm urged him to follow her lead and he did so gratefully.

Pathra Krous' voice was warm and deep. "Thank you. Please, rise, this is not a formal affair. We have much to discuss, young master Lashk."

The Emperor knew his name. The very notion made his ears ring.

Still, the Emperor asked and he listened. He rose and looked at the gathering again. The voice that spoke the next time was not his ruler's but that of the wizard. "Andover, a stranger has come to us. His name is Drask Silver Hand and he believes that he can replace your ruined hands. He cannot heal them, but he can give you new hands."

He gestured to the large man with the oddly tinted skin, as if looking at the strangely dressed brute would somehow clarify the matter.

"New hands?" His voice cracked as he spoke.

The stranger looked at him and then at Tega, his eyes giving away nothing of his feelings. In response the man nodded his head. He gripped the leather glove over his right hand and held the hand out for Andover to examine.

He walked closer, staring at the marvel of metal and flesh, not believing what he was staring at. A sculpted limb. Before he could scoff at the notion of useless metal attachments, the metallic fingers moved, the hand twitched.

Shock didn't begin to cover his reaction.

Andover stepped back and tripped over his own feet. He pinwheeled his arms in an effort to catch himself, but could not. The sculpture moved!

And before he could fall on his backside, the man with the silver hand was in front of him, grabbing his tunic and righting him until he could find his balance. Andover stared at the metallic hand, unable to so much as utter thanks.

"It moves!"

"It is my hand now. It moves, it feels, it is strong." The man spoke directly but the ringing in Andover's ears made the sounds seem distorted.

"How did you do this?"

"The Daxar Taalor did this. The gods of my people."

"You have your own gods?" He felt numb. His fingers reached out, touched the metal of the man's hand and marveled at the warmth, the strange texture.

Metal, yes, no denying it, but there was almost a hint of something else.

"Don't you?"

The Emperor laughed, the sounds a bit forced to Andover's ears. "Don't we all have our gods?"

Drask turned his head to look at the Emperor, his eyes narrowing for the briefest moment before he nodded. He carefully removed his hand from Andover's grasp.

Then the stranger spoke to him. "If you do this, there will be great pain, far worse than you felt when your hands were taken. The gods tells us that life always hurts more than death. That would be the first sacrifice you have to make. Would you accept pain in order to have your hands again?"

Andover nodded without true consideration. What was pain in exchange for being able to work again, to avoid a life as a beggar? There was no question at all.

Drask looked at him for a moment and he realized the man didn't understand the gesture. "Yes. I would accept pain for hands."

Drask stared for a moment longer and then nodded, as if trying the gesture out for the first time in his life. "Good. That is good. There is more. The Daxar Taalor would ask that you visit them in their places of worship, where I come from. The trip is a long one, but you would learn much from your travels. Would this be acceptable?"

Before he could answer, Desh Krohan spoke up, the wizard's words carrying with ease. "You would serve as a sort of ambassador for the Empire, Andover. You would represent the Emperor if you did this. Think carefully before you answer."

"How long would I be gone?"

His eyes moved of their own volition, his head turned without his choosing, and he found himself looking at Tega, drinking in her beauty. To be something other than a beggar, to serve the Emperor in that sort of way, would that not be an important thing? Would that not make her notice him?

"Most of a year, I suspect. The travel time there is months as it is, unless Drask decides to lead you through the worst of the Blasted Lands.

"You come from the Blasted Lands?" His eyes moved to Drask again.

"Beyond the Blasted Lands." The man moved back a few steps and Andover realized for the first time how fast the man must have responded when he tripped himself to clear the distance between them. "Your people and mine are not the same. The Daxar Taalor would have to see you, to understand you in order to make certain that their gift to you works properly."

"You mean I would meet your gods?"

Drask waved a hand in a gesture that seemed to indicate a negative. His words confirmed. "No. You would not meet them. They do not show themselves to any who are not kings. But they would meet you."

"Only your king gets to see the gods?" The Emperor took note of that, his eyes seemed particularly alert.

"Only our kings," Drask corrected. "There are seven kings. One for each mountain. One for each god."

Enough. The Emperor was very important, yes, but Andover wanted his hands.

"I accept! I will go with you. I will be an ambassador for the Empire. I accept." His face flushed red with embarrassment. He had interrupted a conversation between the Emperor and a man from another land. His mother would have been horrified.

The wizard, the stranger, the Emperor all looked at him for a moment in silence so complete he could hear his own breaths.

Then Emperor stood and walked toward him. "Excellent! You are a brave lad, and you do the Empire proud." The older man's hand rested on his shoulder for one moment. "You make me proud."

Andover's knees shook. Despite being very nearly overwhelmed by the praise, it was the thought that he might have hands again that mattered most to him.

Hands.

The ability to once again be seen as something more than an object of pity.

He looked toward Tega and dared a smile.

And the girl he adored smiled back.

The boy did not understand. And he was a boy; there was no denying that. He was soft and untried. Drask looked at the thin lad and took a deep breath. This was not his choice, nor his place to question. The gods did not want his wisdom, only his service and he did not question the Daxar Taalor.

Without another word he moved to the satchel he'd carried with him to this place. Tataya watched him, her eyes glittering in the firelight, and her lips settled into a half-smile he found pleasantly distracting.

Andover Lashk watched him, too. All of them did, even the Emperor of the realm. He had heard stories of Fellein, of course, but had he ever really expected to be here in person? No. The gods had honored him again and again of late, though he did not allow that fact to swell his heart with pride.

He removed the dark iron box from his satchel and set it on a carved marble table. The weight of the thing was substantial, more than he suspected the strangers around him realized. There was the box itself, of course, and then there was the metal within it. An image of a face, a mask of iron with a harsh features and a cruel mouth stared at him. Aside from the face of Truska-Pren – His Might Be Unchanging – on the top of the box, it was unremarkable, unadorned save for two circular openings, one on either side.

He looked to Andover and gestured the boy closer. "This is a gift of Truska-Pren, whose heart is forged in iron, whose face adorns the blessing box. Each god offers a different form of gift. Your hands will not be like mine. They will have a different appearance, but they will be yours and they will never fail you."

The boy looked at him with wide, nervous eyes.

"Do you accept this gift, Andover Lashk of Fellein?"

"I…" He nodded. "Yes, I do."

"Place your arms within the blessing box. Do not move them, no matter how great the pain, no matter how tempting. Life is pain, and if you would have hands that live, you must accept that pain. Do you understand?"

The boy swallowed several times, his throat making a clicking noise each time. The Emperor, the hooded wizard, and both of the women in the room moved closer, drawn by curiosity to see a miracle occur. Who would not be tempted, really? Hundreds had watched when Drask's hand was gifted to him.

Drask prepared himself. The boy thought he was strong enough. Drask did not agree.

Andover Lashk reached into the openings of the blessing box, his face pale and his lips trembling. He pushed forward, his forearms sliding in a bit at a time until the ruined stump and the shattered remnants of his hand were gone, pushed beyond the point where his wrists disappeared into the device as well.

"I don't feel anything."

"Be patient. Truska-Pren must reach a long way to offer his blessings to you."

The wizard moved a step closer.

"Wait. There. I feel something. It tingles. It–" The boy bucked and screamed, his eyes flying wide. He started to yank his hands from the blessing box and Drask responded, grabbing the boy's thin arms at the elbows and holding him in place.

Andover's face grew first pale and then extremely red and he shrieked, his entire body thrashing as he tried to escape.

"No! Stay where you are!" The words were called out to the girl who'd arrived with Andover, who reached out as if to help him. Andover kicked him in the foot, then in the shin, trying to break free. Pain drove civility from the lad and he leaned down and attempted to bite Drask, and rather than fight him, Drask let the boy sink his teeth into the skin of his bicep. The skin broke and the boy worried the wound, did his best to savage the flesh. Drask gritted his teeth and did not move. Life is pain. The boy had to learn that. The gods make their gifts and they make their demands and sometimes the two were intertwined.

Drask shifted his body instinctively and the boy's knee crashed into his leg rather than slamming into his privates. Under most circumstances he'd kill the man who tried that, but not now. He understood the pain all too well.

The blessing box grew hot, the image of Truska-Pren's face glowed white and the smell of burning iron filled the air. The sounds that came from Andover Lashk failed, but to take their place his skin hissed and sizzled within the metallic confines.

When Andover fainted away, his eyes rolling into his head and his mouth falling slack as his body fell, Drask held the boy's hands in place, supporting the added weight and shuddering at the strain. Still he held the boy and when the wizard reached for him – perhaps to help, who could say what sorcerers contemplated? – Drask turned to him quickly. "If you move, if you interfere, I will kill you." The words were spoken softly enough, but the man listened and stepped back two paces.

Finally the hissing stopped and the glow of Truska-Pren's visage faded in an instant. Drask very carefully lowered the boy, keeping his hands within the blessing box as he settled him to the marble floor.

"Let him rest. He will need time to recover." Drask stepped back and crossed his arms over his chest. He saw the wizard staring at him from beneath his hood, but made no gesture, did nothing to apologize. He had done as the Daxar Taalor commanded and held the boy still. Their blessings had been granted. Time alone would tell what form those blessings took.

SEVEN

Desh Krohan paced around the dining hall with his arms behind him and the hood of his cloak thrown back. "Well, that was unexpected."

Emperor Pathra Krous looked at him with one raised eyebrow. "I should hope so. What in the name of the gods were you thinking? Introducing me to the first stranger to see the Empire in a hundred years that way?"

"Well how was I supposed to introduce him? Wait for the entire bloody entourage to show up and then ask you to join the whole merry lot for a picnic?"

Pathra shook his head. His hair moved in a nearly solid wave around his face. "Alright, seriously, Pathra, you have got to talk to that girl. Your hair could almost be a helmet."

The man waved away the annoying words, not willing to be distracted from the matters at hand.

"One of my citizens just fell down screaming in the middle of my throne room. He's unconscious and his arms smell like they've been dropped in a smithy."

"Well, your citizen agreed to the chance to have new hands – replacing hands destroyed by the City

Guard, I might add. You really have to decide what to do with those guards and soon, too. I'd wager a few tongues in the city are still wagging over the fact that they've not been properly punished. Also, as he worked as a smith's apprentice, maybe he always smells that way."

"That's a weak excuse even for you, Desh. I'm not foolish enough to think the smell of molten metal stays on skin for several weeks."

"It was a bad attempt at a jest. I'm a little stressed at the moment." He paced some more, trying to come up with a proper plan of action. "We can't very well arrest this Drask Silver Hand. He's come as an emissary of a king from another land. We don't know a damned thing about them. All I can say for sure is he's a very large man and he looks remarkably capable of eating half the City Guard if they were to try anything foolish with him."

"Well that seems a little…" The Emperor paused and contemplated the man who'd come before him. "Yes, alright. Good point. But sheer size doesn't mean he's a capable warrior."

"There are fifty more of his people coming here to meet with you formally. If you don't handle this the right way, you could very well have a war on your hands."

"Don't be absurd. Who would dare attack the Fellein Empire?"

Desh rounded on the Emperor and jabbed a finger in his direction. Most people wouldn't have dared. The wizard was not most people, but he was also wise enough not to act so casually when there were others around. "We've discussed that. Yes, you have soldiers, but when was the last time you had an actual war on your hands, Pathra? Not in your lifetime is when. It's been close to a hundred years. The Empire is getting along just fine and that's a wonderful thing, but only because we've not had more than a few scuffles with the Guntha since your father built the walls separating their land from ours."

"The Guntha are hardly an issue." Which was true enough, since the Guntha had given up all attempts to attack the Empire, save in occasional skirmishes along the waterfronts of the southlands.

"The Guntha aren't currently the problem." He pointed to the throne room beyond the closed doors of the small dining hall. "He is. He and his people are. We don't know anything about them."

"We know their so called gifts aren't very impressive."

"We know no such thing. Drask said the process wasn't finished."

"Then let's go out there and see what happens when it is finished, shall we?"

"Just be prepared, that's all I ask, Pathra. We have to be prepared for if things go poorly. We also have to be prepared if things go well."

"I am the Emperor, Desh. I've been trained in etiquette."

"Yes, you were trained by me. That's why I'm reminding you to be cautious. I always hated having to follow the rules."

"Well, I've always been less temperamental than you, too, old man."

"Good point."

Desh sighed and pulled his hood back in place. He was still working on looking mysterious for the brute in the next room. "So did you hear about the mount they rode here on?"

"No." Pathra frowned.

"Big as a house. It also ate a horse roughly two hours ago."

"A horse?"

"One of the white chargers you're so fond of."

"Well, that's certainly an awkward step in the wrong direction." The Emperor sounded just a bit pouty about the horse.

"Possibilities of war, Pathra. Just remember that part."

"Stupid rules."

"Yes they are. Perhaps you should change them. Just do it later, yes?"

Pathra opened the door and moved back into his throne room. Soon they'd know how badly things were going.

The entourage continued on, moving across the wasted landscape at a pace that exhausted riders and mounts alike. Human riders and horses at least. The people from the valley seemed just fine and their beasts looked almost as fresh as when they'd left.

Merros and Wollis rode side by side again, both of them sharing a certain anticipation now that they could see the steppes ahead of them. They would be out of the gods-forsaken Blasted Lands soon, and as far as Merros was concerned if he never saw them again he would live a fulfilled existence.

A few things they had learned about the Sa'ba
Taalor: first, they were not much for idle chatter.
Though Merros had spoken on repeated occasions
with all of the retinue traveling with them, they had
spent most of those conversations doing their best to
learn the language of the Empire. Second, they were
very, very determined to learn. Though none of them
could be called fluent in the tongue, they had learned
enough to now have conversations with the rest of the
group. They were formal, they were inquisitive, and
they seldom volunteered anything about themselves.
Maybe it was difficult to open up to strangers when
they had never seen strangers before.

While almost all of the riders wore armor, he also
now knew that easily a dozen or more of them were
women under their gear. It was almost impossible
to tell from a distance, but in speaking with them
he'd noticed the differences in tone – sometimes
a challenge as all of the people from the valley had
the same unusual distortions to their voices – and as
the weather warmed a bit and they came closer to
the Empire, layers of cloth were removed and more
flesh was exposed. The females had smaller arms.
They were still muscular, and a few of the women
had the sort of muscle tone that made Merros realize
he should get more practice time with his weapons.
The time out in the fields had robbed him of some of
his shape.

Third, there wasn't a single one of them that
wasn't covered with scars. When the curiosity got too
much for him he decided to approach a rider named
Tusk who was more curious than a lot of his peers.

Tusk sported a scar around one wrist that wrapped itself over his forearm twice. The scar was a thick, serpentine mess and it seemed almost a wonder that the sort of wound that would leave that scar didn't require the loss of a limb.

Tusk – he wasn't sure if that was a name or a nickname as the man's skull-shaped helmet was adorned with large teeth from some sort of animal, possibly a Pra-Moresh by the sheer size of the fangs – explained without hesitation. "We are trained to defend ourselves from a young age."

"From whom?"

"The Blasted Lands have many threats."

"You mean the Pra-Moresh?"

"They are only one. There are others." The man shrugged his shoulders, sending a rattling effect across all of his armor. "We are also taught to make our own armor and weapons. That often leaves scars."

"You forge your own weapons?"

"You cannot be connected with your weapons if you do not make your weapons. They should be as the claws of a beast, a part of you." The way he said it made Merros suspect he was quoting an age-old adage.

"You forged your own sword?" The notion was damned near ludicrous. It took years to learn how to work a forge and pound metal into something other than a shapeless lump.

Tusk drew his sword, a thick bladed affair with surprisingly delicate inscriptions across the center of the blade. He offered it hilt-first to Merros. Merros took the blade carefully, not only because it was a weapon and should be respected, but also because he suspected he was being given a great honor when he was offered the piece in the first place. The craftsmanship was damned fine, and the balance was perfect. The metal was lighter than he expected, but he could see how well-sharpened the blade's edge was and he had no doubt it was as fine a sword as he'd ever held.

"You do not forge your own weapons?" Tusk's turn. His tone was hard to read. It was hard to tell much of what the man thought under the helm he wore. One tended to get distracted by the amazing array of sharp teeth leering in one's direction.

"Well, no. Not really. We have people who bake bread, we have people who tend animals, we have people who build houses, and we have people who forge weapons. Each is a skill that is learned over years."

Tusk stared at him in silence for a moment as if trying to absorb a piece of vital information. No, as if he were genuinely surprised by the response he'd received.

"Then how do you know your weapon is well-made?"

"You test it, of course. Before you make a purchase. Or if you are in the army, you are issued a weapon."

"May I see your sword?" Tusk's voice was unusually formal.

"Of course." Merros had little choice, really. The man had just offered his own weapon. He first handed Tusk back the sword the man had proffered and then extended his own. Tusk's movements were nearly a blur. He held the weapon, ran a finger along the blade, eyed the edge carefully and then swung the blade several times in arcs above his head and to his side. Merros was unsettled by how little effort the man seemed to extend in the process.

He then handed it back. "Thank you."

"Of course." Merros pointed to Tusk's arm and the thick scars. "May I ask how you came by that one?"

"I was hit with a chain."

"A chain?"

Merros leaned in closer, looking at the scar. He could imagine the sort of chain that had links thick enough to break skin in that way, but he didn't really want to.

"Why in the name of the gods would anyone hit you with a chain?"

"As I said, we are all trained in defense."

"Against a chain?"

Tusk chuckled, a deep sound that came from low in his chest. "If you do not think a chain can be used as a weapon, you have obviously never been hit with a chain." He patted his side and Merros looked at the spot where a length of chain had been coiled several times before being secured to his belt.

"Good point." Merros thanked him for his time and slowed down a bit until he and Wollis were once again riding next to each other.

Wollis looked a question at him.

Merros shook his head. "I'm beginning to understand how Drask killed four Pra-Moresh."

"How is that?"

Merros looked at one of the riders off in the distance. He could see the muscles on her arms and though he could not see her face, he was astonished by the attraction he felt for her. Like Tusk, she had several serious scars on her exposed flesh.

"These are not a people to be underestimated, Wollis. Let's leave it at that for now."

Wollis, ever one to conserve his energies for things more interesting than speech, merely nodded his head and kept riding.

Andover woke up in a different room this time. The ceiling was higher and there were furs on the bed beneath him. Also, he was clothed differently.

Also, his hands weren't screaming at him. For the first time in what seemed like a lifetime, his hands weren't shrieking their tortured agonies into his arms and then through the rest of him. He lifted his arms without thinking and looked at his hands.

And froze in wonder.

They were hands. There was simply no doubting that. The fingers were as long as he remembered, and he stared at them as he moved them. His lips trembled and tears threatened to break from his wide eyes.

His hands were metal. He'd known they would be, if those of the stranger, Drask were any indication, but knowing in your mind is different from knowing in your heart. In color they looked as if they'd been freshly forged from good iron, free from impurities. The "flesh" had a polished, buffed look and was smooth, save where the joints met. That area was a bit rougher, more textured but still impossibly flawless. The real skin of his wrists was heavily scarred, and he could see where metal and flesh were married if he looked, but he did not want to look too closely, not yet. He might think too much, and then he might well start screaming and never stop. A miracle these hands, yes, but many were the people who had said that to look upon the blessings of the gods was to know their flaws and their pettiness. He would not consider the flaws of the deity that had offered this amazing blessing. There were markings along each finger, across the tips, the palms. Everywhere. They made no sense to him, but the marks were there, a language he had never seen, perhaps, or merely decoration. He did not know.

When he flexed the fingers moved exactly as they should, smoothly, without hesitation.

More importantly, oh, so much more importantly, he could feel through his hands. Not the ghost pains that had insisted his hands were still there even after they'd been taken, but real sensations. He closed his eyes and ran his hands across his face. The flesh of his jaw line felt warm metal, not hot, merely warm, caressing the angles of his face. His fingers felt those same angles, read them as well as his fingers had ever read any surface.

Impossible! But there it was. He opened his eyes and sat up on the bed and for the first time was aware of the people around him, looking at him with expectant faces. Tega was there, and the wizard and the Emperor and the stranger, the man with the silver hand. The only person who did not seem surprised by the use of his hands was the man who had a similar limb.

"How do they feel?" That was Desh Krohan.

"Like flesh. Like real hands."

"They are real. The gods do not offer trinkets." Drask spoke softly and in the semi-dark room his eyes offered a faint silvery glow that reminded Andover of the odd way cats' eyes could reflect light.

"How can I thank you?" Andover's voice shook and he closed his eyes for a moment, overwhelmed with a wave of gratitude. Later, perhaps, he would allow himself to feel dread at the sight of his new hands. But he hoped not. Let them look odd. Let others see them as strange. He could accept that. He had hands again, and that was an amazing, spectacular thing.

Drask shook his head. "To me you owe nothing. I am merely a messenger. If you would offer your thanks, offer them to Truska-Pren, God of the Iron Forge."

"When I am at his altar, I shall surely do so."

Drask nodded without saying another word.

Really, there wasn't much to say. Not then. The emissary from the Seven Forges merely crossed his arms and waited patiently while the rest of the group asked their questions. Andover answered them all, and as he did so his smile grew a little at a time.

He had hands!

No one was more surprised than he was when Tega placed her hands upon his and ran her fingers over the metal, surprised and curious.

He had feared that she would be repulsed.

Instead she seemed fascinated. He did his best not to read anything into that, but as is often the case with young men who think they are in love, he was not completely successful.

••••

The steppes were close enough that the air felt almost warm again. Merros couldn't quite keep himself from getting jumpy about it. He'd been away from the world he knew for just a little too long.

Not far away from him the remaining two women who served as the wizard's eyes and ears – and at times as his mouth – had actually left their wagon and were walking alongside the supply wagon. The wind occasionally caught their cloaks and threw the hoods back far enough to let him see the startlingly blonde hair or the midnight black. Without the redhead they didn't seem complete; beautiful, yes, but not complete.

To make up for the difference, they spoke with two of the women from the valley. Although they were also female, they were not quite cut from the same fabric: two ladies who looked like they should be dining with royalty, and two women who looked like they'd spent their lives working the fields.

Wollis noticed him looking and chuckled. "Hard to decide which you prefer?"

"Not at all. After months of dealing with you and sleeping in a tent, I'd gleefully bed your mother."

Wollis frowned. "I have told you about my mother, yes?"

Merros smiled. "And yet I would still bed her."

"Gods, Captain, you are beyond desperate."

"So you can see why staring at four fit women would be a nice distraction?"

Before Wollis could respond, one of their escorts blew three sharp notes on his horn. He was a decent distance away and the winds were still bad enough that all the bellowing in the world might not be heard.

And as fast as the wind, the Sa'ba Taalor were in motion. They looked toward the sound of the horn and then they moved, not so much heading in the direction of potential trouble as stalking it. The two women he'd been admiring a moment before spun away from the wizard's servants and crouched, sliding their bows from their backs and communicating with each other with quick hand gestures between motions. Bows removed, arrows pulled and notched in place all in seconds.

Goriah looked toward him, her eyes startlingly blue. She cupped her hands to her mouth and called out "Pra-Moresh!" Merros nodded and looked toward the horn blower.

It was almost over before it started, really. There were only two of the beasts this time, not seven like they had encountered before. The Sa'ba Taalor devastated the damned things in a matter of moments. The two women who'd started in that direction both fired arrows at the same one and they surely must have spoken to each other, because each of them fired exactly one arrow and each of them planted an arrow in a different eye. The great, screeching beast fell backward amid a thunderous roar of voices, and bucked and thrashed for several seconds before dying.

The horn blower was none other than Tusk, who took the other animal by himself. He did not throw an axe. He did not fire an arrow. Instead he charged on his war beast and drew a great sword unlike any Merros had ever seen before. The blade was well over four feet in length, very thick in the center and with a heavy curve. Merros was still trying to identify exactly what the weapon was when Tusk climbed from his saddle, balanced himself on the back of his moving beast, and then leaped at the Pra-Moresh. One hand held the hilt of the sword. The other was braced along the blade's length, and as Tusk came downward, so too did his hands.

Hard to say who was more surprised, really; Merros or the monster that Tusk jumped toward.

"What is that madman doing?" Wollis' voice cracked as he watched the man from the valley bring the sword down and cleave the blade through the neck and shoulder of the monstrous wall of flesh. He did not completely decapitate the Pra-Moresh, but it was close. The impact ran through hunter and hunted alike and Tusk rolled past the falling creature sliding across the frozen ground as he brought himself to a halt.

Merros was far too busy staring at the dead monster's carcass to answer Wollis' question. The damned things had hides thick enough to slow a crossbow bolt. They had bone plates under the skin in a dozen different places. He wasn't completely sure, but he was fairly certain that the cut Tusk made carved through at least one of the bones.

Tusk stood up and raised his massive sword over his head, roaring to the heavens. "Durhallem!" The war cry was nearly as loud as the roar of the monsters he and his brethren had just slaughtered.

Wollis led his horse in a wide circle. The animal was well-trained and had been steady through the entire time they'd been on the expedition, but now it was edgy and seemed ready to bolt.

Merros could fully understand that. The smell of the Pra-Moresh was potent, made stronger here because the air was cleaner. Leagues away, closer to the Seven Forges, the air was thick with soot all the time, heavy with dust and ash. Here, closer to home, it was almost like his senses were coming back for the first time.

The hunters made quick work of their kills. While Merros watched and Wollis worked on calming his animal – a task he handled expertly – Tusk swept the massive sword clean with a heavy piece of his prey's fur and slid it back into the sheath. Then he took a different blade, smaller but decidedly sharp and sturdy, and began cleaning the carcass. Within ten minutes he'd cut away a good portion of the meat from the Pra-Moresh. He called to two of his brethren who moved over and helped pack the meat into several cloth sacks. While they worked, the mounts they'd been riding stared at the dead beast and shifted from paw to paw. Not one of the creatures moved from where it stood.

The two women were just as fast as their male counterparts, and had cleaned a good amount of the meat away from the carcass in short order. When they were done, they stepped back and one of the women called out with a harsh, barking command. A moment later the great predatory animals they rode on pounced on the bodies. Not all of the Sa'ba Taalor rode the animals, just as not every person on the expedition had a horse. It simply wasn't practical. Still there were a dozen of the beasts, and they tore hard meat and gristle away from the bodies and feasted on the entrails and several dubious looking organs their masters had set aside for them.

Tusk walked around the circle of feeding animals and held two more massive teeth out to show a few of his friends. He spoke in his own tongue, laughing, and Wollis, who had finally calmed his horse down, rode close to Merros. "What is he saying?"

"He's just having fun. He's being a hunter." Merros pointed to the teeth. "He's planning on adding those to his helmet. He's just cracking wise because he can't decide if he wants to merely add them or replace a couple of teeth that have broken in previous combats."

"So he's bragging?"

Merros shook his head. "No. He's just having a good time. He may as well be a woman discussing what sort of fur to line her cloak with."

"I'm thinking referring to him as a woman might be a mistake."

The voice that responded came from Goriah. The blonde woman had crept closer while both of them were busy conversing. "No. I don't think they care. Male, female. It's all the same."

"How so?"

She looked from one man to the other, her eyes drawing both of them. She was, as always, extremely distracting. "They have been learning from you. We have been learning from them. The only thing that matters seems to be how well they obey their gods. If you were to call Tusk a woman, he would probably think you were confused. He wouldn't be insulted. He'd just possibly think you had been hit in the head too many times to think clearly."

"Really?" Wollis' voice was a skeptical.

"You wonder how that could be? Why he wouldn't be offended?"

"Well, yes. No disrespect, Goriah, but most of the soldiers I've met would beat a man into the mud for calling him a woman."

Goriah smiled. Even her teeth were perfect. "That's because most of the soldiers you've dealt with would consider that an insult to their manhood and to their ability to fight."

Wollis squinted at her. He was thinking it through. "Well, yes."

She nodded her chin to the two women who were cleaning their blades and sliding them back into the sheaths on their bodies. Their cloaks were opened to the elements and the numerous straps that held knives, axes and even swords in place were revealed. Once again, Merros found himself watching the smooth play of muscles moving under their scarred skin. Once again, he found himself oddly drawn to their forms. Too damned long away from civilized women. He'd have to fix that and soon. "Answer me this, Wollis. Do either of those women strike you as the sort who would be considered too delicate to fight?"

Wollis shook his head. "Gods no. I don't think I'd want to cross either of them." His tone clearly revealed his admiration.

"Then why would a fighter be offended to be compared to them?"

"Your point is well made, Goriah."

One of the women called out to Goriah and she in turn called back with a fast response. When she was done she looked at Wollis again. "We are apparently in for a treat."

"How's that?"

"Ehnole over there is going to make us a stew from the hearts, eyes and tongue of the Pra-Moresh." The woman looked at Wollis with a certain humor. "Apparently it is a treat."

"I doubt that."

Goriah waved a dismissive hand and started toward the woman in question. "Should I tell her you wish to decline her generous offer? Keep in mind that if she takes offense she might decide you've insulted her honor."

Wollis blanched.

Merros smiled. "I think we'll both be delighted to try whatever dish she offers." His second did not disagree.

They gathered together at the dining hall where Pathra Krous and Desh Krohan often had their conversations in private, joined by a dozen others who simply had to know what was happening.

The Emperor had numerous advisors, most of whom were not present. Some had other engagements, some had families to attend to, some were not invited because at that particular moment Pathra did not wish to see them. To the very last of them the newcomers stared at Drask Silver Hand with the sort of fascination normally reserved for a new and particularly unsettling looking bug. It either said a lot for him that he didn't seem to care, or it spoke volumes about his ignorance of what was going on around him. Desh Krohan reached the same conclusion Merros had earlier: the stranger was not foolish enough not to notice that he was being observed, and carefully. He simply found nothing to be concerned over.

Among the people in the room was an exotic beauty from the far south of the Empire, whose flawless skin was darker by a few shades – in much the same way that Drask's skin was grayer – and whose hair fell in a straight wave down past her shoulders. She had trouble taking her eyes off of Drask, and when she did, it was only to stare at Andover's new hands. For his part, the young man was staring around the room with the same sort of fascination, save when even he found himself drawn back to his hands. The woman had come to the seat of the Empire to seek a solution to a growing problem with the Guntha. Once again the closest kingdom of any size was feeling the need to stretch their legs into the Empire's territories, in this case a tropical zone called Roathes, the domain the young woman's family ruled. Roathes was allegedly beautiful. Desh had not been there in a very long time and no longer remembered it clearly. What he did know, however, was that the girl was one of Marsfel the King of Roathes' daughters, and that she would be staying in the area and making multiple requests for aid until the situation either grew bad enough to require action, calmed down on its own, or her presence offended Pathra. The reason so staggering a beauty had been sent along? To ensure that she did not quickly get on the Emperor's nerves.

"Well, the Guntha are a persistent problem, Lanaie. We aren't ignoring them, but we also have to make sure that the borders throughout the Empire hold against our enemies." That was Pathra, who was currently trying to explain why he wasn't sending troops to help the girl's father. He was talking to her chest as much as he was talking to her face. That was to be expected, as her assets were considerable. The advantage of being the Emperor was that no one would say a word to him about his boorish behavior. Except for Desh, of course, but he would wait until after the meal.

"How many troops do the Guntha employ against your father?" Desh had been about ask that very question. Drask beat him to it.

The dark eyes of the girl grew wider as Drask spoke to her. She looked at him with slightly parted lips and drank in his words, fascinated by him. His face still remained behind the veil he found so important. Tataya had seen him, of course. Well, she had felt his face so she understood what was going on behind that cloth. So too did Desh. What his associates knew soon became his knowledge as well.

"My father says the Guntha have gathered almost two thousand in preparation."

Desh held his breath. That was the last thing Fellein needed at the present time.

"Does your father not have an army of his own?" Drask again.

"Well, of course, but we were hoping for additional forces."

"How many soldiers does your father have?" Drask again. The girl listened to every word he said and answered quickly each time he spoke. When Pathra talked to her she seemed to take forever to get around to answering. Her father had not chosen wisely when it came to a good representative. She was too easily distracted.

"Our numbers are good, but we hope for additional assistance to end the assault before it can become substantial."

Drask turned to the Emperor. "And do you plan to offer assistance, Your Majesty?" He had learned quickly the proper form for addressing the Emperor. Tataya was teaching him.

"Well. It's something I have to consider, of course."

"May I offer a solution, Your Majesty?" Drask stared hard, his face unreadable above the veil.

"Of course." Pathra's expression said he was curious about what the solution might be. So was Desh.

"I could send ten of my fellows to see to the situation. They would like the opportunity to explore Roathes, and to meet these Guntha face to face."

Pathra Krous stared at Drask for several heartbeats, his face frozen at the edge of a smile. He managed to behave himself, but Desh knew him well enough to know that the Emperor was tempted to laugh.

"Ten men?"

"Yes, Your Majesty."

A quick look. A question shot toward Desh with a single expression. They had known each other so long that they needed nothing else for the communication. Pathra asked *What do you think?*

And Desh responded with *Why not see what Drask thinks ten men can do?*

Pathra smiled and lowered his head in a small bow of concession. "I appreciate the offer, Drask. Why don't you send your men?"

Lanaie frowned. She did so very fetchingly. "That is all the help you can offer?"

Pathra said, "Merely as a consultation, another group to offer an impartial consideration."

And at the same time, without any hesitation, Drask answered, "You shall see, Princess, what ten of the Sa'ba Taalor can do."

The look Pathra shot was both amused and shocked. He had the good graces to hide his face from the eyes of both strangers before he stared at Desh.

Desh gave a small wave of his hands in dismissal and hid it behind the act of reaching for his wine. This would be enlightening at the very least, and if the Sa'ba Taalor managed to make a miserable situation more manageable while simultaneously telling something about themselves, all the better.

Of course he'd have to make sure he knew what was going on down there. And he'd have to get the strangers there in one piece. The good news was he already knew how to handle that.

Tataya looked in his direction and he nodded. She knew the way he thought. That was a good thing. It made life much easier when it came to certain things.

The sun broke through the thinning cloud cover and Merros sighed. What a beautiful sight. He'd been granted a teasing glimpse of the sun when he was in the valley of the Seven Forges, but that had been through the perpetual haze that covered the entire

region. When one considered the misery of the Blasted
Lands in general, the fact that any place within the
depths of the frozen hell they were leaving ever saw
sunlight could almost be considered a miracle.

The ground was no longer frozen. Spring was
coming to Fellein, though it was hard to tell this far
north. The air was warmer, sweeter and had the first
scent of green, fertile plants that he could remember
in forever it seemed. Even in the valley the air had a
taint of soot.

Wollis was involved in a serious discussion with
Tusk about the benefits of marinating wild meats. For
reasons Merros didn't begin to understand, the two
had struck a mutual respect for each other. He didn't
quite want to risk calling it a friendship.

Pella called his name, and he turned to the sound
of her voice. Without the winds half-deafening him
he realized again that even her voice had an air of
sensuality to it. How the hell was that even possible?
Too long without companionship, that was how. He
tried not to think about it.

The wizard's servant moved closer and walked
with a woman who either had the name Swech or
the name Soot Hair. Possibly both. He still hadn't
quite grasped all the nicknames versus titles versus
actual names of the people they traveled with. The
differences were once again instantly obvious. Swech
was almost as tall as he was, and she dressed for easy
function in her motions instead of for any semblance
of fashion. In other words, she dressed like a man.
She had longish hair that did, indeed, carry the same
color as the ash from a campfire. Her hair was tied

back at the present moment, and fell in a tail halfway down her back. She also had a body that was as delightfully feminine as he could recall, just in a very well-muscled way he wasn't at all used to. Pella was far thinner, seemed more like a proper lady, but both of them were distracting.

The weather was warm enough that both had discarded their cloaks and were happy to wear shirts instead of thick layers of cloth. That didn't help with the distraction at all, but he still decided to enjoy the show rather than be annoyed. Pella was wearing a long skirt of dark cloth that shimmered around her. Swech was wearing leather breeches that fit almost as well as her skin. Oh yes, she had a feminine shape to her.

She also sported one sword, two daggers and at least one axe that he could see. Judging by the way they were carried, she'd long since adjusted to their shape and weight against her. She was still wearing a damned veil, too. His desire to see what she looked like under that cloth cover was even more distracting than the very shapely curves her outfit revealed.

"What can I do for you, Pella?" He made himself speak to avoid looking like he was staring as much as he wanted to. He also looked away from both of the women and let his attention soften until he was aware of everything around him instead of focusing on any specific details.

"Desh has been in contact with me."

"Of course he has."

She ignored his tone. "He requires additional work from you."

"I believe our contract is fulfilled within the next two days, barring unforeseen occurrences." There was a rather large fortune waiting for him and he intended to get around to spending it. He also intended to spend at least a full day soaking in hot, scented waters.

"Yes." She nodded and he looked at her face. Damn if she wasn't stunning.

"Then what could he possibly require from me?"

"That you lead ten of the Sa'ba Taalor to the southern edge of the Empire, the better to examine the border between Fellein and Guntha. The Guntha seem to want another war."

"And why would I be at all interested?" He was interested, of course. He hadn't been to the southern part of the continent in a very long time, and he was curious about what the Guntha were up to since he and a few thousand others had helped repel them in the past. That was how Wollis got his leg wrecked as he recalled. A spear hurled by a particularly angry Guntha had gone completely through his thigh, bone and meat alike. He had recovered but never completely.

"Double the money you have already earned."

By all the gods, the man had gone mad. With that sort of money a man could buy himself a title and the castle to go with it.

"Yes, you could. But if you keep on Desh Krohan's good side, he might well arrange for the title himself." Pella's voice was soft and amused.

Merros pulled back, not at all aware that he had been speaking aloud. A moment later he realized he hadn't been.

"You need to not do that." He made his voice hard.

"Do what?" Swech's voice was naturally husky.

Merros chose to ignore the innocent question. "Fine, I'll accept the commission, but I'll need to go to the capital at any rate to finish this commission and draw the papers for the next. There's also the matter of supplies and getting a fresh horse."

"There's no time for that. I was discussing the matter with Swech and she's agreed to let you ride along with her."

"Excuse me?" Was he blushing? Gods, he hoped not.

Swech struck him with a companionable cuff across the shoulder. "This horse of yours is slow. My Saa'thaa is faster and can easily carry two. If you are nice, I might even let you take the reins." Oh yes, there was a bit of blushing going on now. He coughed into his hand in an effort to mask that fact.

Both of the women kept their quiet, but he suspected they exchanged an amused look while he wasn't looking.

"So when do we leave then?"

"Immediately. Take what you need from your horse. Wollis will take over the leadership of the expedition."

Wollis would take the maps to Desh Krohan. Wollis would handle the exchange of goods between the Sa'ba Taalor and the Emperor's people. Fair enough. Wollis was his right hand and had certainly earned a bit of credit.

Merros nodded his head and called to Wollis. A few moments later he was removing his bedroll and a satchel of clothes from the saddle. Food, too, though he wasn't sure he'd need it.

Pella came closer as he was gathering the last of his needs from his horse. His sword tapped against his hip as he settled it. Unlike his new friends, he didn't carry the bloody thing around all the time. "Wollis is prepared to make the trip without you?"

"He's probably delighted." He snorted. "He and I are friends, but we have very different opinions on how an expedition should be led. He'll enjoy himself a great deal more now that he's in charge."

Pella reached out a hand and offered him a pouch. He took it and felt the weight of the coins inside. "Expenditures. You're back in the realm now, and the need to eat and sleep can be better accommodated with a few silvers than by pitching a tent."

He nodded his head. "Like as not we'll ride hard. That seems to be the only way these folks like to ride." Pella's ornery smile made him look away and cough into his hand a second time. He hadn't meant it that way, of course.

Swech came up next to Pella as if summoned to make him even more uncomfortable. "The day is half done. If we're to make good distance we should go."

Wollis limped over and stood next to Merros as if for moral support. "We'll be waiting for you when you return." He took the horse's reins and nodded a brisk farewell.

"Go home to your wife instead."

"By the gods, man, why would I do that?" His second walked away without looking back.

Swech started toward her mount, and Merros gathered his belongings.

"Ride fast, Captain. Be safe on your journeys."

"So are we going there merely to observe?"

Pella stared at him long enough to make him uncomfortable. "You are. You are going to observe. The Sa'ba Taalor will follow their own instructions."

"And where are they getting their instructions from?"

Pella pointed to where Swech was standing. "Drask delivered a message to them at the same time as Desh contacted me."

"How?"

"You are endlessly full of questions." She waved a careless hand toward the wagon where she stayed. "Tataya rests in the wagon now, recovering from her journey here."

He frowned. No riders had come toward them. They were in the steppes now and the land was fertile enough in comparison to the Blasted Lands, but there wasn't a tree or even a shrub that could have hidden the approach of a rider or even a wanderer walking under her own power.

Instead of making a comment, he headed for the woman giving him a ride to their next destination. They'd be riding together for a while. During that time he intended to learn more about the Sa'ba Taalor. He'd have time. There was very little else to do while riding.

When Pella laughed behind him he felt himself blush again and wished desperately that if she were indeed reading his thoughts she would do a better job of hiding that fact from him.

EIGHT

"It occurs to me that I have almost no clothes."
Andover looked at the room he'd been staying in and
shook his head. What meager belongings he owned
had been brought to him when Tega stopped by Burk's
smithy to let him know Andover had been assaulted.
That had been a while back now and looking at his
spare clothes – one pair of trews and two tunics – he
shook his head. "Does it get as cold as I've heard in
the Blasted Lands?"

Drask stood in the corner of his small room and
looked at him. The man seldom spoke to Andover,
but he was almost always nearby. "Yes. The cold will
sink into your bones."

"Do you suppose I'll freeze on my way to your
valley?"

"You are to serve as ambassador for your Emperor.
Even if he were not planning on clothing you, I would
find something you could use to stay warm."

"I'm fairly sure whatever you might offer me would
be too damned big. You're really quite large."

He could not see the man's smile behind his veil,
but he could sense it. "Adjustments can be made."

"Do you really suppose the Emperor plans on clothing me?"

"From what I have seen clothes are very important to your people. You would no sooner be asked to represent your Emperor without the proper clothing than I would be asked to come here naked."

Andover looked down at his new hands again and felt the same shiver of excitement. He had hands, which was amazing. They were real and they could feel things. And they were metallic. He shook his head in wonder.

Drask stepped closer. "Do they hurt you? Your hands?"

"What? No. I just. It's hard to get used to them." He looked to the other man. "I can't thank you enough."

Drask shook his head. "Not me. Truska-Pren."

"Then I can't thank Truska-Pren enough."

"You will have your chance to thank him." Drask put his right hand on Andover's shoulder. "I will teach you how to offer your thanks when we travel back to the valley."

"When do we leave?"

"Three days from now. First we wait for the rest of my people to arrive. There are offerings that must be made to your Emperor."

Andover shook his head. "I don't understand this. How have we never heard of your people before now?"

Drask shrugged his thick shoulders awkwardly, mimicking the gesture he'd likely seen from a few soldiers. "Your people have never reached the Seven Forges before now."

Andover stared at his hands again, at a loss for what he wanted to say.

Drask spoke up. "The men who did this to you. The ones who ruined your hands. What happened to them?"

An instant anger swelled in Andover. "Nothing. They sit in a cell and await a decision. They are to be punished, but no one seems to know what their punishment should be."

"They attacked you? They broke your hands because you looked at the girl Tega, yes?"

He hadn't discussed the situation with Drask at all, but obviously someone had. What was there to say?

"Yes. A man named Menock claimed to be her fiancé and broke my hands because he saw me looking at her."

"We have a name for such men where I am from."

"Yeah? What's that?"

Drask stared into Andover's eyes. For the first time he noticed the faint glow inside the stranger's own eyes. It was hard to see until you noticed it and after that it was hard not to see.

"Dead. We call them dead."

"I am not a fighter, Drask. You are a fighter. I am a weapon smith. And I'm only an apprentice."

Drask reached out suddenly and grabbed Andover's hands. He held them fast and raised them until Andover was forced to look at them, to see the fine workmanship, the amazing finesse with which they had been crafted.

"These are a warrior's hands. They are the hands of a weapon smith and a warrior and a man. You are not given these hands without purpose, Andover Lashk. You are given these hands because Truska-Pren, the God of Iron, the God of Armed Combat, has given them to you. He does not grant his blessings without a reason and he does not offer his blessings to cowards. Do you understand me?"

He nodded. He would have nodded just as vigorously if the man had asked him if he wanted to weave butterfly wings from silk and then fly to the Great Star. Drask exuded a confidence that was nearly contagious.

"Your Emperor asks that you serve as his ambassador. That you go to my country and speak to my kings. That you learn to understand our ways and better create an alliance between our people. You understand this, yes?"

"Yes, of course."

Drask nodded. He squeezed Andover's hands and Andover marveled that he could feel the pressure exerted on the artificial extremities. "Then know this. My people, my gods, are not always kind. They do not respect weakness. They respect strength. If you would be respected, you will have to demand satisfaction."

"What do you mean?"

"The guards who hurt you. You must fight them. You must punish them for what they did to you."

"I don't know." Andover shook his head.

Drask shook his head right back. "You do know. I am telling you. If you do not fight them, if you do not restore your honor in this fashion, you will fail your Emperor. You will dishonor yourself in the eyes of my people and the eyes of my gods. You will lose face before Truska-Pren."

"How–?"

Before he could finish his question Drask interrupted him. "If you lose face before Truska-Pren you could well lose the very gift he has granted you."

Andover pulled away from the stranger's grip. "What?"

"You understand already." Drask pointed. "Your hands come at a price. You must now pay it. Demand satisfaction from the men who took your hands. Do this thing, Andover Lashk, or risk losing the hands you have been given."

Andover stared at his hands for a very long time. While he stared, the stranger who had granted him those hands slipped away as silently as a bad dream.

The night found Merros Dulver sleeping in his own country for the first time in months. It did not, however, find him sleeping in a room. They were in the middle of the plains to the south of the Wellish Steppes. Aside from wild grasses and the occasional tree there was little to see as far as the horizon. Two days of traveling had moved them a great distance, leagues farther than he'd expected. The damned things the Sa'ba Taalor rode on were fast and had the endurance of a dozen horses. They also moved differently from horses, which meant that his hips, thighs and buttocks were sore in places he had not been prepared for because he had no idea how to ride comfortably on the beasts.

All of which meant that when sleep finally came for him it came hard and fast. When he awoke he found that several of his fellow travelers were down at the river bathing. Because he desperately wanted to wash the stench of the Blasted Lands from his body he joined them.

Males and females alike washed themselves in the waters of a tributary that ran down from the steppes. The water was as clear as the sky and almost as cold as the Blasted Lands themselves. Just the same, Merros followed the lead of the people around him and stripped down and moved into the stream. To the last, the people with him were covered in scars, except for their faces, which remained hidden behind veils.

Merros shook his head and looked down, moderately embarrassed by both the shape of his body and oddly enough by the lack of scars. If the people with him judged him, their veils hid whatever decisions they had come to.

Within an hour they were on the move again, heading toward the south. Swech sat before him on the saddle and he rode, his hands resting on two runners that seemed designed specifically to allow a second rider. The beasts – he still could not decide if they were feline in nature, but he was leaning in that direction – were larger than horses by at least half again and capable of pulling the carcasses of several heavy animals. He supposed it was possible that they often carried more than one rider with ease.

Swech looked at him over her shoulder and for a moment her veil shifted, showing more of her face than he had seen before. Her nose was straight and slightly shorter than he would have expected; he could not see her mouth. He found the glimpse oddly intoxicating.

"Tell me about the place where we go. What is it like?"

"Very warm." He thought back. It had been a few years since the last skirmish he'd been engaged in. "The land is flat, and the ocean is nearby. The winds are almost always blowing, but not like they do in the Blasted Lands."

"Will there be so much… green?" She waved her arms and he looked around them, He hadn't thought about it, but he could only imagine how different this was for her and her people.

"No." He thought for a moment longer. "Have you ever been away from the valley or the Blasted Lands?"

"No. Never." She looked away from him and he could sense that she was, if not embarrassed, at least uncomfortable with her lack of knowledge.

"Before I traveled there, I had never seen a place like your valley. You will see a lot of things you have never seen before." He pointed. "This, this is just an unsettled area. There are many. But there are a lot of towns between here and Roathes."

She shook her head but made no other response.

Just to keep the conversation going, he asked, "Did you make all of your weapons? Tusk said he did."

"We all do."

The notion still shook him. "Why?"

"That is what the gods demand. The Daxar Taalor say we must learn to forge our own ways, and that means we must make our own weapons, hunt for our own food and till the land if we would have crops."

"Everyone?"

"Yes, of course."

"What about children?"

"Children too. We learn to make weapons when we are small, so that when we are old enough to train we already understand the weapons."

"How old were you when you made your sword?"

"Which one?"

Seriously?

"The first."

Swech laughed. "Seven. It was not a very good sword."

He thought about what he'd seen at the last smithy he'd been to, watching the man hammering away at a length of blazing hot metal, watching the sparks that danced away with each blow. He tried to imagine a seven year-old girl using the same hammer to shape the rough metal, or even the smaller hammers to work on the nearly finished product and shook his head. "I can't be surprised."

"Have you ever made your own weapons?"

"No. I haven't even shoed a horse."

"What did you do when you were growing up?"

"Honestly?" Merros thought about that. "Not really very much. My father was off handling life as a soldier, and my mother stayed busy. She'd find a few odd jobs about the house for me, but mostly just to make sure I wasn't underfoot. When I was old enough I joined the army. Before that, I just did what my parents told me to do."

"What about your gods?"

"What about them?" He shrugged. "I have never been a very devout follower."

Swech turned her entire body to look at him, her eyes surprisingly wide above the veil. "And have your gods had nothing to say about this?"

"I don't think my gods are quite as concerned as yours." He felt his face flush red. "Drask told me that your gods told him where to find me. That your gods spoke directly to him. None of the gods of my people have ever spoken directly to me. Or to anyone that I know for that matter."

Swech turned away from him, shaking her head. "They do not speak to us every day. They speak when there is something that must be said. There were many who were called to look for the travelers. For you." She was silent for a few moments and he looked around them at the other riders, checking for landmarks or signs of a town anywhere in the distance. "Your gods confuse me."

Merros nodded. "That's alright, they confuse most of us." He stared at her back for a moment, mesmerized by the play of solid muscles under skin that varied between nearly flawless and heavily scarred. "So tell me about your gods, Swech. Tell me what makes you so obedient to them."

Swech nodded her head and looked around. The beast under them let out a grunt and then a noise that could have been a roar waiting to happen or possibly just gas.

"The lands were not always as they are now. You know this." Merros nodded his agreement. "When the land was shattered, when the war of sorcerers took place and the city of Korwa was destroyed, everything along with it was ruined too. The lakes were boiled away, the ocean was pushed aside. The great fields of battle were burned to dust along with armies so vast that they spanned the horizons." Her words were passionate, but bore the metered tone of tales recited again and again. "All destroyed by the men who thought they were gods. All that was left was what you call the Blasted Lands. All that remained was dust and ash and smoke. The ground was so hot that it boiled. That is why there are so many uneven places there. Even a thousand years later, the Ta-Wren, the cutting winds, have not smoothed away the waves of earth."

Merros found himself drawn to the story. Possibly it was her passion for the tale, possibly merely boredom. It could have been a bit of both.

"Do you know that not everyone died?" She spoke with a reverent awe. "A thousand years ago the Ta-Wren were harsh enough to polish stone in a few days, but not everyone who was in the fields of battle died. The ones who lived were broken, though. They broke and they bled and they suffered first in the great heat of Korwa's death and then in the biting cold that came afterward. The Daxar Taalor call that the First Forging. The spirits of the people were hammered and leveled until the impurities could be driven from their flesh and bones and then they were allowed to cool off, the better to prepare them for what happened next."

"What was that?" Damned if he wasn't being drawn along. She shot him a look and he apologized before allowing her to continue.

"There was nothing left but wreckage. Dust, ash, the charred remains of too many people to count, and the glass spires of the Mounds. The people who survived tried to go to the Mounds first, seeking shelter in the hidden tunnels where the earth still moves and the air screams. But there were things in the Mounds that could not be challenged. They killed anything that came too close and so the people were forced to move on.

"After they had walked a great distance and traveled through the clouds for too many days to count, the people began to die off. There was no water. There was no food. And finally seven of the survivors got together and decided to move on while the rest fell to exhaustion. They meant to go on, to find a place of shelter for those too tired to move any further. But because they were warriors and because they were human they did what all people do when they are angry. Those seven argued as they walked. They debated what could be done. Finally they all agreed that it was better to die as warriors than to live as victims. When they could no longer move forward they found whatever weapons they could scrounge – mostly melted remains of weapons or the bones of the dead – and they prepared to attack each other.

"The Daxar Taalor saw as they fought in the Cutting Winds and stopped the air from moving long enough to watch. The seven battled until all were broken and bloodied, but so great was their spirit that they would not die. And the gods looked upon them and asked what it was they wanted.

"Two of the people could still speak and they answered. 'We want to live,' said Wheklam. 'We want to grow strong again,' said Ordna.

"And Durhallem, who was the first of the gods to speak to them, asked what they would do if they were granted their lives and the chance to grow strong.

What they would offer in exchange for the help of the gods.

"And Wheklam and Ordna spoke together: 'All that you would have of us would be yours.'

"The Daxar Taalor granted their favor to the seven. They were so impressed with them that they chose to take the names of the warriors as their own. They offered their help. They created the valley by forming the Taalor, what you call the Seven Forges. The Hearts of the Gods were bared to the world, and the shelter they offered was mighty enough to stop even the great waves of fire and ash, the Cutting Winds and the things that came from the Mounds.

"The gods reached out with their hands and carried the people from where they had fallen, laying them within the valley. They gave the people water and clean air. They offered food and protection and most importantly, the offered wisdom and a chance to grow strong again."

"So your gods provided food and shelter?"

Swech nodded. "Yes. For the broken and healing. When they were healed, the remaining people were told to find their own way. This they did but always under the watchful eyes of the Daxar Taalor."

"And then they stopped? They just stopped helping?"

She nodded again.

"Why?"

Swech chuckled and shook her head at the same time. Her shoulders lifted and fell in a shrug. "Why did your mother let you go into the army?"

"Because I needed to grow up and be out from under her feet, I suppose."

"And did she stop being your mother when you left? Or did she still offer advice? How about your father? Did he ignore you?"

"No." He sighed. "I see your point, I suppose."

"The gods are not there to make our lives easy. They are there to aid us when they must and to guide us through the worst of times." She patted the hilt of the weapon at her side. "The Daxar Taalor tell us to make our own way. They also show us how to make our way. When we were at our weakest, they gave us comfort and shelter and food. Now we are stronger because of what they have taught us."

Considering that he'd supped on the flesh of the monster she and her sister had slaughtered without ever breaking a sweat, he had a hard time arguing with her words.

"So what will you do when you meet the Guntha?"

Swech remained silent for a while and he found himself watching the gentle sway of her hips, the play of muscles. When finally she spoke he had to force himself to listen. "We will do as the gods suggest. We will make ourselves known."

"Yes, but how?" Swech did not answer. It wasn't long before he forgot the question and once again let himself contemplate the shape of the woman in front of him.

Pathra Krous looked at the man who had been his advisor since he was born. "And where is this coming from?"

Desh looked back and shrugged. How it was that the man could manage a boyish *aw, shucks* expression with such ease would likely always remain a mystery. "I'm just the messenger. The kid says he needs to confront the men who broke his hands, and I can't blame him."

"I can. What if the damned fool gets himself killed? How will that look?"

Desh leaned halfway across the table and carved a slice from the breast of the bird in front of them. The meat was roasted to perfection and despite the conversation the Emperor reached for the meat when it was offered. A chunk of bread torn from the loaf worked perfectly to hold the hot roast, and a moment later he was chewing contentedly while Desh contemplated his next words.

"The thing is, I'm almost certain that Drask put him up to this." Desh looked at the various dipping sauces and finally settled on a spicy brown concoction. He dipped bread and meat alike and then chewed.

"Almost certain?" Pathra rolled the food around with his tongue, trying to speak and simultaneously avoid burning the inside of his mouth.

"It might have come up in conversation before Drask actually arrived here."

"Why am I only hearing about this now?"

"So as to avoid you being part of any possible incidents that arise from this."

"I rather like being informed of potential disasters before the fact, not after, Desh."

"Granted. But in this case it was a rush decision. I really had no time to consult with you."

Lies. All lies. He had no doubt the damned sorcerer was playing him like a harp. "Fine. I'll accept that. But no more of this, Desh. I have a great fondness for you. I would rather not lock you in a tomb."

"That trick didn't work the last time. It won't work the next."

"I'll make it a better tomb than the last Emperor who tried."

Threats never worked against Desh Krohan. Very few of the royal family wanted to imagine a life without him there to lean on. He'd been a part of the Empire's council for almost as long as there had been an Empire.

The sorcerer sighed. "Either way the facts remain the same. Andover Lashk wishes to conclude his business with the guards who wrecked his hands in combat."

"Well, I don't want him to."

"According to the laws which have not been changed despite numerous suggestions to the contrary, the right to trial by blood is still on the books. Also, as you have already pointed out, you want the boy on your side in this argument because fate has chosen him to be your ambassador."

"Fate had nothing to do with that. I seem to recall your hand being involved."

Desh waved the comment away. "I'm sure I had perfectly valid reasons."

"Oh, don't you always."

"I'm an advisor. No one said you had to take my advice."

Pathra shook his head. "What are we going to do here, Desh? Do I allow the boy to get himself killed in an effort to seek justice?"

"Well, you could hang the damned fools for misuse of authority."

"I'd have to kill over half the Guard," he snorted the words.

"We've had this discussion before, too, Pathra. They need to be put right."

"So fine then. Let this serve as an example to anyone who wants to misuse their position."

Desh cut another slice from the bird for himself and one for the Emperor. "I wonder how long it will take to teach the boy to use a sword."

"Don't you have a spell for that?"

"Probably. Doubt I'll use it though. That would be cheating."

"I thought you said it would be justice."

"No. I said the justice he seeks is still allowed by your rules. I also said you should have changed the laws a long time ago."

"I could order you to fix the fight."

Desh looked at him as he slopped more of the spicy sauce across his food. "That would end poorly."

"Why?"

"Because that sort of sorcery demands a price."

"And who pays the price?"

Desh offered a thin and genuinely unpleasant smile. "That's where it gets complicated."

"Then let them fight. Arrange it for the dawn if that's what he wants."

"Maybe if he doesn't choose a sword?" Desh was staring at his hair again. He could tell that the wizard was going to make a comment. It was something he had to deal with, he supposed, especially if he was going to continue seeing the same girl to do his hair.

"They always choose a sword. It's tradition."

"My good Emperor, have you seen anything at all about Andover Lashk that struck you as traditional?"

Pathra reached for a green fruit the delightful Princess Lanaie had brought with her from her father's kingdom. "There is that, I suppose."

NINE

They didn't look the same as when they were ruining his hands. The clothes they wore were simple cloth pants and jerkins, and none too clean. Menock had a look on his face, a pinched expression that made him appear both older and more like a rodent. And Purb, who was always somehow larger than life when he was strutting around in his Guardsman attire, seemed substantially smaller.

Or maybe it was just the rage.

The gathering took place at the Emperor's Palace. The arena was small, only twenty feet across, which barely even seemed like enough room to pace, but there would only be three of them inside the area when the time came, and that would be enough, he supposed. A deepset pit, the arena was surrounded by perhaps a hundred seats though Andover doubted most of them would be filled. The entire affair was in an area that had been hastily cleaned and prepared. Andover knew that only because he had heard the activities during the night and Tega told him about it as she paced around, working her lower lip with her teeth.

"You can't do this, Andover."

He looked at her and shook his head. "I have to. If I don't…" He looked down at his hands. Tega looked too, with that same morbid fascination. She kept touching his hands, always asking permission first, as if he could possibly deny her, but when she touched them it was with a clinical detachment. Her eyes examined the metal of his new replacements, moved along the odd patterns that had been built into them, but never seemed to want more than to examine them as instruments. She asked questions, of course, and was always surprised when he explained that he could feel everything he touched.

But she did not like touching them. She didn't understand how much it meant to have hands again, even if they were different.

Even if they made him a freak.

Andover was wearing gloves. He intended to wear them a lot.

Twenty feet away Drask stood looking at his opponents. There was also a very large assortment of weapons laid out next to the man, which he was completely ignoring. Andover would have preferred that the man instead point to the best of the tools available to him.

Tega shook her head. "I don't know if I can watch this." Her voice shook.

He looked toward her, once again a frown forming on his face. "Tega? If I don't at least try, I could lose my hands. Do you understand that?"

She nodded her head. "I just don't like this, Andover. I don't want to see…"

She didn't say "you get hurt" but he understood what the silence meant.

And her doubt in him only increased the anger he felt. "There's a difference this time, Tega."

"What difference?" Her eyes searched his. How was it possible that every time he looked into her eyes seemed like the first time? How could she mean so much when they barely knew each other? No. No time for that. He had to focus. He couldn't take solace in her or in anything. Not now.

"I'm not being held down."

"Not yet. But you said you wanted to fight them together."

Well, alright, that had been a horrid notion.

"I know." It was his voice that shook this time.

Drask waved him over. He cast one last look at the girl who always made him feel like he could do almost anything, and then he walked over.

Drask's eyes looked him over from top to bottom and the man nodded. "You seem fit."

"I feel like pissing myself."

Drask chuckled. "That's natural. You're about to fight to the death with two men."

"That would seem to be the problem, yes."

Drask grabbed his shoulder. "Why are you here?"

"To fight those two men." He had no idea what else he should say.

"No. You are here to kill them. Why do you want to kill them?"

"Because they…" Andover looked at the two again, looked hard. He remembered the pain when Purb half-ruined his testicles. The screaming, hellish agonies that Menock brought about when he brought down the hammer on his hands. In that moment the rage grew hotter again and his hands, his new hands, the ones that Drask and his god had given him, clenched into fists. "Because they tried to kill me."

"Pick your weapon."

"I thought you were going to choose?"

The man stared into his eyes, and that odd light burned as he stared. "It is not my fight, Andover Lashk. It is yours. What feels right to me is not what will feel right to you."

Andover looked carefully. There was a good assortment of decent tools, three different swords, and a dozen knives. He cast his eyes toward the other two men who were looking at a similar array.

"None of this."

Drask looked at him and crossed his beefy arms. "You would use your hands alone?"

Andover shook his head. "No. I know what I want."

"It is almost time. If there is a different weapon you should get it now."

Andover nodded his head. A moment later he was jogging away as Drask walked over to the officials discussing the situation. A couple of them were staring after Andover's retreating form.

"Does he forfeit his challenge?" The man who spoke was the Arbiter, the judge of the combat. His sole purpose as far as Drask could understand it, was to declare a winner when the combat was finished.

"No." Drask looked the man up and down. He was soft and heavyset, with clean and perfumed skin. He doubted the man had been in combat in many a year. "He said he had a different weapon in mind."

The Arbiter shook his head, a petulant scowl on his flabby face. "There are no ranged weapons permitted.

He can't go off and get himself a crossbow and expect a proper judgment."

Drask felt a smile pull at his face. "I don't think that's what he intends."

Desh Krohan was there again, wearing his impossible robes and staring from the shadows that hid his face away. "Let's just see what the boy is up to shall we?"

Drask nodded his agreement, and the Arbiter apparently decided that debating with sorcerers was a bad idea and reluctantly agreed.

Ten minutes passed before Andover reappeared. When Drask saw what he was carrying he allowed himself a small laugh and nodded his agreement.

Andover looked at the courtyard and the deep retaining wall designed to keep anyone from escaping judgment.

The Arbiter looked toward him and stared at the farrier's hammer he carried. "That is the weapon you prefer?"

Andover's fingers held the sturdy handle with the ease of long familiarity. He looked at the two men across the small area where each was holding a sword and nodded. "Oh, yes."

"I suppose it's acceptable," he said finally, sniffing the air as if something foul had just occurred. Andover resisted the urge to hit him with the hammer.

The Emperor came into the room and everyone stood at attention, facing him. He waved away the start of a formal bow and settled himself near the pit. Without another word Desh went to sit next to him. Drask walked over and looked at the scarred, heavily used head of the hammer. One side was broader and square, the other side tapered down to a heavy chiseled point that was deeply scarred and scratched. "This is a weapon you know?"

"I've used it many times."

"Have you ever used it to fight?"

"No." Andover's eyes looked to the men across the pit from him. Both of them seemed a little more confident now that he was holding the hammer instead of a sword or axe. "But it's tasted blood before."

Drask patted his shoulder. "That seems a proper justice."

The Arbiter cleared his throat and spoke loudly. "Purb Larfsen and Menock Westerly, you stand accused of betraying your position and attacking Andover Lashk unjustly, causing the ruination of his hands and great suffering." Both of the accused stood and faced the man. "By the traditions established in the time of Emperor Aurent Krous, Andover Lashk has chosen trial by combat to decide your fate. Do you accept this judgment as fair and final?"

Menock nodded and coughed into his hand. "Aye, ho."

Purb sneered in Andover's direction. "Aye. Ho!"

The Arbiter looked to Andover. "Do you accept the fate of these men as fair and final judgment in your case against them?"

"Aye." He looked from one to the other and then finally at the Arbiter. "Ho."

Drask leaned in close and whispered in his ear. "Take the big one first."

The Arbiter ignored the breach of protocol. "Then let the combat begin and may the gods be just."

Two guardsmen stood at each entrance to the pit. Menock and Purb entered on one side of the small battlefield and Andover entered across from them. The sand was soft under their feet and yielded with each step taken. Andover would have preferred a solid footing. Whatever they were thinking as they stepped down those stairs, all three men seemed solemn enough.

Both of the accused held their swords at the ready, taking proper stances. Drask eyed them carefully, studied their positions, the way they held their weapons. Andover did the same as he held the hammer in his hand then carefully stepped to the left.

Purb did not wait to be approached. He charged toward Andover with a roar coming from his throat. The guard was a large man, heavily muscled and capable. He hefted the sword and prepared to cleave Andover in half.

Andover let out a much smaller sound as he scrambled to the left a second time.

Purb took a chance and swung the sword in a wide arc aimed at Andover's chest. Andover dropped to his knee, ducking under the hard swing, and as Purb was drawing the sword back a second time, he brought the heavy hammer down across the man's leg. Hard metal met meat and bone with a mild slapping noise. The sound that came from Purb's mouth was much, much louder as his kneecap exploded and slid sideways under the flesh.

Purb staggered and dropped his sword, gasping at the pain. Before he could attempt to right himself, Andover brought the weapon backward in a hard arc, growling and nearly spitting. The tapered side of the hammer's head caught his enemy across his face and tore skin before shattering teeth and the bone of his lower jaw.

Andover stood back up, shaking the hair that had fallen into his face away from his eyes. He hefted the hammer with practiced ease and then yelped as Menock came for him, moving with far greater stealth than Purb had managed.

Menock swung a blade with even better skill than he did a hammer. Andover dodged as best he could and hissed as the sword's tip slashed across his ribs. Had Menock scored a better swing that would have been the end of the fight. Instead the apprentice blacksmith bared his teeth in pain and stepped back as his side started bleeding.

All around him the people he'd come to know stared intently, many with worried expressions. Not Drask. Drask simply watched the action, his eyes moving from one opponent to the other, seldom staying on Andover.

Purb was down on the ground trying to recover, trying to stand up again, his ruined leg buckled under him and his face a bloodied ruin. He reached for his sword again, not finished with yet. How could he be? The fight was to the death.

Menock was eyeing Andover cautiously and weaving the tip of his sword a little to the left, a little to the right. Not quite feinting, but not standing still either.

Most of Andover was in a panic. He was bleeding! Gods only knew how badly he was cut, and he didn't have the time to examine the wound, despite the warmth he felt running between his fingers. But part of him was unsettlingly calm. That was the part that held the hammer. His hands worked. His new hands, the ones given to him by a god called Truska-Pren. His hands *worked*. The hands that replaced the flesh and bone that Menock had taken from him because he dared look at a girl. That small part, the voice in his head that kept speaking of the insane actions of the man facing him across a sword's distance, did not speak softly. It bellowed inside his skull, outraged that the bastard was alive and infuriated that he had drawn blood.

His side hurt? In comparison to the agonies he'd suffered since his hands were ruined the scratch was nothing. He remembered that pain and the cut faded away to a minor inconvenience.

His hand on the hammer shifted and he hefted the comfortable, familiar weight. His hair fell in front of his eyes and this time Andover let it, looking past it at the face of his enemy.

The man who took from him without reason.

The panic fell away, brushed aside by a strange calm that felt alien to him. He would not die today. He would have his retribution.

Andover stepped forward and grinned.

Menock's face twisted into an ugly expression that was half sneer of contempt and half a wince of panic. The sword drew back a bit and then lashed forward.

Andover's left hand reached out to block the blade. The edge of the weapon carved through his glove and then screamed across the metal palm and fingers of his hand. He clenched a fist around the piece and pushed it aside as he stepped closer to Menock.

Menock's eyes flew wide open in shock. The sword was wrenched sideways, half pulled from his grasp as he struggled to right his grip. Andover stepped closer still and brought the hammer up between his straining arms and drove the head into the guardsman's stomach with all the force he could muster.

The hammer struck him in his sternum. Metal met cartilage and muscle with bruising force and Menock grunted. He did not let go of the sword, but Andover pushed in closer still and wrenched the blade free of his hands.

Menock looked at his weapon as it fell and lunged, determined to take back his prize.

Andover brought his knee into the man's exposed side and sent him sprawling. While Menock tried to collect himself, Andover stepped in again and this time brought the hammer's broad side down on his enemy's left shoulder. The bones of the joint separated and Menock fell on his face, grunting, gasping, overwhelmed by the pain. He retched, his stomach revolting against the unexpected damage to his body.

Andover did not stop. The fury grew larger inside him, exploded into a full rage, and he swept the hammer down on Menock's arm, breaking the bone between elbow and shoulder. Without pausing, he lifted the hammer and dropped it again, this time smashing in his enemy's ribs.

Menock screamed, but could do little else.

Andover paused and looked down at his foe.

And while he was staring at Menock, Purb stabbed him in the side of his thigh. He might have been aiming higher, but it was the best he could manage. The pain was immediate, and Andover gasped as the blade cut deeply.

He hopped backward, felt the blade pull free of his muscles, and a second after that felt warm heat running down to his calf.

Purb scrambled toward him, crawling forward with one hand and one leg, holding his sword carefully, and looking up at Andover. His face was a swollen, broken mess and his leg apparently wasn't working. Andover considered that fact carefully as he looked at the man.

And then he limped as quickly as he could to take advantage of the situation. Purb was a big man, physically much stronger than he was, but the guardsman was also wounded. Andover's leg threatened betrayal but held its own as he moved around the man. Purb tried to move as quickly and failed. He was still trying to adjust himself to a new position when Andover stomped down on his bad leg and then dropped forward.

The guardsman screeched and tried to swing his sword from an impossible angle. Andover landed on his back and brought the hammer down again, again and then a third time on his enemy's skull. After that Purb no longer tried fighting him.

Andover stood back up and looked down at his opponents where they lay broken on the ground. His body shook with adrenaline and exhaustion, his leg throbbed and he shifted most of his weight to the uninjured partner.

The Arbiter cleared his throat and Andover looked toward the man who was considerably paler than he had been before.

"This battle is not yet finished, Andover Lashk. You have won the justice you sought but you must decide if the accused have been punished enough."

They were alive, the both of them. Broken, yes, crippled, to be sure, but alive. Would they ever recover completely? Doubtful. Would they ever serve as guardsmen again? Not possible. Would they suffer? Oh, yes.

"Let them live." Andover didn't bother looking at either man again. Instead he walked away from the arena and headed back to the smithy. He had a weapon to return to its rightful owner.

He managed five yards from the arena before he collapsed. Tega ran to his side a moment later, followed by Desh Krohan. The visitor did not move. He merely stared at the downed men.

The Emperor sent out twenty men with full regalia to meet the travelers and guide them through the city. Those twenty men rode out in polished armor, carrying the Imperial banner and riding proudly on white chargers. As it wasn't very often people saw that sort of thing going on in the capital city, quite a few people watched the procession and spoke of it.

They came back two days later with a caravan. There were more horses, of course, and a few wagons. But there were also the people who quickly got dubbed the Outsiders by the citizens of Tyrne.

They rode great beasts; monstrous things that were decidedly not horses. Those creatures were covered in armor and saddled as if they were somehow tamed, though a good number of the things turned their heads and let out warning growls to the people who gathered on the streets to watch them pass.

The dust of the Blasted Lands still fell from riders and mounts alike, and the air around them seemed to carry a cloud of its own as they moved past. To the last, none of the Outsiders looked at the people on the streets. They kept their eyes on the riders ahead of them, or occasionally eyed the buildings around them, but the people seemed of no consequence.

And those riders? At first there were some who claimed they had no faces; later it was decided that they hid themselves behind cloth veils and sported helmets that hid still more of their features. And all of them wore armor, carried an array of weapons, and did not seem like the sort who should be approached for any reason.

Though several of the Outsiders rode on their great beasts, still more of them marched, moving with steady precision and once again ignoring anyone nearby, save those foolish enough to try touching them. There was some confusion as to exactly how many of the Outsiders there were. A small but vocal crowd insisted that there were enough to invade. Calmer voices actually took the time to count and revealed that there were exactly forty Outsiders and twenty beasts.

They did not dawdle.

Though a great number of people were curious to see where the strangers might go, what they might look like, and what they might have to say, the guards at the palace had different ideas, and the masses were stopped at the gates.

Once beyond those walls, the procession finally wound to a stop. The escort climbed down from their horses and presented a man named Wollis to the

Captain of the Guard. Wollis in turn nodded his head to the wizard Desh Krohan.

Krohan nodded back and gestured for the three women who had ridden along to join him. When they had done so, he gestured for Wollis to approach him.

"You have done well, Wollis March. I appreciate your services. Can you introduce me to the leader of this band?"

Even as he spoke Drask Silver Hand stepped out into the courtyard and placed his hands on his hips as he looked at the group. Wollis stared at the man for a moment and then nodded to the wizard.

A moment after that an enormous man came toward them both. He was wearing less armor than most, primarily because he had a beast he could leave the armor with. He left behind his great helmet, but wore a veil covered with small metal rings and sported a necklace covered with an intimidating variety of long, pointy teeth.

"Tusk, this is Desh Krohan, the man who hired us to examine the Seven Forges. Desh, this is Tusk, the leader of this particular expedition."

Tusk nodded his head and very carefully followed the bowing method that he'd learned from Wollis. Step back on one foot, bow at the waist, spread the arms to the sides.

The wizard returned the gesture.

"I know that you and your people must be tired. You've ridden a great distance. We've prepared rooms for you and an area for your mounts. Can you possibly tell me what they like to eat?"

Tusk looked around, the veil over his face tinkling softly. "Mostly meat, but if they are hungry enough they've been known to eat almost anything."

The wizard was hidden away within his robes, but he nodded his head. "So best to feed them well before they get any ideas. Duly noted."

Tusk contemplated the words for a moment and then laughed, nodding. His hand reached out and swatted at the man's shoulder good-naturedly. The sorcerer staggered a bit but did not fall. A moment later he was leading all of them into a courtyard and a wing of the palace that had been set aside for the use of the visitors.

Wollis shook his head and grinned. He was exhausted, no way around that, but he was also excited. They had traveled a great distance to reach this point. He was ready to celebrate.

That was to happen later, as he soon found out. First there was rest and a chance to clean up. The meeting with the Emperor was delayed by several hours. That notion didn't hurt his feelings in the least.

The blonde woman who had been with them from the beginning of the quest was in the chambers they'd arranged for him when he stepped through the threshold.

"Goriah?"

She smiled at him; it was a curious expression, neither promising nor friendly. Polite. That was the word. She did not want to be there. "I know you are tired. There will be time to sleep soon."

"What is it you need from me?" He wasn't much in the mood for her or her riddles. Merros found her enchanting. Merros found most women enchanting, but mostly Wollis just thought she was trouble. She and her sisters, too.

"We're not your enemies." Her voice held just the finest hint of reproach.

Wollis shrugged. "Neither are you my friends. You are merely women who serve my employer."

"I'm here to warn you, Wollis. There will be a great number of noblemen at this dinner. It's a formal affair, and very significant. The people you have traveled with will be scrutinized very carefully and the people who will be looking them over so carefully will be looking you over as well. Comport yourself appropriately and your future is made. Act the wrong way with this lot and you might well wind up swinging by the neck, or more likely poisoned when you turn your head."

"Who is supposed to be there?"

"The Emperor, or course, but also his closest advisors and his family. The Emperor is not the problem. His closest advisor is your employer. He is not the problem."

"So you want me to watch my back?"

"Be smart. Observe." Her voice was distant. "Do not offer answers unless you are asked. To do otherwise would be ill advised." Without another word she swept past him and moved into the corridor beyond his room. He let her go.

But he was wise enough to listen.

They came into the city of Larnsport without fanfare. That was the way Merros wanted it. This was really the first chance that the Sa'ba Taalor had to meet up with the people of Fellein and he wanted the situation to be uneventful. We seldom get what we want from the world. They were low on supplies and while the people with him believed in hunting for their food, they were not in an area that made that easy. There were cattle around, to be sure, but they were owned by the people raising them. Since he rather liked the idea of avoiding an incident, they went into Larnsport, and because the notion of a bed appealed to him, they stayed at one of the larger inns. He had the good sense at least to make sure that Saa'thaa and the rest of the mounts were placed in a stable that was cleared of other animals. And because he'd been given money he arranged for a local butcher to deliver a lot of raw meat. A lot. The beasts were sated – or at least he hoped they were.

After that, it should have been easy enough to handle matters. He and Swech and a lean, hard man named Blane went shopping for supplies.

Perhaps he'd grown too accustomed to being with the Sa'ba Taalor. Perhaps he was simply tired, or perhaps it was a combination of the two. Whatever the case, Merros failed to give enough warnings. The people with him stared at everything as much as he had surely stared at the great keep where he met the King in Iron. There was little about Fellein that resembled their valley, their world. While they were purchasing supplies and Merros was haggling with a very determined baker regarding the need for at least two dozen loaves of bread – he had a passionate need for freshly baked bread after the last couple of months – Swech wandered off.

He looked for the woman who had become his new right hand for this trip and, when he couldn't find her, he asked Blane where she had gone.

Blane was looking at an assortment of cheeses as if they were a complete mystery. He turned to Merros and pointed to his right in a vague way. "She went there."

"Where?"

"In that direction."

The baker looked in the same direction with a frown on his face. "Your friend is a woman? That is not the right place for a lady."

Before Merros could ask what the man meant, there was a loud scream. It did not sound like Swech and that was a good thing, but it most decidedly sounded like trouble.

The second scream? That one sounded like Swech. Merros was moving a moment later, and without even thinking about it, he drew his sword. The blade felt comfortable in his hand, as it always did after the years he'd been carrying it. Later, after everything was done, he would remember what Tusk had said when they talked about how the weapons he had forged himself felt like a part of him. For now he concentrated on Swech and protecting her from whatever might try to hurt her. She was a stranger here, and he felt like a fool for letting her wander off.

The pathways between buildings grew narrower in the area off the market square. There were additional vendors to be found, of course, but they were the ones who could not afford shops or who sold merchandise of more dubious natures. Like as not the reason the baker had warned him was because someone was selling women. Or possibly there was a gang who felt they had the right to take what they wanted from women by force. Either way, Merros would make them pay dearly for hurting Swech if they managed.

He came around a sharp corner just in time to watch Swech drive her elbow into a thin man's throat hard enough to crush his trachea into a new shape. The man fell back, clutching at his ruined neck and rapidly reddening in the face. His eyes were wild and rolled desperately. He fell back against the wall and fought for his balance and his breath alike, with no success.

While that man was choking on his own internal injuries, Swech caught another man with a swipe of opened fingers across his face that made him scream in pain. While he was trying to recover from the assault, Swech moved against him a second time, her arm moving fast enough for Merros to just make out the way she caught the stranger's arm with hers and then brought her free arm in to shatter the bone between his elbow and his shoulder.

While the first man was collapsing on the ground and turning redder still, on his way to a dark purple, the second man was shrieking while she bent his arm into a shape it was never meant to take. Bone fragments punched through muscles and the gods granted the man the mercy of unconsciousness.

Three more men were in the area. One of them was dead on the ground, his head canted at an unnatural angle from his neck. The other two were staring at the woman who had just destroyed their friends with wide, terrified eyes.

Merros knew exactly how they felt.

For a second he'd forgotten himself, forgotten the people he was traveling with. In a fit of madness he'd let himself think that Swech was anything like the women he'd been raised with. Had he not seen the weapons she carried? Her proficiency with a bow?

Swech dropped into a crouch and stared in the general direction of the two remaining men. They did not stand still. They ran for dear life. Really the sort of vermin that would team with four others to tackle one woman would hardly be expected to stay around.

Swech looked like she was thinking about chasing after them but changed her mind at the last moment.

Merros looked at her – marveled at her, really.

Swech turned to look in his direction and when she saw who was staring at her, she relaxed. The way her body moved was quickly becoming a second language for him. Merros seldom realized how much he depended on facial expressions until he dealt with the Sa'ba Taalor. With only their eyes to go by, he was beginning to understand how much the way a person stood or even sat could convey a great deal.

"You are angry with me?" Her words were curiously soft.

"What?" He looked at her. "No. Not at all. You were defending yourself, obviously. I'm angry at myself for not warning you."

The man whose throat she had crushed thrashed and shuddered behind her, and a moment later was as still as the death that had come to claim him.

"Do the men in your land always try to mount women they do not know?"

"No." He spat. "No but some of the men think they have that right."

"They are wrong." She shook her head and then moved toward him. She dismissed the dead and dying as if they did not matter. In truth they didn't, not really. There would possibly be trouble if they lingered and less if they moved on, so he moved with her, back toward the bakery.

"What made you come this way?"

Swech looked at the small carts where vendors were suddenly reappearing. They had been gone as soon as the trouble started and now they were back as if they had remembered it was rude to watch a woman get raped. Now that the possibility was gone they were glad to once more hawk their wares.

"That one." She pointed to a flat cart where a withered crone of a woman crouched over a collection of baubles and tokens. There were medallions and rings and an assortment of well-crafted leather works, all meant for decoration rather than any practical use.

Merros smiled. Of course a woman would find the jewelry. He shook that thought away. The woman in question had just killed three men with frightening ease. Best not to underestimate her. "You see something you like?"

"What does it do?" She pointed to a bronze medallion with a feathered serpent adorning it. The craftsmanship was exemplary. Like as not the lady in question had either stolen a few of the pieces or she was dealing with someone from the Guntha. The winged snake was one of their symbols.

"The items she sells? Nothing. They are meant to be pleasant to look at and to wear. That is all."

Swech stared at him for a moment, her eyes wide with wonder. "They mean nothing?"

"Well, I suppose they mean something to someone." He pointed to the medallion she'd been looking at a moment ago. "This is a symbol to the people we're going to observe. Here? In this area? It is just a pretty piece to wear around the neck."

The old woman tending the cart looked from Swech to Merros and back again and then snatched the medallion that had struck Swech's fancy and held it out to her. She chattered in the local tongue – same language but a sharp, fast dialect that even Merros had to listen to carefully – offering the prize up as a reward for having stopped the group of men from hurting anyone else.

Swech stared hard at the woman for a moment while Merros translated and then waved the offer away. "Tell her I did not do this for her, but because they offended me. I would no more take her offering than I would steal from her."

Merros conveyed the message and though she seemed puzzled, the woman nodded her head in understanding.

As they walked the short distance back to the bakery Merros kept his eyes peeled for signs that the two who got away might want to come back with reinforcements, but he saw nothing.

"She merely wanted to say thank you."

"No." Swech shook her head. "She wanted to feel better about not stopping the men or reporting them. I am not here to make her feel less guilt."

Merros chose not to argue the point. Instead he asked, "Where did you learn to fight that way? Without weapons?"

"Wrommish tells us that we must never forget the body and mind are weapons before the tools are weapons."

"Wrommish is one of your gods?"

"Of course." He resisted the urge to roll his eyes.

"But who taught you?"

Swech stopped just before they reached the bakery. "We are taught. From the time we can stand we are taught all the ways of the Daxar Taalor. We are always taught. We are always learning." She patted the blade on her belt, and gestured to the short sword he knew was strapped to her side. "Before we can forge a blade we are taught. When we walk we are taught. When we hunt, when we grow crops. We are always taught."

He nodded and smiled. This was one of the differences he was trying to understand. The Sa'ba Taalor seemed to take for granted that everything they did was about learning the ways of their gods. Everything. From the way they walked to the way they trained their mounts, everything seemed directly connected to their deities. He wasn't sure if he envied them their connection to their gods or pitied them their delusions. Time would tell, he supposed.

The baker called to him. There were negotiations to finish.

Blane nodded. He seemed indifferent to the events that had unfolded. As far as the man was concerned it was simply another day and Swech had never been in danger. Then again, considering what she had done to three men, Blane seemed to have the right mentality.

TEN

Desh Krohan stood next to the Emperor and looked out at the sea of people. There were five great tables, each capable of seating twenty people, and every last one of them was seated to capacity. The only exception was the table where he and Pathra would be sitting soon.

"What have you learned about our guests?" Pathra gazed past the simple spell Desh had placed on the wall. The men could look upon the dining hall and see all that needed to be seen. The people on the other side of the wall could only see the tapestry that covered the stone. The spell was permanent and had been set by Desh before Pathra Krous was born. People without the right jewelry could not use the scrying portal. There were exactly three pieces of jewelry that had been ensorcelled at the same time. Two of them were on Desh's person. The third was the ring that bore the Emperor's seal.

"Which ones? The Sa'ba Taalor? Or your family?"

"My family I know all too well." The Emperor's voice was dry and bitter. "Tell me about the strangers."

"I've only just met them myself. They're not like us, I can certainly tell you that much. They are more direct, for one. From what I've seen so far they tell a soul exactly what they think and what they feel."

"That alone should make this an interesting feast."

"True enough, Pathra." The Emperor's kin were a very large assembly of liars and collaborators. The path to the throne was murky at the present time and everyone knew it. There were no heirs as yet. The Emperor was a widower and his wife had passed while delivering a stillborn child. To date he had not successfully sired an heir and that was a pressing matter. In reality, in comparison to other issues it was hardly urgent, but it was a consideration in almost every discussion. Thus the young princess from Roathes, Lanaie, was meant as a messenger, true enough, but she was also offered as a consideration for a bride. No one was openly saying anything, but everyone knew that was the situation.

There were many women at the Emperor's table. Most of them were guests from the Valley of Seven Forges – Taalor, Desh reminded himself, was the proper name as far as anyone could tell – but there were a few exceptions. Lanaie was sitting to the Emperor's left. To his right his cousin Nachia was already seated and waiting. She had changed since last Desh had seen her. She was always a beautiful girl but now she had grown to full womanhood. Her red-blonde hair was falling in curls around her face; the difference between her and her cousin was that her curls were natural, and her cousin's were the product of rare oils and a hairdresser he desperately wanted to bed. Her eyes were clear and her skin was flawless. Most of the men in the area looked at her with open admiration, but they did so most often when she was not looking at them. Nachia was not a woman known for keeping her tongue.

Desh rather liked the idea of keeping the woman company. Nachia's claim to the throne was the most legitimate. If anything happened to Pathra before he sired an heir she would likely take the throne. She was not overly concerned about it one way or the other, and that made her the exception. As far as Desh Krohan could tell, Nachia genuinely liked her cousin, despite the decades of difference in their ages. She had been raised at the Emperor's side for several years before heading off to her own place on the other side of the great city. Her parents had rudely decided to die at a fairly early age, and left her in Pathra's care.

Certainly she would have Desh's backing if something happened. But that didn't mean there weren't a dozen others who felt they had claim as well. That was the problem with the Krous family: there were a lot of them and it seemed most believed they should be in charge of the Empire. Pathra didn't take the threat seriously enough for Desh's liking. Towdra Krous, a bilious waste of breath as far as Desh was concerned, was even now wandering around and leering at the various members of his family. He didn't much seem to care if they were male or female. He just leered and pretended to know what everyone was talking about.

Aside from Towdra, most everyone else in the family was at least pretending to behave. Pathra had made clear that this was a very serious situation. He had no intention of letting his family cause an incident. Desh looked at them just the same: Nachia, the heir apparent; her brother Brolley; a few withered men who had once been important and now were merely decorations. The men in question dressed in finery and smiled and nodded at all the right times, but they knew the situation well enough. They were there mostly to show their support for the throne.

Further away from the head of the table a very heavy man – portly, but also muscular – sat scowling at his plate. His hair was also dredged in fine oils and formed into tight curls. Desh scowled. He hated the latest fashion. There had been a time when Laister Krous had been considered a possible heir to the throne, and there were still a few who believed he should be on the throne right at the moment, but his backers lacked the power to place him there when Pathra was younger and the Emperor had done an excellent job of making sure that fact didn't change.

There were other members of the family there, but mostly they preened and did their best to look at everyone around them without being seen to show any curiosity.

Desh spoke softly as he looked away from the family members. "You've met Drask. He seems to be a rather tolerant example of his people."

Pathra looked at him. "Seriously?"

"Oh, yes." Desh nodded. "The Sisters assure me that the Sa'ba Taalor are a very direct people and from what they have gleaned, the people as a whole do not appreciate anything but direct answers and brutal honesty."

Pathra stared at the visitors again. Almost half the
seats were occupied by them. There were forty-one
in total in the town and they were all present. All
of them came offering gifts, and all of them came
wearing clothes that seemed positively barren. To
be sure, a few sported jewelry, but most wore only
simple outfits and even the women wore outfits
better suited for farming or riding than for the palace.
In comparison the Krous family was wearing insane
finery at the very height of fashion. The only exception
was Nachia, who wore comfortable clothes that were
well-crafted but bordered on being scandalously out
of fashion. She liked to walk her own path, and as
one of Pathra's favored relatives she could get away
with a great deal.

"Are we sure about this?" The Emperor of the
Fellein Empire gestured down the length of his body,
which was currently sporting a nice pair of leather
breeches and a tunic of blue silk. He did not wear
his crown, nor did he cover himself with robes, as
was the tradition. The wizard sported his robes as
he always did, but they both understood that was
for show.

"We discussed this. You want to make these people
feel welcome, then you should dress as they do. To do
otherwise might well prove insulting to them."

"And you wear your robes because…?"

"Because half of your family remains in the dark
about me and that's for the best. They don't need to
know more about me than they already do."

"And I don't need to wear a veil before these
people? Because I would rather not."

"No. The veil is because their gods have decided we don't need to know their faces for some reason. It's not an insult, it's just the way of their people."

"It still feels like an insult."

"They're a very direct people. If they wanted to insult you, I suspect they would have spit at you or just possibly sent one of those great slavering mounts of theirs to piss on your leg."

Pathra chuckled. "They are outrageously large things, aren't they?"

"Do you know they feed on the Pra-Moresh?"

"That's a terrifying notion by itself."

"Let's go, Pathra. It's time to eat and to meet your new neighbors."

The Emperor shook his head. "Why do I think I'm going to regret this?"

"You say that whenever your cousins are around."

"Yes. And I'm normally right."

"You're the one that decided not to have them all executed on general principles."

"You know, I am never quite certain if you're joking when you say that."

"You know, neither am I."

They entered the room and dealt with formalities for nearly twenty minutes. Pathra nodded and listened to half of his family making speeches and praising him, and while that went on, Desh settled himself at his normal location to the right of the Emperor and flirted shamelessly with Nachia. Shamelessly, but subtly, because there are only so many ways you can misbehave in front of the royal family.

He paid better attention when the visitors came

forward and introduced themselves. The surprise came from the first man he'd met aside from Drask, the fellow who'd been introduced to him as Tusk. The man was dressed in black breeches and a black tunic. He sported no finery. His presence was enough. Everyone looked at the man as he rose from his seat.

The stranger stood, took four paces toward the throne and bowed formally to the Emperor, his pose flawless, the scars on his body made more prominent as a result of his lack of accessories. There was nothing to hide every wound he'd suffered, except of course for the veil that covered his face below the eyes.

"I am Tuskandru, Chosen of the Forge of Durhallem and Obsidian King." Well, that was a surprise. "I come to you with my brethren, the Sa'ba Taalor. We bear gifts from the Seven Kings in your honor and a hope for a long and lasting friendship."

He nodded and the first two of his people came forward bearing a metal box of apparently impressive weight. Neither of the men carrying it was small, but they strained with the burden. Once the box was set down the men raised the lid. Inside the crate was a small fortune in gold, presented as a gift from N'Heelis, Chosen of the Forge of Wrommish and King in Gold.

Next the Emperor was offered a shield made of what seemed to be pure silver. The craftsmanship was as brilliant as the metal itself and sported an image of an oak tree planted on a mountain top. A gift from Ganem, Chosen of the forge of Ydramil and King in Silver.

There were more offerings, different metals and different designs. It was the last offering from Tuskandru that stuck out the most. Four of the Sa'ba Taalor brought forth the offering, the skull of a beast, a truly terrifying thing by any account. The head was as long as a man and nearly as tall. The entire thing had been cleaned and preserved, and was adorned with gold and gems. Every surface had been meticulously carved, and even from a distance Desh could see the loving detail that had gone into the work.

Several of the Emperor's kin looked upon the offering with contempt, but not Pathra. He rose from his seat and walked a slow circuit of the great skull, marveling. Pathra had always loved the idea of traveling, had longed to explore his realm and well beyond it, but had never been given the opportunity.

"What sort of beast is this from, friend Tuskandru?"

Tuskandru – "Tusk" as he corrected – called it a Mound Crawler. "They are glorious enemies. We have only seen two in my lifetime, and they always bring with them great carnage and bloodshed." Tusk walked to the head and rested one scarred hand on the largest of the canines. There were rows of the things. "This Crawler came from the Mounds and found entrance into Taalor through the Gate of Durhallem, my kingdom. Once there it killed my father, my uncle, my mother, my brothers, and seventeen of my people."

Pathra Krous looked at the man with horrified eyes. "I am so very sorry. Your sorrow is mine."

Tusk nodded brusquely. "Their names and their stories adorn the skull of my enemy. This Mound Crawler earned the name Kingmaker and Kinslayer. Its actions brought it to my attention and so I was forced to kill it. That was when I was made king of my people. I offer this to you as a gift. It is my greatest prize and my greatest sorrow. It is the cause of my pain and my ascension. I ask that you do me the honor of caring for it."

Pathra Krous looked at Desh Krohan and remembered their earlier conversation. "It is I who am honored by your request, Chosen of the Forge of Durhallem. It is my hope that we will long remain friends and allies." He offered a formal bow to the king who had come before him and after a moment the king returned the gesture.

And after that there was feasting.

The meal was excellent, some of the finest food that Andover had ever consumed, but he was far more interested in the people he would be joining on their journey back home. All of them had the same odd tint to their skin, though the amount varied. Drask had a strong shade of gray. But Tusk looked to have been rolled in ash in comparison.

Tega sat at the same table during the meal and though she was friendly enough there was a distance between them now. Maybe it was his imagination but it seemed she frowned upon his dubious mercy when it came to his enemies.

That was hardly important. His hands were his now, and Drask assured him that Truska-Pren was satisfied that he had paid the price to keep them.

Blood, yes, but not necessarily lives. He would remember that.

When the meal was done the groups moved around and celebrated, conversing about their different lands and about every subject under the sun. Several of the men in the room stared at the Sa'ba Taalor women with open curiosity. Many of the women did the same regarding their men. Their cultures were different down to the way they dressed and no one missed the fact that every last member of the visiting people was heavily scarred.

The pain in Andover's thigh reminded him that he would soon be sporting a severe scar himself. The wound had been cleaned and tended to by the women who studied under Desh Krohan, and while the wound was severe, it was well on its way to healing. Not because Andover was a special case, but because the circumstances demanded that he be in relatively healthy shape for his coming travels. He had looked at the wound before the meal started and even though not a full day had passed, he could see that the damage was substantially healed.

He shadowed Drask Silver Hand around the event. Drask introduced him to Tusk – The man did not stand on formalities – who heard the story of how he lost his hands and how he fought for the right to keep them and then nodded his satisfaction. Then in the language of their people the king rattled a series of words at Drask and congratulated Andover on his victory. He felt rather like a simpleton being congratulated by a scholar: the man had killed the sort of beast that had a head large enough to sleep in and his praise seemed directed at making Andover feel more comfortable with his own inadequacies. Still, he supposed that was courtly manners. He honestly didn't understand half of what went on around him when it came to the matters of the aristocrats.

And he was supposed to be an ambassador. The very notion made him more nervous than fighting his attackers had.

Drask tapped his arm. "The forge where you got your hammer earlier, it's near here?"

Andover frowned and nodded. "Yes, of course. Burk's smithy is on the premises. Well, just off them, really. He's the smith to the City Guard."

Drask looked past him and nodded. "We should go there."

"Why?"

"You know how to use a blacksmith's hammer, yes?"

"Yes."

"Then you must use it now. It is time to forge your first weapon."

"My what?"

"Tuskandru is a king. He says you will travel with us, but you will do so as an equal, not as a burden. For that you must have a weapon. Now you must forge that weapon."

"Burk will not be pleased."

Drask looked directly at him. "Burk will understand. You must do this thing, Andover Lashk. You must."

Andover looked around the dining hall and nodded his head. There was little he wanted that was in this area anyway, except of course, for Tega. But he wasn't foolish enough to think that anything would happen with her. Dream yes, expect, no.

The Emperor himself had asked that he go with the strangers and they had gifted him with new hands. He would do as Drask asked for now, if only to ensure that all who expected from him were happy with their decisions.

An hour later the forges were burning brightly and Burk was watching him with the shrewd eye of a master smith. He was also watching with several small gold coins in his pocket, which had done wonders for stopping the man from being upset about being disturbed.

At first Andover had no idea what he was going to do, what he was going to make for his weapon of choice, but eventually the answer came to him as he stared at the raw materials around him. What else would he use but what he had used earlier to win his combat?

Of course he would use a hammer. But there would be modifications, oh, yes. There would be changes a-plenty.

Both Drask and Burk watched as he first gathered the materials and then began the work of making his weapon. He looked to Drask and asked three questions. First, "Why do I have to make my own weapon?"

"Because a weapon should be as much a part of you as your arm." The brute pointed. "Or your hands."

"I am to choose the materials that are used in forging my weapon?"

"Yes. Of course." The man's expressive eyes showed little comprehension.

Andover nodded. "If I am to have a connection with the weapon, and the weapon is to be a part of me, then I want the weapon to actually be a part of me. May I have the metal from the blessing box?"

"Of course. It is only metal. Why?"

Andover smiled. "If I am to have a weapon that is as much a part of me as my hands, than let it be the very same metal that forged my hands."

Drask went back to his room and brought the box with him. They waited together while the metal slowly melted into the crucible where the blacksmith did his work.

There were three people present, but to Andover it seemed like a great number more watched him as he worked. His new hands got a great deal of exercise and his arms strained as he worked the metal after casting it. The weapon had a good number of metallic parts and he worked on each one, seldom letting himself think as he brought down the very hammer he'd used earlier to mete out his justice. The metal had tasted the blood of his enemies and that seemed to him a very important thing. Before he was finished the sun was nearly ready to rise and his leg ached from standing on the wounded limb for so long. His shoulders and arms burned with the hard work, and the small stings of a dozen sparks burning his skin remained to annoy aggravated nerve endings.

And he felt content, as if he had finally accomplished something worthwhile.

He had one day to recover and part of that was spent being fitted for his new clothes. A small army of tailors went to work making sure he was prepared for the trip, supervised in part by the Sisters who served with Desh Krohan.

And while he was allegedly recovering from the work of creating his new weapon, Drask examined the device and then began schooling him in the best way to use the bloody thing. The man seemed to understand instinctively how Andover meant to employ it, and he expanded on those ideas.

Despite the discomfort in his arms and the exhaustion he felt, Andover reveled in the new weapon and learning its potential.

It felt as if the weapon had been waiting all along for him to make it and then wield it.

It felt right in his hands, as surely as his hands felt natural and right attached to his wrists.

They traveled for days before they finally reached Roathes and days more before they made their way to the great stone keep of King Marsfel. It seemed at least half the time that the people with him were mesmerized by the ocean. Considering where they'd come from it must have seemed an impossibility. Merros could still remember the first time he'd stared at the vast expanse of choppy waters. He'd been nearly overwhelmed and he'd at least known of the ocean's existence. Swech kept looking it over and shaking her head as if, even after days, she had trouble accepting the reality.

Though Merros hadn't been in the area in a very long time little had changed, really. The people in the area lived a fairly routine life and aside from a few structures like the castle and the town center outside its walls there was little aside from well-designed huts to run across. Very elaborate huts, granted, but built from materials that seldom seemed like they'd hold up in a strong wind, despite the evidence to the contrary.

King Marsfel received them with a dubious expression. Reading the note that was passed over by Merros didn't seem to help much, really. On the other hand, no one threatened to execute them. You take your victories where you can find them.

Within an hour they were settled at an inn not far from the palace. The rooms were small, the air was hot and humid, and it was still a welcome change of pace from sleeping on a bedroll. One wing of the rather large affair was set aside for them. The cost seemed prohibitive at first, but then there was the feeding of the mounts to consider. They did not eat grass or hay, and as they'd learned in the last village, sometimes the damned things went off hunting if they were not fed in advance. On the bright side, the money was provided by the Emperor.

He would let kings and emperors work out the bills.

When they had all settled in Merros called the Sa'ba Taalor to join him and laid out a map of the area that the king had finally provided after a bit of haggling. There were limits and a map of the affected area didn't seem too much to ask.

The map was clear enough. There was a large stretch of ocean; on one side of it there was Fellein, on the other was nothing. Somewhere in the middle of that vast ocean there was a long stretch of islands that had been unified under the Guntha flag. The problem seemed to come from the notion that the islands the Guntha called home were sinking. Seemed they wanted to live on dry land. In the defense of the Guntha, he could understand their dilemma. King Marsfel on the other hand seemed to find the notion of giving up his lands to accommodate their desires reprehensible. His father before him had felt the same way.

So he had to explain the situation to Swech and her friends. And once he started, the group immediately began expressing opinions.

Swech said, "They cannot come and simply take the land?"

Merros countered with, "Well, we're here to assess that situation, to see if the Emperor has enough forces here already to repel the invasion or if he needs to send more troops."

Swech shook her head. "No. We are here to stop them."

"I don't think so. We're here to examine the situation."

Swech shook her head again. "We are here to show your Emperor what ten Sa'ba Taalor can do. That is what Drask Silver Hand said."

He pointed to the map. According to Marsfel, the Guntha had already claimed an area to his south, less than a day's travel away. The land was considered inhospitable and it was hard to actually do anything there but settle a few hundred tents. However, that was where they were amassing a fighting force.

"Why does he not send his soldiers there to stop them?" Swech asked.

"Well, Roathes doesn't really have an army. They have soldiers, yes, but more as a force to guard against possible attacks from the land. They don't really have enough men to have an army and to tend to the villages as well as they should. They have many ships, and they're certainly very good at sailing, but they don't have an army. They depend on Fellein to handle issues where they might need an army." He could see the way they looked at each other. They weren't getting it, so he clarified. "As part of the Empire they've made negotiations in the past to guarantee assistance. They provide ships for transport of goods to different areas, and in turn the Empire is supposed to offer defense in situations like this."

"Then why does your Emperor not offer soldiers?" That was Blane.

"We're here to assess the situation. To see if soldiers are necessary."

"How many of the Guntha have already settled here?" Swech pointed to the area on the map called the Blade of Trellia. The jutting finger of land was a harsh area, covered with rough terrain and a good number of easily defended rock outcroppings. Oddly enough, the Guntha almost always chose that spot. Apparently somewhere back in time it was sacred to their people. He had long since given up trying to understand why as he found it genuinely unattractive and uninhabitable.

"According to King Marsfel, the Guntha have over a thousand people there right now."

"A thousand?" Swech looked at her friends.

"Over a thousand and more showing up daily."

"We should go there. We should investigate."

"Well, yes, that's the idea. We just had to present ourselves to the King first."

Swech nodded her head and slapped him on the shoulder. "Good! Then let's go see these Guntha."

"Well there's more to it than that."

The whole lot of them were already standing up and getting ready to move. Swech looked at him again. "What more is there? They are here." She jabbed a finger at the map. "We are here." Another jab. "We need to be there."

"And that's true, but no one here has ever been to the Guntha homeland and that includes me."

"And?" Blane leaned in closer, his eyes watching every expression, every motion of Merros' face to the point where Merros was nearly made uncomfortable.

"We know that there are people resting on the shoals, here." Jab at map. "We do not know how many for certain, and we do not know if that is all the people they can spare, or if it is an advanced scouting party, or if this is a carefully laid trap to make sure the Guntha have good reason for declaring war. No one has been attacked yet. They have merely posted themselves on an inhospitable piece of land."

"Did the king's people not ask for help?"

"Yes, they did. But they are not the Emperor. He must know what forces are against his people before he decides to commit himself to an act of war." They were a direct people, the Sa'ba Taalor. They didn't really seem capable of understanding duplicity. That was a good thing when it came to relationships, but a bad thing when it came to understanding the fine art of backstabbing, also known as politics. Years in the military had taught Merros that much.

"No one has ever been to the islands of the Guntha?"

"No. Anyone coming close is normally not heard from again. The Guntha are not a gentle people."

The people with him looked at each other and then back to him if trying to assess why, exactly, he was addled. There comes a point where you simply can't make your point any clearer. Tomorrow, they would see.

Merros sighed. "Yes, well a good night's rest would be the right point for starting this."

"Come. We have a long ways to travel."

That effectively ended the debate. The Sa'ba Taalor wanted to head on and he was supposed to be their intermediary. That meant he had to move along as well.

Within the hour they were well away from the castle and the town and moving along the shoreline. They rode through most of the day and stopped only well after the sun had set.

The weather was delightfully warm, even with the sun down and the breeze coming off the ocean. Tents went up quickly, more as defense against the sand and the breeze than because they needed any real shelter. The mounts were sent out to find their own food. Merros hoped they didn't find anything that would cause problems later, like a herd of cattle or possibly a small village. There seemed to be sign of neither around the area; that would have to do.

Ludicrous. He was riding with strangers and heading into a strange situation. He'd have packed his bags and walked away from the situation, but the money was simply too damned good. He was still contemplating the money situation when he drifted off to sleep.

His sleep was interrupted sometime later when Swech entered his tent and climbed on top of him. He looked up at her sleepily and she looked down at him. Her fingers found his mouth and she shushed him before he could protest.

"We come closer to battle, Merros Dulver. Tonight I feel restless." She leaned down closer, her words spoken softly. "Make me tired and satisfied." Her hands, strong and callused but still feminine, ran across his chest and shoulders as she spoke, feeling the texture of him through the shirt he wore. His hands reached out as well and soon they were exploring each other more thoroughly. They did not make love; they rutted, neither pretending that what they did was meant to have a greater meaning.

When he woke in the morning, pleasantly sore, Swech was still beside him, but dressing herself. Some communications do not require words. They dressed in silence and worked together to break down the tent they'd shared. If anyone with them failed to notice what had occurred, it was simply because they were all just as busy breaking camp. If anyone did notice, they chose discretion when it came to making comment.

They rode for a good portion of the next day, moving across the land without fear of being seen by much aside from the occasional fisherman. Neither Swech nor Merros spoke of what had occurred the night before though there were many opportunities to do so. They did not avoid the subject either. It was simply something that did not need discussing, not now at least. Perhaps after they had dealt with what was coming when they made camp.

"What do you intend to do when you see the Guntha?"

"Drask Silver Hand wants us to work on behalf of your Emperor. To handle the matter. We will handle the matter."

Frustrating. The woman was frustrating. "Yes, fine, but how?"

Swech shrugged. "I will know after we have seen these Guntha and assessed what they are capable of."

The conversation continued along those lines until they finally stopped at the Blade of Trellia. The land was mostly dark rock, black sand, and thick patches of grass that often stood as tall as a man. Occasionally, to break the monotony, there were trees laden with a thick gray moss that was almost the same color as Swech's hair. Merros had thought there would be no proper places to hide the great mounts or the group as a whole, but he was wrong. There were enough hills and enough patches of the thick saw grass to allow a substantial gathering to hide. As they were almost a mile distant from the camp of the Guntha it was easy enough to conceal their location.

The great mounts did not roam or wander off as they sometimes did when they were finished for the day. Instead they lay down and slumbered, but Merros could tell they were not asleep so much as they were waiting. Blane and another of the group left the area, heading toward the beachfront where the Guntha were supposed to be camped. They came back when the sun was setting and nodded. "They are there. There are many."

"Are they armed? Do they prepare for battle?" Swech spoke softly, but it was easy to hear her. None of the Sa'ba Taalor spoke out of turn and most barely moved as they listened to the discussion.

For the first time Merros realized on a conscious level what he'd noticed and acknowledged silently before: Swech was the leader of this group. It wasn't unheard of for a woman to be a fighter, not even a solder, but it was rare. Never had he run across a female who was in charge of any sized group of soldiers before.

Still, considering her talents, he could not exactly blame them for choosing her. Her skills as an archer alone would have made her a just choice.

He had been gifted with the ability to understand their language. For that reason he was genuinely surprised when Swech spoke again and not a single word she said made any sense to his ears.

After several minutes of the group conversing they broke apart, each moving back to their mount and quickly undressing, gathering different clothes and then different weapons.

"What's going on, Swech?"

Swech spoke as she stripped out of her clothes and changed into darker fabrics. "We are going to investigate the camp. And then we are going to handle the matter of the Guntha for King Marsfel."

"What do you need me to do?"

Swech shook her head and took off her shirt. He looked away out of old habit, despite their recent intimacy. "You are here to observe for your Emperor. You are not here to be a part of this. We are here to handle the matter as Drask has requested."

"I am to do nothing?"

"You are to wait here." She patted the face of her mount. "And you should avoid getting eaten." The beast made a rude noise. Sometimes he was certain the things understood every word said around them.

"Why are you changing your clothes?"

Swech looked at him as she pulled on a dark gray blouse that fell loosely around her. "We do not need armor for what we are about."

"And what is that?"

"There are times when a warrior needs shields and swords, Merros Dulver, and there are times when silence and a short blade are better suited. Now is a time for silence and fast actions."

"What?" He shook his head. They couldn't actually mean to attack, could they?

"Do not think about this. Simply know that when we return it will be time to leave."

Within moments Swech had gathered a small collection of weapons and was on her way. The others moved with her, slipping into the night and running along the beach where the sounds of the tide quickly washed away any noises they might have made.

Merros waited exactly long enough for them to move out of sight before he followed. He prayed very hard that the great beasts had not been told by their masters to keep him there. Apparently the gods listened, because he was not torn apart for his insolence.

ELEVEN

Swech moved quickly, her feet barely touching the ground before lifting again, her body crouched low and when necessary falling to hands and feet alike to maintain her balance and speed.

Behind her and around her, nine others moved much the same way, all of them following her subtle orders.

There was no speech. None was necessary. The language they used was the one every Sa'ba Taalor learned as soon as they were walking, the language of the body. Wrommish and Paedle moved with them, of course, guiding them in their time of need. The gods always watched. That was what Merros Dulver could not understand.

Swech pushed thoughts of the stranger from her mind. He was a pleasant distraction, but now was not the time to be distracted. Now was the time to move with the speed of the Cutting Winds and to move just as effectively.

They crested the last small hill between the ocean and the shoreline and saw the tents spread across the beach for what seemed an impossible distance.

Apparently a thousand souls required a great deal of cover. The notion would have been amusing if it weren't being used to the advantage of the Sa'ba Taalor. The leather hides and canvas that made the tents offered excellent cover. Swech and her charges took full advantage of that fact and spread out.

Most of the camp was sleeping, but there were exceptions. They would handle the ones who moved around as they came to them.

The wind from the ocean was blowing harshly, whipping the hides and making them thrum with their own music. She liked the noises. They were pleasant to the ears and they also provided cover for the sounds of her feet moving over the ground. The breeze itself provided cover should the Guntha have guard animals that might smell their approach.

She found no guard animals.

She found few guards and those she did locate were easily avoided if that was her choice.

It was not.

The first guard she encountered was staring at the distant waves with a bored expression on his tanned face. He never had a chance to grow excited. One hand covered his mouth. The other jammed the long, thin needle blade of her dagger through the base of his neck and into his skull. He stiffened for only a moment and then fell. She helped him to the ground with the care of a mother tending to a child, and then moved on. He would eventually be discovered, she knew that, but before then they had much work to do.

To her left she saw Jost lock her arms around a guard's throat and drop the man in a quiet slump as her hands cut off the flow of blood to his brain. She had Jost staying close to her because this was the first time that Jost had ever been taken for a group expedition. The young girl was doing brilliantly. One more move and the man's lifeblood was puddling on the ground around him, a crimson shadow to match the shape of his prone form. Jost moved on without seeking approval, a sign that she had earned this privilege.

Beyond Jost she saw another guard fall quickly and knew that Ehnole was moving with her usual efficiency. Ehnole was first and foremost a follower of Paedle. She could have run through a room full of wind chimes and trinkets and no one would have heard her.

Around her the other Sa'ba Taalor moved quickly and efficiently. There would be no room for error. The odds against them were grave.

There would be no mercy for the exact same reason.

Once the guards had been dispatched the group began the serious work. Swech opened the first tent and slipped in as quietly as she could. Four people rested within the cramped space.

She struck four times.

The sleepers did not awaken.

Far away from her yet with her in her soul, the Daxar Taalor watched on. She felt them in her mind, in her heart, and knew that they approved.

Merros followed from a distance and kept it that way. There were ten very dangerous people moving ahead of him and while he had every intention of watching what they did, he had no desire at all to get them annoyed.

The Great Star was rising and that helped a little with following their tracks, but despite the fact that there were ten Sa'ba Taalor, he had trouble finding tracks to follow. Their footprints were deceptively light and as often as not they ran where the waves came to wash away evidence of their passing. He had been worried that they would leave an obvious trail back to the camp, but the worry was wasted.

He kept himself from running into them by being as careful as he ever had been. In time he followed their ghostly trail to the last of the small hills above the vast camp of the Guntha, and there he waited.

The Guntha were an interesting people. They seemed perfectly content to live on their islands, but for the fact that those islands were sinking. That did not mean that they were easy targets, as he'd learned when the Empire had demanded they be driven back previously. They were hard, violent fighters and they were not to be taken lightly.

That said, the camp was almost silent now. To be sure there must be lookouts and guards stationed around the area, but he saw none of them and they did not see him. Instead he saw their people gathered around fires or moving to the tents they'd pitched, or in a few cases preparing for whatever their next day was supposed to bring. They had not attacked the Roathians that he'd heard of, but they were in the kingdom and they were not welcome. There was something to be said for their current dilemma. There was also something to be said for his personal theory that they were waiting for the Roathians to make the first move.

But for now, there was this odd silence and the calm of the air, the gentle sighs of the surf and a cool, clear night. Were it not for the sure belief that he would soon be hearing screams he would have possibly gone to sleep.

Merros waited, moving just enough to keep himself alert. Above him the Great Star rose and reached its zenith, then began to slide toward where it would eventually rest for the night.

He stared at the camp without looking at any one thing, the better to see any possible changes. He was rewarded with small motions, subtle hints that something was going on. Far in the distance he saw one of the Guntha moving back away from the fires. He also saw the shadow that rose from the darkness and seemed to swallow him whole. Moments after that the shadow moved again, but the Guntha did not. It could have only been his imagination, but he didn't think so.

He almost missed the guard that came for him. Almost.

The man came up from the surf and moved toward him from behind. He would have never heard a thing, would never have noticed him at all, if the Great Star's light hadn't cast a shadow for warning. The man was crouched low, one hand holding onto a knife designed for cutting and filleting fish. It would do a fine job on a fool's throat and that was exactly what the man must have intended because he was creeping up from behind and almost standing atop Merros before he was noticed.

Merros grabbed a handful of sand and rolled. The man had been very careful and he was probably firmly of the belief that his target was as good as dead. Instead of cutting a throat he got sand in his eyes and his face, enough to blind him and to leave him spluttering. And as he tried to recover, Merros kicked a heel into his knee. There was a cracking noise and then a bark of pain. That could not be avoided. Merros reached for him and felt the man's knife cut across his forearm. The strike was more luck than anything else and the line of blood it drew was annoying but not fatal. He aimed to hit the man in the face and missed, instead punching his knuckles into his attacker's throat. Sometimes the gods are kind to fools. The blow was enough to leave his enemy gagging.

The Guntha fell forward and Merros rolled from under his weight. He had feared a second strike but the man continued to struggle for air.

And while he was struggling, Merros drew the dagger from his boot and carved a hole in the man's neck. There was nothing clean about the kill. The man grunted and fought and Merros held him down, felt him thrash and fight to live. It was one thing to defend himself against a great beast like the Pra-Moresh and another entirely to kill a man. He did not regret his actions. He knew that either he would live or the Guntha would, but he'd been a soldier long enough to understand the consequences of his actions. Somewhere, possibly in the camp below, that man had a family. They would mourn the loss and curse his existence. If they were determined enough, they might even come looking for him. It wouldn't be the first time in his life.

Blood stuck to his hands, coated his arms, soaked his shirt and pants. He dared not move just yet. The Guntha had made a good deal of noise and someone down below or another guard might have heard something. He had no choice but to wait a few moments and listen for sounds that an alarm might have been issued.

Stupid. His actions could well have endangered the Sa'ba Taalor. He was up here on a hill. They were in the campsite doing the gods alone knew what.

But he had suspicions, didn't he? Shadows moved and people vanished down below. Yes, he had suspicions.

After almost three minutes had passed, after the blood on his body began to cool, Merros finally allowed himself to rise from the sand and look at the camp again. Nothing seemed to have changed. The man under him had dark skin and hair that the sun had bleached nearly white. Several tattoos covered his arms, his chest. He was a fisherman according to the marks on his body. And a warrior. Though Merros didn't understand all of the markings, he knew enough to know that the man left behind a wife and two children. Their names were marked on his chest.

He dragged the Guntha away from the camp. The sand was loose enough. Though it took a few minutes he managed to hide the body in a new sand dune.

By the time he was done burying the body, the screams started to come from the encampment.

At first he thought he'd been discovered, but then the fires bloomed below. He dared a look and saw that the tents on the far side of the camp were burning, the canvas flaring in great sheets of flame that let him clearly see the dead bodies lying around them. The boats of the Guntha burned as well, not one or two, but seemingly all of them. Impossible that any of what he was seeing was an accident.

The tents that were closer to him bled shadows as people moved to investigate the screams, the blazes. Some of them moved toward the fires. Others fell to the ground without warning and occasionally twitched a time or two before growing still.

He didn't mean to stare. He meant to move, but the sight froze him. He watched as the Guntha died, some dropping without apparent reason, others swallowed briefly by shadows or merely touched by them before they grew still. Some had time to draw weapons before they were felled, but fall they did.

Not enough of them. There were a great many tents, but not many of them showed life or movement. He shook his head and worried. The Sa'ba Taalor were fighting down below and they were apparently doing very well, but there were too many tents and sooner or later the people in those tents would come out, and when they did the ten who were with him on this journey would die. There was no other way around it.

Even as he contemplated that, however, another dozen tents caught aflame. The blaze ran like water from one to the next and they burned furiously, fairly exploding into brilliance.

From some of those tents he finally heard screams, and saw movement. Oh, how they moved as they burned.

Merros wanted nothing more than to look away, but he did not dare. The gods sometimes demand witnesses, and he had been ordered here for the purpose of witnessing exactly this, hadn't he? He had been bought and paid for that he might witness exactly this.

And so he watched as the Guntha died, and as he watched he remembered Swech's words from the day before. *We are here to show your Emperor what ten Sa'ba Taalor can do. That is what Drask Silver Hand said.*

Eventually Merros rose and walked to the water's edge. Once there he washed the blood of the dead man from his clothes and from his skin, and then he headed back for the camp where he was supposed to be waiting for the Sa'ba Taalor. He made no attempt to hide his tracks. He doubted there would be anyone left to follow him, at least not any of the Guntha.

The great beasts watched him as he entered the camp and not one of them made a noise of warning or a threatening move.

It would be untrue to say he slept when he got to the camp. But he closed his eyes and managed something like rest. When he opened his eyes again, Swech was moving into his tent. She was freshly scrubbed, well cleaned and dressed in different clothes. She looked at him without speaking for several seconds. He looked back, uncertain what he should say, what he should do.

"You watched us." It wasn't an accusation, but a statement of fact. He nodded his agreement.

"You understand now? We did what we were sent to do."

He looked at her more closely and saw the bandages on her left arm and on both legs, as well as across her neck. She had received several injuries to his one scratch. Then again, he had only killed one man. Who knew exactly how many she was responsible for?

"Will they go back to their people and say they were attacked?"

"There are none to go anywhere."

"What do you mean?"

"There are no survivors." Her words were calm. Merros felt a deep chill creep through him.

"All of them?"

She reached out and touched the wound on his arm. "You should tend to that. There is always a risk of infection."

"You killed all of them?" He had to ask a second time, had to make sure that he had heard what he thought he'd heard. Madness, it had to be.

"They cannot go home and claim they were attacked by King Marsfel and his people. They cannot go home and report anything to anyone." Her logic was flawless, of course.

Oh, and terrifying. Absolutely terrifying.

Desh Krohan ate breakfast surrounded by four beautiful women. Three of them worked with him. The last was his apprentice. They ate together because they could and because it was likely to be the last time they were together for some time to come.

Tega picked nervously at the fare, though all of the foods presented were excellent.

"You should eat, Tega."

"I know." She nodded and looked at the table, not meeting his eyes.

"What's wrong?" He reached out and caught her chin with his fingers, making her look up at him. One thing he did not tolerate from his apprentice was a sudden need to be shy. Shyness and sorcery of any sort did not mix well. That was a lesson he had learned the hard way and one he insisted that his students learn.

"I'm not ready for this."

"Of course you are," he countered. "If I had any doubts I wouldn't be sending you."

"My parents–"

"Will miss you horribly while you are gone, but you are an adult, and you chose to be my apprentice, and that means you have offered yourself to my guidance, yes?"

"Yes, Desh."

"Then look forward to this. It's an amazing adventure you're going on. You're one of the first people to ever see the land where the Seven Forges join together. How could that not be an amazing thing?"

She fidgeted and pulled her face from his hand.

"Ah. It's the boy, isn't it?" It was hardly a difficult guess to make. That was one of the reasons he'd decided to send her along to the Taalor Valley. The boy. Andover Lashk was an interesting lad, with an unusual situation. "You know that I need someone to watch over him, Tega. You also know that you're about the perfect choice for that task."

"I feel like I'm spying on him."

"That's because you *are* spying on him, my dear. Among other things, granted, but that's one of your tasks." There were other things, of course. She was there to be his eyes and ears when he couldn't be there and if the Sooth weren't lying, he'd be a very busy man in the near future, far too busy to go running off through frozen wastelands for the next few months, much as he might like the notion.

"But the Sisters–"

"Will also be far too busy. Also, they've just come back from spending over two months traveling. They deserve the chance to rest as well, yes?"

Oh, how she wanted to argue the point, but really, what could she say?

"I'm scared." She looked at him with wide eyes, and trembling lips and Desh had no doubt that Andover Lashk would have killed for her in that moment.

He shook his head. "I've seen you handle worse situations and you know that if you have to, you can summon me." He did not need to add that doing so would be meant strictly as a last possible option scenario. She knew that. They all knew that. Those that didn't understand how much he preferred his privacy learned very quickly.

She wanted to say more, but one look at his face and the young girl knew better.

"You have time before you leave, Tega. Go, see your family again and prepare yourself." His voice was not unkind as he sent her on her way. There would be no ignoring his orders, not if she truly wished to learn from him. He had taught her some things already, but she knew there was much, much more that he could teach her, would teach her if she obeyed.

She nodded her head and managed a smile before leaving them. The Sisters watched her go, but said not a word. Desh stood from the breakfast table and stretched.

"I suppose I should go have a chat with the Emperor." He smiled as he looked at the Sisters.

"How long will you be, Desh?" Tataya pouted playfully. "We're already getting bored."

"I doubt that. You have new toys to play with." He chuckled as he spoke.

Goriah shook her head and reached for one of the soft cheeses and the knife Desh had left impaling it. "Hurry. We don't get to see you enough these days."

"As much as I can, sweet."

"Bring us back presents." Pella's voice was teasing. There were many, many rumors about Desh Krohan and the Sisters. None of them much cared what the rumors were, but from time to time they found them as amusing as they were inaccurate. Their relationship was… complex.

He waved and snickered as he pulled on his robe and headed for the door. There were too many strangers around, and too many familiar faces, in addition.

He walked quickly through the corridors and kept his silence. Really, a loud and boisterous magician held remarkably little air of mystery about him. Though a good deal of the staff and the servants knew that he could be bit sarcastic, and yes, even loud from time to time, they also knew better than to wag their tongues.

Pathra Krous was in his offices, behind the main

area where he received guests and handled business. This was not one of his days scheduled for handling affairs of state, which meant that he was entertaining himself with paperwork and looking over the maps that had been delivered by the expedition.

That was good. The maps were exactly what Desh wanted to talk to him about. He came into the room without announcing himself and Pathra gave a half smile as he leaned back in his chair. "I was wondering how long I'd have to look these over before you came along."

"I was nice. I let you play with them for a whole day." He dropped his ceremonial robe across the back of the wooden chair where he settled and leaned over to look at the map facing the Emperor. The writing and images were upside down, but that was hardly an issue. He had been reading upside down since he could remember.

He touched the map at the entrance of the mountain range, at the base of what the Sa'ba Taalor called Durhallem. His mind tried correcting his casual nature and reminded him that the proper title was the Heart of Durhallem, but he waved the thought away like so much white noise. Really, he tended to fend off a lot of his own thoughts these days and found himself wondering if that was a sign of senility, or merely too damned many years walking the planet. Either way, he waved that thought aside as well.

Back to the maps.

"If these measurements are correct, we have grossly underestimated the size of the Forges. We have also never begun to consider that there might be a fertile valley here, or that it would be large enough to accommodate seven separate kingdoms."

Pathra snorted. "They could be very small kingdoms, couldn't they?"

"They could indeed, but from what we've seen, they have wealth and they have soldiers."

"We've seen a few burly folks in armor. That hardly makes for an army."

"By all the gods, Pathra, you've been hanging around me far too much. You're getting positively snide."

"I'm trying to be a realist. You said there might be people and we've seen that there are. You said they could be dangerous. That's likely a given. They came offering gifts, and that's a positive sign, yes?"

"Hopefully. Again, we don't know much about them. By the way, what have you prepared as gifts for their return?"

The Emperor frowned. "I have no idea what to offer them? I mean, I hardly have any great trophies that I've earned in combat…"

"May I suggest an offering of emeralds from the mines of Canhoon? Perhaps a dozen of the Alacar eggs?"

"A dozen?" The man's voice cracked as if he were an adolescent.

"Then make it seven, one for each of their kings." Desh waved away the regret in the Emperor's tone. Yes, the eggs were a rarity, but they were hardly impossible to get. "Honestly, Pathra, what the hell are you going to do with all of the eggs you're already stocking up in your larders?"

"But they're…" The Emperor sighed. "Fine."

"Don't be that way. Each of the seven kings offered you a treasure. You have to do the same in return."

"A fruit basket isn't enough?"

"They're kings, not your relatives. You have to treat them with the proper respect. Maybe if you're lucky they'll let you have one of those great, hairy brutes they ride around on."

"Gods! Wouldn't that be lovely?" His eyes grew wide at the prospect.

"And if you establish a proper relationship it's always possible that you could wind up visiting their kingdoms. So make sure you get a good friendship working here."

That was really all it took. Pathra's fascination with the Blasted Lands made him putty when it came to working out a proper accord with the inhabitants. Even if he wasn't much of a statesman when he was in a mood, he was almost guaranteed not to get too moody if he was thinking about the unknown wonders from another land.

Desh looked at the maps again. Really, the area was much larger than he would have expected possible. At least assuming that the map was an accurate representation. There was little doubt in his mind. The craftsmanship and the attention to detail made him think that the map had been around for a while. There was no reason to assume that the people living in that valley would have time to draw a fake map, or for that matter good cause.

He studied the lay out, his fingers running over the multiple rivers that seemed most likely run off from the mountains themselves, and then working toward not one but five separate lakes within the massive valley.

"There's nothing they couldn't do here, Pathra. Do you see that?"

"What do you mean?" The Emperor leaned in closer, the oils in his recently restyled hair threatening to rain down on the map. Happily they didn't quite saturate his tresses to that level.

"I mean they have forests, they have farmlands, they have clean water, and apparently they have food aplenty. There is no need for them to ever leave their valley. It's small wonder we never knew they were there."

"We've never been able to get to them. How could they get to us?"

"We never knew for certain that they were there, Pathra. There's a difference. They either knew of us or at least suspected we existed, as best I can determine."

The emperor rose from his seat and walked to his window, looking toward the Blasted Lands as if there were any possibility that he could see them from where he was. On particularly clear nights it was possible to see the glow from the Seven Forges on the horizon, but that was a rarity.

"Do you know I never really thought you'd find anything out there, Desh."

"I didn't spend my money on the sure bet that there was nothing, my friend."

"True enough."

Desh returned to the map again, looking even further to the north. The land seemed to continue on well beyond the valley of the Daxar Taalor, but the map itself ended. It was his curse that he was already wondering what was on the other side of that map and how long it would take him to arrange an expedition.

Pathra laughed, "You really need to work on one goal at a time, old man. First we establish a good relationship and then you use the valley as a starting point for the next expedition."

"That obvious?"

"To me? Of course." The Emperor looked at the map, leaning over the surface of the desk to study. "Do you suppose the scale is accurate?"

"I see no reason for it not to be. The details between where we are and where they are seem to follow a consistent scale." Still he frowned as he spoke and looked carefully at the map. Even allowing for the violent storms and horrid environment, it seemed that more of the expeditions he'd sent over the years should have reached their destination.

But, again, sometimes the lands between the Forges and Fellein seemed to change. The distances seemed smaller now than they had. And there was a rather large icon on the map that, according to Wollis March was an affair called the Mounds. The man said the Sa'ba Taalor were forbidden to go there.

He'd have to look into both situations properly instead of merely considering them as possible causes of trouble. Mysterious ruins and shrinking distances were not the sort of notions he found at all comforting.

"What are the plans for today, Pathra?"

"I'm supposed to meet with Tuskandru and his retinue for a meal. I assume you'll be joining me?"

"Of course." He waved the very idea that he would be elsewhere aside. There were some things that were simply too important to overlook. "Have you ever known me to turn down food?"

"Not in my lifetime."

Andover Lashk looked at the brutes around him and swallowed hard. Drask was a giant of a man, no two ways about it. The one next to him Tusk, was even larger. They were the biggest, to be sure, but none of the people facing him were small, and that included the women.

They were standing in the courtyard that had been set aside for the Sa'ba Taalor, and a dozen of the strangers were looking at Andover and his weapon, giving both a long and nearly silent scrutiny. He had not changed. The weapon was what they were examining most closely. The handle was a little over three feet in length, and on one end was a heavy barb for stabbing. On the other was the hammer head he had fashioned. One end was a heavy, blunt head. The other was a blade, more properly fitted to an axe. The challenge had been to make the two sides of the head balance out, as well as making the entire weapon balance out. He'd done it by adding iron rings along the base where the barb rested. When he was completely finished he would be able to balance the weapon in the palm of his hand without having to worry about it tipping one way or the other. The metal bands were also studded, allowing them to cause extra damage should they strike flesh. He'd made the bloody thing and now they were staring at it like it might be a lump of carrion he was holding instead of hours of intense labor and the cause of several small burns on his forearms from working the forge.

Tusk reached forward and plucked the weapon from his hands without asking, without warning and so quickly that Andover could not respond.

Drask looked at him with knitted brows above his veil. His expression said that Andover had just lost respect in the eyes of the newcomers by so easily forfeiting his weapon. There was nothing he could do. The man who had taken the weapon would snap him as easily as a twig.

Tusk whipped the weapon around between his hands, moving in fluid motions that seemed nearly impossible. The hammer head alone weighed enough to make wielding it a challenge to Andover, but to the man holding the weapon it seemed as light as air.

Drask stepped closer. He leaned down just a bit as the monarch from the Taalor Valley continued testing out the hammer's balance and weight.

And then Tuskandru called to two of the surrounding Sa'ba Taalor. They nodded, came forward, and drew their weapons. The one on the left of him, a smaller man – which meant he was only enormous – swung a one-handed axe. The other was sporting a well-used and weathered sword.

"What are you…?"

Tuskandru ignored him and brought the hammer around in a savage arc, swinging at the swordsman's head. The man deflected the blow, grunting with the effort, and immediately countered. Even as Tusk was knocking the attack aside – and continuing to swing the long hammer as if it weighed nothing – the axe-wielder swept his blade toward the monarch's head.

Tuskandru ducked down low and brought the hammer in close to his chest before striking out with the barbed end, knocking the axe away from the wielder's hands with a loud clatter. The axe man immediately stepped back, his arms held wide apart.

Two steps and a spinning motion that Andover could barely follow and the swordsman was on the ground, his weapon a few feet away and Tusk's boot planted on his chest. The hammer came down and stopped inches from where it would surely have splattered the man's skull.

All around them the horde of Sa'ba Taalor roared their approval.

"He seems pleased with the work you put into the weapon." Drask's voice was low, just barely audible. "That is good. Likely he will throw the weapon to you. Do not let it fall to the ground."

Andover began to look toward the foreigner who had become his advisor, but stopped himself when, exactly as Drask had predicted, Tuskandru hurled the weapon in his direction. He did not throw it in an attack, but instead threw it with the head pointed toward the skies.

Andover moved forward and caught the weapon. The weight was almost enough to stagger him, but he braced himself and managed to keep his feet.

And found Tusk staring at him with scrutinizing eyes.

The giant bellowed out five words in the language of his people. His eyes were smiling behind the veil he sported.

Drask put a hand on Andover's shoulder. "He likes your workmanship. He approves. Now he wants you trained with it."

"Trained?"

The man nodded his head and looked around the courtyard. He seemed incapable of not looking around constantly. "Oh yes. You will be learning to fight with the hammer you forged. It is to be a part of you and you have… limitations."

"What limitations?" He wasn't sure, but suspected he should be offended by the comment.

"You do not know how to fight. You do not have years of practice. You must be readied for the journey to Taalor."

"What do you mean 'readied'?" He didn't much like the sound of that, or where any of this seemed to be going. When he heard the term readied, he immediately thought of the rare occasions when his mother would make roasts and spent hours seasoning the meats and preparing them. It was not a comforting notion.

"You are meant to be an ambassador for your people."

"Yeah?"

"That means you will need to know how to fight."

"But, why?"

Drask sighed and pointed toward Tusk. The king was looking from one person to the next, talking softly and moving with the easy confidence that seemed afforded only the finest warriors. "Would you willingly risk a fight with him?"

"By the gods, no. He'd kill me."

"Yes, he would." Drask looked at him closely. "He would kill you with one blow. And that is the problem. Tuskandru, Chosen of the Forge of Durhallem and King in Obsidian does not negotiate with weaklings and those who cannot defend themselves in simple combat." He paused to let that sink in. "Neither do the other six kings. Nor do their emissaries. If you would deal with these people on behalf of your Emperor and your Empire, you must be able to fight and defend yourself."

"Are you saying I'll have to fight the kings?"

Drask laughed and slapped him on the shoulder. "Not at all. They would not fight you. But their appointed representatives almost certainly will."

"But how?" Andover couldn't find the words to finish his question. "I mean, what, exactly is my job going to be?"

"We have never had ambassadors before. Almost certainly you will make arguments on behalf of your Empire."

"Alright…" Andover worked that over in his head. "How does that lead to me fighting anyone?"

"You handled your dispute with the men who attacked you, yes?"

"Yes, of course. You made me do that. You told me I had to do that to keep my hands."

Drask nodded his head. "That is how disputes are settled where we come from."

"All disputes?"

"Yes. Though sometimes the fights are to the death."

Drask called out to three of his people. Two women and one man came forward. All of them looked at him expectantly.

"Delil." He pointed to the first of the women. She was younger, and carried herself with more swagger than half of the City Guard. Next was the male, a brick wall of a man, with scars that looked like one of the great monsters they rode in on had tried to chew him to pieces covering one arm and half of his neck. "Bromt." The last of the three was a woman whose helmet bore great horns that curved down toward her shoulders. "And this is Stastha. They will be your instructors today."

"My instructors?" He hated the way his voice broke when he looked toward Drask.

"Yes. They've been instructed to beat on you until you learn to defend yourself." Drask stepped back and clapped his hands together. Delil came forward, dropping into a crouch as she started circling Andover. She carried no weapons. "Delil will go first."

"Wait!" Andover stepped back, gripping his hammer fiercely and looking at Drask when he wasn't keeping a wary eye on the unarmed woman facing him and moving slowly around him, assessing his movements.

"Yes?" Drask already sounded bored.

"Am I supposed to go up against an unarmed enemy?"

"She is not unarmed. Her body is her weapon."

A moment later the female slid forward and punched Andover in the side of his head. He staggered back and almost lost his grip on the hammer. Before he could recover properly she came at him again and boxed him on the other side of his face. After that, Andover started defending himself very vigorously. Every time he thought he was ready for whatever the

woman might do, she came from another direction.
Within five minutes she had disarmed him and
handed him back his hammer no less than four times.

The girl was kind to him. She didn't hit him very
hard. At least not at first.

By request of the Emperor himself, Wollis March was
in attendance at the dinner with the Sa'ba Taalor.
He sat at the same table as Drask Silver Hand and
a few others, including the boy with the new metal
hands, Andover Lashk. Currently the young man
was looking a bit like he'd been dragged behind
a runaway carriage for a few leagues. His skin was
marked with scratches and bruises, but he was clean.
Wollis stared at the gloves covering his new limbs for
all of a minute and then decided the hands beneath
them didn't much matter. The same could not be said
for the boy, who kept fidgeting and fussing with the
supple leather.

They were all sitting and the Emperor was not yet
in attendance. Neither was the sorcerer, who it turned
out was a rather nice fellow, all things considered. He
was grateful for the maps and offered a handsome
bonus to Wollis. Being a fairly decent sort himself,
Wollis divided the money between the rest of the
expedition. Well, not all of it, but a decent portion.
Some he set aside for himself, some for Merros, and
because he knew it would be what Merros wanted, he
even set some aside for the families of the men who
had died on the journey. Merros was a good man.
That was one of the reasons that Wollis continued to
serve with him even after they left the service.

The hall where they took their meal was another large affair, with marble walls, a few statues of previous emperors in the corners, and a dozen different sigils from various kingdoms of the Empire scattered along the walls almost as an afterthought. All in all it was a bit overwhelming, and so Wollis concentrated on the other people dining instead.

And there were a lot of them. One of the Sisters sat at the table as well: Pella, she of the midnight hair and hypnotically dark eyes, sat to his left. From time to time she pointed out the names and positions of some of the other people in the room to him and Drask alike. She was probably talking to Andover as well, but the boy barely seemed to notice.

The largest of the tables was set aside for Tusk – who the hell would have guessed he was a king? – and four of his retinue, as well as the Emperor, the wizard and a few of Pathra Krous' cousins. The king, the Emperor and the sorcerer were conspicuously absent but the rest of the table was occupied by a group that appeared to have more money than common sense. One or two of them seemed to have been raised to understand the sort of manners that even Wollis was raised with – one does not deliberately outshine a guest in the house, and if these were truly members of the royal family, they seemed determined to show as many jewels as they could in an effort to prove that they were worthy of being noticed – but the ones dressed in more casual clothing were the exceptions, not the rule.

Pella leaned in close to him and did that thing where she seemed to read his mind. "You are not wrong. They seek only to impress the Emperor, and as a result, fail to follow proper decorum."

Rather than taking offense from the possible ability to hear his thoughts – she was an associate of a sorcerer and Wollis understood the implications, even if Merros did not – he was pleased to hear that his beliefs were being confirmed.

"So they are failing in the eyes of the Emperor?"

"Oh yes. But they do not see it. They see only that they have a chance to get his attention."

Wollis chuckled and Drask looked his way. "It is one thing to get the attention of an authority, my friend, and another entirely to get the attention you desire."

Andover laughed bitterly at that. The boy's eyes looked toward him and he wagged his fingers. "On this you and I agree." Then the lad went back to looking at his hands. He was almost the same age as Nolan, and Wollis felt a twinge at the thought. It had been a long while since he'd seen his son. It might be a very long time indeed, as Nolan was now of age and likely already off to serve in the army.

Laughter erupted at the table to their left and the royals looked over with surprised expressions. Pella smiled indulgently and, at that table, Tataya laughed along with several of the Sa'ba Taalor, who were apparently exchanging anecdotes about fighting. It seemed that almost everything the people from the valley did involved fighting. Wollis remembered watching them when they were heading toward Fellein, still dressed in their weapons and armor, and had little trouble understanding that the people around him were warriors. The noblemen seemed less likely to ever fully understand that notion.

They were not soldiers. He doubted most of them would properly understand which end of a sword should be pointed at an enemy. Oh, to be sure they had been taught the ways of weapons, had likely been taught by the finest swordsmen around, but having a good teacher did not guarantee that a person was among the finest students.

The Sa'ba Taalor did not carry any weapons on them. They were unarmed. A few of the royals were sporting daggers or other small bejeweled pieces that were supposed to be weapons. In any situation that involved bloodshed Wollis would have banked his entire newly acquired fortune on the visitors from the Seven Forges. That included the slightest of the females, who, sadly, had gone off with Merros on his merry little adventure in the south. Jost. That was her name. Young enough to be his daughter, but oddly sexy, even with her face hidden away.

He looked toward Drask and wondered what, exactly, was hidden behind that veil. His curiosity was mild enough to avoid him risking life and limb to find out.

Of course Wollis would have been the first to say he had a great deal of common sense and a powerful sense of self-preservation. He wouldn't have been wrong on either account.

Sadly, the same could not be said of the nobles.

A young buck at the main dining table was sitting to the left of a stunning beauty who had the common sense to dress appropriately for the guests of the

Empire. She had the sense. The young buck was a dandy, dressed in finery and actually sporting a thin sword that, while likely quite deadly, didn't look like it could take a blow from an axe without being reshaped. His hair was over-oiled and curled in the latest dubious fashion, his clothes were of shiny silks, and his face was still round with the last of his baby fat. He would likely be handsome enough someday, but like Andover Lashk, he was barely of age to be called a man.

He spoke exactly loudly enough to be heard by everyone. "What sort of swine come to an affair like this and bray like broken mules?" The four members of the Sa'ba Taalor at the same table looked toward him with wide, shocked eyes.

Wollis bit his lip. It was bad enough that the young fool was speaking that way. It was worse that he spoke that way during one of those sublime moments when it seemed that everyone in the room stopped speaking at the exact same time. All of the background murmurs faded away just as he posed his deliberately rude question.

The beauty next to the buck looked shocked. "Brolley! What has possessed you?" Her voice was soft, her chastisement meant only for the offender's ears.

Drask's voice, on the other hand, was sharp and loud enough to answer the challenge that had been thrown. His accent in that moment was thick, and the distortion that all of his people spoke with was particularly loud. "What sort of whelp barks when he should keep his mouth shut and save himself sorrow?"

Wollis reached out a hand. "I'm sure he did not mean—"

Drask brushed the staying hand aside gently. His eyes locked on the younger dandy. "He knew exactly what he said. Didn't you, boy?"

Oh, yes, this was going poorly indeed. Wollis looked to Pella, and she in turn looked at her sisters, possibly trying to find the best way to calm the tempestuous situation.

The young noble bristled. "How dare you?" His face reddened.

The beauty next to him called out sharply this time. "Brolley! Think carefully before you speak!"

"Enough, Nachia! I'll not have a dirt farmer like this speak to me with that tone!" Brolley stood up and faced Drask where he sat. "I'll not be called a boy by a savage!"

Wollis started to stand up. He would, by the gods, not stand by and allow a foolhardy boy to start a war between nations. "That's enough! Hold your tongue, lad!"

Drask stood up. And up. And up. And for the first time the boy with the fine clothes and the fancy sword realized that he might have made a mistake. It was one thing to see Drask when he was settled comfortably at a dining table and another entirely to see the man when he was ready to handle a situation.

"You offend me. You offend my people. You disgrace your Emperor, your family, and yourself." Drask spoke softly, but every last soul in the room heard him clearly.

"Apologize, Brolley, immediately." The woman, Nachia, spoke with frosty warning in her tone. The whole group of them knew better than to let this go on any longer. Their faces spoke volumes of how well they understood the situation.

Wollis could see it on the boy's face. He wanted to apologize. He wanted to make the situation go away, but he also couldn't stand the idea of losing face in front of his family, his peers. He was humiliated. He'd been chastised by a man he certainly considered a savage and he'd been called out by none other than Wollis himself, a lowly peasant and soldier. The sting of the situation was worse than a slap across the face.

One sentence and the entire affair could likely have been forgiven. One simple apology and the incident would go away. But youthful pride is always a stone in the boot of an arrogant boy.

"I don't apologize for speaking the truth. And I don't apologize to pigs."

It was then that the Emperor, the sorcerer, and the King walked into the room. They were just in time to hear the boy's words.

Nachia shook her head. "Brolley, no!"

Drask looked at the boy and took three steps forward. The first stride seemed to cover half the room. The second had him in front of the dandy. The third had the boy driven against the table, pinned in place by Drask's hands.

The boy tried to draw his sword. He had it halfway out of the scabbard before Drask slapped his hand aside and then threw the weapon to the ground with a clatter.

"Drask!" Tuskandru's voice was thunderous.

Drask lifted Brolley from the table and shook him. Brolley's eyes were wide in his round face and he yelped as surely as a dog that has been beaten. It was obvious even from where Wollis stood that Drask was doing all he could to restrain his rage.

"I demand satisfaction from this cur!" Drask roared the words. His veil shuddered with the force of his angered breaths.

Emperor Pathra Krous looked to his cousin, and then to the king beside him and finally to Drask.

Desh Krohan spoke softly, but the words carried far enough to let Wollis hear them. "I told you to change that stupid law."

The Emperor of Fellein looked at the warrior holding his cousin off the ground by the front of his shirt. His cousin looked at him with wide, worried eyes.

Tuskandru looked at the Emperor. Pathra Krous looked at the king and then at Drask. "You shall have your satisfaction. You shall have your blood trial."

Nachia looked at her Emperor in horror. Wollis knew just how she felt.

TWELVE

King Marsfel's demeanor changed radically when Merros Dulver came back to his throne room and explained that the Guntha had been taken care of for him.

The man was not exactly arrogant the first time round, so much as he was bored with the notion of dealing with political nonsense. That was the impression Merros had when he met him at the beginning of the journey. When the King heard that there were ten observers attending on behalf of the Emperor, he grew cold and distant, and offered remarkably little by way of assistance.

When Merros and the ten Sa'ba Taalor came back to him, and Swech and her companions reported that the Guntha had been taken care of, the man positively fell over himself with gratitude, which, Merros observed, really was most of what he was supposed to do. Merros also translated a few phrases when Swech and company didn't quite catch the nuances of the language. There were only a few incidents and none of them would have been trouble so much as they would have been awkward. All told, the travelers had done an incredible job of learning a new language, but time and context limited what they absorbed.

Marsfel looked at the ten from the Valley of the Forges and smiled. He stood and strutted around them. He clapped his hands and did everything he could to make them know he thought they were amazing. He insisted on a feast on their behalf, and when they tried to refuse, Merros stepped in and accepted for them, then begged a moment with Swech.

She was not angry, but she was decidedly formal when he pulled her to the side. "Why do you make us eat with this man?"

"It's his way of offering thanks."

She shook her head and her eyes half pinned him in place. "He is like the old woman at the cart. He wishes to thank us for his weakness."

Merros nodded. "I thought you might see it that way and that's why I wanted to speak with you." He paused and tried to decide the best way to answer without getting his head separated from his neck. "He offers you a feast because this buys him time to see if you are telling him the truth."

Her eyes flared behind the veil and her hands twitched as if preparing to seek the comfort of her weapons.

Merros stepped in closer, until they were as close as lovers. "It's not what you think."

"I think he insults my honor."

"It's not that at all. That is why he offers the feast, to avoid offending you. But your claim is very unusual for him. Ten of his soldiers could not have done what you and the others did. They are not as skilled as you.

For that reason he must send someone he trusts to confirm what you have said."

"And if we lied?"

"The feast would be your last." Some truths are simpler to state than others. She could understand the idea of being punished for lying, it seemed, with more ease than she could understand the concept of being accused of lying.

"And if we have told the truth?"

"Then you have earned his gratitude, and made the Emperor look good and your own people look good. You might even have earned an ally in King Marsfel."

That stopped her. Her eyes locked on him again, this time trying to read any possible secrets he might be hiding from her. There were none. He had come initially to observe, but had amended his reasons for being there to include making whatever this task of theirs was as amenable as possible for all parties.

"Very well then. We will allow this feast."

"And I'm sure the king and Drask appreciate your tolerance." He sighed. "Now let's go back to being congratulated and then we can get back to Tyrne."

"Are you so tired of us already?" Her voice was teasing. He knew she was jesting. Or at least he suspected strongly at that. It was sometimes difficult to know what anyone was thinking when half of her face was constantly hidden.

"Not hardly. But I have earned a great deal of money and I would like to go about the business of spending it."

Her fist cuffed him lightly in the arm. "Wise answer. There's hope for you yet."

She headed back for the main group and he watched her go. He knew her to be a passionate lover. He also knew she could kill without remorse. His eyes tracked the sway of her hips and the play of muscles along the part of her back that was bared by her tunic. Scars and smooth flesh, muscles and just the right amount of softness to remind him that she was decidedly a woman.

He shook his head. No. He would not allow himself to fall for a woman from a country where everyone carried enough weapons for five soldiers. The first argument they had would surely be the death of him.

Within a few hours of their arrival with their news, the feast was under way and Marsfel seated them with his immediate family, including three daughters who were, to be kind, stunning. Each was lovelier than the last. It might well be true that Roathes had little to offer by way of military might, but if all the women were as striking as his daughters, the man should seriously consider hiring a few extra armies for their protection.

Merros hardly had time to get to know any of the ladies in question. The king had many questions for his guests and Merros had to be ready to provide translation at all times. Mostly, however, he simply listened and took in what there was to hear.

And he worried. Much as he wanted to believe that all was well, his mind refused to accept the notion. He looked around almost constantly and could find no source for his unease, and that too worried him.

As he contemplated what might be wrong, he saw a man who had left earlier, immediately after the king announced the feast, come back and speak softly in Marsfel's ear. The monarch's eyes grew wide for the briefest moment and then he nodded and relaxed a bit. It seemed the news that the Guntha were well and truly finished with their attempt at an invasion had reached his ears.

No, Merros did not think it would be that simple. He thought it far more likely that the Guntha would retaliate, or, worse, start planning a proper invasion instead of merely landing on a strip of shoreline. But Marsfel seemed quite pleased with what he found out, and that had to count for something.

It seemed there was something amiss. Now all he had to do was figure out what it was. Beside him Swech was talking to Ehnole, their voices clear enough to hear if he wanted to, but instead he focused on Marsfel. There was no reason that he could see to be worried. Still, he couldn't help but think that the king of the region was up to something.

"What are you thinking?" Swech's voice broke his contemplations.

He looked at her and thought carefully before answering. "I think we might need to be cautious."

"About?" He had her undivided attention.

"I'm not sure yet. But something is not right here."

Swech nodded and her hand tapped the table three times, a casual enough gesture, but not a nervous habit that she normally used. Merros had been around the woman for weeks and had observed her when she was eating, when she was speaking, even when she was sleeping. Her gesture wasn't exactly out of character, but it wasn't casual, either.

Around him the other Sa'ba Taalor continued doing what they were doing, eating or conversing with one of the locals, but all of them responded in small ways. Hands patted the table or made gestures that would have meant nothing at all to most people, including Merros himself had he not been watching for it. Still, he had no doubt at all that the people were communicating with each other. Tataya had used her sorcery to allow him to speak the language of the Sa'ba Taalor, but only one of the languages. As near as he could figure, they had at least three separate languages. He could only guess that she had alerted the others to be aware and that they, in turn, were reporting back.

Swech leaned in closer to him and her hand ran suggestively across his forearm. Her eyes did not show affection. When she spoke it was in her native tongue, almost ensuring that no one else would understand outside of their party. "No one is certain what is wrong, but a few of the others have sensed there might be trouble brewing. We are alerted. We will keep a close watch." Her voice was low and the tone light, as if she were merely making a suggestion between two lovers.

He smiled and nodded and leaned in closer himself. "We should not stay here."

"You suggest we leave during the feast in our honor?"

"I think it would be best if we leave as soon as the feast is done."

She nodded her head, keeping her tone light. "We will do so. We will also expect troubles."

Marsfel stood up and cleared his throat. Immediately the people under him quieted and with moments everyone was looking toward the monarch. His voice was clean and deep when he spoke – actually a good deal deeper than when he talked normally. "We have asked Emperor Krous for a solution to our troubles with the Guntha, and he has responded by sending us the very people with whom we now dine." The king bowed formally. "I can but offer our thanks for the generosity of the Sa'ba Taalor, who have taken care of the threat to our kingdom."

Swech stood up in response, and carefully repeated his bow. "We are grateful for the feast you have offered in our honor. We welcome the chance to call the people of Roathes our friends." Her words were met with a small round of applause from people who looked uncertain as to exactly what was going on. Merros found himself wondering if most of the locals knew of the troubles with the Guntha or if that trouble had been kept from the general populace. He'd been with the royal army long enough to know that not every ruler felt the need to share news of potential problems with their people.

Marsfel smiled and excused himself a few moments later as the celebration continued. Merros watched on as the people around them consumed food and drink alike.

"We are leaving now." He spoke a command without even thinking about it. He had no authority over the Sa'ba Taalor and he knew it, but his sense of urgency was growing, not dwindling.

Swech did that trick with her hand again and nodded her head. Within moments all of them were ready to leave.

There was no subtlety to it. They rose and they left. If their host took offense, Merros intended to be well away before he could do anything to make his dissatisfaction known.

"Explain to me again why we are running away from the man we just helped." Swech's voice was tense, annoyed. Merros couldn't really blame her, but they had to do it this way. The wind was cutting across them as they moved, and Merros had to lean in very close to hear her and to be heard. Their bodies were pressed half together and he did his best to ignore the situation. Among the Sa'ba Taalor there was no apparent awkwardness about the way his body responded. At home he would likely have been hearing about the inappropriate and discourteous actions he took for weeks. Then again, he would not have been riding behind a woman on the same animal at home. At least not without extreme circumstances.

"Because if he decides to do something to us, we are vastly outnumbered and it could lead to problems between your people and mine."

"What sort of problems?"

"Well, if the king of Roathes decides that we should all be executed for killing the Guntha on his beach, we all die. That's rather a problem for me. I don't much care to die. I'll do it if I have to, of course, but I prefer to keep living." Swech looked over her shoulder at him her eyes narrowed a bit as she contemplated what he'd just said. He smiled to show he was jesting. "There's also the problem of your people taking offense to having you killed by strangers. We have no idea how they would respond to that."

"Of course we do."

"Really? And how would that be?"

"They would take it as a challenge against the honor of our people and our kings."

"Meaning they would send more people down here to deal with the king and the executions."

"Of course." Her voice was casual as she answered. There was no doubt in her mind.

"So why wait around in a situation we know is not going to end well?"

"Because there is never a good reason to run from a fight." Her voice was strong with conviction.

"I don't agree. If there are four thousand people ready to hang you for a crime you did not commit, it's a good time to run."

"That is not a fight. That is a mob."

"Semantics. There are people who would use this situation as an excuse to cause troubles between your people and mine and I wanted to avoid that."

Swech nodded, satisfied. "Then I can accept your wisdom in this."

He resisted the urge to respond with sarcasm and instead enjoyed the view of their surroundings and the speed of the animal moving under them. The great beasts were in a running mood apparently, and were charging across the land at a hard run.

They were almost to Tyrne, and would likely not stop until they got there. That suited him just fine. It wasn't that he didn't enjoy the company. It was that he wanted to be home, sleeping in a decent bed and not worried about whether or not he was going to be killed for any possible slight.

"You understand that I am not upset with you. I simply do not like running from a fight." Swech's tone was conversational.

"I did what I felt was necessary. I wanted to keep you safe."

"I would have been safe." She shook her head. "It is not my time."

"How do you know that?"

"I just do." Her voice was teasing. He wished he had that sort of confidence.

"Not to worry. I didn't think I'd offended you. I would apologize if I had."

She tilted her head. "Why?"

"I do not mind offending my enemies, Swech, but I don't consider you an enemy."

"That is good." She nodded her head and said no more.

Twenty minutes later, as the ride was beginning to lull Merros into a semi-doze, a horn sounded three short, sharp blasts. He woke right up.

"What the hell?"

"We are followed." Swech's voice was calm. No, it was more than that. She sounded almost happy about it.

Merros turned his body and looked back. In the distance a fair way down the king's highway, he could see horsemen. A good number of them.

He called out to Swech, "Do you plan to stop?"

"Not yet. We will slow down and give them the opportunity to make themselves known to us."

"I don't think that's wise."

"I know this about you." Her voice was positively amused.

Swech raised her left arm above her head and waved it slowly back and forth. Behind and around them the other riders slowed. Blane rode closer, his long hair free-flowing for the moment, but even as he pulled alongside them he drew the hair back and quickly tied it down with a thick band of leather. "We wait on them?"

Swech nodded her head. "Merros is hesitant of starting a war."

Blane looked toward him and shook his head. "You are worried that they should strike the first blow if this is to be an attack?"

"We don't know what they want. I merely think we should find out."

Blane shook his head a second time and the great beast under him mirrored the gesture. "Then we should stop. I grow impatient."

Swech looked toward Merros. "Blane grows impatient." She raised her hand again and this time made a fist. At the same time Saa'thaa slowed and then stopped. Blane's great beast did likewise. In a moment all ten animals had come to a rest, many of them panting lightly, barely giving credence to the notion that they had been running for hours. His admiration for their stamina went up a few notches.

Blane dropped from his mount and immediately the others did the same. Merros watched Swech nimbly shift her body until she was sitting sideways and looking at him. "You will join us?"

"Of course."

He hastily slipped from the saddle on Saa'thaa's back and the animal grumbled a small sound of relief. Aside from that noise you'd never have noticed a change in the animal's demeanor.

As he watched, the Sa'ba Taalor gathered their weapons of choice. Few of them were the same from individual to individual. There were several devices that he could barely recognize as particular weapons, though there was little doubt that each and every device was designed for combat.

The girl Jost carefully tested a length of chain between her hands. At each end of the chain was a weight with several spikes and Merros was reminded of what Tusk had said about how deadly a weapon a chain could be. He also remembered the long line of scars on the man's arm from a similar weapon. He resisted the urge to shiver, even as adrenaline began kicking into his system.

The riders came closer and Merros tried counting. He lost the exact number but it was greater than twenty. They rode their horses with the sort of posture that came from working on horseback a great deal. They wore armor and carried weapons of their own. What they did not do was wear any particular colors. Every regiment in the Empire sported indicia, but not this group. And while they were wearing military issue armor, in most cases they most decidedly were not soldiers. Not anymore at least.

Mercenaries then. He understood all too well. He was a mercenary himself these days.

"And a good day to you." The head of the riders pulled up slowly, his eyes staring almost exclusively at Merros. His accent was clipped, sharp. He was not from Marsfel's kingdom. At a guess he was from much further to the west, and just possibly from as far away as Morwhen, much farther west than Merros had ever travelled. Morwhen was best known as a land of savages. The soldiers out there earned their pay. As he stopped, the rest fanned out with careful deliberation. The road was wide here – it was the king's highway after all – but even so a few of the riders left the road proper and moved around to the sides until they had better access to Merros and the Sa'ba Taalor.

"And to you. What can we do for you on this day?" Merros kept his hand on his sword hilt. The gesture was obvious and the intent clear. The head of the mercenaries noticed it, too. His lip twitched upward in a half-smile for only a moment. He was very, very confident.

"King Marsfel feels that you left rather abruptly. He wished to extend his offer of hospitality." The man had a lean, hard face. He was weathered and he was scarred. He was, in short, a military man. There was little doubt that he and his knew how to use their weapons. All of the men held their hands in their laps. They were armed and prepared to use those arms immediately.

"And while we would hardly wish to offend His Majesty, we are on business for the Emperor himself and must return home to make our reports."

Swech listened intently, her eyes moving from one man to the next. Around her the rest of her people were similarly alert.

The head of the mercenaries nodded his head. "Marsfel seemed quite insistent."

"Emperor Krous will be certain to explain the urgency of the situation when the time is right."

Swech stepped closer to Merros, her hand resting on the hilt of a rather heavy looking bladed weapon. He couldn't really call it a sword. More like an axe with a very long blade. "King Marsfel has been assisted. We are done. We are leaving." That pretty much put an end to the argument as far as she was concerned. The way she spoke left no room for debate.

"No, lady. He was really very insistent." The mercenary smiled. Behind him the rest of his men lifted the crossbows that rested across their laps and took aim at the individuals around them.

"Why don't we settle this as gentlemen?" Merros looked at the man intently. He was still trying his best to end this as bloodlessly as possible. "Just you and me."

"I am flattered, of course, that you would consider me a gentleman. But alas, no. I have been told to bring you back. If I fail to bring you back, I am not paid."

He was still considering the remaining coin he'd been offered to cover expenses when Blane answered for him. His arm slid almost casually toward the closest bowman and a moment later the man screamed as his crossbow fell from a useless arm. A blade vibrated in the man's wrist and a streamer of blood fell freely from the wound.

And the rest of the Sa'ba Taalor responded as well.

There are times when the world moves too quickly. Merros dropped down and to the side, praying to the gods he claimed to seldom follow that no bolts would enter his body. His prayers were rewarded but barely. A bolt cut across his ear, taking a small divot of flesh when it passed.

He hissed and drew his sword and then he charged the leader of the mercenaries. The man had a distinct advantage. He was on horseback. His enemy drew a sword as well and while he was preparing to hack away at Merros with the long blade, Merros came in closer, close enough to feel the heat of the horse, and jammed his dagger into the rider's inner thigh.

The rider let out a roar and swept the blade of his sword at Merros, who barely managed to block.

And then he stepped back as the blood from the man's severed artery fountained freely. The rider looked down and realized he was dead around the same time that Merros got clear of his weapon.

There are a few places where, when a man is cut, he simply cannot be saved. The open wound in the man's femoral artery guaranteed a quick death. Still, he dropped his sword and tried to staunch the flow and Merros left him to it. There were others to deal with.

There was both good and bad news by the time he'd finished his simple exchange. The good news was that the riders around them had finished with their crossbows. The bad was that several of them were good shots. Blane moved past him, a bolt stuck in his chest. He roared as he pulled a rider from his horse. The man looked understandably terrified by the unexpected move. Blane was not nearly the biggest of the Sa'ba Taalor that Merros had seen, but he had strength enough to haul the rider from his seated position and drag him to the ground. That was all the time that Merros had to look around before another rider was coming for him, charging forward, his horse knocking aside one of the people from the valley. Whoever it was cursed as he fell under the animal and an instant later the horse let out a scream and staggered to the side. The rider tried to compensate for the sudden change in direction and was thrown for his trouble. He fell and rolled to his feet quickly, holding a short sword in a tight grip, his eyes wide and his mouth drawn down in a rictus scowl.

Merros covered the distance between them and brought his own sword up from below. The man blocked and did his best to strike in return, and then they were both swinging, blocking and doing their best to kill their new enemy.

And damned if it didn't feel good. Merros wanted to deny it, but it felt good to be fighting instead of merely existing.

And the Sa'ba Taalor seemed to feel the same way. Jost moved in a near blur, her body half-dancing as she swept her chain around a man's arm and pulled hard. He screamed, fought to free himself and was unhorsed in the process. He did not recover quickly enough and the other end of the chain struck him a hard blow to the face, which tore his mouth into a bloody shred and shattered teeth besides.

Blane rose from the body of his enemy, his hands both covered in gore, with no apparent weapon in sight.

Swech brought her odd looking weapon down in a blow that shattered her enemy's sword and drove the deadly tip into his collarbone. Before he could finish falling she hauled the weapon forward and split his skull sideways.

Merros felt his enemy's sword tip cut into his forearm and hissed. He pushed the man back as their swords scraped each other and then stepped in closer, until the swords were useless. The dagger swept in again leaving a trail of red across the man's chin. Before he could move in again his enemy stepped back and took a defensive stance. Once was all he was going to get with that particular trick.

The roar of voices, the clash of steel and the screams of a dying horse came together in a cacophony of bloodshed. Merros drove forward, slashing again and again at his opponent, not letting the man take the offense. He felt himself grinning despite the situation and watched as his enemy's eyes grew wider. Merros was a captain in the royal army. He'd earned that rank by training constantly and by fighting well enough and long enough to live to achieve it. The mercenary was a good swordsman, but Merros was better. The fight ended when the point of his sword punched through the man's throat.

And by the time that fight was done, the battle was finished as well.

Merros stood still, his sword held at the ready and looked around, breathing through his nose in harsh gusts. Swech leaned against her weapon, panting. The point of the odd blade was still buried in a man's stomach and his body twitched as he died. She looked toward Merros, her expression hidden by that damnable veil. Jost looked at the horses around them as she cleaned her chain with an oiled cloth. She eyed the animals with curiosity and it occurred to him that she might well have never seen one up close before. Even the ones from the expedition had been kept mostly away from the beasts that the Sa'ba Taalor rode.

Blane called out and one of the others came to him, immediately inspecting the bolt stuck in his chest. It looked to be buried deep, but judging by his stance Blane had not been hit crucially.

Another of the people was not looking quite as well off. Unlike Blane he was another wall of flesh and this time someone had done their very best to knock that wall over. Merros realized he was the one that had been trampled by the horse and had apparently managed to gut the horse in the process. He bore several bleeding wounds that looked like indents from the beast's hooves. He stood but shook, and blood came from his left arm in a heavy flow. Merros moved toward him but another of the group beat him there. And then another still. Within moments they had the man on his back and were removing a crossbow bolt from his side.

Merros looked around and realized that all of them were bloodied. It was nearly impossible to imagine how they could have come out of the combat unscathed. For every one of them there had been two of the enemy, and the assault had started with crossbows from the opposing side.

On the ground, one of the mercenaries started to rise, doing his best not to be noticed. He was not fast enough or careful enough. Swech lifted her weapon and brought it around in a hard arc that cleaved his torso nearly in half. She did so without hesitation, and looked down at her enemy with eyes burning as she used his tunic to wipe the blade clean.

"Well. That didn't go as I'd hoped." Merros spoke mostly to himself.

Blane heard him and laughed. "Liar."

"What do you mean?" Merros scowled as he stared at the other man. Wounded or not, comrade or not, he didn't much take kindly to being called a liar.

Blane stepped closer and Merros could see the laugh lines around the man's eyes. "Your heart is beating hard, your face is smiling and you've grown hard in your pants." The man looked closely at him. Studied him. Dared him to disagree. "You are a warrior. You act the part of being soft, but everyone here can see how much you enjoyed that fight." Completely ignoring the wound on his side, he slapped Merros in the arm with affection. "It's why we respect you. You know how to fight."

Ehnole called out to Blane. "Yes, he can fight. Now get over here and let me patch you up, you damned fool. You'll bleed all over yourself again."

Blane laughed and headed back to her. On the ground the one who'd been injured the most grunted as the others held him down.

"We need to fix him." Swech looked over at the fallen warrior. "Does he need metal?"

"Of course I need metal! I'm bleeding like a drunk man pisses!" The words were hissed out as one of the two pulled the crossbow bolt from his side. The bolt did not come out cleanly, but took a piece of meat with it. "Damn but that hurts!"

Swech shook her head. "You cry like a newborn, Lorroth." Her voice held surprising humor as she walked over to Saa'thaa and rummaged in the various saddlebags.

"Just hurry! I have no desire to die in these lands." His protests were weaker.

Swech merely nodded and then pulled a metallic bar from her bags. The rod of metal was oddly shaped, with markings along the sides that Merros couldn't see clearly from his distance. It looked to be pure gold. He moved a bit closer and saw several of the others were now watching Lorroth intently.

Swech crouched next to the man and gestured to the others around her. "Hold him."

Rather than argue the point, Lorroth went limp and allowed his fellows to grab his arms and his legs. Merros could see the depth of the gash in the man's arm. He could see sinew and severed muscle and bone clearly through the open wound. He was surprised that the man was conscious at all. Blood loss alone should have sent him into a deep sleep.

"Wrommish, bless this man for his service." Swech held the bar up before her face as she spoke, and then moved quickly, one hand grabbing the wound on Lorroth's arm and pinching at the flesh. She was not gentle and as she grabbed, the man tried to fight against the pain. The ones holding him in place did their part, pinning him properly as Swech pushed the metal against his arm.

Merros had no idea what they were planning on doing, aside from apparently angering a wounded man. Lorroth bucked harder and screamed, roared as the metal touched him, and then the dual scents of burning metal and burning flesh reached Merros' nose.

Where the gold touched the man it glowed and liquefied, spilling into the wound. The metal hissed as it mingled with flesh and blood, cooking, cauterizing as it bubbled and pooled into the cut. Lorroth did his very best to break the grips of the ones holding him, and they fought harder still to keep him still as he rocked his body and his limbs, screaming.

"Hold still! I'd like to keep my fingers!" Swech hissed the words as the white-hot metal dribbled from the melting rod, narrowly avoiding taking her fingers along with it.

Merros stared, horrified. It was impossible, of course. It couldn't be happening. He was watching it and couldn't begin to look away, but it couldn't be happening. Still it continued until the last of the gold had fallen from Swech's fingers and puddled into the grievous wound, sealing it shut. The skin around the metal was nearly blackened from the heat, and yet as he watched, the discoloration faded down, and the gold cooled and seemed to mix with the flesh.

He thought of Drask's hand and wondered if the same sort of sorcery was responsible.

He'd heard tales of people using gold as a slow poison, heard that it could kill and cause endless misery in the process. But here the people of the valley were using it to seal a wound that surely would have killed Lorroth.

And it seemed that Lorroth was feeling better almost as soon as Swech finished. He lay back for almost a minute, during which time Merros continued to stare at his wound site and the scar that rapidly formed where before there had been a deadly cut. By all rights the man should have been as dead as the mercenary whose leg he hacked open. Instead after that short span of time the man was sitting up, rolling his shoulder and testing the area that had been roasting a few moments earlier.

Merros looked around at the dead around them. He was still contemplating what he had just seen when Swech tapped his arm. He looked at her for a long moment, still half lost in thoughts. All around him the Sa'ba Taalor acted as if nothing miraculous had occurred.

"Patch me up?" She pointed to a cut along her hip. "I can't quite reach."

"Yes, of course." He forced a smile for her. While he worked, she stood perfectly still and then made quick orders for several of the others when they were stitched and mended as best they could be.

"Well, I'll be letting the proper authorities know about this."

"Good." She nodded her head. "We'll leave soon. After."

"After what?"

"Saa'thaa!" The great beast turned its head to regard her, the eyes glowing within the metallic mask it wore. "Feast!" Without another word the animals rose and did just that. Horses and dead mercenaries alike were torn apart by the great animals.

Merros did not protest. He just did his best not to think about what was happening instead.

There were differences between the races, he knew that. Still, it was unsettling to see how little regard the Sa'ba Taalor held for their fallen enemies.

THIRTEEN

Pathra Krous stared toward the distant Seven Forges. Really, it seemed to be about his favorite thing to do.

Desh Krohan watched him in silence for a while and finally shrugged. "Listen you can stare out that damned window for a dozen years and it won't change a bloody thing. Why don't we discuss what you want to do here?"

"I want this to go away. That's what I want." His voice was waspish.

Desh stood and stretched then looked around the Emperor's private offices. "Much as we might want that to happen, it won't."

"Then what do you suggest, Advisor?" His Majesty's voice positively dripped with sarcasm on the title.

"I suggested a good time ago that you change the damned laws. You should have." Desh's voice dripped nothing but frost and Pathra stared at him for a moment, shocked by the tone. He was not used to anyone taking that tone with him and for just one brief moment he forgot himself. He opened his mouth to say something he would likely have immediately taken back, but instead he looked at the expression on the sorcerer's face and remembered that the man before him had been advisor to generations of emperors, and had powers great enough to do him grievous harm without ever lifting a finger.

"You're right of course, Desh. But it's too late for that now." He looked at Desh with wide, fearful eyes. "It is, isn't it?"

"You could change the law this instant if you so desired; you're the Emperor. But you would regret it. You would lose face before your kings, your people, and your new acquaintances."

"Brolley is a damned fool!"

"Yes, we both acknowledge that. That's one of the reasons he was never much of a consideration as your replacement. His sister is far wiser than he is and also a good deal more level headed."

"Nachia is not happy about this."

"I can't say as I blame her for that, Pathra. You agreed to a duel between her brother and a man who looks like he could wrestle a mountain. A man, I might add, who has made sport of hunting down and killing Pra-Moresh."

"What have I done?"

"Doomed your younger cousin, unless you can find a way to placate Drask Silver Hand that doesn't involve him bathing in the boy's entrails."

Pathra blanched. "That seems rather vivid, don't you think?"

"I like to make clear exactly how grave the circumstances are here. You risk offending seven kingdoms with one gesture, Pathra. Seven. An Empire's worth of enemies if you handle this the wrong way."

"Perhaps you could reason with Drask?"

"It's not my place to reason with anyone, Your Majesty. That falls to you and your finest diplomats."

"You trained my finest diplomats, old man."

"Then you are well and truly roasting over a fire pit. I am hardly a diplomat." He sighed. "I'll have Tataya look into what might or might not placate Drask, but I have doubts it will go the way you want it to."

Before Pathra could answer, the doors to his office opened and in came Nachia, her face set in a rather fearsome expression of anger.

The Emperor looked to Desh. "Any help at all would be appreciated."

"Of course."

"That gigantic bear will eat my brother alive!"

"Very likely he will, Nachia, but what am I to do about it?" Pathra looked to his cousin and immediately there was a scowl on his face. There had always been an interesting relationship between them, one that Desh knew more about than either of them understood.

"Nachia, we're trying to work out a way to avoid your brother's unfortunate circumstances." Desh tried to placate the young woman, but she fired a look his way that was pure venom. He crossed his arms and shut his mouth. She would have her say.

Pathra held his hands up. "I did not ask your brother to offend the visiting dignitaries. Nor did you. I believe, in fact, that you were telling him to shut his foolish mouth when we came into the room."

"How could you let that beast challenge Brolley?"

"How could you let Brolley offend the guests of the Empire?" Pathra stood his ground and stared hard into his cousin's eyes.

"Damn your logic!"

"I didn't invite this. Brolley has done this to himself. I'm investigating how to avoid his error becoming fatal without starting an incident between nations, Nachia, but at the end of the day if I have to choose between your brother and my Empire there is very little choice."

Nachia looked away first.

"I don't want my stupid brother gutted by that man." Nachia looked at the desk.

"Neither do I." Pathra put his hands on her shoulders. "Neither does anyone."

Desh slipped from the room as quietly as he could, which was very quietly indeed.

Drask Silver Hand stared into the fire as his hands moved, carefully sharpening the edge on his axe. The weapon had seen a great deal of combat over the years, and if he could be said to have a favorite, the great double bladed axe was it.

Tataya knocked and slipped into his room. He caught the scent of her musky perfume and allowed himself a small smile.

"You are here to plead for the boy's life?"

"No. Not exactly." She slipped closer to him, but did not touch. The whetstone sang softly as it scraped along the edge of the axe's blade.

"Then what is it I can do for you, Tataya?"

"Desh Krohan asks that I see what will satisfy your honor, short of killing a foolish boy."

"Should the boy prostrate himself before me tomorrow, I will allow him his life." He examined the blade and then turned the axe around. The whetstone met with a dab of oil and then again began its soft song along the edge of the weapon.

"That is all?" Her voice was mild, but he sensed the reproach. "All you ask is that a man of royal lineage fall to his knees before you and beg forgiveness?"

"He offended me. He offended my people. He offended the Seven Kings I serve." He watched the stone caress the blade. "What else would you have me do?"

"How would you handle the situation in your homeland?"

"I would have killed him where he stood." Drask looked up at her, stared into her eyes. They were an odd color, like her skin, like her hair. She had the colors of autumn locked within her flesh and that puzzled him a bit, as all of his people held the color of stone and steel and ashes.

"Are your people that unforgiving?"

"My people are direct. The boy spoke of me and mine as if we were not supposed to hear him but he did it with deliberate volume. He did it to offend as much as he could, to gain face while causing me to lose face. He called me to combat with his words." He chuckled. "It was for the sake of diplomacy that I did not gut the child where he stood."

"And yet you have said it yourself. He is a child."

"Then why did he dine with warriors?"

"The only warriors at that table were your kin."

"Has this Brolley ever been in real combat? Has he even been forged once?"

"What do you mean? What do you mean has he been forged?"

"Every life is forged. We start as raw materials and we are made stronger by the forgings of life. Like the tempering of steel. Andover Lashk is not the boy he was before his hands were shattered. That was his first forging."

"Brolley Krous is not Andover Lashk. He has lived a sheltered life."

"Then his family has done him a great disservice."

"Will you consider his inexperience when you deal with him?"

"He has but to apologize. He need only bow before me and withdraw his words and I will let him live."

"And if he does not?"

Drask sighed and set his axe aside. The blade was so sharp that he could shave with it should he so desire.

"If he does not apologize, I still demand satisfaction. Perhaps I will kill him. Perhaps I will break his bones. Perhaps I will cut out his tongue to remind him that only a fool wags an appendage if he wishes to keep it."

"You understand that he is cousin to the Emperor?"

Drask stared at her for several long moments. "I did not know this."

"Does it change anything?"

"I will speak with Tuskandru. I will seek his wisdom on this matter."

"It's late. Will you need time to discuss this?"

Drask shook his head and smiled behind the veil. "You and yours are a subtle people. Had you wished more time for the boy and his family to prepare, you simply could have asked."

Tataya smiled and her hand touched his shoulder, her fingers unconsciously tracing the scars that crisscrossed the flesh there. "Would you have granted it?"

"Possibly. We will never know." He stared into her eyes for a moment. "Two days. I will take two days to consult. At the end of that time, if the boy prostrates himself and apologizes I will spare him. Should my king make other demands I will change my mind."

"You are kind, Drask."

"No, Tataya. I am sensible to the political winds. Nothing more."

She slid in closer to him and her lips pressed against the scars on his shoulder. Her lips were warm and soft and soothing.

He allowed himself to be soothed.

Pella came to him in his room. She knocked and waited for him to answer, then stepped into room. Wollis March looked at her for a long moment, puzzled that she would be there.

The room was large and airy, and yet as soon as she entered he felt the area suddenly cramped and the atmosphere stifling. She was distracting him from his plans to do as little as possible.

"What can I do for you, Pella?"

"You tried to prevent the disastrous events from happening." Her dark eyes regarded him carefully, staring into his.

"Well, yes. I would rather not see a war." He stood up, unsettled by her scrutiny. He didn't like that the woman could stare at him and make him the least bit uncomfortable. It made him feel like he was being unfaithful to Dretta, though he'd done absolutely nothing wrong.

"It might happen anyway."

Wollis shrugged. "I can hardly stop a foolish boy from getting himself killed." Why in the name of the gods was he blushing now? He could feel the color creeping up his face.

"Do you think you could teach him to defend himself?"

"In two days' time?" It hadn't taken long to hear about the delay. "Against Drask Silver Hand? Not the least bit of a chance."

"Enough to let him save face in front of his uncle, the Emperor?"

"I'm not a teacher, Pella. I'm a mercenary."

"Desh Krohan wants someone to teach the boy."

"He carried a sword. Surely he's had better teachers than me already."

"He has never been in a fight."

"There are soldiers aplenty here, Pella."

"They cannot be seen teaching him. It would be embarrassing for Brolley."

"I think I cmbarrassed the lad enough when I called on him to still his tongue." He shook his head. The last thing he needed was to involve himself in the work of nobles and dignitaries. He was a soldier, a mercenary and a bit too old to get embroiled in the politics of the Empire.

"We need your help, Wollis. You know how to fight. You've seen Drask in combat."

"I have, which is why this would be foolish. Drask will kill the boy. That's all there is to it."

The woman stepped closer to him her dark eyes searching through him as if observing his very soul. For all he knew she was.

"Do this small thing, Wollis March. Do this, and help the boy save face."

"It's not saving face if Drask carves his face away. And the man can do it, Pella. You saw him, too. You were there when he took on the Pra-Moresh."

Damn, but he couldn't look away from her eyes. She stepped closer still and he felt himself flush again. She made him feel young and foolish.

"Fine. I'll do my best for the boy."

"That is all that anyone could ask, Wollis." She stepped back and her lips and her eyes united in a smile. "You have my gratitude."

A moment later she was gone without another word.

Wollis sat at the edge of his bed and closed his eyes and reminded himself that he was a married man, faithful to his wife, and not the least bit interested in other women. That was Merros' specialty.

With Pella gone from the room he could almost believe his own words.

Of course, now he had to train a boy to fight like a man. Or at least die with dignity.

Nachia and Pathra looked at Brolley with barely veiled anger. Desh stared indifferently. The boy had never been much of anything in his eyes. He lacked common sense, maturity, skill of any sort… oh, and longevity. He most decidedly lacked longevity. Unless something could be done to avert disaster.

"It was the wine." Brolley's voice was very small. He was a strapping lad, really, solidly built if a little on the heavy side. And he knew his way around a practice arena well enough. Now, however, he was supposed to fight a trained soldier, who in turn was supposed to prepare him for a death match.

"Perhaps if you consume enough spirits in advance you'll find it easier to grovel for your life?" Nachia's voice was winter-cold.

"Nachia, don't be that way."

Pathra Krous looked down his nose at his cousin and shook his head. "You have no idea of the situation you've put us in, you damned fool." Brolley flinched. Pathra seldom spoke in a harsh tone to his relatives. He was a man who genuinely loved his family despite the politics of running an Empire. And in his entire life, Brolley had never heard the man sound angry. Brolley was young; he was only newly considered an adult.

"Please, Pathra." Brolley blinked his eyes.

"You've offended visiting dignitaries!" Pathra rose from his seat, his face reddening with anger. "Your little flapping mouth has caused me no end of humiliation! And in order to placate the visitors, who, believe me, I want to have placated, I have no choice but to either order you to fight to the death, order you to grovel for mercy, or go back on my word as the Emperor and lose face before an entire nation!"

Even Nachia, who usually was the first to defend her little brother, looked at Pathra with wide eyes and silence.

"What would you have me do, Brolley? You called them a race of pigs in front of their king! What choice does he have? What choice do I have?"

"I will fight if you want me to." Brolley blinked his eyes fighting against tears that threatened to fall. Desh felt a small amount of pity for the boy, but it was very small. "I'll fight. Or I'll beg for mercy. Whatever you decide, my Lord."

He was getting it. He was beginning to truly understand the gravity of the situation.

Desh cleared his throat. All three looked his way. "I have done what I can. I've asked that Drask consider the politics involved here and speak directly to King Tuskandru before deciding anything." He held up a hand before anyone could speak – all three wanted to – and continued. "As near as I can tell, we're dealing with a people who solve most of their problems with the sword. They came here making good faith gestures, and they've been deeply offended." He looked at Brolley and the boy stood his ground but his lower lip trembled again. "Deeply. This might not end without bloodshed. To that end I have asked one of the mercenaries who went on the expedition to train you, Brolley. You have a two-day reprieve. During that time you're going to have to either learn to fight or prepare to die." He sighed and shook his head. "Or crawl on your hands and knees in the arena and beg for forgiveness for the insult you cast. It's exactly that simple. All we managed was to buy you time to decide."

Brolley shook his head. "No. My Emperor decides."

Nachia's eyes were dry, but her face spoke of wanting to shed tears.

Pathra stared at his younger cousin for a long moment. "Prepare for your fight. While you do that, I'll decide what I expect of you."

Without another word the Emperor left the room. Nachia stared after him and then looked at her younger brother. A moment later she left the room, too.

There was only the boy, and Desh Krohan, the advisor to the Empire. The sorcerer who could, according to many, perform miracles.

"Can't you do something, Desh?" The boy spoke softly.

"Possibly. If the Emperor demands it." He left a chill in his voice, expressing his disapproval for the situation.

"I've heard that you... that you can make me a better fighter?" The boy's eyes expressed his desperation.

"It's possible, but that sort of magic requires sacrifices."

"What sort of sacrifices?" Was that a glimmer of hope in the boy's eyes? Of course it was.

"Nothing comes for free, Brolley." He could see the boy practically reaching for his coin pouch. "No. Not that sort of cost. I mean the skills have to come from somewhere. I can't manufacture knowledge and years of practice. If I were to offer you that sort of skill, it has to come from another."

"So I could borrow someone else's talents?"

"No." Desh shook his head. "No. It doesn't work that way. I can't simply ask someone to loan me their knowledge and then give it back. It has to come from somewhere and it can't be given back when you're done with it."

"Can you do it? Can you make me a warrior?"

Desh stood up. "You're not understanding me. Someone would have to die for you to have their skill, their knowledge."

"But you could do it?" Ah, desperation. The boy was desperate. The boy wanted an easy way out of his predicament. Desh Krohan was disgusted.

"Could I? Yes." He looked down at the boy. "Will I? No." And then he left the room.

And wondered exactly how long he would have to wait before he was summoned by another member of the royal family, and which member it would be.

He did not have to wait for long.

He was not surprised by who, exactly, summoned him.

Merros Dulver looked at the palace and felt an odd thrill. He had never been past the gates, but as soon as he and the Sa'ba Taalor reached the edge of Tyrne they found an entourage of men in armor waiting to escort them the rest of the way. He felt every grain of sand and dust that stuck to him as he rode, and around him the people of the valley sat up straighter in their saddles, the great beasts below them eyeing the crowds lining the street with wariness.

And through the elation, exhaustion crept along the edges of his being. They'd ridden hard to get back, stopping only once for a few hours' rest. Now that the ride was over, even the thrill of entering the great palace was only small, hardly enough to keep him from wanting to sleep.

Desh Krohan was waiting for him as he slipped down the back of Saa'thaa. The wizard was impossible to miss. His robes shimmered and moved, and his face was lost in shadows darker than sin. All around him the Sa'ba Taalor looked at the sorcerer and eyed him with the same sort of wariness their mounts had displayed on the street. He was an unknown quality.

Tusk and Drask waited nearby and welcomed their brethren. And before Merros could say or do much of anything, the Emperor himself stood in the courtyard, his lean face smiling warmly. The smile did not reach his eyes, which looked worried. Very worried.

Merros had planned on sleep.

His plans fell apart very quickly.

FOURTEEN

Formalities were gotten out of the way quickly and after that Merros was called into consult with the leaders of his nation, people he had never thought to meet in his lifetime.

It was not a comfortable meeting.

"First, Captain Dulver, we need you to speak frankly. We need you to tell us all that you can about the Sa'ba Taalor." Merros stared at the Emperor and tried to figure out where to start. It must have shown on his face.

Desh Krohan sighed. "Let's go about this a bit differently. There's going to be a duel. It's not going to go well, unless we know how to handle it."

"A duel?" He looked at the man for a long moment. "Between who and who?"

"A member of the royal family offended Drask Silver Hand."

"I can't see that ending well at all."

"Yes, well, that would seem to be the general consensus." Pathra Krous mumbled the words.

"I... I'm sorry, your Highness, I truly am, but if a member of your family has challenged Drask Silver Hand–"

"Actually, Silver Hand challenged him."

"Why?"

"Well, my cousin was a bit–"

Desh Krohan spoke up. "Let us get to the point. Listen, Merros. May I call you Merros?"

"Of course."

"Merros. Let's put aside rank and everything else. We're going to speak frankly, as men. We need to make the best of a bad situation. No matter what happens, I don't see this going well, but we need to make the best of it. For that reason we're bringing you in and talking straight about this, no politics. No rank. You're a well-seasoned soldier and we need that. More importantly, you've spent more time with the Sa'ba Taalor than anyone else and they seem to think you're very important." He saw the look on Merros' face and quickly corrected himself. "I'm not saying you're not important, understand, but their gods apparently asked to see you. That puts you fairly high on their list right now, yes?"

"Yes, of course. That is, as you say."

"Excellent. So let's get this taken care of. Pathra's cousin is a spoiled brat. It's just that simple. He acted like a clown and he offended Drask and all of his people. And he did it in front of Tuskandru, who's one of their kings."

"Which king?"

"Excuse me?"

Merros looked at him and shrugged. "Which king? I'm not exactly sure how all of this breaks down, but there seem to be different rules for each of their gods and each of their kings. Near as I can figure from my discussions with the Sa'ba Taalor, each king follows the dictates of a god. So, that might help us to understand exactly how to react."

Desh Krohan looked at the Emperor and smiled. "You see, Pathra? Just like that, we've already learned something important. Something that might make this work out better." He looked back at Merros. "We have absolutely no idea which king. No, wait, that's not true. His full title is 'Tuskandru, Chosen of the Forge of Durhallem and Obsidian King.'"

"Well. I would have to ask one of the others."

"Are there any members of the group you think will give you an honest answer?"

"All of them. But I think the best one for this might be Swech. She's the one who led the expedition on your behalf. Well, for Drask. Also, I think we need to discuss that particular situation as soon as you feel comfortable with it."

"Soon."

"Good, because, honestly, I don't think this situation is quite resolved as yet."

"First, why don't we meet up with this friend of yours, Swech, and discuss matters?"

"She's going to expect acknowledgement of what she and the rest of her people did on your behalf."

Pathra Krous spoke up. "Did they settle the affair with the Guntha for King Marsfel?"

"They eliminated the Guntha."

"They convinced them to leave?" Krous looked at him, frowning. He was starting to get it.

"No, Highness. They killed them all."

"The Guntha? But I thought there was a small army."

"Near as I can figure there were over one thousand Guntha in the camp."

The Emperor stared at him, his mouth open, and his eyes unblinking.

Desh Krohan cleared his throat. "I'm sorry, did you say over a thousand?"

"According to King Marsfel there might have been as many as two thousand, but I feel that must have been an exaggeration. That said, yes, I believe it was over a thousand."

Krohan's voice rose. "Over a thousand soldiers?"

"Well, to be fair, I can't say with any certainty that they were soldiers. Only that there were guards, and that, according to Swech, they left no survivors."

"None?"

"None." Looking at their faces Merros had to bite his tongue. There was nothing at all funny about the situation, but seeing their reaction he felt laughter bubbling inside of him, a sort of frothing hilarity that he suspected came close to madness. He'd seen his share of madmen in his time and he couldn't help but wonder if any of the lunatics he'd met on the battlefield got that way as a result of seeing something deeply impossible take place before their eyes. His teeth chomped down harder and he felt a sharp pain and a taste of blood. Yes, that did it. That was just enough to stop him from starting to cackle.

"How many came back with you?"

"Ten. Ten came back with me."

"And how many left with you originally?" The Emperor was squinting. The math was hurting him.

Oh, damn, but the look on the man's face was making it hard not to laugh at the absurdity of the situation.

"That would be ten, Your Highness."

"Were they particularly large soldiers?" Desh Krohan's hooded face turned in his direction. "The Sa'ba Taalor, I mean?"

"Well, no. I believe four of them were women. And one of those was a girl. I think she just had her seventeenth birthday not long ago." Both stared at him in complete silence for so long that he felt compelled to add, "If it helps, I think they snuck into the camp when most of the Guntha were sleeping."

Desh Krohan lowered his head to the table. The hood covering his face nearly pushed against the polished surface and his entire body shook. It was only when the wizard's hand slapped the surface that he realized the man was laughing.

And really, that was all it took. Merros started laughing himself, laughing at the sheer absurdity of ten people executing a thousand, at the thought that the ten walked away from the killing with little more than scratches on their bodies, and at the thought that those ten were likely not even the finest soldiers that were along on the expedition to Fellein.

The wizard looked up, his face turning toward Pathra Krous, who was now staring at his advisor as if to check whether or not the man had lost his mind completely.

"So, was Marsfel happy with the results?" The Emperor's question seemed innocent enough, but thinking of the mercenaries and their fate only added to fuel to the fire.

Merros laughed so hard he fell out of his seat. The thought that his actions might well cost him his head if he wasn't careful couldn't stop the hysterical fit.

Fifteen minutes later, after all three of them had gone through their moments of laughter, the Emperor included, he brought Swech back to the room to discuss the matters that were going to most decidedly have to be handled soon.

Swech entered the room and bowed as Tusk had bowed the first time, her arms swept out, and every new wound and fresh scar showing.

Pathra Krous rose from his seat and returned the bow. "Captain Merros Dulver tells me that you and your associates have done me a great service. You have ended a potential problem with the Guntha. I am in your debt."

She bowed a second time, carefully considering her words. "There is no debt owed. What we did was merely a demonstration, as asked by Drask Silver Hand."

"Just the same you have done me a great service. If I can return the favor, you have but to ask and if it is within my power to grant your request I shall do so." She nodded her head in acknowledgment and sat where indicated. "Now I must ask a few questions if I may, Swech. We need to understand your people better, in order to avoid causing offense in a delicate matter."

Swech listened as the details were laid out and nodded her head a few times.

Finally, she asked a few questions and weighed the answers carefully.

"Who is the boy to you?" she asked the Emperor.

"He's my cousin. He is blood."

"Is his father alive?"

"Alas, no. Both his father and his mother died a few years ago, taken by fever and plague."

"He is an adult then? Or is he raised by another?"

"He is an adult now. He celebrated his birthday recently."

"He is aware that he caused insult with his words?" She spoke stiffly and it was clear to all three men that she considered the words insulting herself.

"Oh, yes. He has been made very aware of that, you may rest assured." Desh Krohan spoke. He sighed and waved a hand lightly. "Even now he is practicing his combat skills in an effort to make him understand exactly how grave his insult was."

"Does your culture permit a substitute? A…" She looked around for a moment and struggled to find the right word. Merros was taken again by how quickly she had learned the language. "A champion?"

Pathra Krous looked toward Desh Krohan. The wizard looked back. "I don't recall any rules dispelling the notion…"

Swech tapped the table. "Let me explain my people. Let me explain how they believe all matters should be handled. If I were to offend you, Desh Krohan, your recourse is simple. You attempt to punish me. If you succeed, you have made clear your stance on my actions."

"That's it?"

"Yes. That's it. You attempt to administer your punishment. I attempt to defend myself against your punishment."

"What if I steal from you?"

Swech stared him in the eyes. "Then I kill you."

"You have no courts? No judges who decide these things?"

"We do not need these things. If you wrong me, I take back what is mine. If you offend me, I take back my honor myself."

"Well," Merros cleared his throat. "The arena where this is to happen is a similar idea. The difference is it is in front of witnesses."

Swech held one hand up and tilted it side to side, imitating the movements of a snake. He knew the gesture likely had meaning to her people, but it meant nothing to him or the other men at the table as far as he could tell. "You say this as if it is unusual. If people are there to see a fight, they are there. If they are not there, then they are not there. This does not change the outcome of the fight."

"Yes, but Brolley apparently offended all of your people." Pathra was doing his best to explain the problem.

Swech stared at him. "This I know. I am offended by his words and I was not even there. But Drask Silver Hand has chosen to defend the honor of all of our people with his actions and we will respect that. If we did not, most of my people in Tyrne would have welcomed the chance to punish your cousin."

"So, regardless of how this ends, once Drask and Brolley have had their fight, the situation is resolved?"

"Yes." She spread her hands apart and then settled them on the table. "There is no longer a situation to resolve. Drask has taken the affair into his hands."

"If Brolley apologizes, what happens?"

"That depends on the dictates of the Daxar Taalor."

"Could you explain that, please?"

"There are seven Daxar Taalor. Seven gods of the forges. One for each mountain, yes?"

All three nodded their understanding.

"Each of us follows all of the gods through the course of our lives. Sometimes we follow different gods for different circumstances. That is our way." She was struggling again, but the men waited patiently. "I follow Wheklam. I follow Paedle. They are the gods I choose to follow. They are the gods who want me to follow them. That is the way of my life. Drask follows Ydramil, his king is Ganem. Ydramil gifted him with the silver hand that is a part of him. For that reason, he will always follow the dictates of Ydramil. But he also obeys the other Daxar Taalor. He merely chooses to favor Ydramil. Ydramil understands the concept of mercy. That is a good thing for your Brolley."

"What do you mean?" Merros frowned.

"Well, Tuskandru is the King of the Forge of Durhallem. Durhallem is also called 'The Wounder.' He is unforgiving. He does not accept mercy as an option. To offend Durhallem or his followers is to invite your death. Had your Brolley faced Tusk and made the comments that he made, Tusk would have killed him on the spot."

The three men looked at each other and ruminated on that.

Swech's voice grew lighter. "So you see, Drask did your cousin a favor. He was being aware of what you called a delicate situation. He has a chance to survive, depending on what he does."

"If he apologizes?"

"Drask will probably forgive him. And punish him."

"And if he fights?"

"Drask will probably kill him, but the offense ends with him."

"And if he fails to show?"

Swech stared at the Emperor and contemplated the question very carefully. "Then the offense continues. Should Brolley not show, he is marked as a coward. The next member of his bloodline would be allowed to stand in for him, and that would pay the debt of honor, but Brolley would always be marked as a coward."

Pathra Krous rose and walked over to Swech. He bowed before her one more time, a formal gesture, not a sign of obeisance and no one would have mistaken it for anything else. "Thank you for your time, Swech. You have enlightened us."

She rose and bowed again, obviously uncomfortable with the formality. A few minutes later Merros led her from the room and thanked her separately.

And then he moved back into the room.

Desk Krohan shook his head. "He apologizes, he loses face, and he lives. He fights, he loses his life. There's really no other way around that."

"He has a right to a champion. I could pay one of the finer swordsmen to be his champion."

Merros cleared his throat. "If I may?"

Both men looked at him and he made himself speak. It went against a simple tenet that he had lived with his entire life: do your job and avoid getting noticed too often. Still, the situation was delicate.

"Make your cousin face this."

"He's just a boy!" Pathra's voice was stressed, loud and worried.

"Yes. He is. He's just a boy. Take a chance on that fact. Accept that there's no special honor for Drask in schooling the boy. I don't believe he intends to kill your cousin. I think he intends to give him a lesson in manners."

"They're monsters on the battlefield, Merros! You said so yourself!"

"Your Majesty, if Drask Silver Hand wanted to go to extremes, he'd have killed me and he'd have killed Wollis March before we ever reached the Seven Forges. Both of us interfered with him, and Wollis, may the gods always watch over him, actually challenged the man. Instead of killing Wollis, he gave him a warning." He closed his eyes remembering the look on Wollis' face as the bullwhip snapped the spear from his hands. "Believe me, he could well have killed us both with ease."

"He's my cousin, Merros."

Merros thought hard for all of a second and finally nodded. "Then let him take this lesson. Let him learn that there is a price for lacking diplomacy. If he's to be a man and possibly a leader of men, you must do this, Majesty. You must."

Desh Krohan nodded under his hood. "Agreed."

The Emperor looked from one man to the other.

Merros played a card he would rather have avoided. "I stake my life on this, Emperor Pathra Krous. I stake my life on Drask Silver Hand doing the honorable thing here. I think he will mete out a punishment, but I do not believe he will kill your cousin."

Krous looked at him for a very long time. "So be it."

Merros let out a breath he hadn't been aware he was holding.

Andover Lashk watched as Wollis March schooled Brolley Krous. The area where the boy was training was the exact same spot where, ten minutes earlier, Andover had been practicing with his hammer. His muscles were shaking from the exertion and his hands ached. But today he had fewer scrapes on his face and less areas of his body were sporting new bruises.

Tega stood near him, looking on as Brolley's sword was knocked aside and sent skittering across the stone floor.

Wollis March shook his head. "Hold the damned thing like your life depends on it."

"I am!" Gods, the boy was already whining.

Wollis pointed toward Andover. "He's had less than a week of training with that new weapon of his. You've had years of training with a sword. Even a novice knows the sword does you no good if it's halfway across the field from where your hand is!" The older man limped over and grabbed the sword by the hilt. He hurled it toward the young man, who flinched but scrambled to catch it just the same.

"Why are you yelling at me?"

"I haven't begun to yell, boy!" The man came toward him and drew his sword. "You want to fight Drask Silver Hand? I saw that man kill a Pra-Moresh with one blow! And then he killed two more!" He swung his sword and the boy attempted to block and flinched as the sword he carried flew from his hands again. Rather than stopping, Wollis slapped the teenager in the arm with the flat of his sword and roared, "Pick it up, boy!"

On the verge of tears, Brolley ran to his sword, flinching as the instructor slapped him again and again.

When Andover looked away, trying to gather the nerve to speak to Tega, the girl was gone. In her place, another of the Sa'ba Taalor was standing. A younger woman, one he had not met yet. His disappointment must have shown on his face, because the girl chuckled. "I am not here to fight you. I am merely here to watch."

"Oh, it's all right. They have the field." He waved and the girl looked at his hands. He was wearing his gloves, but they didn't hide the spots where metal and flesh merged.

"You're the one blessed by Truska-Pren." She stepped closer and looked at his hands. He looked too, seeing them for the first time all day, really. He would have never expected that staring at his new limbs would lose its marvel but it had.

To the side, the boy had finally regained his sword and was swinging madly. Both the girl and Andover shook their heads. Wild swings were a waste of energy. Energy was a precious commodity in combat. Andover was just learning that, but it was a lesson he took to heart.

The girl's hands on his wrist caught his attention. Her fingers were strong and callused. "Do they hurt?"

"No. They did. Before Truska-Pren gave me the new ones my hands were in constant pain."

Her eyes regarded him levelly and she spoke softly. "May I see them?"

He shrugged and held his hands out. She peeled the gloves off and he watched her, stared at her eyes as she in turn stared at his artificial hands. They gleamed dully in the daylight, and he could see the rough skin where they fused to him. He could also see that the skin where the hands were bonded to him was changing color.

That was something new.

Andover leaned in closer himself, staring at the flesh that had taken on a grayish hue. And he looked at the exposed brow of the girl across from him and realized that her flesh was almost identical in color.

Her fingers traced along the band of coloration and she looked at him. Her eyes smiled behind the veil. "We are not so different a people, after all."

Part of him was horrified, but it was a small part. Miniscule, really. He looked at the discoloration and saw that it was not even. It rippled.

A small price to pay, surely, for having working hands.

In the small arena the Emperor's cousin was panting, red faced and on the verge of tears, but he had a death grip on his sword.

One step at a time.

The girl stepped back and nodded her head. "So. I am to instruct you on how to use your weapon."

"Excuse me?"

"I am to teach you." She shook her head. "Your hammer is not unlike my axe. I will instruct you."

"I thought I was finished for the day." He frowned.

"No. You are merely allowed to rest for a few moments. Drask Silver Hand says you are not ready to travel yet, and that you must be instructed."

"But the arena." He gestured toward where Wollis was commending his young charge, even as he struck the boy across the thigh.

"We can learn right here." She laughed at him and shook her head. "Why does everyone here think you can only fight in special places?"

The girl walked away from him and moved to a collection of different weapons. She found a long handled axe that was, in fact, fairly close in size and shape to his hammer. The head of the hammer was substantially heavier – a fact he was learning to live with despite the protests of his muscles – but close enough that he could see where she would be able to show him a thing or two.

She spun the long staff around her hips and tested the weight for a moment.

"Grab your weapon, Andover Lashk of the Iron Hands." She spoke in a harsher tone of voice.

He listened. Just in time to parry the blow she aimed for his skull. Unlike Wollis March, she didn't use the flat of the blade when she aimed for him. The good news for Andover was that he was a fast learner. The bad news was that Jost was an aggressive instructor.

"Have you thought over my request, Desh?" Nachia's voice was soft, barely a whisper. The wizard paused and tilted his head. Normally one or more of the Sisters would have been in his quarters, but they all had their own tasks to handle, tasks that he had asked them to take care of.

Now and then a man needs to be alone.

"I have. My answer is not changed, Nachia."

"Please. He's my little brother."

"I know that." He shook his head. Nachia stepped from the shadows of the heavy curtain closest to the door. She was dressed in the height of fashion and the silks fell in ways that accentuated her assets while showing nothing. She knew and understood the use of fashion to tantalize. Being a man, despite his many years on the planet, Desh took note.

"I don't want to see him dead." She stepped closer and looked into his eyes. Her gaze was direct. She was not attempting seduction. She'd tried that a few times in the past and found that the sorcerer had the good sense to say no to her advances. One did not stay advisor to the leaders of the Empire by having foolish reactions to the advances of youth.

"I have it on good authority that he'll be fine. He might have his pride bruised, but he certainly won't end up dead."

"Then why is he being trained so diligently?"

"Because he needs to take the situation he's in very seriously, my dear." He smiled, and took a step closer, taking her hands in his. "Your brother has led a very pampered life. I'd wager most of his instructors in combat have willingly let him win, merely to keep him happy over the years."

Nachia looked away, a flush of guilt coloring her cheeks.

"Yes, I rather thought so. It's fine to protect your brother, but he's of an age where he might be called to war. As a Krous he might well be called to lead an army someday. What happens if he can't understand the simplest strategies?"

"You could use your sorceries."

He turned on her, and shook his head. "I told you, I can grant your brother the skills of any man, but that man dies in the process. I'm not willing to do that."

"But you could." Her voice took on an edge. "If I become Empress and make that demand of you, you could do it."

"Anything is possible, Nachia. But there is always a cost. In this case a man's life. I do not take that consideration lightly."

"Neither do I, but–"

"No. I think you do. You are saying that the life of your brother, the dignity of your brother is worth more than another person's life. That's not the sort of decision that should be made and if it is made it must never be made without consideration of the sacrifices."

She stared at him and said nothing. She knew better. That was what this came down to. Still, there was a very real chance that she would rule the Empire someday.

"If I were to do this, who would you recommend I use? General Hradi is getting up in years, true, but he spent thirty years practicing with a sword almost every day of his life. Surely his skills would be formidable. Of course, that leaves us without a skilled commander to lead the armies should anything happen. Perhaps Captain Merros, who has so diligently served me of late. Surely his value as a mercenary is less than the value of your younger brother, who tried to start a war with his careless words." Desh shrugged his shoulders and then sighed. "Listen. Nachia. I will be there and I will be watching. I can assure you that your brother will not die. What he should do, what you know he should do, is apologize. It's not a sign of weakness to admit that you acted foolishly. I have certainly apologized many times in my life."

She turned away from him, offering silence as her answer.

"If there's nothing else then, Nachia, I grow tired. I've had a busy day of politics and ensuring that your brother lives through the next few days."

He out-waited her. She left two minutes later without speaking another word.

Desh made a note to locate and seal any hidden passages leading to his chambers. It didn't do to have the family feel they could come in unannounced whenever it struck their fancy.

Wollis stared at Merros over a mug of ale that was, to be sure, the finest he had ever tasted. He was feeling a pleasant warmth from the drink and his muscles ached from a hard day of instructing the pampered royal in the fine art of not dying too quickly.

"Did one of the Sa'ba Taalor strike you with a hammer while you were traveling?" He squinted a bit as he looked at Merros.

Merros looked back and rolled his eyes to the ceiling. "No."

"Have you been smoking in the Sin Dens?"

"What? No, of course not. I wouldn't and never have. You know that."

"Did a Plague Wind sneak from the Blasted Lands and give you a great fever when no one was looking? That no one noticed?"

"Now you're just being an ass."

"No, Merros. I'm trying to understand why you would wager your life on a man you don't know not killing a boy who, frankly, could use a good killing."

"You only say that because he busted your knuckles." Merros nodded his head at the damp cloth wrapped around Wollis' left hand.

"No, I blame myself for that one. I got cocky. Not so cocky that I have thrown away my life, granted, but still, careless enough."

"It seemed the thing to do at the moment."

"Have you written instructions for the placement of your possessions? I shouldn't mind at all having your share from the expeditions."

"You're plenty rich enough."

"One can never have too much gold."

"I have no intention of getting myself killed, Wollis."

"Have you even spoken to Drask about this?"

"Well, no. I didn't feel that was appropriate."

"You just wagered your life on his actions. It's very damned appropriate."

"And how does one bring up the subject without sounding like a whining babe left to fend for himself?" Merros reached for his own ale and took down a deep gulp.

"One doesn't. Just let the man know where you stand with this."

"I don't know if I can do that." Merros shook his head and looked around the tavern. There were several other tables that were occupied, but no one was paying them much mind.

"Did they really kill over a thousand...?" Wollis' voice trailed off in wonder.

"Oh. Oh yes." The other man shook his head.

Wollis mirrored the gesture. "Here's hoping we avoid a war."

Merros chuckled. "We'll avoid it."

"What makes you so sure?"

"No one wants a war."

Wollis stared past Merros' head and looked at the wall of the tavern. The place was well enough lit, the walls regularly cleaned, but lacking in decoration of any sort, they were rather uninteresting to stare at.

"I don't know if you're right about that."

"What do you mean?" Merros set down his now empty mug and gestured for the woman serving them to bring another. She nodded from across the room and vanished into the area where the kegs were kept.

"I mean have you noticed that there isn't a single person from among our new friends who doesn't have more weapons than a squadron of soldiers?"

"They do seem to have a strong affection for their knives and bows."

"No, Merros. They have a strong affection for everything. If it was just bows and knives I would think they liked hunting. Even if the Pra-Moresh is the animal they like to hunt, a lot of those weapons are not designed for going after dinner. They're designed for killing enemies in armed combat." He snorted.

"Hell, man, they have weapons that I've never seen before and I'm rather proficient at my trade."

"They make their own weapons. Maybe they just make whatever comes to their minds."

"Then they have damned scary minds. You saw that bloody cleaver Tusk used on the Pra-Moresh. I asked him about that. He made it just for situations when he runs across something that needs to be whittled down to a manageable size. Those are his words, not mine."

"Well, to be fair, he was dealing with a Pra-Moresh."

"Ever hear of a Mound Crawler?"

"No." Merros shook his head.

"No one else has, either. But they brought the skull of one for Emperor Krous. Tusk said something about it killing about half his village before he took it down." Wollis thought about the size of that skull and shivered. "That sort of nightmare might well feed on Pra-Moresh. Like a bear feeds on rabbits."

"Hardly a pleasant notion."

"It isn't meant to be a pleasant notion. It's meant to make a point. We don't begin to know these people, Merros. We don't have a hope of knowing them as more than deadly soldiers. You should not risk your life on one of them doing what you would do in the same situation."

"We have people who hunt down whales. That doesn't make them the greatest warriors alive. Hell, most of the whalers I've met have never held a sword."

"Tusk has held a sword. Hell, he carries two of them regularly and has a few more on the saddle of his ride."

"Well, yes, alright. I can see your point on this."

"And Drask?" Wollis waved his arms around the room. "You saw him. I saw him. Big doesn't begin to cover it. And armed? He makes his own bloody hunting bows and those little spears he uses to hook his latest kills."

"I get it, Wollis. I have possibly made a horrid mistake."

"Did you notice that Tusk's biceps are actually wider than my thighs? I did. I looked at his arms and then I did a little measuring. The man could probably bend a sword around his arm. Hell, he probably pounded that bloody great helmet of his with his bare hands."

"Now you're just being preposterous."

"Only a little."

Merros nodded his thanks as the server brought his ale. He smiled at her before she left and then looked back at Wollis. Wollis knew from the look on his face, the look that lacked that long lingering and silent desire he'd seen in the man's face for months, that Merros had recently had sex. Under some circumstances he might well have made a crass comment about it, but it was neither the time nor the place for that. Instead he merely acknowledged that something had happened on the road and wondered if it had happened with one of the gray-skinned women from the valley.

Not that it mattered.

Merros held up his ale in salute. "Here's hoping our new friends don't get me killed."

"That I will drink to."

The two men settled back in their seats and into a comfortable silence. After a few moments Wollis looked over at his captain again. "Over a thousand? Honestly?"

"I swear it on my father's name."

Wollis stared at the distant wall again and repressed a shiver.

The sun would be up soon enough. Drask had spent a day in silent contemplation of what was to happen and then a night in conversation with Tuskandru.

There were contemplations to make. His actions were justified, yes, but not necessarily the best for the Sa'ba Taalor.

Time would tell.

Drask Silver Hand spent the next day practicing. He used each of his weapons as he maneuvered around the courtyard that the Fellein had set aside for them, often working alone and occasionally sparring against another of his people.

He saved the final fight for Tusk, who looked as restless as he felt. They grappled, no weapons wanted or needed. Neither of them tended to much like the idea of facing the other with a blade. They had done so before and possibly would again, but it never ended without them both bloodied. Tusk beat him. It was not a contest, really.

Tusk looked at him when they were done and shook his head. "You are distracted."

"Yes." He nodded.

"Don't worry. I am sure the boy will show you mercy." Tusk's voice was teasing.

"I suspect I will survive the encounter."

"They are a strange people, Drask." Tuskandru's voice was low.

"Mmm. I have not yet decided if they are soft."

"They are soft. But I am not sure if they are weak."

Drask contemplated the meaning of the words and nodded his agreement. The people they spoke of ruled most of the world, if their maps were accurate. He had looked at several of the maps and Desh Krohan had offered him a set of maps showing the Empire. He took them, of course. He was not a fool.

"What will you do?" Tusk meant regarding the duel, or course.

Drask looked at the man for a long moment. Were they friends? He wasn't sure. Friendship was not an easy thing for any of the Sa'ba Taalor. The Daxar Taalor did not consider friendship when they gave their orders and none of his people disobeyed their gods.

Drask grinned. "I will do as the gods demand."

Tusk nodded his head. "Probably that is wisest."

The monarch rose from his seated position in the courtyard and stretched. "We will leave soon. That's for the best."

"As you say." Drask lowered his head in acknowledgement and then stood as well. There were mere hours left before the fight and he wished to be presentable for the occasion.

Tusk left without another word. None were necessary.

The arena was the same one where Andover Lashk had fought for his justice. He looked at the ground and saw that the blood had been washed away. That was just as well, though he felt no remorse for what he had done to either Purb or Menock. They had deserved their fates.

Around him the seats were filled. That was the biggest difference. There had been plenty of empty spaces when he sought his justice. There were people standing behind the last row of seats now, doing their best to get a good view of the small battlefield.

Emperor Pathra Krous sat in a reserved box along with his cousin. Andover stared several times. The woman was beautiful. For the first time since meeting the man Andover saw guards positioned around him. There were four men in armor that glittered with fresh cleanings, all of them sporting spears and with swords strapped to their hips. Their helmets bore crests of black and red feathers and they looked intimidating.

Across from the Emperor and his retinue, the Sa'ba Taalor sat, none of them wearing armor or carrying weapons. They did not appear the least bit intimidated, but it was hard to say as they continued to wear their veils.

Tega sat with Desh Krohan, her face as pretty as ever, but she looked away from Andover and seemed determined not to notice him. He set his face as neutrally as he could manage and did his best to return the favor. The Sisters took seats near the sorcerer as well, and though everyone seemed impatient, no one seemed in a hurry to commence the fight.

Well, *slaughter* would be a better word. Brolley Krous was standing in one corner, his hands locked behind his back in an effort to hide the fact that he was terrified. His skin was pale, his brow covered with sweat, his eyes were wide and seemed incapable of looking at any one thing for more than a second. Except when he focused on Drask Silver Hand across from him.

Brolley was wearing a formal dueling outfit. Snug leather pants, boots and a dark leather vest over a long sleeved shirt.

Drask was wearing leather pants and boots. And his veil. Otherwise he was bare. His upper body showed the numerous battles he'd been in, scars overlaid by fresher scars, many small, some of significant size to show a serious past trauma. Unlike other times, he had taken off his gloves and the silver hand flexed as he moved, pacing slowly back and forth, looking not at his opponent, but at the other members of his people. From time to time one of them spoke to him and he answered, but the incidental sounds of the crowd kept Andover from hearing the words.

The heavyset arbiter that had judged the trial for Andover was present again. He stood at the edge of the round arena and looked around. His pinched features spoke more of how good an impression he wished to make in front of the nobles and others than of how important the battle itself was to him. His lips moved as he practiced his lines.

Andover shook his head. Not that he suspected he'd be less worried in the same situation. He just felt more concern for Brolley Krous than for much of anything else. He'd seen the man trying to fight. It had not gone well.

Wollis March walked to the circle, nodding as he passed Drask. Drask nodded in return as Wollis walked over to his student and patted his shoulder.

Tuskandru sat with his people, leaning forward in his seat, his elbows rested on his knees as he studied the young man in the arena and the man offering last-minute advice. Andover wondered if the king was as curious as he was to know exactly what was said.

Finally, the portly arbiter waved his arms and the people around them began to collect themselves and grow quieter. Just as he was about to make his announcements, Drask walked forward and called out clearly, "No. You are not needed here. He knows what he did. He knows why I have called for a challenge."

"But–" The arbiter started to speak and Drask cut him off.

"No. My King and your Emperor are here. They know why this battle takes place. They do not need a judge or an announcer. Leave before you offend me as well."

The arbiter looked toward Pathra Krous, who in turn shrugged his shoulders and raised his hands. The arbiter stepped back, looking very much like a child deprived of his after-meal treats.

Drask turned to the man he'd challenged. "Brolley Krous! You have called my people swine who bray like broken mules. You have called me both a savage and a pig. You have offended me, my people, my kings. What say you to these charges?" He gestured to the weapons lined along the stone wall behind the boy. "Answer with words or weapon, but answer me now."

Brolley looked at Drask for a moment and stepped forward. He licked his trembling lips and bowed from the waist. Holding his hands out to his sides. "I have done you an injustice, Drask Silver Hand. I have offended you a… and your people and, and your kings. I regret my foolish words and place myself before you to face your judgment." The words were stuttered, but spoken with enough volume for all to hear.

Drask stepped forward and grabbed Brolley by his shoulder, not unkindly, and made him stand. When he spoke it was for the boy alone, but Andover was close enough to hear. "Ask me how I lost my hand."

The boy looked around, uncertain how to respond. And finally nodded. "H… How did you lose your hand?"

"I insulted a man's daughter. He cut my hand off to remind me to watch my tongue." Drask stared hard. "When I got back up, I cut his throat for his troubles."

Brolley stared at him with eyes that were even wider than before.

"This one time, we will call this a lesson learned. Is that acceptable, Brolley Krous?"

Brolley nodded very, very vigorously.

"Should you open your mouth to insult me or mine again, should I even think you have considered the notion, I will take more than your hand. I will carve you apart very slowly and dye my boots with your blood."

Drask patted the boy on the shoulder hard enough to stagger him and walked away from him. He stopped exactly long enough to bow formally to the Emperor and his retinue before leaving the arena.

Brolley Krous stared after him, shaken to his core. Andover doubted it was a lesson he would forget anytime soon.

FIFTEEN

Lanaie of Roathes dropped to one knee before the Emperor, more in keeping with the ways of her people than the current fashions of the Empire, but still an acceptable showing of loyalty.

"My Emperor, may I speak on behalf of my father?"

"Yes, of course, child." Pathra smiled and the girl rose. Desh looked on, hidden behind his hood. They had spoken briefly of exactly how well Drask had handled the situation with young Brolley. He'd have been in his rights to beat the boy or even to kill him if the boy had decided to attack. Instead he had offered a warning against further insults and accepted the boy's apology. Even Nachia was pleased, and that was a challenge at the best of times.

"King Marsfel of Roathes wishes to thank you for the assistance you offered, Majesty."

Pathra Krous smiled. He and Desh had spoken of this very matter. "I merely offered witnesses to assess the situation. Any actions taken were done so free of my command."

That got her. She was looking puzzled. "But did you not send the Sa'ba Taalor to aid my father?"

"You were here, Lanaie. Drask Silver Hand made the offer to assist your father as a demonstration. You agreed to it."

Sometimes it was good to have ears everywhere. Marsfel had indeed been grateful for the assistance, but instead of sending a note of thanks he'd attempted to take the visitors into captivity. His reasoning, according to all Desh could learn, was to have someone to blame for the deaths of over a thousand soldiers on his beachfront. It seemed there was some issue as to whether or not the Guntha had been invited to the area by the king in an effort to gain additional funds for handling the military in his area.

Pathra had been amused. Desh was a bit more worried. Either way, if the Guntha decided to take offense, it might well come down to a war.

"I thought they were sent on your behalf, Majesty."

"No. They were sent as a demonstration of what ten Sa'ba Taalor could do. They were sent by Drask as assistance to your father. If your father would like to thank anyone, he should thank Drask Silver Hand, and perhaps King Tuskandru, the dignitaries who were gracious enough to offer your father assistance in his hour of need."

He held up his hand and Desh moved forward handing him a small sheaf of papers. Pathra gave them a cursory glance, signed his name at the bottom of each page, and then sealed the entire affair with a wax mark. After waiting for a moment, while fanning the seal, he offered the bundle to Lanaie. "These papers offer the formal explanation to your father. I am glad that the matter has been resolved to his satisfaction."

"But, sire, the Guntha are very angry."

"As they should be. Over a thousand invading soldiers were killed on your father's behest. I suspect they are very angry indeed, but now they must surely know better than to offend your father with foolish attempts at invasion."

"Can you not offer assistance at this time, Pathra Krous?"

"If there were a need, of course, but the invading forces have been repelled. Your father's right to rule has been made extremely clear to the invaders and he has time to redistribute his forces before any more attacks can be considered, surely."

The girl was lovely, and her brow was troubled. She considered the Emperor's words carefully and then bowed before leaving his presence.

"That went better than I expected." Pathra spoke softly to Desh. There was no one else in the room, but one could never be too careful.

"All in all, this week has gone remarkably well."

"I suspect you are to blame for most of that, Desh."

The sorcerer shook his head. "I do what I can. Nothing more."

"I understand you might have let a bit of information fall to Drask's hands regarding the life offered on his behalf."

"Nonsense. I merely let Tataya know that the good captain had placed a small wager on the decency of Silver Hand."

"Mmm. Well, at any rate, I suspect I owe you thanks."

"What you should consider, Pathra, is why the offer by the good captain would make any difference at all to the Sa'ba Taalor."

"What do you mean?"

"Why is he important to them? What is so very special about Merros Dulver that he could change their minds about anything at all? Why did they seek him out in the Blasted Lands? Why did one of their kings meet with him and another come back with him as an escort?"

"You ask too damned many questions." Pathra's brow knitted in concentration.

"I ask the questions you choose to ignore."

"Precisely my point."

"That's why I'm your advisor."

"You came with the crown. Don't flatter yourself."

"Have you stricken that damned law yet?"

"Oh yes! No more duels to answer insults. No more duels to handle charges of assault. No more duels."

"Good. Excellent. Now if you can change the rules regarding nephews of the Emperor drinking to excess at formal affairs…"

"The boy learned his lesson. He's still dealing with multiple bruises from the beating Wollis March gave him."

"You should promote that man. Him and Dulver both."

"They're no longer with the military."

"You're the damned Emperor. Pull them back into service and then promote them."

"I wish I thought you were joking."

Desh looked around the empty throne room. The Sa'ba Taalor would be leaving soon. They had plans to head for their distant homelands. The great skull from the thing called a Mound Crawler gleamed in the western corner of the room. Pathra was smitten with the thing and looked at it almost constantly. It fed his desire to travel. "I don't joke about that sort of thing. It comes back to the fact that Dulver is respected by the valley folk for whatever reason. And the fact that March just spent two days showing your upstart nephew how easily he could be bested in combat. A much needed lesson in humility, I might add."

Pathra Krous rose from his throne and stretched his back. He hated the throne. Not being the Emperor, but the throne itself. No matter how he sat or what sort of cushions he used, he always rose with a sore back. That was one of the finer and subtler magicks Desh had ever employed. No one sat there without feeling a bit of the weight of their authority. He felt it left the crown-bearers properly humbled. He had no idea if that was an accurate feeling or not, but he wasn't about to go and change a spell that had worked for the last four hundred years. "What else is on your mind?"

"That's it, really. I think if they have brought us allies they should be rewarded. If they have earned the attention of potential enemies – and I'm not saying they have, but we never know, do we – then we should make sure they are in positions to keep the attention of said enemies."

"Write up the papers. I'll sign them." Pathra looked askance at him and moved over to the skull again. His fingers touched the gold-plated surface, skimmed over rough gems of differing values. Even without adornment, the value of the skull to the academics in Canhoon would surely have been enough to feed the army for a few months. The Sa'ba Taalor had offered a phenomenal amount as their way of saying hello. "But Desh? Make sure that's what the men want, please. I have no desire to reward anyone with consignment into the military."

"I'll make sure, Pathra." He watched the Emperor's hand play around the eye socket of the great skull and then move down to touch a tooth larger than the blade of most swords. "I've asked that artist you're so fond of, the one who handled your portrait, to render images of the Mound Crawler based on notes from Tuskandru. The work should be done soon. Tusk was very generous with the details."

Pathra's face lit up in a broad smile. "I can't wait to see it."

Sadly, that would never happen. The Emperor of the Fellein Empire would be dead before the work was completed.

Sometimes the world moves smoothly. Other times the world trembles.

SIXTEEN

The morning after Drask Silver Hand spared a young man his life, he and several other members of the Sa'ba Taalor stood on the Western Field, a large area not surprisingly to the west of the Emperor's Palace, and watched an impressive gathering of soldiers going through exercises. They watched avidly, seldom speaking, as over a hundred soldiers went through basic maneuvers with sword, shield and bow. The men were dressed in standard uniforms, not wearing armor, and all of them were on their very best behavior when they realized they had unexpected observers.

There were none among the soldiers who failed to recognize the travelers, and though none of the observers had said a word, rumors had already begun to circulate about what had happened to the Guntha in Roathes.

After noticing that several of his people were spending as much time looking at the people watching them as they were actually practicing, the sergeant in charge of the maneuvers walked over to the group, feeling remarkably self-conscious.

The man, Morton Darnaven, was a long-timer, having spent over fifteen years in the military and a good portion of that along the borders handling skirmishes before being recently brought in to train some of the newer recruits. There was a real chance that he might have been absolutely pissy about the entire situation, but he recognized Wollis March and spoke to him instead of getting into an argument with the visitors.

Wollis was there because he had been asked, again, by one of the Sisters. He was beginning to think Pella liked using him as a buffering agent between civilians and the Sa'ba Taalor. He was not wrong in his assumptions. That did not make him the least bit happier about the situation.

On the other hand, the wizard was still paying him handsomely, and he definitely liked making money.

Wollis and Morton spoke the same language; both were grunts, had seen their share of combat and understood that now and then you just plain had to follow orders. Wollis was also smart enough to introduce him to Tuskandru, who was watching the entire operation with crossed arms and the air of a man who was not the least bit in a hurry to go anywhere.

Morton took Tusk's measure with one glance. Tusk did the same back. Five minutes after that, Morton had invited the strangers out on the field to practice with the troops if they were so inclined. Starving children offered the finest meals could not have responded with more enthusiasm.

The Sa'ba Taalor were among the soldiers in short order, except for Drask and Tusk, who walked with Morton and Wollis for a while.

"Do your people have a formal military?" Morton was looking at the king, craning his head just a bit to meet the man's eyes.

Tuskandru shook his head. "No. We don't have armies."

"How do you defend yourselves from enemies?"

Tusk grinned under his veil, the crow's feet around his eyes immediately becoming laugh lines. "We are isolated. Mostly we don't have friends or enemies outside of the valley."

Wollis explained exactly where the visitors were from, and both of the strangers were amused by the reaction. Somewhere along the way the rumors had started that the strangers were actually from the far south, well beyond where the Guntha lived on their islands, and where Roathes ended and Brellar began. No one had ever been that far south. It was one thing to know that there was a place called Brellar and another entirely to have been there. The people were said to have strange skin and to cover themselves with scars. The confusion was understandable.

Drask shook his head when the mistake was clarified. "So the people in Brellar scar themselves on purpose?"

Morton nodded. "They are said to tell stories with the scars. That each one has a meaning."

Drask laughed. "Ours do too."

"How so?"

He ran his gloved finger across a thick scar on the left side of his chest. "Here I survived my first encounter with the Pra-Moresh." He stroked a deep indentation on the ribcage on the same side. "This is where Tenna hit me with a spear."

"What did you to this man, Tenna, that made him try to kill you?"

Tusk laughed at that and slapped Drask hard enough on the back to earn him a withering stare. When he was properly balanced again, Drask responded, "Tenna is a woman. We had a disagreement about whether or not she was going to be with me as a life mate."

Wollis stared at him for a long moment before he started laughing. Morton took a while longer. "Wait. Are you saying she tried to kill you because you wouldn't move in with her?"

"To be fair, she was my first. I was the one trying to make something more serious of the relationship." Wollis laughed so hard he couldn't stand for several moments. Whatever, exactly, Tusk said in response was in his home tongue and neither of the local men had the vaguest clue, but Drask roared a challenge and rather than fight him, the king merely laughed harder.

When they had finally calmed down, Morton continued his questions. "So, no one in your valley is in an army?"

Tusk contemplated that before answering. "We have seven kings. I am a king. If I tell my people it is time to fight, I expect them to take up arms for me."

"Has anyone ever said no?"

"No."

"No one?"

"Why would they?"

"Well, I think if I went down the streets outside of this palace and told people to take up swords and prepare to fight, most of them would tell me to sit on the tip of my sword." Morton scratched the back of his neck as he spoke, and shrugged.

"If the people of Roathes came today with swords and spears and attacked the palace, the people outside of the palace would not fight?"

"Well, to be sure a few would, I suppose, but most would expect the army to do the fighting for them."

Tusk shook his head. "How many soldiers are in this army of yours?"

Wollis coughed into his hand. "I don't really know. Thousands and thousands, I mean if you add all the soldiers from the different kingdoms of the Empire together, of course."

"How many soldiers do you have here, in Tyrne?"

"Well, there's the City Guard, the Imperial Guard, and I think close to a thousand if you added in the reserve soldiers."

"Reserve soldiers?"

"Aye. Citizens who are trained with sword and shield and can be called on to support the Guard."

Tusk nodded. "I suppose that is what we have instead of an army. We have many reserve soldiers."

"You would expect a lot of your people to come to arms if you called?"

Tusk shook his head and stared hard at Wollis as he answered. "No, Wollis March. I would expect *all* of my people to come to arms if I called."

"All of them?" Wollis shook his head. "The women, the children?"

Tusk gestured to the field where the Sa'ba Taalor were currently testing their archery skills against a good number of the soldiers of the Guard. The locals used crossbows. The visitors used mostly long bows though a few seemed content to merely try their luck with the weapons that the soldiers showed them how to use. Crossbows seemed a fairly novel idea to the lot of them.

Tusk said, "There you see the women and men of my people. Some from my kingdom and some from others."

"All of your people know how to use weapons?" Morton sounded perplexed.

Tusk looked long and hard at Morton and sounded just as puzzled when he responded. "Don't all of yours?"

From that moment on, Morton paid much closer attention to the people working alongside his soldiers during his practices that day.

Andover looked at his belongings and sighed. There really weren't that many of them, aside from his clothes, which were really quite nice, he supposed.

It was almost time to go. In the morning they would be heading out and in the meantime he was packing his belongings into proper bundles. There were wagons, of course, two of them with supplies, and those supplies would include his possessions and the gifts that were being offered to the Sa'ba Taalor by the Emperor.

He almost went to visit his parents. He almost went to tell them that he would be going away, would be headed to a foreign land to serve as ambassador for the Empire, but in the end he decided against it. He hadn't told them when his hands were ruined, hadn't told them when he made his apprenticeship, hadn't spoken to them since they had kicked him out from their home and told him never to come back. Did he miss them? Of course, but they had made their point clearly enough, hadn't they?

Servants had been sent in to pack his belongings. He'd sent them on their way. He could pack all by himself and he had done so before. Also, Tuskandru was a king and he packed his own things and took care of his own animal. He would probably frown on anyone who couldn't manage that sort of stuff by himself.

The bundles were deceptively heavy, so he made two trips down to the wagons and packed away everything that needed to be packed.

And as he was feeling the butterflies gathering together in his stomach to swarm again, he saw Tega heading toward the wagons.

She faltered when she saw him, but managed to force a quick smile.

"I did not expect to see you, Andover."

"I just wanted to finish packing my things. What brings you down here? Did Desh Krohan ask you to check over the arrangements?"

"No. Not exactly." She looked down at the ground, once again carefully avoiding looking at him. "I am to make the journey to Taalor on his behalf."

"What? When was that decided?" His voice cracked and he felt himself blush the slightest amount. He sounded like he was excited by the prospect of traveling with her and that wasn't what he wanted. He was excited, of course, but he didn't want to be and he didn't want her to know it, either. Being near her was a wonderful drug, but it was like the wine his uncle Brann consumed. It was deceptive. It felt so good you didn't know it was doing you harm. Being around Tega was distracting and he thought he'd need his wits when dealing with the Sa'ba Taalor.

Tega looked at him for a moment and looked away again. "It was not my choice. Desh and the Emperor decided for me." Her lips pressed into a thin line. "I'll try not to be in your way." She quickly shoved her belongings into the wagon and turned away.

"Tega. I didn't mean that the way it sounded. It's just, the Blasted Lands are dangerous." As if the explanation was any less foolish than his initial reaction.

She waved off his explanation as easily as he might wave aside a persistent insect, and headed away from him.

Andover did not follow her. He wanted to, but what would he possibly say?

It was annoying, really: he could fight two men in combat, beat them both to pulps, receive wounds in the process and keep fighting, but the idea of talking to a woman almost a head shorter than him was enough to make him quake inside.

He continued packing away his belongings, unsettled by the fact that Tega coming along on the trip was putting him in better spirits and simultaneously making him miserable.

"You want to reinstate my commission in the Imperial Army?" Merros stared at the wizard. For a change of pace the man's hood was down and he could see the rather unremarkable face, which normally hid in a darkness that seemed more than mere shadows. The eyes that looked at him did so with a certain amusement.

"That's correct. With a promotion, of course."

"By the gods, man, why would you want to do a thing like that?"

"Well, Emperor Krous would like to thank you for all of your loyal service." He could smell the lie coming off of the man.

"Mmm. Hmm. Perhaps you might try telling me the actual reason?"

Desh Krohan sighed. "Fine. You have more experience with the Sa'ba Taalor than anyone else."

"By a fortnight. It's hardly like I've studied them for years."

"No, but you have studied them." The wizard leaned in closer and pinned him with a stare. Unremarkable? Hardly. The man just did a very good job of hiding his personality behind a veil of average. "You can deny that if you'd like, Merros, but I know it. I can see it on your face when you look around any place where you are standing, that you see everything. It's an excellent trait and one that few people have."

"There are plenty who do. Most any career soldier."

"Not true. Most career soldiers merely manage to get through their routines without consideration for what goes on around them. If they did otherwise they'd demand substantially more pay for what they face."

Merros shook his head in response. "Look, I'm really very flattered, but you've just paid me enough money to let me retire in comfort. Why would I want to go back to work?"

"Because you aren't designed to sit on your backside and relax, not any more than I am."

"I would hardly compare what I do with what you do."

"Why's that?"

"You're a sorcerer! You're advisor to the Emperor."

"You'd be advisor to me."

"No, I'd be a captain. You'd have me telling troops what to do and planning out budgets and doing all of the things I've so carefully avoided since I retired."

"Not a captain. A major. And really? Didn't you have to budget out that entire expedition before you hired men to go with you?"

"Not really, no. You offered an obscene amount of money."

"Which I then doubled when you had to do additional work."

"Which is why I no longer feel much of a need to work as a soldier any more. We've just discussed that very fact."

"You're really very good at this negotiation business, aren't you?" The wizard stared at him for a long moment. "Very well then. Colonel. And all of the requisite increases in salary."

"I've just explained that I don't need the money. I don't want…" He blinked. "Did you just say 'colonel?'"

"I might be able to arrange for general as a rank, but really, I think that's a bit excessive."

"Now you're just playing with me." Merros crossed his arms. "I don't really much appreciate being toyed with. I know you've been very generous as an employer, but there's no reason to tease a man."

Krohan leaned in closer and smiled a thin, cold smile, "I can arrange general. For that matter I can also arrange a royal title. I have that sort of clout you know. I have friends in very high places."

"I don't really think you need friends in high places. That is to say I'm fairly certain you're doing just fine in that arena by yourself."

"True, but I hate to brag." That one earned him an arch expression from the retired military man. "Look, I want you nearby and in a position where you can do some good. That means around here, and with enough rank to make waves if I need you to."

"You could use anyone at all for that."

"I already know you and what you're capable of handling."

"I'll consider the notion very carefully." Merros leaned back in his seat and stared hard at the sorcerer.

"What more can I ask?" The smile said it all, really. The smile on the man's face said he knew Merros would eventually agree, if only to stop his life from standing too still. Some people simply aren't meant to have stationary lives and Merros couldn't very well abide the notion of settling down.

He hated that the man was right.

There was one last meal for the visitors on the night before they left. The great banquet hall was opened and well over four hundred people were in attendance, many of them officials within the government, many others merely people of influence who wished to see the strangers before they were on their way. The latter group was wide-eyed with excitement, and smart enough, to the last, to know better than to cause troubles.

Noticeably absent was the younger brother of Nachia Krous. It would likely be a while before he was invited to any official encounters. That was also to ensure that there would be no troubles started. Most of the people at the feast were there to enjoy the food and see the strangers before they left to go back into the most inhospitable place anyone could imagine.

That is not always the case with visiting dignitaries and family members.

The Sa'ba Taalor had prepared as best they could for their long trip back. They'd been offered extra supplies, which they accepted, and even a military escort, which they politely declined, and come the sunrise the following day they would be heading back into the Blasted Lands and the valley that nestled in the heart of the Seven Forges.

Pathra Krous made clear that he would do his best to visit them sometime soon, circumstances permitting.

Nachia Krous stared at her cousin with an expression of tolerant indulgence, and then promptly told her assistant to plan to stay in town for a while. More often than not she'd have already headed to the family palace in Canhoon, but if her cousin was feeling the need to explore, she might well be asked to stand in for him.

Three times in the past she'd changed her plans to accommodate the Emperor's whims. Three times she had wasted her efforts. She did not mind in the least. Her life was relatively placid in comparison and the change of pace was hardly a bad thing in her eyes.

Pathra was in his element. He seemed fully a decade younger as a result of it, too. His face was constantly smiling and his wit was sharp, but pleasant. He could be cutting with his words when it suited him, but at the moment he was, instead, a perfect host, even to that little wench from the south, Lanaie.

Nachia did not like Princess Lanaie and had, for Pathra's sake, held her opinion in, but she was glad to see the young girl preparing to go back to her father in Roathes. As an added bonus, the girl seemed positively puzzled by everything around her and the expression on her face was quizzical enough to make her cousin stop looking at the girl like she was a prize flower reading for plucking. That, or the hairdresser had finally slipped into his bedchambers and satisfied him. Either way, the enchantment the princess had been casting seemed greatly weakened.

Desh Krohan looked at her with that damnable smirk of his in place, the one that said he knew exactly what she was thinking and that she should likely be ashamed of herself. Part of her remained convinced that the man was a charlatan, but not enough of her to ever test that theory. Really, it was rather like dealing with the gods as far as she was concerned: Likely they did not exist, but she said her prayers and offered her tithings, just in case. The difference was, at the very least she knew Desh Krohan had substance and enough money hidden away to buy most small kingdoms.

Speaking of which, the princess came and settled next to her as the desserts were passed around. There were several choices of exotic fruits – mostly what the Sa'ba Taalor seemed interested in trying – and easily a dozen different forms of cake and pastry. Nachia plucked a round pink pastry from a tray and sampled it with small bites. It was as delicious as it looked.

Lanaie looked at her and gnawed on her lower lip. Like as not Pathra would have found the gesture intoxicating, but Nachia just acknowledged that the girl was too young to know better.

"May I bring to you a delicate matter, Nachia Krous?"

"Of course," she smiled. It was her duty to her cousin and to the Empire to behave herself. Unlike her little brother, she performed her duties faithfully.

Lanaie looked around carefully and leaned in close enough to have have kissed the heir apparent's cheek. "There have been… untruths between my father and the Emperor."

Oh and didn't that sound appropriately juicy? She kept her face carefully neutral and nodded. "Tell me."

"My father has claimed that the Guntha came to him and said that their lands were sinking."

"Yes, I'm familiar with the stories." She had to be familiar with the stories. As with her cousin she had been raised to understand the machinations of the Empire.

"There are other stories, tales that have not been told because, well, because my father sought financial assistance and to handle the rest himself."

And wasn't that often the case? That was why so many requests for assistance were investigated before any resources were put at risk. "What tales, Lanaie?"

The girl actually leaned in closer. Pathra would have been beside himself as the girl's lips brushed her ear lobe lightly. Knowing Pathra, he'd have been delighted just to watch. He was a bit of pervert, truth be told, but as the Emperor he was also wise enough to be discrete about his unusual habits and tastes. Besides, in comparison to a few other members of the courts her cousin was practically an innocent. He might like watching, but he would never instigate.

"There are stories that the Guntha came seeking help against a fleet of ships, raiders who come from time to time and slaughter anyone who gets in their way."

"A fleet of ships?" Nachia had to close her eyes for a moment and orient on a mental map of the world. To the south was Roathes, and beyond that the waters of the vast Corinta Ocean and the islands of the Guntha. In the waters to the west of the Guntha? No one could say for certain, because the Guntha had always been a bit on the aggressive side and tended to destroy anything that came too close to their lands.

Corinta to the south, to be sure, but to the north? She had to think for a moment. To the north would be land, yes, but the only land north of the Guntha would be the Blasted Lands and the great frozen wasteland was not exactly an area that had been carefully examined.

"The ships, my lady, are supposedly vast ships, warships of a size not seen anywhere else. They are said to be nearly indestructible."

"The Guntha make these claims?"

"Yes, my lady."

Pathra was laughing not a dozen feet away. Something that one of the visitors had said had him first chuckling with delight and then actually laughing out loud. The sounds were welcome and unexpected.

"You say that the islands aren't sinking? That they've been under attack for all of these years and your father has kept these alleged invasions as his secret?" Pathra was laughing. That would change as soon as he heard that accusation.

"Yes, my lady." The girl nodded her head and looked down at the ground below her feet. "It was wrong, of course, but the claims the Guntha made were preposterous."

"What sort of claims?"

"The great ships, of course. I mean, of course they could be true stories but they always said the invaders came from the north, and there is nothing to the north but the Blasted Lands." The girl looked around and then once more leaned closer still. "The claim that my father refused to believe was simple, however."

"Yes?"

"The Guntha said the invaders had gray skin. Skin like slate. Skin like ashes. And eyes that glowed in the darkness." She moistened her lips. "And the faces of demons."

Nachia listened to the words and considered them carefully as she looked toward the Sa'ba Taalor. Finally she nodded her head. "I will mention this to my cousin. He will decide whether or not the words are truthful. He might wish to speak with you before you leave." The girl nodded her head and looked oddly relieved though Nachia certainly had given her no reason to relax. "Why do you tell me this now? Why would my cousin believe your words are true where your father's were lies?"

Lanaie looked surprised by the very notion. "Why would I lie?"

Nachia shrugged and picked up a wedge of pabba fruit that has been sprinkled with honey. "Why did your father lie before if what you say now is truth?"

"He thought the Guntha were making up ghosts to convince him to let them have a place to stay."

"So he decided to make up a lie about the islands of the Guntha sinking?"

"Yes."

"My cousin will want to speak to you."

The girl nodded her head and looked around the room.

Nachia managed not to roll her eyes. Like as not she would have let the matter go, but the fact was simple: as far as she could tell, Lanaie was too stupid to make up a lie, but exactly smart enough not to tell the truth without good reason.

From across the room Nachia saw the one called Drask looking at her. His face was hidden, his eyes were half buried in shadows, and the pupils seemed almost to glow, much like the cats she kept in her room.

She contemplated those eyes as she thought about the princess' words. And like many people before her, she wondered what was hidden by the veils the visitors wore.

••••

Merros and Wollis leaned against the wall of the courtyard and watched in silence while the Sa'ba Taalor gathered their belongings and placed them in the appropriate spots.

After several minutes of observing the insane efficiency of the group, Wollis spit. "I've never seen anyone who could pack that much nonsense onto a riding animal and still find a place to ride."

"Fair enough, but when was the last time you saw anyone who rode a monster the size of those things?"

The closest of the mounts, Swech's great beast Saa'thaa, cast its eyes toward them and snorted. Merros stared at the face of the thing, hidden though it was behind the skull-like metal and leather mask it wore, and smiled. "I shall miss you, too, you great lumbering thing." He meant the words only for himself, but damned if the animal didn't seem to smile in response. At the very least it bared those massive fangs that could make the average dagger feel inadequate.

Swech sauntered around the animal's flank and slapped it affectionately. The tail of the beast swished and slapped at the back of her legs.

The woman looked toward Merros and nodded. "You came to see us off?"

Merros looked into her eyes and shrugged. Wollis looked away but not before Merros caught the start of a smile on his aide's face. The bastard knew more than he should. He normally did.

"Well, I could hardly let you leave without wishing you a safe journey." He deliberately kept his voice casual. It was best not to show too much affection in his experience. Women tended to expect it after a while. Then again, Swech was hardly like most of the women he'd met. And also, his personal experience with long-term relationships was dubious at best. Most times he tended to be the one to call off anything that might seem like a romance.

Swech regarded him and stepped closer, her hand resting on his chest. He felt the heat of her fingers over his heart and she leaned in until the veil over her mouth was close enough to tickle his ear when she spoke in her native tongue. "I shall miss you too. You are an inventive lover."

She stepped back and nodded a quick farewell before moving to step onto the saddle on Saa'thaa's broad back. Even as she prepared to mount, Tusk was bellowing his orders. "We head for home! It is time!" Without so much as a glance around, the Obsidian King started forward. The rest of his people were quick to take his actions for their own.

The great animals and the people started off, only a small number waiting until the wagons had moved out of the courtyard before they left.

Wollis watched with Merros for several heartbeats in silence, and then his voice broke that blissful void. "So you're imaginative now? I shall tell my mother she should expect nothing less than satisfaction when the two of you finally satisfy your carnal lusts."

Merros laughed. "She said 'inventive,' and you're a jealous bastard."

"Maybe." He shook his head. "You may rest assured it's been a while since Dretta called me 'inventive.'" He tilted his head. "Actually, it's just plain been a while."

"Will you go back home then?"

"No." Wollis shook his head. "Apparently I'm deserving of a promotion and a commission within the Imperial Army."

"Krohan?"

His second nodded. "According to the wizard it was the Emperor's idea."

"So you'll be staying here?"

"Messengers have been sent to gather Dretta and my belongings. She'll positively have a fit. She's always wanted to see Tyrne."

"Where will you stay?"

"There's a nice little villa in the northern quadrant, not far from the cavalry barracks. You know it. The one with the red brick wall around the entire affair."

"Indeed I do." Merros looked to his friend. "You'll be saying there?"

"I should say. I just bought the damned place."

"My mind acknowledges that both of us have that sort of money these days, but my heart is still having trouble accepting the notion." Merros shook his head. "Maybe I should look into finding a place of my own."

"You? Owning property?" Wollis snorted.

"What?"

"I just thought you'd rent a room at the local brothel and work out a deal. You know, work as bouncer and sample the wares whenever you like."

"If I didn't know you were joking, I might have to take offense to that, you northern savage."

"I'd call you rude, but that would hardly be anything unusual." Wollis looked away and grinned again. "Planning on settling down with Swech, are you? Going to call her back from her homeland and make an honest woman of her?"

"Gods! I can only imagine." He spoke with a laugh in his voice that he didn't completely feel. For the moment at least, he would actually miss her. Perhaps it wouldn't last, but the woman was interesting enough to keep him alert and exactly mysterious enough to make him want to know her better. That was a rare combination for him.

"Just think, you could have a dozen babies and raise your own little army."

"Is it just me, Wollis? Or are they possibly the scariest fighters you've ever met?"

"No. Their women are the scariest fighters I've ever met. Their men are just the biggest fighters I've ever met." He looked at Merros and carefully slid a step away before he continued. "I mean, did Swech even notice you were in there? Because if she was with the likes of Tusk first I'm surprised she'd notice."

"You're a swine."

"I've seen you naked. I'm not saying you're inadequate in that department, but be fair, Tusk is, well, Tusk is just plain large everywhere."

"I didn't look."

"The man had no shame. Saw fresh water and stripped down in front of everyone. I had trouble not looking."

"You really have been away from Dretta for too long."

"You have no idea. Those great beasts of theirs were beginning to look appetizing."

"You have very strange appetites, Wollis."

"Like I said, it's been a very long time."

Merros slapped his arm. "Dretta will be with you soon."

"Not soon enough."

"There are always the brothels."

"Dretta would wear my manhood as a necklace."

"She doesn't already?"

"You should talk. Was Swech wearing something around her neck as she left?"

"That was just the veil." He sighed and looked along the path the Sa'ba Taalor had taken. Swech was gone and suddenly he found he was quite tired.

Wollis stared at him for a moment and put a hand on his shoulder without saying a word. That was one of the things he liked about the man. He knew when to quit cracking wise and when to just stay silent.

"Well, no, Nachia. The islands of the Guntha are sinking. I've checked on that myself. It's a slow process, but they are falling back into the sea and nothing can prevent that from happening." Desh Krohan shrugged. "Well, magic, I suppose, but I haven't really looked into the matter."

Nachia rolled her eyes and looked out the window to her suite. The sorcerer was there by her request and she could feel his eyes examining her form. In his defense she was dressed to be noticed. It irked her quite a bit that the man was barely reacting at all.

The sun was rising behind the walls of the palace and the shadows stretched out long fingers that pointed toward the distant Seven Forges.

"So what do you think of the claims that the Sa'ba Taalor have been attacking the Guntha?"

"It seems rather a stretch, doesn't it?" He paused. "You've seen the same maps that I have. I suppose it's possible that the Taalor have access to the sea, but they certainly don't have the supplies to build ships of any size, or if they do, they'd have to haul the raw materials for a great distance."

"The stone that built this castle came from the Wellish Steppes and was carried here by horses and many, many wagons."

"True enough, but there was a great deal of expense and effort involved."

"Yes, but how much effort to carry wood to build ships, even if the ships are very large?"

Desh sighed behind her. She turned and saw him staring directly at her face.

"What? Say what's on your mind, wizard."

"Even if the Sa'ba Taalor are off and running around on ships, what has that to do with us?"

"The princess spoke as if the Guntha made claims of a vast navy."

"Secondhand innuendo and suppositions from a girl who has just confessed that her father has been lying to the Emperor." He shook his head. "Even if it's true, the Guntha have never been our allies."

"This isn't about alliances. This is about not knowing what they are capable of, or what their intentions are."

"I can see your point, Nachia, but, really, we've only just met these people." He stepped closer and she held her breath. It bothered her, too, that as much as he seemed indifferent to her, she found herself drawn to the sorcerer. She'd have thought the man was using an enchantment on her, but knew better. He had always held a fascination for her, even when she was a child. His hand pointed out the open window to the courtyard below. "It's almost irrelevant, really. There they go."

Off to the left the long line of animals – horses and stranger things – were in motion, the great beasts of the Sa'ba Taalor were heading for the distant Seven Forges. A trip that would take weeks at the very least according to what she knew.

"I think I'm relieved."

"I'm not sure how I feel about them yet." The man's voice drifted lazily as he looked toward the caravan. "They're a fascinating people."

"They are different."

"Well, yes, that's rather what makes them fascinating."

"Why didn't you go along?"

"For the same reason that your cousin is still here instead of traveling along with them. I have far too much to do around here."

"Like what?"

"At the very least I have to advise the Emperor on the changes those people have just brought around."

"What changes?"

"Weren't you paying attention?" His voice was teasing. His voice almost always seemed to be teasing. She hated him just a little for that. "Our new neighbors have apparently been killing off our other neighbors to the south."

"They aren't new." She watched them as they moved away, none of the small figures seemed the least bit interested in looking back toward the palace and that suited her just fine. "We just weren't aware that they were there."

"Is there a difference?"

"Oh yes." Her voice was very soft. "We were unaware of them. We should not for a moment think they were unaware of us."

Desh Krohan nodded his head slowly, never looking away from the winding line of animals and riders. "Congratulations, Nachia. I do believe you're learning."

"You said it yourself, Desh. One should never stop learning. Or studying the world."

She closed her eyes as she felt his hand pat her back softly for a moment. Oh, how she hated that the contact felt so damned good. "I stand corrected. I know you're learning. That's what I like to see."

In the very far distance there was a flare of light and both of them looked. For just a moment the illumination from the Seven Forges was bright enough to be seen on the horizon. Neither of them was looking when the faintest vibration from the same location reached the palace.

SEVENTEEN

The first night they traveled until they reached the edge of civilization. Andover looked around in awe. He had never been outside of Tyrne in his life, and though he knew the world was large, he had no idea just how immense it truly was. The wilderness, the darkness of the sky and the vastness of the same were intimidating.

Tega rode in a separate wagon, one that was marked with odd symbols that meant nothing to Andover, despite the fact that he could read a little.

She did not leave her wagon on the first night, but instead locked herself away. There were more wagons than he had initially assumed, four in total: three of them carried supplies and one of those had a bunk for Andover. The others carried the larder and gifts for the kings of the Seven Forges.

When the group made camp, Drask found Andover and called him over. In the open spaces and near complete darkness, the eyes of the Sa'ba Taalor and their mounts seemed to burn. It was an unsettling image, as if they carried a bit of the fire of their homeland within them.

Drask had made a fire and he and two others settled near it, the deeply scarred Bromt and the girl, Delil. Bromt had been hunting earlier and the meat of three rabbits roasted over the fire.

"Join us." Andover nodded. Really, when Drask said to do something the idea of disagreeing seldom came up. The warriors settled around the fire and mostly sat in silence, but it was a comfortable quiet, something that Andover was not really accustomed to.

Bromt peeled one of the rabbits from the spit where he'd been cooking them and used a knife as large as the animal itself to cut it into quarters. Without speaking he offered the meat to each of his companions and Andover nodded his thanks when the offering was made. His stomach rumbled and he realized that he was ravenous.

As he ate, Drask picked the meat from his piece of the animal and tore it into small pieces that he slipped under his veil. All three of them did that.

And when they were done eating Drask looked toward Andover and sighed. "When we wake in the morning, we will be walking."

"Where are we walking to?" Andover gnawed the last of the meat from a leg bone and licked his fingers.

"Home."

Andover stared for a long moment. "All the way to the Seven Forges?"

"Yes."

"Why?" It was all he could think to say.

"Because Tuskandru demands it."

"Excuse me?"

"Tuskandru believes that you must be... tempered."

"What do you mean?"

Drask sighed. "You have been healed. You have been broken and you have been healed, and that is the First Forging for you." Drask leaned in closer. "By the beliefs of my people there are many stages to becoming what you should eventually become. The First Forging is..." He waved his hands around and squinted into the fire. "The First Forging is the first step into adulthood. I know that for you, for your people, you are an adult. But to the Sa'ba Taalor, you are still a child. It is time to be tempered. It is time for your mind and body to be strengthened."

"The Seven Forges are a great ways off, Drask." He stared at the man for a long moment. "You're from there. Even riding your mounts it took you weeks to reach Tyrne. It would take months to reach your home."

"This I know. You will walk the entire distance."

Andover shook his head. It was madness, of course.

Drask placed his heavy hands on his knees and leaned in closer. "Allow me to explain this. You will walk. There is no question of this."

"But why?"

"Because Tuskandru speaks for all of the Kings. And none of the Kings will acknowledge you until you have proven yourself worthy. You will walk. And while you are walking, we will train you with your weapon and with a bow. I have a spare and you may use it. You will learn to hunt for yourself. You will learn to feed yourself. You will learn to fight and to defend yourself."

Andover closed his eyes and thought hard about the situation. "If I say no, what happens?"

"You will stay here."

"What? You mean I won't be allowed to come to the Seven Forges?"

"Yes. You will not be allowed."

He looked back over his shoulder, back toward Tyrne, so far removed now that not even the glow from the city could be seen.

"You will not be allowed to walk to your home, Andover Lashk."

"What do you mean?"

"I mean you will either walk to the valley of the Seven Forges or you will stay here." Drask stomped his foot into the ground. "Right here. You will walk, you will obey the orders of Tuskandru, or I will kill you myself."

"You're serious."

"Truska-Pren has given you new hands. You proved yourself worthy of the gift of those hands when you fought your enemies. That was your First Forging. You must be seen as an equal by my people, or you will not be accepted."

"I'll never find my way!" He waved his arms around. "I've no damned idea where we are now! How do you expect me to find the Seven Forges!"

Drask leaned back. "I said 'we' are walking. The four of us. We will show you the way to the Seven Forges and we will teach you what you need to know if you will be an ambassador to the Sa'ba Taalor."

The silence between them grew. Bromt cut apart another rabbit and despite his lack of appetite – a very sudden change indeed – Andover had the good sense to eat. If he was going to be hunting for the food he'd be eating, he wanted to build up whatever stores he could in advance.

Desh Krohan lay in his bed for a long while and stared at the ceiling. The world was moving on again; he could feel it and it was not a sensation he was very fond of.

His skin shivered and the sorcerer rolled into a sitting position as his flesh goosepimpled. "What in all the worlds?" He looked around and tried to orient himself as his vision blurred. The Sooth often told him of potential calamities, but this, whatever exactly was happening, was coming out of the darkness.

"Tataya! I need you!" Tataya was close by, the others, even Tega, were all gone, sent off by him on different tasks that needed to be tended to as surely as he needed to watch over the Empire.

Tataya flowed into the room, her robes fluttering around her form as she came to him. "What is it? What's happened?"

"I am not sure, but something is wrong." His head throbbed. His vision would not focus. For a moment he felt every year of his existence and the weight of those years dropped him to his hands and knees on the cold marble floor of his suite. Tataya's hands caught him before he could fall completely, and her strength helped him regain his feet.

Around the room, around the palace and the entire capital city, glass rattled, small items shook and still waters rippled with fish scale waves.

Tataya spoke under her breath, quickly weaving protection for the both of them and for the room. As she cast her words into the world the air around them calmed and the delicate glass and crystal items around the area steadied themselves.

And then it was merely a matter of minutes before Desh could stand on his own again, could think again as the pain that held him eased its violent grip.

He tried wiping at his flesh but his hand came away stained with a thin patina of blood-sweat. Tataya grabbed a soft cloth and pulled his robes open, wiping the reddish stains from his body with careful strokes.

Desh stood still for it, mostly because he was not yet convinced that the worst of the seizure was over.

"Desh, what did you do?"

He shook his head. "This wasn't me, Tataya. Not this time. This was… I don't know what. But something has happened. Something I need to investigate."

She nodded her head, her red hair falling loosely around her face. "I will prepare the chamber."

"Thank you." Desh moved carefully. His strength was recovering nicely but his hands still shook. He made his way to the end table near his bed and poured clear, cold water from the pitcher there. He drank four full glasses before he felt more himself again.

By the time he'd dressed himself Tataya returned, carrying his shimmering robes and four black stones that Desh had carved himself, each covered in delicate markings that were etched deeply into the spheres.

He stared at the stones for several seconds. Each was the size of a small apple. "Do you think four?

Really?" he grimaced at the notion. The effort to make them had not been expended lightly.

"You were just sweating blood, Desh."

He nodded and instead took three from her after he'd put on his robes. Then he slipped one of the round stones into the pockets of his robe.

"Two for now. A third if I need it."

"You know best." Her voice said otherwise. He ignored the tone. He was used to it from the Sisters. Part of their mission in life was to keep him humble and they did an excellent job. That did not mean he always listened to their suggestions.

"Let's just finish this." He mumbled the words for himself, really, to bolster his sense of self-confidence. Dealing with the spirits was never an easy thing, and the odds were good that they would be very agitated by whatever had just happened.

"Have a care, Desh. I've grown rather fond of you."

"I always do, Tataya. Watch over us please."

He moved into the small room that she had prepared for him. The walls were unadorned iron. The floor was cold silver, polished to a mirrored finish. The ceiling above him was red and wet and rippled as he looked at it.

Desh set two stones on the floor before him and sat cross-legged.

Deep inside, hidden well away from the faces of the people he knew, Desh allowed himself a small shiver.

The Sooth could be very demanding when they wanted to and he suspected there would be a cost for whatever questions he asked. He just hoped the stones were enough of a payment.

The tide of red that came down from the ceiling covered him in a matter of moments and he resisted the instinct that told him to breathe.

The answers would come soon enough.

First, however, was the pain.

Desh Krohan managed not to scream. At least on the outside. In his mind he howled with agonies few would have believed possible to endure.

Goriah walked along the beach and looked at the ruination. There was little that had not been picked over by seagulls, crabs and other creatures, but there was enough. Skeletons remained half buried in sand, scoured by the wind and rain and cleaned by the vermin. Some of the remains still had jewelry and weapons alike.

The Guntha had come to do battle. They never had the chance.

Far off across the waters the islands of the Guntha were slowly sinking into the depths of the ocean. In another hundred years there would be little left of them, but for now they were still inhabitable. She would be heading over to the islands soon enough.

Even now, she knew, the Guntha were planning on coming to Roathes. They were angry. They were confused and they were scared. All she had to do was look at the remains of their camp to know why.

"All true. None of them survived. Not a single one."

She closed her eyes and felt the echoes of the dead. They were not ghosts, exactly, though to be sure there were a few of those around. No, these were merely afterimages of the carnage. Reflections of the pain that ran through the Guntha as they died.

Most of them never even knew what happened. They slept through their deaths. She supposed that was a blessing.

Goriah opened her eyes when she heard the men coming her way. She did not bother looking toward them. She knew what they wanted. They wanted to know who she was and why she stood among the ruins of well over a thousand corpses.

Really, she cared very little what they wanted, but she had to play by the rules that Desh Krohan offered her.

When she finally looked toward the small gathering of men, they stared at her with open surprise. She was as pale as snow in comparison to them. Her skin was pale, her hair was nearly white and there were likely none among them that had ever seen anyone as far removed from their own body types.

They were dressed in pants and shirts, not in the more casual skirt-like outfits that so many of the Roathians preferred. Like as not that meant they worked for the king, who was trying, slowly and without much success, to make his people more like the rulers of the Empire.

Pants did not make sense in the heat and humidity, nor did the heavy cloaks and greatcoats favored by Tyrne at the present time.

One of them finally came closer to her, his eyes wide. He was not scared, exactly, but he sensed that she was not quite what she appeared.

"No one is supposed to be here. This area has been declared unclean by King Marsfel."

"And yet here you are and here I am."

"Well, but we are here because you are here."

"I have been summoned here to examine this very place. By order of Emperor Pathra Krous." She held up the golden seal of office that he presented to his managers.

The man stepped back and bowed down quickly. "If we may assist, you have but to ask." His voice did not agree with his words. Like so many, he disliked being made to help strangers to Roathes. The king wanted the Empire. The king wanted the prestige and wealth of Fellein. The Roathians seemed to prefer the idea of fishing and farming. She could see the appeal.

"Your offer is kind, but I am merely here to examine this and then I will leave you in peace."

He opened his mouth to respond but stopped when a peal of thunder hammered the horizon. The sound was not expected, certainly not normal. Goriah turned to the water and stared as a column of flames flashed in the distance. Leagues of water separated the Guntha from the shoreline, enough distance to make sure that most of the time the two peoples never met by accident. The sound came from a great distance away, just possibly as far away as the Gunthas' islands.

The man closest to her stared at the burning pillar in the distance. Like the stem of a flower it began to grow petals, but these were made of smoke, of flame, and touched the ceiling of the world as nearly as Goriah could see.

She turned to the man and pointed. "Has this ever happened before?"

He shook his head even as he was backing up. He might have been saying no. He might simply have been denying the impossibility of that great fire roaring toward the sun. Either way he turned and ran a moment later.

The winds from off the ocean grew stronger, and even from where she stood, Goriah could see the way the waters were dancing. There would be great waves in the near future, the sort that leveled whatever stood in their way and washed aside all but the greatest structures. She had once walked where the castle of Queen Harper had fallen to such waves and no one had ever thought that great structure capable of being damaged by man or the elements.

Goriah knew better.

With one last look around, she surrendered her investigation. She had other places she needed to be, other sites to examine. And truly, what she stared at now would be gone when the waves came ashore. Somewhere between the fiery fountain and the shoreline great waves were swelling and bucking, growing in size and fury.

And exactly that quickly the problems between the Roathians and the Guntha were solved.

And the questions about the gray men were swept aside just as easily as the corpses from the massacre were cast into the waves.

Goriah moved on.

Pella looked upon the Blasted Lands from the highest point along the Wellish Steppes. That was the large collection of flat gray stones that marked where the Wellish Overlords had met their end fully a hundred years before the Great Cataclysm.

Though the steppes were flat, they still looked down on the great crater that marked the Blasted Lands. The pitted, scarred rock walls that rose from the devastated area were a natural barrier against the raging storms that used to come from the Blasted Lands and carried Plague Winds and worse. As cold and bitter as the Steppes could be, they were home to many a thriving township.

From her position she could see into the vast area of ruination for quite a distance before the perpetual storms hid away the secrets that had remained lost for almost a thousand years.

Though she stood at the very edge of the area, she could see the distant light of the Seven Forges. Even from the final resting place of the Overlords, the skies to the west were ablaze with their glow. And at the moment that glow seemed brighter than usual.

She was not here to enter the damnable area again and she was fine with that. Though Pella found no particular dread of the Blasted Lands within her heart, neither was she fascinated by their unrevealed enigmas.

Somewhere out there, Andover Lashk was walking. She knew that. She could sense it. He had been marked by her, by order of Desh Krohan, and so she watched over him from a distance, with no intention of helping him in any way.

She was not his custodian, merely an observer.

Far more importantly, she had to take care of delivering a message to Dretta Marsh from her husband. That was a task she looked forward to. The village he came from, where his wife still waited for him, was only a few hours away. For the moment she rested, tired from her constant motion.

In the distance, closer than she would have expected under any circumstances, she heard the mournful cries and maddened giggles of Pra-Moresh. Pra-Moresh... in the old tongue their name translated to the Crying Death. The name fit. The noises came from the Blasted Lands, of course, but it was rare that the damned things ever came this close to civilized lands. She would have to warn the Imperial Watch when she reached Stonehaven.

Trecharch was to the north. The great forests of that area could be seen in the far distance as a dark line on the horizon, a frozen wave that seemed forever ready to run toward the steppes. There were stories that the Pra-Moresh sometimes roved those ancient woods. She hoped against the idea.

The ground trembled beneath her feet. Pella looked down at the vast stone she stood on, noting as she often did that not even lichen grew on the wind-polished surface. Sometimes, according to local legends, the Overlords still moved within their tomb. She didn't think that the case, not now at least. No, the vibration was distant. She called out to her Sisters and both responded. In moments each knew what their Sisters knew and she understood that something powerful was happening in the distant ocean.

Something that seemed to mirror almost exactly the pulse and flickering, shimmering lights of the Seven Forges which painted the underbelly of the sky to the west.

"Interesting." She gnawed lightly at her lower lip as the Pra-Moresh wailed their mad sorrows to the skies. It sounded like a lot of the beasts, enough to make her know it was time to move on.

Would they climb the almost sheer walls of the Steppes? Perhaps. They had done so in the past. It could well happen again.

Either way, she had no intention of being there when the time came.

The wind caught her cloak and Pella spread her arms wide and dreamt that she was a storm-crow, comfortable with the knowledge that sometimes dreams really do come true.

The Emperor looked at the princess and smiled. She was a lovely girl, of course, and most decidedly a temptation. Her body was young and firm and she would likely produce beautiful children, and those were all things he was supposed to care about, but, sadly, she was also a bit stupid. Oh, he could have accepted naïve and possibly even found a certain appeal in that aspect of a woman's personality, but she was just plain dumb, and the thought of being wed to a woman he could not hold a conversation with was worse to him than not being wed.

That was part of the problem, really. There were few women who held his attention for long.

He stopped thinking about possible wedding ceremonies and focused instead on the girl's words.

"What you're saying to me is that your father lied to me in an effort to gain money."

She nodded without actually speaking. Her deep dark eyes were moist with unshed tears. She was terrified. She should have been. It was well within his power to either punish her or her father or punish the country her father ruled over if he thought the actions necessary. Battles had been fought based on lies. Resources used and soldiers laid to rest for the claims of King Marsfel.

Unless, of course, she was lying now. There was the rub. That was the problem. He had to decide if her new claims were legitimate or not, or even if the entire situation was worth the effort of a proper examination.

"Why not simply ask for assistance? Why claim the Guntha invaded if they did not?"

"They did invade, majesty. But they invaded after they were attacked as well. Attacked by people who sound much like the Sa'ba Taalor."

He nodded his head. "And what would your father have me do about this now?"

"He fears that if they are the same people, they might well attack Roathes. The stories of the Guntha claim that the gray people are merciless."

Pathra Krous looked at the girl and sighed. Nachia sat nearby, observing without speaking. That was exactly what he wanted from her at the moment. She had been gone too long and he wanted his cousin nearby, the better to observe and learn, because the more he thought about it, the more he rather liked the idea of journeying to the Seven Forges to see the lands that almost no one had ever seen before.

Pathra leaned across the table and stared at Lanaie, his eyes locked on hers instead of on her warm and welcoming form. It was one thing to flirt with a visitor, and another to let his personal desires get in the way of running an empire. He knew better than to mix the two and even if he had not, Desh would have cleared that issue up a long time back.

"I do not believe you or your father need be worried in this circumstance. I will overlook the issues of why he called for assistance and accept that when he called for aid he felt it was the best action he could make." The girl let out a breath and offered a tentative smile. Before she could open her mouth to offer thanks, however, he held up a hand for silence. "And as luck would have it, your kingdom has an excellent recourse to possible attack."

"We do?"

"Oh yes. You can call on the Guntha and make peace with them. That way, if there is an attack, you already have a naval force to back up your father's navy."

"I…" Oh, she wanted so much to protest. He could see it in the expression on her lovely face, and the way her body was positioned, but she knew better. One did not argue with the Emperor. That was one of the rare benefits of being in charge. When you made a decree, you seldom had to justify it to the people around you.

Unless Desh Krohan was in the room, of course. Happily the mage was elsewhere. He would have likely agreed anyway.

"You are very welcome, Lanaie. I know you are eager to return to your father's side and bring him the good news. I suspect that after their recent setbacks the Guntha will be delighted to come to a peaceful accord."

The princess left a few moments later, the puzzled pout not quite leaving her face.

Nachia smiled. "That was harsh."

"Do you think so? I thought I was being rather diplomatic. I'm not sending the army in to take Roathes from that fat buffoon."

Nachia stared at him for a moment, a smile playing around her lips but not quite manifesting. "I sense hostility."

"I don't like being lied to. It makes me look foolish, especially if I don't punish the liars."

"I think it makes you wise and just."

"You haven't ruled yet."

"I've had a bit of experience." She spoke without rancor, just as he did. They were not only relatives but friends. It helped.

"True enough, Nachia, but believe me, there are differences."

"You'll understand if I'm in no hurry to find out, I hope." He nodded.

"So what you call harsh, I call just. I sent her on her way with instructions for her father to make peace. I've committed enough troops in the last four years to his needs. He lied about the reason for the attacks, if actual attacks truly happened."

"Assuming she is not lying?"

"Always a possibility, but in this case, if she is lying, she merely heads home with no changes in her position and no extra commitments from the Empire.

Once again a simple message to handle the matters on his own goes to King Marsfel."

"And if the Guntha attack Roathes in force?"

"Then he has only himself to blame for putting himself in this position in the first place. He should have attempted to make a peaceful truce with the Guntha."

"What if the gray people are actually the Sa'ba Taalor?"

"Even if they are, they have not attacked the Empire. They have had a skirmish or two with the Guntha." He shrugged. "And I don't believe the Sa'ba Taalor have any sort of navy. They live in the Blasted Lands. Where the hell would they harbor their ships?" He pointed to the duplicate map that Desh had given him. "Do you so much as see a river outside of the Seven Forges?"

"I'm not disagreeing with you. I'm pretending to be Desh Krohan for the sake of argument."

"Please," he sighed. "One Desh is enough."

"True." She rose and moved closer. "What do you make of these 'gray men?'"

"Probably old wives tales from the Guntha. Half the seafaring people claim they've seen specters on the ocean. Why should the Guntha be any different?"

"Well, I believe I'll get in a little rest before it's time for dinner. Is this to be another large affair or merely a few family members sharing a meal?"

Pathra smiled. "For a change of pace it will be a small meal. You can even bring Brolley if he promises not to act out."

"Brolley remains very humbled."

"Humility has its charms."

Nachia laughed and touched his arm briefly before she headed for the archway leaving his offices. "I shall see you when the meal is called, Pathra."

"I look forward to it." He rose from his seat and walked to where he kept the bottle of sweet wine hidden behind a suit of armor that had never once been worn into combat. He seldom indulged but it was nice to have a small sip when he was done handling tasks he did not enjoy. He always disliked having to say no to a beautiful woman, especially one who so obviously wanted him to say yes.

His fingers had just closed on the bottle when the blade slid though his neck as quietly as a whisper. The Emperor was dead before he hit the floor.

The Emperor Pathra Krous was not a small man. He was quite a bit larger than she was, in fact, but that did not change the plans for him in any way.

He was to be an example. He was to be a warning. She had very little time to make that warning clear, but she would make the best of the time she could spare.

The knives slashed deeply. The symbols took shape on his chest, on his face. And when she finished the grisly message, she looked around the room very quickly and then caught the dead man's wrists and pulled him toward the window, straining with his size. Dead weight, indeed.

There are plenty of people who would argue that a woman is naturally weaker than a man. It might be true but there were ways around that problem.

Sometimes it wasn't merely the weight of an object that mattered, but also how that weight was approached.

She used her arms to balance his mass. She used her legs to propel his corpse through the open window. He fell almost forty feet to the pavement below and landed with an audible slap. A moment later the screams began.

And then she slipped back into her hiding place to wait out the chaos that would be coming her way.

The military leaders of Tyrne were not amused.

Newly appointed General Merros Dulver did not much care. Rather than dealing with the crusty old bastards who were waiting to speak to the Emperor or his First Advisor, Merros called the troops to assemble on the Western Field where they often practiced. With Wollis at his side, he began a complete inspection of the troops. By most standards they were in fine form. By the standards of the Imperial Guard they were sloppy and unkempt. He made note of that fact to Wollis and knew that his second would see the matter attended to immediately.

The day was close to ending, the sun would set soon enough. That did not mean that Merros intended to make life easier for the troops. They had been living a bit too easily as far as he was concerned, and that included him. Thinking back on the Sa'ba Taalor was enough to bring that point home.

It was time for a change. There would be more serious practice sessions. He might well instigate proper war games. The weapons he inspected were functional, yes, but some of the edges were not what they should have been, and a good number of shields and breastplates were in need of repair. There was a smithy on the premises for the love of all the gods. It was time to make the blacksmith there earn his keep.

And again, he trusted Wollis to make note of all he said and he trusted that his second would make it happen.

Several of the soldiers looked too young to shave.

"Wollis?"

"Yes, General?"

"Make a note. Find out where Nolan March is stationed and have him transferred to the capital."

He turned to stare at his second and smiled at the shock on the man's face. "What are you doing? I mean, can you do that? I'm grateful of course, but–"

"I can do that. I can order that. I'm a general. Make it happen. I think I rather like the idea of him being a part of the Imperial Guard."

"Aye! Ho, sir!" Merros' smile grew broader. His friend had more than earned the right to see his family again, all of them.

When the inspections were done, he prepared to make a short speech to the troops. There were going to be a good number of changes and he wanted them to understand why those changes were taking place. He wanted them to understand that though the Sa'ba Taalor seemed inclined to be allies, they could not be ignored as a potential problem and they were, hands down, far superior fighters to most of the soldiers he'd been with over the years. And that could not be tolerated. It was time for the soldiers to become everything they should have been all along, especially the soldiers who guarded the crown city and the Emperor himself.

He planned to make a speech. Instead he turned with almost everyone else when the alarm bells sounded from the palace.

The great bells were sounded only rarely, and normally with a great deal of warning. There was no warning this time, however, and the sound shocked the regulars and the newcomers alike. Merros had heard of the palatial bells, but had never before heard them. They were indeed incredibly loud notes and the sound rang across the field and echoed off the closest buildings without losing much of their initial volume.

To the last, every soldier on the field grabbed their arms and headed for the palace at a run. He was gratified to see that response and horrified by the lack of organization involved in the same.

Finding out that the Emperor had been murdered, however, made his previous dread seem inconsequential.

EIGHTEEN

To say the death of the Emperor came as a surprise is to say that the wind will blow or the sun will rise: It is a simple statement of fact.

The impact, however, was immediate and on a few occasions violent.

Pathra Krous was dead. By rights his successor had to be chosen and Pathra Krous had already made accommodations to that end. He had carefully groomed his cousin, Nachia, to take over upon his death. Heartbroken though she was, she knew that she would have to assume the mantle of Empress.

There were matters that had to be taken care of, naturally. The death of an emperor is as serious an affair as a coronation. Messengers had to be sent out, officials throughout Felleln had to be prepared for the changes that would be coming their way, and regardless of all of the paperwork, all of the endless details, life had to continue on and daily events had to be handled.

Desh Krohan knew all about that sort of thing. He was extremely helpful in making arrangements. There were letters of instruction from Pathra Krous himself, details about the funeral services he wished taken care of, and details on how to handle the transition from his reign as Emperor to Nachia's ascension to the throne. A great deal of the work that Nachia had ahead of her had already been mapped out, not only by the sorcerer but by her deceased cousin.

It should have made her life easier, but it did not.

First, there was the disaster that had come about almost at the same moment that her cousin was murdered. The Guntha were gone. Decimated by a volcanic eruption. The seas to the west of Roathes were raging with storms and the kingdom was beset by disaster after catastrophe. Great clouds of ash were coming from where the Guntha had once been and drifting across the shoreline of Roathes, coating everything in gray waste. The people were falling ill to the toxic air that carried those ashes, and while not everyone was affected, enough were to make the matter urgent. Whatever falsehood may have existed in previous claims, the fact of the matter was simply that the small kingdom now needed the assistance of the Empire and that assistance could not be ignored.

The stories of exactly what had happened to the Emperor were uncontrollable and made worse simply because no one knew much, aside from the fact that he had been murdered. That could not be denied, really. And the rumors were growing by the day.

And then there was Laister Krous. Laister, another cousin, who was even now making noises about exactly who should be ascending to the throne in the immediate future.

Desh Krohan was not amused by the man's presence.

That did not change the fact that the man demanded to be heard. Laister and several of his family members gathered together and glowered as menacingly as they could manage at the sorcerer. Despite their best efforts, he remained unintimidated.

"My claim is legitimate." Laister sucked in his gut and squared his shoulders, perhaps in an effort to somehow look even larger. It didn't change much of his physical appearance. Laister was a large man, and in his time he'd been an accomplished swordsman. Likely he was as skilled as ever, but not quite as fast. Too many years of rich foods and sweet wines had taken their toll on his physique.

"Indeed it is. Your claim is quite legitimate. You have a right to state your case and I have listened very carefully. And I have considered your words. And now that I have, the decision remains unchanged. Pathra Krous made very clear that Nachia Krous, your cousin, was the rightful claimant to the throne. He wrote it down, he signed his declarations. He told me personally on a dozen different occasions. I have borne witness to his desires and I have agreed to follow them."

"Well, yes, but I don't agree with them." Laister crossed his arms and scowled some more. Really, it was likely a very good tactic for him in most circumstances. Just not now.

"Yes, you made that clear, as did your mother, your father, your sister, and your most recent consort. However, as Regent, as First Advisor to the Throne of Fellein, as Council to the Emperor for the last few hundred years, I am afraid that I have just a bit more authority than you do in this situation, and I have to respectfully decline your desires to be the new Emperor."

Laister looked at the gathering of people who had come with him to show their support and leaned in closer to his sister. Danieca was a bloated lump, but she carried a surprising amount of support. Also, though he wasn't present, there was Towdra Krous to consider. Towdra had his hands in everything and he could, potentially, cause troubles.

Of course, Desh could, potentially, wipe out every last one of them. That was the sort of fact that made most of them behave to a very real extent.

When they had finished whispering among themselves, Laister looked at Desh with a nearly desperate hope. "I don't suppose the right to challenge is still on the books?"

"Blood duel? No. I had that particular law stricken three generations back." He waved a hand. "Really, it would hardly matter. Even if Nachia couldn't fight you herself, she'd just choose a champion."

"Really." Laister planted his broad hands on his hips. "And who do you suppose she'd choose? Brolley?"

"Probably she'd choose me." Desh crossed his arms and stared past the shadows of his hood.

"Oh." That seemed to take a bit of the arrogance from the man's stature.

"Your cousin Nachia will ascend to the throne within the week. First we take care of the funeral. I know it isn't to your liking, but it will happen, Laister."

The group made more noises, but ultimately left the offices that Pathra had occupied.

Desh shook his head and leaned back in the chair where he had often sat across from the man. He would not, at any point, willingly sit on the throne. That was not a position he wanted.

Tataya slipped closer to him. "Do you think they will be trouble?"

"Of course they will." He sighed. "It's what Laister likes to do. Without Pathra around, he will likely do everything he can to cause issues."

"Why do you allow it?"

"I don't allow anything. I'm nothing but an advisor."

Tataya snorted.

He ignored the derisive noise.

There was still a lot to be done.

There was always a lot to be done.

Desh would have denied how much he enjoyed the troubling times, but those few who knew him best understood that his protests were hollow.

Some people thrive on chaos, even when they choose not to generate it.

Merros shook his head and looked at the ranks of soldiers. "We're missing a few hundred people aren't we, Wollis?"

"Well, not really. No. They were sent out."

"Who were sent out and exactly who sent them? Also, where were they sent?"

Wollis looked around the Western Field and gestured. "General Hradi sent the First Imperials to bring the Sa'ba Taalor back to Tyrne." He spoke very softly, as if, perhaps, by keeping a level head he could will Merros to do the same.

"He did what?"

"I'm not repeating myself, Merros."

"Hradi did that?" Merros had met the older man for the first time the day he was promoted. The meeting had not gone well. Apparently the general did not agree with retired captains being promoted to the rank of general without any warning. Really, Merros could hardly blame the man. He was having trouble with it himself and he was the one who'd been promoted.

"He is the actual head of the army, you know. He has that authority."

"Well, yes, but still." Merros looked around the field and shook his head. "What was he thinking?"

"I should suppose he was thinking that the strangers might be responsible for the murder of the Emperor. Someone has to check on these things."

"Well that's just fine, but I suppose there are procedures that should be followed for this sort of thing."

"I'm not sure about any of that." The tone of voice Wollis used added a silent subtext about merely being a soldier. Merros understood the sentiment automatically, but, of course, these days that wasn't exactly true for him.

He looked over the troops and continued to speak softly, not wanting to cause any undue alarm. "Has anyone told Krohan about this?"

"I have no bloody idea. Maybe Hradi did."

Merros looked at his second. "Do you suppose I could get that lucky?"

"Not remotely."

"How do you think the Regent of the Empire will react to the news?"

Wollis stared his way for a moment and then looked at the ranks of troops that had gathered for inspection. They were looking a bit better, what with the uniforms being worn properly and the inclusion of proper armor. They were looking a bit more like an army, really. "You've heard about the situation in Roathes?"

"The volcano? Of course."

Wollis kept his face calm and expressionless and Merros had to wonder if the man was joking when he spoke. "I've heard a few people say that the eruption occurred at exactly the moment he heard about the Emperor's assassination."

"Is that so?"

"Well, that's what I've heard. If it's true, he might not react well to a few hundred soldiers being sent off to drag back the Sa'ba Taalor and accuse them of murdering the Emperor."

"Yes, well, I suppose I should go have a chat with our employer."

"What about the troops?"

"Have them practice some more. I suspect they're going to need it if Hradi causes an incident."

"If?"

"I'm trying to be optimistic, Wollis. Let me have my delusions."

"I always do."

Four days out, the cold became a vicious, living thing, and the air grew bitter and chalky. The first part of the journey had been comfortable, but this? This was a special little assortment of discomforts. Every part of his body ached. Not just his legs, which he would have expected with the amount of walking he was doing, but everything. Andover Lashk moved forward, one step at a time, his eyes squinted against the wind and the grit and the endless damned dust.

The bad part? They weren't even in the Blasted Lands proper as yet. Merely on the outskirts. The temperature had been rising when he left Tyrne, but here where the ruined lands met up with the Empire, the temperatures were colder and the sky was already constantly dark. And he was beginning to understand the veils that the people he traveled with wore. He'd taken to doing the exact same thing.

The caravan was gone. They'd already moved on into the Blasted Lands proper and now there was only him, Drask, Delil, and Bromt. None of the great beasts were with them at the moment, though he suspected that could change with as little as a call out from Drask, who sent the great animal of his off without a rider when they left the main group. Exactly how intelligent the creatures were he had not yet determined, but he had suspicions.

They carried everything they needed as far as Drask was concerned, and apparently that was the end of the discussion. The others listened to the man without question, and Andover suspected that if he wanted to live to see the Seven Forges he would do well to follow their lead.

Their days were already starting to take on a certain routine. They rose when the meager light of the sun punched through the clouds, then broke down their camp, and began walking. When they had walked for a while, Drask or one of the others, under his command, would begin the instructions for the day. Most of the time the practice with his hammer or with the bow was done while they were walking, because, in the words of Drask, "The world does not wait for you to be ready to engage in combat and therefore you must simply always be ready."

The Sa'ba Taalor were always ready, it seemed. How did he know? One had merely to look at them. The three that were traveling with him had changed as they moved toward the Blasted Lands, seemingly growing layers of fur and armor as they walked. All three sported helmets now, and armor and cloaks of fur and hide that hid most of their bodies away and simultaneously sheltered them from the worst of the constant winds. Each bore easily thirty or more pounds of additional garb plus their weapons and supplies and carried the weight without noticeable effort. In comparison he barely seemed to carry anything. Andover had thought the clothes being selected for him were excessive when he started the trek, but now he knew better. Drask had made him take the heavy fur-lined cloak that had been provided and now he was grateful for the extra weight.

The hammer was a different beast. He had adjusted to carrying the excess weight strapped to his back by a thick leather brace Delil had helped him put together on their second night, when they were done setting camp. Now it rested comfortably enough against him, and with practice he'd learned how to unsling it in a hurry. Once again Delil helped with that. She kept coming at him until he got very good at defending himself.

He was also damned hungry. That was almost a constant thing. They carried a few provisions, but mostly they intended to hunt for game out in the Blasted Lands. That seemed impossible, of course. As far as Andover could tell, there was nothing to eat in the entire area, nothing to eat and nothing to hunt, unless one decided to hunt the shifting clouds of dust that filled the air, or the ice that pelted them from time to time.

Delil stepped closer to him and tapped his shoulder. She seemed nearly alien with the helmet over her face, shielding her head. Little but her eyes could be clearly distinguished in the semidarkness. He looked her way and she pointed. "There are riders coming this way. Do they wear the markings of your people?"

He scanned the horizon and after a moment saw the shadowed forms coming through the haze of dust and sleet. He couldn't make out any standards and told her so.

She nodded and jogged forward to speak to Drask, who looked even less human than Delil did in the perpetual twilight. The horns on his helmet and the heavy cloak that swam around his shoulders brought to mind a few of Andover's least favorite childhood nightmares.

Drask stared at the column of horsemen and considered them carefully, not speaking for a long while. Finally he shook his head. "We will not meet with them."

Andover was surprised by the decision. "Why not?"

Drask turned to face him. "You are not ready yet."

"You think I'll run to them and ask for aid? Ask for safety?"

"You are not ready yet. That is enough." Drask pointed at the group moving past them. "They follow the caravan's path. They are interested in Tuskandru and the rest."

"Then shouldn't you see what they want?"

Drask shook his head. "No. We are here to help you learn. That is all."

Andover sighed and then turned away from Drask. One foot forward and then the other. One step after the next. More than that was more than he wanted to think.

A short time later, after the riders had vanished from sight, Bromt approached him and distracted him from his walking. "You and me, we go hunting now."

"Hunting for what?"

"Dinner."

"I mean, hunting for what? What is there to eat out here but dust?"

Bromt laughed as if hearing a delightful joke, and punched him lightly in the arm. "Come on then! Let's go find out."

Andover turned to see what the others were up to, but they were gone.

"Where are they? How will we find the others when we're done?"

"We will find them. I'll show you how."

There was nothing else to say, really. Andover learned his first lessons about hunting in the Blasted

Lands. There was bloodshed long before the hunt was finished.

Tuskandru watched the riders coming and finally decided that they would wait for the soldiers who seemed so determined to catch up with them. While they waited, he checked the wagons that were being drawn along and most importantly, he met up with the sorcerer's apprentice. The girl, Tega, looked at him for a long moment after answering his knock.

"Yes?" Her eyes were very wide in her face. She stared up at him as if he might suddenly lean down at take a bite from her face, but still she stood her ground. He liked that. The boy, Andover, was easier to startle. The walking trip would either make him a fighter or it would kill him. Until the Daxar Taalor decided, he was no longer the king's concern.

The approaching army was.

And to that end, he spoke to the girl with the frightened eyes. "There are soldiers from Fellein coming. I would ask that you stand with me and translate. I do not wish to cause an incident."

She looked back the way they had come and stared at the dark forms moving closer. They rode in close ranks, four horses deep, a good number of them carrying horseman's pikes. Though the likelihood of being attacked by the Pra-Moresh was small, the soldiers seemed as prepared as they could be. That or, just as likely, they were expecting troubles from the Sa'ba Taalor.

"Yes, of course. I will assist gladly."

The Sisters had opened a language door between Merros Dulver and Drask Silver Hand. The apprentice and the king did not share that luxury. While Tega could manage to speak the Old Tongue derivative of the people she traveled with, her limited abilities didn't allow her the same sort of skill that the Sisters had used. She could merely translate, not fix the situation.

The riders came closer and Tusk stood his ground next to her wagon. As the column came closer, he called out in a language she was not familiar with – the same one the Sa'ba Taalor used to speak to their animals – and his people responded. Several of them moved closer. The rest stayed where they were, but Tega could see them reacting, some checking their weapons, others actively preparing arrows and settling their bows across the broad shoulders of their mounts. Had she not been looking she would have missed many of the actions.

The first riders were directed to Tusk by one of the Sa'ba Taalor; Tega had no idea what the man's name was, but she could barely recognize any of the people she rode with. Somewhere along the way they had begun sporting their armor and that completely changed their appearance. They had seemed odd but friendly enough in the palace. Now they seemed different, far more dangerous – even the ones who had made no actions to worry anyone.

She recognized the man at the front of the column, not by his name but by his face. He was one of General Hradi's men, a lifer with high hopes of moving up to replace the old man in a few years.

Tuskandru stood with his arms crossed and waited, not bothering to speak first. The man climbed down from his horse and looked at the king for a moment. Tusk stood easily a head taller, not including the great fanged helmet that covered his head. The man was lean and weathered, with dark hair cut short, and a neatly trimmed beard and mustache. His face was not unkind, but his eyes were hard. He was either a man expecting trouble or a man who sought it. She could not quite decide which.

"You are King Tuskandru?"

Tusk nodded.

Tega cleared her throat. "This is King Tuskandru. I am Tega. I work with Desh Krohan."

That caught the man's attention. He'd already dismissed her, was barely even listening to her speak until she said that. No matter how some might find her attractive, or find the possibilities of her having sorcerous skills impressive, none of them gave those thoughts a second consideration when they heard who she worked for.

"There has been…" The man struggled for a moment, trying to decide what to say. Finally he started again. "Emperor Pathra Krous is dead."

"What?" Tega had trouble believing what she had just heard.

"Pathra Krous was murdered. He was thrown from his private offices a few hours after the Sa'ba Taalor left Tyrne."

She translated quickly for Tuskandru, who seemed little affected by the knowledge.

The man looked to Tusk. "My name is Colonel Wallford. I am tasked with bringing you back to the courts to answer questions."

"What sort of questions?" Tega's voice was sharp and even as she spoke her hands slipped together. Desh had to be told of this if he did not already know and that meant she would have to call for him. This situation was exactly the sort of thing the wizard did not want. Though she would never claim to know her mentor's every desire, of that much she was certain.

The colonel looked at her for a moment, his eyes half-lidded as he contemplated whether or not she was worth the trouble of answering. Then he remembered whom she worked for.

"There is some concern as to whether or not the Sa'ba Taalor had any part in the Emperor's death."

Direct and to the point. She could understand that and knew by the change in Tusk's stance that he understood every word the colonel was speaking.

"You would accuse a king of murdering the Emperor?" She made sure her voice was a challenge. He needed to know that he was treading on dangerous territory.

"I accuse no one of anything. I am merely following orders. I have been tasked with bringing the Sa'ba Taalor back to Tyrne."

"By whom?" Oh how her heart was thundering in her chest. Madness! Desh would surely be outraged. He had worked hard to make the first meeting between the two lands a peaceful, fruitful encounter.

"By General Hradi."

"Who is General Hradi to order King Tuskandru to come to him in this manner?"

Tusk looked from her to the colonel and back again as they spoke, but did not answer or respond otherwise.

"General Hradi is in charge of the Imperial Army."

"General Hradi is not in charge of the Empire."

"No, but the army is his to command and he has ordered us to bring King Tuskandru and his retinue back to Fellein."

"And if the king should refuse?"

And there it was: the question that would change everything, depending on the colonel's answer. The Sa'ba Taalor stood ready, though apparently the colonel did not understand that fact. Tega did not know the ways of the people she was with very well, but she knew that they had been willing to fight a young man to the death for an insult. Accusing them of murder? How would that go for Colonel Wallford? For the troops with him? For her or the people she was with for that matter?

She desperately wished that Desh Krohan was there with her.

He was not and that left her with only one option. The blade she slid along her palm drew a hot line of blood in her flesh. She clenched her fist tightly on the small offering and reached out with her mind. For the briefest moment she felt nothing and then, thank all the gods, she felt Desh's attention turn to her and her offered blood from leagues away.

"If His Majesty is not prepared to come back willingly, I am to bring him in by force. To that end, I have brought a very large retinue of soldiers." Wallford spoke to her as if to a slightly addled child.

Tusk shook his head. "I have matters of my own to attend to in my kingdom. I cannot come back with you. You may join us on this journey if you will, but that is all." The man's voice brooked no argument.

Wallford looked at the king for a moment and rested his hand significantly on the hilt of his sword. He made sure to let the gesture be seen.

Tuskandru looked to her for a moment, his eyes narrowed, and then looked back to the colonel. "Do you have gods?"

The colonel nodded. "Yes. Of course."

"Then should you draw your weapon, pray to them."

"Do you not understand the situation? The Emperor is dead!" The colonel's voice was outraged.

Desh's voice rang in her head, a distant echo that grew clearer, became a significant sound. "I will speak through you." The words were for her alone and she nodded and closed her eyes.

And a moment later she felt herself displaced from her own body, felt her essence rise into the air above the group as Desh Krohan's will possessed her form.

From her new height she could see the transformation. A thick shadow rose from the ground and surrounded her form, cocooned her in its darkness and from the depths of that odd black cloud the voice of Desh Krohan spilled forth with a dark, echoing quality, "There is no need for this."

Tuskandru stepped back three paces, his eyes growing wide beneath the beastly visage of his helmet. The colonel fell back as well, not merely startled by the unexpected change in her form, but also by the voice of a man who was feared as much as any legend ever has been. Around them the Sa'ba Taalor and the soldiers of the Imperial Army reacted as well. Several of the horses made noises and threatened a panic at the rumbling voice of the sorcerer.

"Colonel Wallford," Desh continued. "You are here under orders of General Hradi. I am acting Regent of the Empire. My word supersedes the word of your commander. Stand down."

"The Emperor is dead!" Wallford's nerves were not holding well, but his discipline could have been admired under different circumstances.

"The Emperor is dead, yes. That does not allow General Hradi to take command of the Empire."

Wallford pointed a hand at Tuskandru. "This man is accused of murdering the Emperor!"

"Not so!" Desh's voice lashed out, demanding attention.

Tuskandru's hand lashed out, slapping Wallford's accusing hand aside. "You dare?"

And that was the moment that war broke out between the People of the Seven Forges and the Fellein Empire.

Wallford's reaction could easily have been expected. He grabbed the hilt of his sword and began to draw the blade from the scabbard.

The heavy blade of King Tuskandru's sword cleaved the top of the colonel's head from the rest of his skull.

Desh Krohan stepped back, taking her body along for the ride, and Tega stared on, horrified, as the soldiers who followed Wallford grabbed crossbows and aimed, or leveled the horseman's pikes they held and prepared to charge at Tuskandru. The King did not step back, but instead moved toward the closest soldier behind the colonel's falling body. The man's crossbow bolt fired at Tuskandru's chest even as the warrior swept his great sword in another tight arc and hacked into the soldier's leg and into the horse under it. The sword cut deep. The crossbow bolt dug partially into the armor on Tusk's body and vibrated where it stopped.

Tega felt her essence pulled backward, as Desh did something with her body, and suddenly rose into the air. He tried to speak again, tried to gain the attention of the soldiers and warriors alike, but it was far too late for that.

War cries came from the mouths of the Sa'ba Taalor and their great mounts alike. Arrows and bolts lashed through the air, striking some targets and missing others. The cavalrymen turned their warhorses toward the enemy and discovered that the enormous beasts their enemies rode not only ran fast, but also pounced. The warriors held onto their mounts with hands and legs alike as the animals ran and jumped, moving over the first rank of riders and into the columns of horsemen who were jostling for position as the first line tried to brace for an attack that never happened.

Thick claws and powerful teeth ripped into horses and soldiers alike and even as they did so the Sa'ba Taalor drew weapons as varied as their armor. Men screamed, women screamed, horses screamed, and the great beasts howled out in voices that seemed too large for their enormous bodies.

Tega had little chance to see more before her body rose higher still, sailing away from the sudden explosion of combat, moving at a maddening speed and dragging her anchored spirit along for the ride. Had she eyes she'd have closed them. Had she a mouth, she'd have screamed.

The wizard tried to warn them, but failed. The soldiers of the Empire approached with threats and then the foolish one insulted him. And Tusk responded as he had been raised to respond. There was no question in his mind of right or wrong. The gods made their demands in exchange for all they did for the people. The first demand was obedience. Durhallem did not believe in mercy and so Tuskandru, King of Durhallem's Heart did not believe in mercy. The accuser died first. And then the one who'd followed him so closely. The point of the crossbow bolt cut at his chest and so he pulled it free, even as the next of the fools came for him, charging with a long pike. The rider was good at riding his charging horse. He was not quite as good at holding the lance on target. Tusk stepped to the side and blocked the weapon before it could hit him, felt the impact run up his arms and stepped back enough to alleviate some of the force.

He whistled and Brodem, his mount, roared in response. The animal would not follow him, would not come to his aid, but because of his call, was now free to hunt the enemy. He did not bother further with Brodem. If they survived the battle, they would reunite. Until then, there was only one thing that mattered: the fight.

Tusk's sword cut through the flank of the great war horse and it fell, toppling along with the rider. The man who had tried to impale him with the pike was pinned under the horse at it screamed its way to the ground. He struggled to rise, perhaps to fight or merely to stand. Tusk stomped down on his skull and felt bones shatter beneath his foot. The horse thrashed too much and so he carved its head from its body and moved on.

A pike rammed into his helmet and skidded off. His head rang with the force of the blow but not enough to stop him. He grabbed the pike with his free hand and held it as he pulled the rider closer to him. The man could let go of his weapon or he could fall off his horse. Foolishly he chose to hold the weapon. Instinct told him the weapon could save his life. Tusk knew better. To depend on any weapon alone was to weaken yourself. That was the first lesson taught by Wrommish, and none of the Sa'ba Taalor lived long without knowing the lessons Wrommish made them learn. His sword stuck in the chest of the man when he shoved it through the armor of his enemy. Rather than fight the sword free he surrendered it and reached for the chain held against his hip. The heavy links sang and rattled as he swung them.

A crossbow bolt found its way into his thigh and he roared as he faced the man who'd fired the thing at him. The soldier surrendered his crossbow and tried for his sword. The chain shattered his lower jaw before he could pull the weapon from its scabbard. The enemy seemed skilled at the weapons they used, but only employed a few. That was a mistake in Tusk's eyes. Many weapons, many ways to kill. That is what the Daxar Taalor demanded and a wise man did not argue with his gods. The chain lashed out a second time and the soldier fell.

Around him, his people grinned and roared and called the names of the Daxar Taalor, celebrating both the injuries they sustained and the ones they delivered.

The Daxar Taalor were gods of war, and they had been training for so very long for this moment, for this time when the gods would finally unleash them on their enemies.

Sometimes the gods are kind.

Tuskandru, Chosen of the Forge of Durhallem, called out his god's name and celebrated the offerings he made to his deity. Around him blood spilled across the half-frozen ground of the Blasted Lands, which had waited as patiently as the gods for this day, for this time.

At long last the time for war had come.

A soldier screamed as he caught the man's fingers in the links of his chain and pulled, breaking the digits and tearing the flesh around them. While he was screaming Tusk drove his elbow into the man's windpipe and shattered the cartilage there. The man began coughing and trying to breathe. He was still dying while Tuskandru moved toward the next sacrifice he would offer to his gods.

Truly, he was blessed.

NINETEEN

Desh Krohan released the body of his apprentice, Tega, and watched her slump across the bed where he'd set her down. She was exhausted. That was hardly surprising. She was not used to the rigors of anything but the most minor sorceries. There was a reason it took years to learn the more powerful spells.

Tega made a slurred noise and he regarded her. "Sleep. You're safe now."

He'd hated to release her from being with the Sa'ba Taalor, but had no desire to see her harmed and had little doubt that she would have been if she had stayed. They seemed an honorable people, but he didn't know them well enough to know how they treated anyone they associated with their enemies.

Enemies. He shook his head. That damned fool, General Hradi, was about to learn what it meant to have enemies.

Desh moved back to his body where it lay within the safety of his guarded room. As he fell back into his flesh, his lungs breathed again and his heart beat, and the cloak that sheltered him once more began to shimmer and pulse.

And Desh moved his body, rose quickly to his full height and left the room he kept locked against troubles, barely allowing himself time to recover from the disorientation of jumping bodies. Anger made him a little less cautious. Anger made him reckless. And he was so very angry.

He stormed down the corridors on the way to the Emperor's chambers and those who saw him coming did their very best not to get noticed by him.

General Merros Dulver looked at the other men at the table and scowled. Currently all of them were sitting in the Emperor's throne room, which for the moment was not being used to run the country and was therefore available. That would change soon, but until then it was the only bloody office that Merros knew well enough to find.

"Which one of you actually decided to start a war, and why?" The two men facing him were both longtime commanders of the military forces. He had, on rare occasions, received commands with their names, signatures and formal seals. Generals Olec Hradi and Dataro Larn were not the least bit impressed by him. He should have been terrified.

Instead he was well and truly pissed off.

Hradi sat a little taller in his seat. The man was old, much older than Merros expected, with a heavily weathered face, perfectly tailored uniform and a gut that could not be hidden by the by the very finest of tailors. His white hair was thinning on his head and he'd worked hard to comb it over so that it might seem fuller. He was failing in all efforts.

"Who are you to talk to us that way, Dulver?" He sneered. "You're a nobody! The only reason you're here is because you managed to cull favor with the Emperor. Perhaps you heard the news that he's dead?" Hradi leaned forward, his hands planted on the table as if he might decide at a moment's notice to leap into action and come across the grand marble surface at a full charge.

General Larn looked on, not saying a word. His eyes watched one man and then the other as they spoke, taking their measure and doing nothing else.

Merros stood perfectly straight and stared daggers at Hradi. "So you decided the best way to take care of his death was to send two hundred soldiers off to start a war? Have you lost your mind?"

"How dare you?" Hradi's voice cracked with outrage, or just possibly age. It was hard to clearly decide while the man was bellowing and red-faced. "I took control of the situation! It's very likely that the person responsible for Emperor Krous' murder was moving with that caravan! They had to be made to come back here."

"The caravan left before the Emperor was assassinated. I was there. I watched them climb on their animals and leave." Oh, yes he was liking the general less by the moment.

Hradi's eyes nearly bulged from their wrinkled sockets and he found himself wondering how it was that he had ever feared or admired the man who had sent him off to a dozen different border skirmishes over the years. There was nothing about the man that spoke of military strength or of anything remotely like discipline. He stank of perfumes designed to lure women to his bed and his hands were soft and his nails manicured.

"They need to account for themselves!"

"So you sent two hundred armed men to politely ask a visiting king and his retinue to come back and answer to whom, exactly? You?"

"If needs be, yes!"

"You're not the Emperor! You're not in charge of the Empire!"

"No I'm in charge of the greatest army in the known world." Hradi's voice grew cold and calm and he rose from his seat with an oily grace. His eyes were clear and his expression was calm and that worried Merros more than anything else.

Merros looked toward General Larn, but the man was still merely watching. His facial expression had not changed in the least.

Merros frowned. Actually, it should have changed at least a little. In fact, the man's eyes should at least move a bit or blink.

"General Larn? Are you well?"

Hradi looked over at the other general. "Answer him, Dataro. You agreed with my decision, after all."

There was no response. Larn remained in the same position, but he trembled a bit, his hands shaking ever so slightly.

"Oh, damn."

Merros walked toward the man and called out at the same time, "Wollis! I need you!"

Wollis March opened the doors to the room immediately, and two other men were right there with him. Surely there was no such thing as a general without an assistant. Merros barely knew the generals by name and likeness together. The assistants were lost to him.

His hand reached out and touched Larn. The man's flesh was nearly like ice and though his heart was beating it was a close thing. The small needle in the back of his neck was all the hint that Merros needed to know the man was poisoned and likely already dead.

"Poisoned. We've an assassin around here." Larn had entered the room after Merros. He had been lively enough when he sat down. That had only been a few moments before. Merros took in the details of the room. There were a great many items within the place. Tapestries on the walls, suits of armor – really, he was beginning to wonder if anyone ever actually wore the armor or if it merely lay around waiting to be used as decorations – several different globes and tables covered with documents and maps.

Halfway across the room the great skull of a thing Merros hoped never to run across sat like a centerpiece. It was adorned with gold and crusted with gems of every type. It was enormous.

It had also been moved recently. The last time he'd been in the room the nostrils of the thing faced directly at the door and now they were slightly to the right of where they had been.

Without speaking he pointed to Wollis and his second nodded, drawing his sword before heading for the great skull.

Larn slid from his seat with a soft sigh. Merros wanted to check on him again, but not now. There simply wasn't time.

He pointed to the two men standing in the doorway: "Close that. Block it."

They listened without asking. Hradi made a rude noise and started looking around the room himself. His eyes didn't bother with the skull, he knew that someone was already looking. Instead he focused on the draperies around the area. They ran up to the ceiling in most cases and were loose enough that a person could likely hide with little or no difficulty. Good. The idiot was keeping himself busy. That meant that Merros didn't have to worry about doing it himself.

Instead Merros approached the skull himself, looking into the cavernous eye socket that stared blankly back in his direction.

There was nothing at all pretty about the beast.

He ran his hand along the eye socket, felt the contour of the bone ridges and saw what he'd half-expected. The inside of the thing was hollow, as most skulls would be, granted, but there looked to be a larger cavity inside than in most skulls he'd seen. His fingers kept sliding over the surface, feeling the gems, the markings and carvings, and he kept looking for…

There. His fingers pushed on a gem near the hinge of the massive jaw and a clicking noise followed. "Wollis. Help me with this."

Wollis came to him, his face serious, and looked at the spot where Merros was touching. He lowered his head to examine the spot where the skull seemed to have a hidden compartment.

While he was looking the assassin slipped from under the table and threw a dagger directly at Hradi. The general never even saw the weapon that killed him. The blade rammed into his temple and he let out another little harrumphing noise before he crashed to the ground.

Merros turned at the sound – compounded by the shocked screams of the two men at the door – and watched the commander of the Empire's army fall dead.

The figure moved fast, doing exactly what he'd imagined Hradi might do earlier and sliding across the polished marble surface of the table. Slim, possibly female, and shorter than he'd expected, the way she moved was telling, even if he hadn't recognized the pattern of scars on her left hip, where his hand had rested more than once.

"Swech!"

She ignored him and moved for the door, both hands already in motion, throwing glittering objects that drove into each of the men at the door. One fell back with something vibrating in his bleeding eye socket. The other staggered to the side and tried to stop the blood that was flowing from a fresh wound in his throat. Still she did not stop moving. She carried herself toward the door and potential freedom.

"Swech! Stop! What is this?" Impossible was what it was. He'd seen her climb aboard Saa'thaa, had watched her leave the city with the caravan of riders. Yet he looked at her now, saw the scars he'd damned near memorized, the way her gray hair moved in a slow wave of curls.

Swech spun and cocked her hand next to her shoulder. He could see another blade, small but no doubt deadly, resting amid her fingers.

Merros raised his hands, wanting to talk this out somehow, wanting not to get a knife through his eye or throat or any part of his body, really.

And while he had her attention, Wollis took a chance and charged, his sword drawn back for a killing stroke.

Three seconds, at most. The hand holding the blade moved with a casual flick and the blade cut into Merros' jaw, sliding across bone and carving a trench. The pain was immediate and exquisite. He hissed and stepped back his hand moving automatically to staunch the blood, the fire, the pain.

Wollis brought his sword up in an arc and down toward Swech's head. By rights he should have taken a large portion of her features away from the rest of her skull, but she moved out of the way, sliding sideways and striking the descending blade with the palm of her hand. Swech kept her balance with ease. Wollis staggered forward, trying to compensate for the unexpected change in his weapon's direction.

Had he been there, and instructing, Tuskandru might well have pointed out Wollis' mistake. The sword is only a weapon after all, and none of the Sa'ba Taalor lived long without knowing the lessons Wrommish made them learn.

Swech hit Wollis in the throat with her hand. He staggered back, coughing, and she struck again, her elbow driving into Wollis' surprised face and shattering bone. She struck one more time, and Wollis fell as surely as a tree taken down by the foresters of Trecharch. Swech did not look back. She pulled open the closed doors leading into the hallway and ran.

Merros ran too, but only as far as Wollis. The man was his friend. They had been on a good number of journeys together.

One look told him that they would not journey together any further. Wollis was dead. Really, that was all it took to slow Merros down for the moment. Wollis was dead and he was left wondering exactly what had just happened.

Desh Krohan arrived in the chambers exactly too late to be of any assistance at all.

Merros would be a long time deciding whether or not he could forgive the sorcerer for that.

Goriah rode on the bow of the small vessel, staring at the mountain looming out of the waters ahead of her. She did not need to get much closer to see all that she needed to see. The islands of the Guntha were gone, swallowed by the newly born land still steaming and growing. The towering center of the freshly formed land burned and above that fiery pit the skies were filled with sulfurous ash and lightning crested, turbulent clouds.

She stared at that sky and was immediately reminded of the Seven Forges.

There had been no warning. The Sooth had not given so much as a cry of the threat that this moment brought with it, and that was beyond unusual. While the spirits were hardly the most reliable creatures, they tended to offer too many possibilities not to remain quiet about disasters of this scale.

The islands of the Guntha were gone and so too were the Guntha themselves, burned away when the explosion birthed this new place.

But was it new? While the land looked fresh, the mountain did not. It struck her as remarkably similar to one of the Forges, the one farthest to the west on the maps she and her sisters had studied with Desh Krohan. It was impossible to say, of course. She had not circled that one particular mountain as she now circled this one, but at certain angles she could almost be certain. If Desh was correct in his guesses, that would be the mountain closest to the ocean, though to be fair it was purely guesswork on his part.

"Do mountains move?" She whispered the words, not expecting an answer.

The captain of her small vessel cleared his throat. "Lady, we are in danger here. The storms are growing again."

They were indeed. The storms were gathering above and they would grow wider and more violent soon. The shore where she had rented the services of the captain and his crew were covered already with heavy ash blown over from the new island. Surely there would be more of the same covering their homes in the near future, covering them as well if they did not return to the docks and soon.

"As you say, Captain Whelan." Goriah studied the peak for a moment longer and stared at the clouds painted the color of blood that brooded above it. "Let's return to the harbor. I have seen enough."

The man was quick to accommodate.

Desh Krohan would find the news very interesting. She intended to tell him just as soon as she could get to dry land. The turbulent sea was making it difficult for her to concentrate well enough for long distance communication.

The sun set on Tyrne, and instead of stars there were only clouds. The storms were coming from the south, from where the Guntha once lived before flames swallowed them. Their shroud seemed to want to cover the world, at least for the moment.

Guards moved in close precision throughout the palace, moving in groups of three or more and checking everywhere they could, for there could be no doubt that somewhere nearby a murderer crept, perhaps even now seeking a way to reach Nachia Krous, or another member of the Imperial Family.

Swech did indeed move through Tyrne, but no longer moved to strike against anyone. It was time to go home, her mission was complete.

The Daxar Taalor had visited her, their voices softly whispering for her alone. It was not King Tuskandru who guided her to kill, though likely he'd known of what was planned. Had it been Tusk she might have listened. She might not. She was not overly fond of him, though she bore him no particular dislike.

But one did not disobey the gods. Not if one wished to continue living.

She looked back at the palace, at the torches that burned around the structure and the distant shapes of guards that had not been there before she did as commanded.

She had no regrets.

The men she'd killed meant nothing to her. They were not Sa'ba Taalor. They were not her people. Still, she felt a little sorrow. She had been fond of Merros Dulver. He had been a pleasant distraction and had taught her a great deal about his people while they journeyed together. Also, he was a fun lover.

Saa'thaa still waited patiently for her, exactly where she had left him. Her hand patted his muzzle and his warm breath greeted her fingers. He breathed in her scent and let out a pleased rumble.

"We go now, yes? We head home." She sighed the words into his ear and then climbed into the saddle he bore without effort. Her muscles ached from hours staying in one position, barely breathing, waiting patiently for the right times to do as the gods commanded. She was grateful for the chance to rest for a moment. The work of the faithful could be exhausting, but was, as always, rewarding.

Swech rested her head against Saa'thaa's neck and he rose moving with a steady gait that very gradually increased in speed.

Merros Dulver.

Unconsciously her hand drifted to her abdomen, to the child she felt growing within her womb. He was an interesting man. She remained uncertain what she should feel about the child within her body, but she also knew that the Daxar Taalor willed that she carry the baby, and so she would.

Would her child meet the man who had helped with its conception?

If the gods willed it, it would be so.

Some of the plans she had for the future were accurate, but not all of them. The gods had different ideas.

Nachia Krous looked at the crowd of people around her and kept her composure through sheer force of will. Pathra would have expected no less of his successor. Though she did not yet wear the crown of the Empress, only a few considered denying her the position. They did not matter. Desh Krohan kept telling her as much and she believed him.

Merros Dulver stood to her left, the sorcerer to her right. It was time to deal with affairs of the state and that meant having her forces gathered and with her. There were other generals, of course. The Empire was too large to have only three men in charge of the armies, but the others were in other places and not yet even aware of everything that had transpired.

They would know soon. The wizard had sent his messengers and there were others like him who would receive the messages and inform the appropriate parties.

"Like as not the rumors of your cousin's death will reach the other side of the Empire before the messengers arrive. That's the way of it with bad news and gossip."

She managed a small smile for his jest, but only barely. Even the sorcerer's acerbic wit would only go so far right now. Too many things were going wrong. They were at the very edge of war, and possibly they had already gone over that precipice. Most of the armed forces were in disarray because of the assassinations, and there were several forces gathering around the area that would very likely add to the chaos rather than detract from it. Her cousin, Laister, was behaving himself, but only barely, and there were other members of the Krous family who were already being vocal about their support of his claims to the throne.

Desh had said the situation would resolve itself. He had not promised it would do so without bloodshed.

And the closest thing she had to a commander for her armies at the moment was staring around with half-lidded eyes and a seething anger in his soul. Merros Dulver seemed intent on something, but she didn't know him well enough to know what that something was. That worried her. Pathra had always said it was best to know the minds of your closest allies.

Pathra. Damn but thinking about him hurt. He wasn't supposed to be dead. He was supposed to be here, with her, making her laugh with his quiet humor and his deliberate antics. Instead she was mourning his loss and sitting on the throne that had been his for over a decade.

She felt like a graverobber.

That's me, she thought, Empress of the Dead. She meant the notion as a joke, of course, but found it not at all amusing.

It felt too much like the truth as the bodies of her cousin and two of Fellein's greatest warriors were prepared for their final rest.

Truth, she knew, was often not as solid as it appeared. She had only to look at the sorcerer at her hand to know that fact.

Three months earlier his life had been a frozen wasteland and the promise of wealth if he survived a trek to the Seven Forges. Since then he'd gone into a land no one from Fellein had ever been to, met with kings, gained a larger fortune than he'd ever imagined and become the nominal head of the Empire's armies. He had met with a fascinating woman, gotten to know her intimately, and then watched her murder his best friend. A friend he had not really considered very much through his journeys, because like all good friends, the man was simply there when he needed him.

And now he was gone.

Tataya's words came back to haunt him: the prophecy she claimed Desh Krohan had received about him. *You will lose your hand, find your fist and gain an ally. You will also meet your enemy face-to-face.* He did not know of prophecies or of the ways of sorcerers. He did, however, feel as if he had lost a vital part of himself with Wollis' passing. He had in fact lost his right hand man.

Of fists and allies he had no such claims. Perhaps that was the problem with prophecies: they only came true after you looked back at them. As for his enemies, he had only met them face to veil, really, so that could hardly be a proper choice of words.

Dretta March would be arriving soon. She would be followed by her son, Nolan. It was very likely that they would blame him for the death of Wollis. Even if they did not, he felt to blame. His friend had been following his orders, had been trying to protect him. Tears threatened to sting his eyes and he forced them back.

Tears were for men, not soldiers. He did not have time to be both. Currently the scariest fighters he had ever seen in action were heading back for their homeland and they would likely be gathering an army to come back to Fellein and seek retribution for whatever had caused them to assassinate Pathra Krous in the first place.

Were there any prophecies that claimed he would win the coming battle? He did not know and he was afraid to ask. The answer might terrify him a bit too much.

Nachia Krous stirred in her seat near his side and he turned to look at her.

"Call in the first claimant, please."

Once every month the Emperor heard from his people. The lords and ladies and the courtesans as well as a select few of the commoners, all of whom had matters they felt needed his attention.

That day had fallen again and the Emperor would not be able to answer. But the woman who would soon be crowned Empress would stand in, along with the Regent to the Throne and the First General of the Empire.

First General of the Empire. Merros wanted to run screaming at the very notion. Not all that long ago he'd nearly wet himself at the notion of facing seven Pra-Moresh on the frozen wastes of the Blasted Lands. Currently he found himself longing for the good old days when the only thing at stake was his life.

The Princess Lanaie of Roathes was led into the throne room. Her eyes were wide and her lips trembled. She was terrified.

"Yes, Lanaie?" Nachia waved away the formal protocols for this particular occasion. No one would hold it against her.

Lanaie fell to one knee and lowered her head. "M... Majesty, I come on behalf of my father, King Marsfel of Roathes."

"Yes, I know. What is it your father seeks?"

"Only to inform Your Majesty that the Guntha seem to have been telling the truth."

Nachia frowned. "What truth is that?"

"On the horizon, near where Guntha used to be and where the great island of fire now burns, many people have now seen ships. Great black ships, Majesty, and they are headed for Roathes."

Nachia frowned. "And where do these ships come from?"

"From the north and the west, Majesty. From the Blasted Lands."

Merros frowned as well. The Sa'ba Taalor could not possibly have a navy as well, could they? He shook his head. Navies took time to build.

Of course, the people of the Seven Forges had been alone for a thousand years. They could have planned anything in that time.

He cast his eyes toward Desh Krohan, but the man's cloak was on, his face lost in shadows and unreadable.

Damn. What the hell had he gotten himself into?

Three days without food, and he was running low on clean water too. Drask Silver Hand and his cohorts had abandoned him, and Andover Lashk walked slowly toward the distant fires of the Seven Forges. The winds had picked up a great deal and he was grateful for his fur-lined cloak and the scarf he'd now used to cover most of his face. He squinted through the grit trying to blind him and oriented himself on the Forges. He'd have turned back, would have tried for home, but he didn't quite dare. There was a chance that Drask was waiting for him to do something like that. There was also a chance, no matter what the Sa'ba Taalor had said, that he would lose the gift of his iron hands if he tried to return to Fellein. He doubted that last, but faith was as new a concept for him as having artificial hands that could feel and could move at his command.

Faith takes time to cement itself in a wary heart.

The sun had set, or if it had not the clouds overhead were too thick to let the light shine down. Either way the world was mostly darkness and Andover found the light in the distance as attractive as a moth finds the glow of a lamp in the night. He walked faster whenever he let himself look up, as if he might somehow make his way to the Seven Forges magically shorten by increasing his speed.

There would be no rest. No stopping. He would prove himself to the people who demanded to know his worthiness, or he would die trying.

The air around him shifted and danced and he heard the sound of weeping coming from his left. A moment later laughter came from his right.

His skin crawled. There was an element of insanity to both sounds and he made himself stand still and truly listen.

The sounds came again from in front of him and from behind as well.

His hands reached instinctively and he pulled the hammer slung across his back into his hands. For one brief moment the air calmed itself and he could hear skittering noises as something in the darkness sought to properly gain purchase on the icy ground.

The darkness was almost complete but he could see shapes, far larger than he was as they moved along the edges of his vision.

His hands gripped the hammer the way he'd been taught.

Andover released a breath and drew back for a proper swing as something giggle-screamed and charged him from the right. Another something wept as it came from behind.

ACKNOWLEDGMENTS

Special thanks to everyone at Angry Robot for taking a chance on my first Fantasy novel. It's always a bit unsettling trying something new and they've been a pleasure from beginning to end to work with.

Thanks also to Maurice Broaddus for his invaluable help.

BUY STUFF, LOOK COOL, BE HAPPY